The R(

Somorі ostro

Julia Slack

Happy reading,
Celia

xx
Julia
x

Book cover design: © Nuria Zaragoza

Front image: © iStock image
Back cover: Somorrostro, 1950/ © Alamy

www.juliaslackauthor.com

For Jacques Leonard
1909 - 1995

1

Carmen Garcia Marquez puffed her way from the cramped third-floor apartment she lived in with her seventeen-year-old daughter, Margarita, down the stone steps worn smooth and shiny by decades of use. On each level, she leaned against the gritty, flaking plaster on the wall, trying to relieve the ache in her arms from the bags of food scraps and empty wine carafes weighing her down. Heat rose up her body, her hands becoming sweaty against the plastic, the smell of rubbish nauseating. Catching her heel on a step in the dim light, she stumbled, the bottles clanking as she wobbled.

She muttered under her breath, cursing Don Calvet, the nefarious owner of almost all the buildings on the street. Each week when he came knocking for the rent, she told him that the bulbs on the stairwell needed replacing and that her toilet dripped incessantly. That the intercom hadn't worked for months.

Every week he nodded his greasy head, a permanent sneer on his sweaty, pitted face. And nothing was ever done.

She hated him even more than she hated the mouldy

walls and the cockroaches that shared the building with them. Specks and streaks of dried blood decorated the walls where one of the residents had managed to swipe the dirty bastards with the satisfying crunch of a slipper or a rolled-up newspaper.

At the bottom of the stairwell, Carmen placed the rubbish bags on the floor so she could tug open the front door with both hands, wincing as the brightness of the day stabbed like needles into her temples. The area around her kidneys ached as she bent to retrieve her bags, licking her lips with a tongue fuzzy and dry, sour with the aftertaste of last night's wine. Dizziness triggered more nausea as she straightened up, unable to shield her eyes from the glare.

Calle Sant Pere, in *Ciutat Vella,* the Old Town, was narrow and cobbled. And though rarely touched by the sun's rays, the summer months were stiflingly oppressive, the winter depressingly grim. The tiny balconies, separated by just metres, meant all but the brashest exhibitionists had their shutters permanently closed. On one side of the street were two rival butchers, one of which was Carmen's place of employment, where she gutted chickens and bagged the innards ready for the day's customers. Blood had seeped into her cuticles, leaving her nails permanently stained, even in August when the shop was closed for summer.

Dumping the bags with a clang in a metal container at the end of the street, Carmen squinted at the harsh brightness. It was Margarita, leaning against the side of the chemist, a cigarette in one hand and twirling a strand of her brown hair with the other. The young man, who had his arm proprietorially on the wall above her head, was whispering in her ear, and Margarita giggled vacuously.

Tutting loudly, Carmen marched towards the pair. 'Margarita Marquez, get home right now; the house is in a state! And stop making a show of yourself with Miguel Perillo where everyone can see you.'

Carmen glared at her daughter, swallowing down an insult, as Margarita stamped on her cigarette, smiled flirtatiously one last time at the boy, and with a flick of her hair, walked away without even a glance in her direction. Carmen gritted her teeth before turning to the butchers to begin her afternoon shift, her hangover crushing her skull. It was going to be a slow afternoon.

***

Margarita rolled her eyes as she stalked away from her mother towards home, her jaw clenched. She didn't care about Miguel; he was only a friend. But even so, she burned with humiliation at the way her mother had spoken to her. How would she ever find a boyfriend with a mother like Carmen Garcia?

She knew she wasn't as pretty as Clara Artola, one of her childhood friends. And she suspected her lack of popularity had something to do with her grubby clothes and the odd meaty-bread smell that lingered on her hands and hair, no matter how much she scrubbed. Clara had once told her she'd overheard her parents talking about Carmen Garcia and how the apple didn't fall far from the tree.

'They said your mum was "fast" and had no idea who your father is,' Clara had told her, her face lit with an almost indecent glee which had, at the time, made Margarita lower her eyes, her cheeks burning.

As she had never known who her father was, malicious tittle-tattle like this was nothing she hadn't heard a thousand times before. Her mother had always remained tight-lipped, leading Margarita to conclude that Clara's poisonous observations were true: her mother had no idea who Margarita's father was.

Several ridiculous rumours had circulated at different times, from a torrid affair with a high-ranking military commander to the pregnancy resulting from prostitution and the father being one of hundreds. As Margarita grew older, these taunts became water off a duck's back. She wondered why the neighbours were so invested in her parentage when she herself barely cared.

Margarita unlocked the door to their building and blindly made her way up the dark, uneven stairway, her hands feeling along the familiar walls. The stench of stale cigarette smoke hung heavy in the air when she entered the apartment, tossing her keys onto the dining table. Tamping down her disgust, she emptied the overflowing ashtray and piled up the greasy plates to

4

carry through to the kitchen, dumping them in the sink.

As she made her way to her bedroom, she kept her eyes straight ahead, ignoring the layer of dust over the tatty furniture and the dark, plastic sofa with its stuffing hanging out. She took a few short steps to her bedroom, deliberately turning her head away from the scuttling sound of cockroaches which made her skin crawl. Shutting the door firmly, she wedged a blanket against the gap at the bottom to keep the disgusting insects out of her space.

She sank onto the end of the single, metal-framed bed that took up almost the whole space in the room, along with a battered old chest of drawers. It was hers, though, and she fiercely treasured her scant possessions.

Looking up at the wooden cross her mother insisted on mounting on the rough walls in all the rooms, she pulled the colourful shawl her beloved Yaya had knitted into a bundle against her chest. She swallowed the ache in her throat, and her vision blurred as she pressed the shawl into the tightness under her ribcage.

Earlier that day, Clara had told her she was starting to work full-time in her parents' Colmado shop, serving dried rice, beans and olives and filling customers' carafes with Priorat and Rioja. Margarita's heart had sunk into her scuffed shoes when Clara had haughtily informed her that she wasn't allowed to have friends in the shop anymore. Margarita loved helping Clara at the weekend, giggling at the customers, pressing the tap on the barrels and passing the money to Clara's mother, who sat like a statue behind the till at the end of the counter from morning until night.

But Margarita was neither blind nor stupid. Now, as she reflected on the looks that passed between Clara's parents whenever she was there, shame vied with indignation. Was she no longer welcome because she brought the tone of the place down with her unwashed clothes and rank odour? Or was it because she was the daughter of Carmen Garcia, a slave to drink with the morals of an alley cat?

Margarita had never felt close to or cared for by her mother. Her only memories of being held or having her hair brushed were of her maternal grandmother, Yaya Rosa. Carmen had given Margarita her mother's surname when she was born – an unorthodox move that only served to take local gossip to a new level but made Margarita feel even more connected to her adored grandmother.

She had concocted a plan to go somewhere she was wanted, and she would take her grandmother with her. Her dreams took her to the wealthy north of the city, towards Tibidabo, a place she and Yaya had visited years before. As they had travelled through Sant Gervasi and Sarriá, climbing up on the rattling tram towards the big church in the Collserola hills, Margarita had gasped at the luxurious mansions they'd passed. Lush green spaces and modern apartment blocks with huge balconies that looked down onto communal gardens. Right then, she decided this was where she would find her husband and where they would live.

Although this had been years ago, and she could barely remember how to get back there, her dream never once wavered. Margarita wiped her eyes on her damp sleeve and took a deep, shuddering breath. If she didn't get moving, she would be late for work. She changed into her waitress uniform and, in minutes, was on her way to the bar at the end of the street.

Hours later, after a busy shift, her feet throbbing, Margarita arrived home close to midnight. The apartment was cold and empty, the plates where she'd left them in the sink. She ignored them and went straight to her bedroom to change into her nightie. She sank into bed, gratefully closing her weary eyes. Sleep took over almost as soon as her head hit the pillow.

She was woken a few hours later by the sound of the door to their apartment closing with a resounding bang, followed by mumbled cursing. Margarita tracked the sounds of her mother staggering around in the dark, making her way to the toilet, where she peed as loudly as a horse and cackled when she farted.

Margarita's face scrunched up in distaste. She pulled her thin blanket over her head to try and block out the sound of cupboard doors slamming as her mother searched for more to drink. Then, her bedroom door opened. Unsteady footsteps headed towards her before a hand shook her roughly. 'Are you awake?' Her mother's voice was slurred, and even through the blanket, the stench of alcohol was overpowering.

Margarita was too tired – in both body and soul – to have yet another spat with her mother. She lay stiff under her blanket until her mother tutted loudly and shuffled out of the room.

She waited for ten minutes until rasping snores echoed from the living room and crept out of her room to conduct her nightly search for money. She didn't need to worry about waking her mother as she scrabbled around, searching by touch through the contents of her bag. But that night, she was unlucky and only found a scrap of paper and a filthy handkerchief. She pocketed the piece of paper and got back into bed, hugging Yaya's shawl again. For now, her plans would have to wait. She'd have to remain content saving money from her two jobs and pilfering *céntimos* from her mother's purse. She closed her eyes and allowed her drained body to rest.

Margarita Marquez was leaving, and the day she finally did was getting closer.

2

'Margarita! *Madre de Dios*, stop chatting and start serving!' hollered Bernat over the din of the crowded bar.

It was late on Saturday evening, and Margarita had been working since lunchtime with only a half-hour break to cram her sandwich and take a breath of air. Her feet ached, and her hands were chapped from collecting and washing dozens of glasses, but she didn't mind. She loved talking to the customers and listening to their conversations about everything from football to Franco. Day to day, in and around the neighbourhood, people didn't take much notice of Margarita. But when she was behind the bar, serving customers, she had power of a kind. It was she who decided which customer to serve first. It was she who got their drinks and took their money. She was the centre of their world for a short time as the liquor she dispensed eased their worries and cares.

Most of the customers were regulars and had known her since she was a child. They all knew what a rough time she'd had with her mother, and many of the male clientele knew Carmen Garcia more intimately than they would admit to anyone, especially their wives. But even they, through the permanent fugue of alcohol from which they never quite seemed to sober up, could

9

see   Margarita Marquez was made of stronger stuff than her hapless, irresponsible mother.

Now, she loaded a tray with glasses and empty carafes of wine to be carried to the sink behind the bar to do the tedious final round of washing up. A last group of regulars were convulsing with laughter at something Jorge Perilla, Miguel's father, was telling them.

'He's back then, I heard,' Jorge said, propped up at the bar.

'*Si,* apparently he is,' Bernat nodded. 'Same smooth-tongued, shifty bastard he always was by all accounts.'

Margarita carried on cleaning the tables, not paying much attention until she heard something which made her ears prick up and the hairs on the back of her neck twitch.

'Has anyone told Carmen Garcia yet?' Jorge sniggered. 'Though I was never convinced when I heard the rumours.'

Bernat shook his head. 'She probably won't remember – doesn't even remember she has a bloody kid most of the time!' And they all roared with laughter.

Margarita came out of the back kitchen, noticing their discomfort when they spotted her, their eyes lowered. The place was almost empty now, the men having spent their last *céntimos* and already wondering how they would find more for tomorrow's session. They grunted their goodbyes and slowly straggled home.

'Before you leave, make sure you empty all the

10

ashtrays in the metal pail and put the uneaten sardines and *tortilla de patatas* back in the pantry,' instructed Bernat as he began cashing up the evening's takings. 'And take those sacks of rubbish to the bin on your way out.'

She finished as quickly as possible, carefully washing her hands before smothering them in the thick emollient cream she kept in her bag. Her hands were always red raw, and if she didn't put cream on every time she dried them, they would crack and bleed. It didn't help that she picked at the cracks when she was anxious, which made them worse. It wasn't the pain of her chapped hands that bothered her; she hated how ugly they were.

Shouting goodnight to Bernat, Margarita slipped out of the door, pulled the shutters halfway down behind her and turned in the opposite direction to home. After dumping the sacks into a container, she hurried through the narrow streets, staying close to the wall.

A few old drunks sitting in the plaza were shouting out crude suggestions to passers-by. But Margarita was used to their cussing and knew they were mostly harmless. She lowered her head, praying her mother wasn't among them and kept going.

Margarita's heart beat faster as she reached the corner of Via Laietana and Plaza Urquinaona. She rarely came this far up on her own at night. Too many tales from Yaya about suspicious goings-on had put the fear of God in her. The lights of Plaza Catalunya glowed comfortingly, reassuring her as she headed towards Las Ramblas. She used to visit the vast square when she was a child to feed the pigeons with Yaya Rosa. They would buy little bags of birdseed for a few *céntimos* from an old lady who was there every weekend. Margarita loved it when the birds landed on her hands and shoulders, pecking at the seeds. But Yaya always kept a safe distance, grimacing and shrieking at the fluttering attack of *'ratas voladoras'* and scrubbing Margarita thoroughly in the tin bath as soon as they arrived home.

As Margarita skirted around the bottom of the plaza, she wasn't thinking about feeding the pigeons. Jorge and Bernat's scathing remarks had triggered a memory from years and years ago when she'd been shopping in Santa Caterina market with Yaya.

Waiting in turn at Yaya's regular fruit stall, Yaya and the stallholder had been gossiping, guffawing at something or other. Margarita had been playing a game which involved reaching in front of Yaya and carefully plucking cherries from the stall. She'd eaten a few, dropping the sticky stones on the ground, and then started putting them in the embroidered pocket on the front of her school smock to eat when she got home. When Yaya grabbed her arm and pulled her close, Margarita thought her game had been discovered, and she was about to feel the back of Yaya's hand. But that didn't happen. She peered from behind Yaya's coat to see a strange man standing beside them.

She didn't like the look of him at all. His hair was long and shiny, as black as a raven's feathers. When he opened his mouth to speak, she saw a flash of gold glinting under the fluorescent lights of the market. Uneasy at how Yaya was holding her, almost suffocating her, Margarita tucked her chin in, hunched her back and stood as still as she could.

A cacophony of noise assaulted her ears; vendors shouting to customers, people laughing, and the whoosh of the coffee machine in the bar next to the fruit stall.

But even above all the noise, Yaya's hiss was menacing. 'If you ever go near her again, I will kill you with my bare hands, you shifty beggar.'

Margarita giggled at Yaya's words, but only in her head. She could tell Yaya was furious.

As Yaya yanked her out of the market by her arm, Margarita glanced back to see the man's eyes following them, his shoulders slumped and a beaten look on his face. Although he made her nervous, as they walked away from him, she felt a pull she hadn't entirely understood.

Later the same day, at home, Margarita snuggled up to Yaya, her head resting on her grandmother's lap while they listened to the radio. There was a tap at the door, and Yaya gently laid her on the sofa, thinking she was asleep. She wasn't, though, and overheard the hushed whispers of her mother and Yaya, angry murmurs about that 'lousy devil'. She instinctively knew they were talking about the man with gold teeth and hair as black as a raven's feathers.

Dismissing the memory with a shiver, Margarita

reached the corner of the Rambla and Calle Pelayo opposite Plaza Catalunya and crossed the road to wait in the shadows of a doorway until there were no passersby. Then she emerged, squinting up at the second floor of the grand modernist building to check for shadows at the window. She whistled three times, jigging from one foot to the other until she saw a candle flickering behind the thin curtains. A ghostly face appeared, and Margarita waved, the tension in her shoulders easing. The figure stepped out onto the balcony, glanced back into the room and quietly closed the door.

Eva Sanchez Ruiz. Her supporter, protector, and the most trustworthy friend Margarita had ever had. But their friendship was clandestine and had been since the first day they met in the hospital all those years ago. As a result, their encounters were planned meticulously. Both girls knew that if Maria Ruiz, Eva's mother, got the slightest whiff of their ongoing friendship, she would do all she could to prevent it.

'Margarita! It's late. Has something happened?' the girl murmured, her hair shining like a sunset under the streetlight.

'I need to see you, Eva. It's important,' Margarita whispered back. 'Can we meet tomorrow at the bench at five o'clock?'

Eva looked over her shoulder, saying brightly, 'I'm coming now, Papa.' She nodded briefly to Margarita and turned to go back inside.

Margarita scuttled back down the street towards the

old town, her steps lighter now that she'd seen her best friend.

***

As Margarita was hurrying home, Carmen had already arrived to find the apartment cold and dark. It was almost midnight. Even in her drunken stupor, Carmen's addled brain alerted her that something wasn't right. Margarita always left the kitchen light on. Lurching across the poky lounge, she opened the door to Margarita's room. It was empty.

Where the hell was that damn girl now? She went into the kitchen and tore off a piece of bread from a fresh loaf that Margarita had brought home from the bakery. Carmen thanked God that even when the larder was empty, they always had bread.

She wasn't hungry, but she needed something to soak up all the gin she'd drunk, or work tomorrow would be another misery to endure. She was already supposedly on her final warning for arriving half-cut. Although, for all his blustering, she knew Eduardo – a humble, kind-hearted man who once upon a time had been Carmen's saviour – would never get rid of her.

In a moment of painful clarity, she admitted to herself how tired she was of this life – exhausted and despondent at what a damn mess she'd made of everything. And she couldn't seem to find a way back out of the hole she had created. She sighed, all too aware she had no one but herself to blame. Sinking onto the plastic sofa, she rested her head in her hands as self-pitying sobs escaped her.

Carmen longed for her mother's approval, yearned for it with a pain that took her breath away at moments like these. Although she would never admit it to anyone, especially her mother, Carmen thought she was the loneliest, the most misunderstood person in the world.

She had no friends, having alienated and pushed away all those closest to her. Since Margarita was an infant, everything and everyone from before had disappeared, leaving Carmen in a downward spiral of loss and self-loathing.

Her mother, Rosa, knew that Carmen would spend every *céntimo* in the bodega and had stopped giving her money years earlier. Margarita was hardly ever around these days and was simply another mouth to feed. Not that Carmen ever bought much food.

Another sob wracked her body. The only thing to numb her pain was to drink. Laying down on the squeaky sofa, she wriggled until she felt comfortable on the rigid plastic and hugged herself hard, taking deep, shaking breaths. In under a minute, she had passed out.

3

I was finishing a late supper with my father, my twin sisters and two of my brothers. The eldest, Iker, was currently serving a stretch in the Modelo prison after being caught breaking into a house in well-to-do Pedralbes.

I was glad he wasn't here. All of us were enjoying the respite. Iker was a violent bully, quick with his fists, and I'd been on the receiving end of his punches more times than I could remember. Sometimes I resented my father for not standing up to Iker, but like all of us, he was wary of his eldest son.

'How was work today, Pa?' I asked, refilling his glass with the rough red wine we bought in giant carafes from Manolo's bar around the corner.

My father, Pichi, finished eating and immediately lit a cigarette from the one still smouldering in the overflowing ashtray on the table. I couldn't remember a time when my father didn't have a cigarette dangling from his lips.

'Same as always,' he replied, his kind eyes squinting through the curl of smoke, 'though they're looking to hire. I spoke to the foreman and told him you and Kiko would jump at the chance to work. You have to be there at the end of the morning shift tomorrow for an

17

interview.'

I was eleven when I began helping my father, collecting bits of old scrap in the Poblenou district, but my best friend, Kiko Perona, had been just seven when he started working alone – roaming the streets for bottles, metal, wood, anything his father, Paco, could sell to earn a few pesetas. Although I'd grown tired of collecting metal to sell for a pittance at the salvage yard, the prospect of working at the port didn't excite me either. My father worked as a stevedore and had been trying to get me in for a couple of years, but with so much unemployment, there was always someone stronger and more experienced than me. I feared that once I started, I'd never be able to leave and that my passion for medicine and working with Tia Rosita to heal the illnesses within our community would come to nothing. But we needed the money, and I knew it would please my father.

'That's good news. I'll go round to Kiko's right away and tell him.' I swallowed the last of my rice, chugged down the last drop of beer, and left.

As I headed to Kiko's house, I dodged muddy puddles, my shirt sticking to my back. Despite the approach of winter, it was a humid evening, and neighbours sat outside, eating or playing cards. The soulful strum of a guitar floated in the air. Before long, we would be forced back inside as the weather turned, cramped and overcrowded in the shacks we called home. Our front doors opened right onto the shore, and our lives were ruled by the sea, with the sting of salt always on our lips and in our hair. In the summer, the corrugated iron roofs began warming up early in the day. By midday, heat shimmered off them in mirages, rendering the inside suffocating until late into the evening. In the winter, we were tortured by bone-chilling dampness. The waves often came up and over our houses, an unstoppable tidal wave destroying our scant possessions.

The shacks joined onto each other, spreading outwards like a virus as far as the eye could see. We used wood, metal and anything that could be nailed down or tied. We hoped against hope and offered up prayers to Saint Florian for protection that our flimsy barrier against the sea and the world would be strong enough, unyielding. But in reality, it was a paper castle, fragile and useless, protecting us from nothing and no one.

Two minutes later, I was rapping on the front door of Kiko's house. The dogs on the other side of the door began howling. Hearing a shout, I cautiously opened the door and batted down the two mangy dogs that jumped up at me excitedly.

The scene that greeted me was as far removed as could be from the tranquillity of the one I'd left at home. Three generations of ten people, crushed elbow to elbow and seated around a rickety table made for four. Filthy fingers reaching hungrily to grab chunks of bread were slapped back. The noise was overbearing. 'Santi, come in!' shouted Kiko over the din, moving along to make space for me on the bench.

Loli, Kiko's mother, smiled at me. 'Have you eaten, *chico*? Do you want some stew?'

I shook my head. 'No thanks, Loli, we've just finished supper. I wouldn't say no to a drink, though.' I squeezed in beside Kiko and lightly punched him on the arm.

'What's going on? It's not like you to brave the chaos around here. We're celebrating Papa's saint day, so it's worse than usual,' said Kiko, pouring me a tepid beer.

'*Felicidades,* Paco,' I shouted over the chatter and held up my glass in a toast. Paco looked over at me, a tight smile on his face, and raised his glass.

Turning back to Kiko, I lowered my voice. 'There's an opening at the port for work, and my father has put our names forward. Are you interested? We have to go tomorrow afternoon when he finishes work to speak to the foreman.'

Kiko's eyes widened, and he glanced over to check his father wasn't listening. 'I'm interested. Papa has been working in the Barrio Gòtico doing some bricklaying, but last week the site manager caught him with some copper wiring down his trouser leg and threw him out. And I'm sick and tired of collecting scrap. It isn't enough to keep us going, and God knows when he'll find something else. He's been in a foul mood since he got sacked, and Mama's exasperated.'

I turned in Paco's direction. It was true. The corners of Paco's mouth were turned down, his shoulders

20

hunched as he slumped on his chair. It was clear he was getting quietly and steadily plastered. Loli had also noticed the state of her husband, and I saw her glare at him, tutting through her teeth. Suddenly one of the dogs jumped up, snatching a piece of bread from the baby's hand, and all hell broke loose. The baby began to scream, the other children started chasing the dog around the room, and Loli began yelling at Paco to do something. Only La Bati, Kiko's grandmother, who was as deaf as a post, looked unperturbed as she slurped her stew.

'Kiko, get those bastard dogs out of here before I break their necks and skin them for tomorrow's supper,' Paco roared as the noise level became thunderous.
Hearing his threat, the four-year-old twins joined in the screaming. Loli turned on Paco, berating him for upsetting them, her finger jabbing at him accusingly.
'Oh *Benito Santo*, don't tell the poor mites that, you brute,' she cried, trying to soothe the twins. Kiko jumped up, and I followed, each of us grabbing a dog. As I passed Paco, I saw him close his eyes, his face pinched and drawn, running his fingers through his greying-black hair, just like a raven's feathers.

We took the dogs outside and tied them up at the side of the house with the goats. I passed Kiko a cigarette, and we inhaled deeply, both relieved to be away from the chaotic atmosphere of Kiko's house and walked down the street towards Manolo's bar on the corner. Some of the regulars were sitting outside on upturned crates and old plastic chairs, playing cards for *céntimos*.

'Hey, *Qué pasa, chavales*? Come and have a game,' called out Raul, an old friend of Pichi and Paco, the candle on the table illuminating a mouthful of gold teeth.

'Not with you cheating rogues!' I laughed, shaking hands with a couple of the men.

'Ach, you're too chicken to put your money where your mouth is,' said Raul, good-naturedly, his attention turning back to the game.

We ordered a couple of beers and went to sit on the damp sand by the water's edge in front of the bar. A glow of light came from a fishing boat that had just upped anchor. Kiko was unusually quiet and stared off into the distance as if his thoughts were miles away.

'What's up with you?' I asked, taking a deep drag on my roll-up.

With a frown on his face, Kiko exhaled smoke. 'I've met someone,' he said, cracking his knuckles. 'A girl… and I don't know what to do. My father will kill me if he finds out.'

'Come on*, tío*. You're nearly eighteen. He'll be proud of you. You know he believes he's Don Juan himself! He'll be glad you've finally got a girlfriend!' I laughed, slapping him on the back.

'You've got to promise you won't tell anyone about this, Santi.' His eyes were fixed on the horizon, and I nodded, unnerved by his grave demeanour.

'Her name is Eva Sanchez, and I think I'm in love

with her.' He flicked the ash off the end of his cigarette and blew on the lighted end. 'She's a *paya.'*

I couldn't hide my reaction. I stared at him in silence, with my eyebrows raised, for what seemed like an age until Kiko began to squirm uncomfortably under my scrutiny. Eventually, I let out a long whistle. 'Uff, *Madre mia*, what the hell are you thinking?' Kiko rubbed his jaw, his eyes narrowed.

So I continued. 'Well, you're right about one thing, Paco will hit the roof when he finds out – and what about your mother?' I shook my head. 'A *paya*? Kiko, if you don't marry a gypsy, they'll never forgive you.'

Kiko sat with his arms resting on his knees and hung his head. 'I don't care,' he said, his voice heavy with emotion. 'I won't stop seeing her for anyone.'

We stayed there for a long time, smoking our cigarettes in silence and watching the fading lights bobbing out on the horizon.

4

The next afternoon when Margarita had finished work at the bakery, she hurried to the corner of Passeig de Gràcia to meet Eva. She arrived a few minutes early and flopped down on their favourite bench.

They could spend hours sitting there, admiring the elegant clothes and hairstyles of the wealthy shoppers going in and out of El Corte Ingles department store, followed by maids carrying their bags. But today, she didn't notice anything. Earlier that morning, she'd checked the jar where the rent money was kept and had discovered her self-centred mother had filched the lot. Margarita didn't get paid for another five days, and Don Calvet was coming tomorrow. She was tired of going through the same thing each week but was reluctant to dip into her secret stash. Resentment smouldered inside her.

Lost in her thoughts, she jumped as Eva sat down heavily beside her, huffing dramatically.

'God, it's such a relief to be out of that apartment. They treat me like a five-year-old.' She turned to face Margarita, a scowl on her smooth face. 'Do you know Eulalia still lays out my clothes every morning as if I'm incapable of dressing myself?'

Margarita bit her tongue. Having heard the story of

Eva's adoption many times, she believed that Eva was the luckiest girl in Barcelona. She'd been found outside the police commissary in Plaza Espana when she was a week old, wrapped in a thin cotton pillowcase, naked and malnourished.

As dawn broke, she'd been discovered by a street cleaner, who'd mistaken the bundle for old rags. He'd almost thrown her in his rubbish cart, another piece of flotsam and jetsam from the street, but quiet snuffles and snorts had alerted the cleaner it was alive. He'd taken the infant to the commissary, leaving it in the care of two bewildered police officers who had immediately rung the hospital. A doctor checked the baby over and declared that she was in good health apart from being extremely hungry.

When Eva was two, she'd been adopted by the very same doctor, adored and spoiled, living a life Margarita could only dream about. She knew Eva's mother was a cold fish who withheld her love from her adopted daughter, but this, in Margarita's opinion, was preferable to the love that came pickled and stinking of alcohol from her own mother.

She snapped back to the moment as Eva spoke again. 'Anyway, is everything alright?

Margarita sighed, crossing her arms and slouching further down the bench. 'Mother has spent the rent money again. I can't stand her drinking, the lying, or the state of the apartment anymore. And, God, she stinks worse than I do!' They began to giggle, and some of the unbearable tension Margarita had been feeling since the previous night eased.

Biting her lip, Eva looked at her. 'I can get some money from my savings bank. You know I'll help you.'

Margarita shook her head. Part of her was grateful to Eva, but at the same time, it annoyed her that Eva would never truly understand her situation, which she knew was unfair criticism of her best friend.

'I know you would, but it's happening week after week. It's never-ending. Why is she like this?' They'd had this same discussion many times, but neither knew the answer. 'Anyway, I only found out about the money this morning. It's not the reason I came to see you last night...' She paused for a moment, biting the inside of her mouth. 'A bizarre thing happened in the bar yesterday. One of the customers, Jorge Perillo, was talking about someone who knows my mother, someone who's "back".'

'Back from where?' asked Eva, picking at an invisible thread on her skirt.

'Well, I don't know, do I? We need to find out,' Margarita replied, with a flicker of irritation, but then brightened. 'Maybe it's my father! Oh, imagine if it was! I could move in with him – or perhaps he's rich, and he'll be able to help us pay the rent.'

Eva frowned. 'How will we find out, though?

Margarita reached down into the band of her skirt and pulled out a piece of paper with a flourish. She didn't want her friend to know the depths she'd sunk to, stealing from her mother, so she bent the truth a little.

I was rooting in her bag this morning to see if the missing money was there. It wasn't, but I found this.' Eva took the scrap of paper, looking puzzled as she read it out loud. '*El Paco, Barraca 47*. Who's Paco? Which barracks? Is he a soldier?' she asked, her brows knitted.

'I don't know yet,' said Margarita sitting back on the bench and folding her arms, her eyes narrowed. She would get to the bottom of this.

5

When Kiko Perona told me he was in love with a *paya,* my heart almost stopped beating. Even then, I knew things would change, although neither of us could have imagined how much. Kiko had always been so level-headed. As the eldest, he was the man of the house when his impetuous father was missing or off doing dodgy deals, often for days on end, and Kiko worked all the hours he could to put food on the table.

I loved him like he was my brother, more than the three I already had. Although he was often quick to judge and easily angered, he was loyal and hard-working, and I trusted him with my life. We'd always been together as children, playing football in the rain and the sunshine, even in the fog that curled up from the beach, hiding the horror of our squalid streets and slum housing. We played outside for hours, returning home only when our bellies cramped from hunger. My mother, Merce, or Kiko`s mother, Loli, would give us slices of homemade bread with olive oil and sugar sprinkled on top to tide us over until supper. Or simply to get us out from under their feet. We would sit on the breakwater, eating our bread, our filthy feet swinging off the pier as we sheltered from the cold wind or the fiery sun, planning our escape from here.

Somorrostro. The only place we'd ever known. But we were sure, even back then, that there was something better for us than this. Men came from all corners of Spain, searching for work with nowhere to live and nothing in their pockets. My father, Pichi, had arrived from the Basque country when he was fourteen.

Along with hundreds of others, he found not only a place to live in the derelict slums but also acceptance and friendship on the grim streets. The gypsy population welcomed the immigrants with open arms and kind hearts, knowing how it felt to be pushed to the bottom of the scrap heap without a voice. And they would help anyone who asked. Most of our neighbours were gypsies, and after living there for so long, my father gradually became one of them. I don't remember when I first realised my family, my friends, and myself were different from those who lived in other parts of the city.

Kiko glanced over his shoulder before beginning to explain. He'd been hanging around Las Ramblas one day several weeks earlier. Pick-pocketing from the well-heeled weekend visitors was something we both regularly did. There were always plenty of pickings to be had in Las Ramblas, and we went whenever we could.

'The first time I saw her, she was coming out of the Bar de la Opera, hanging off the arm of an older, dour-looking man. He had grey hair and those weird little glasses that sit on the end of your nose.' Kiko tapped the end of his nose, taking up the pose of a fussy old man. 'I didn't like him; it was like he owned her. I decided to

29

follow them. *Tío,* they were slow, stopping every few steps to smell roses and orchids at the flower stalls, and further up, she seemed captivated by the caged birds for sale.' Kiko's face took on a look of adoration as I glanced at him, and I stifled the urge to laugh.

'Didn't they spot you?'

Kiko tutted. 'Course not! I stayed a few steps behind. But I swear, I couldn't take my eyes off her, Santi. It was like I was in a trance, pulled along by an invisible thread held by the prettiest girl I'd ever seen. She looked like a little porcelain doll.'

I'd never seen my friend like this before – and I didn't know what to say to him. I'd seen the wealthy girls out with their parents or governesses parading up and down Las Ramblas in their fancy clothes, and I was sure this girl would look nothing like the ones we knew. In our world, the girls used whatever they could find to make clothes, scraps of coloured material fashioned into a skirt or a headscarf.

'So where did they go?'

'I followed them until they reached the top of Las Ramblas. They entered a domed building on the corner. It was so elegant, just like her.' Kiko's voice grew soft, his eyes turning heavenwards as if he were talking about having seen an angel. Maybe he thought he had.

'Before she disappeared through the door, she looked right at me and smiled the most dazzling smile I've ever seen.'

Kiko told me he'd sat on the corner of Las Ramblas

and Calle Pelayo all afternoon and long into the evening. No one had taken much notice of him, although several passers-by had given the scruffy, shifty-looking boy a wide berth. Still, Kiko hadn't taken his eyes off the doorway. It was only as night fell and the streetlamps came on that Kiko looked up towards the lit apartments and saw the girl standing at a second-floor window, looking down right at him.

I sniggered. 'But Kiko, *tío!* Have you ever spoken to this girl, or do you just go and stand there looking up at her?'

'Stop interrupting and let me finish the damn story,' he replied, scowling. Lighting another cigarette and passing it to me before lighting his own, Kiko carried on talking.

'Day after day, I went and stood there. Even when I needed to piss, I didn't move. Then on the fifth day, she came out with an older woman I thought must be her sister. They walked along Calle Pelayo, and I was right behind. I swear to God that she kept looking back at me. The woman, who I found out later was her governess, went into the butchers alone, and I knew it was the perfect time to speak to her. But I was struck dumb, Santi, standing there like an imbecile! We stood there staring at each other, and before I'd even blinked, she walked toward me and pressed a piece of paper into my hand. Then she turned around and walked back to the shop doorway!'

'What was on the piece of paper?' I asked, a spark of

31

interest making me pay closer attention to my friend's love-sick ramblings.

'Well, I didn't understand it at first. You were at work, so I dropped in to see Tia Rosita on my way home,' said Kiko. Like most people we knew, Kiko hadn't learned to read. I was one of the lucky ones. Along with teaching me about plants and herbs, Tia Rosita also taught me to read. Everyone in Somorrostro went to see the ancient matriarch when something significant happened in the community, and she often acted as an intermediary in disputes between families and neighbours. She may have been as old as the hills of Collserola, but she was the wisest person any of us had ever known. I was proud of my close relationship with her and the work we did.

'She stared at the piece of paper for so long, I was worried about what it would say, but then she said, "Kiko Perona, who gave you this? It wasn't written by one of ours. It looks like Payo writing." I told her I'd found it on the floor and that if I could find out whose it was and return it to them, I might get some *céntimos* for my trouble. But how the devil could she tell who'd written it?'

'Because she just can. You should know that by now. But anyway, what was written on the piece of paper?'

Like the cat who had got the top of the milk, Kiko's grin was triumphant. '"Meet me on Saturday afternoon on the steps at Plaza del Rey. I will be waiting at 4 pm. Yours, Eva Sanchez Ruiz".'

***

Margarita stared at Eva, her mouth agape. 'No, Eva! What will your parents say? *Dios*, they'll kill you.' Despite her horror, Margarita was intrigued. 'What's his name, then?'

Eva's ordinarily pale face flushed red. It was two days after Margarita had shown Eva the note about *El Paco* at the barracks. They hadn't talked any more about it, both at a loss how to find out who and where it was, wondering if it even meant anything. Her mother hadn't mentioned the note was missing, which made Margarita conclude it had no significance. But today, Eva had revealed her secret as if she couldn't contain it for a moment longer, giving Margarita the shock of her life. They may well have two problems to deal with now.

'His name is Kiko,' Eva said breathlessly, her eyes lighting up. Margarita thought she saw her friend hug herself a little.

'Kiko who? Do we know him? Is he our age?' asked Margarita, eager for all the details.

'I don't know his last name; I didn't ask. I suppose he's around our age,' replied Eva vaguely, chewing her lip and avoiding Margarita's eyes.

'What does he look like?'

Eva stared into the distance, her eyes taking on a faraway look. 'He's quite short, actually,' she said

33

after a pause as Margarita nudged her expectantly. 'His eyes are otherworldly, and his hair is to die for.'

'Ohh', exclaimed Margarita, a touch envious. She'd do anything to have a boyfriend. 'And how does he dress, Eva? Is he very dapper?'

'Just normal, really.'

Margarita thought Eva's reply was evasive, and she frowned. 'I thought you were smitten with him? Don't you want to tell me everything about him?' Margarita asked, hurt her friend might be holding back. She'd share every detail with Eva if she had a boyfriend.

'Don't be silly. I hardly know him. We've only seen each other a couple of times,' Eva tailed off, glancing to the side.

Margarita cracked her knuckles. 'Where does he live, then? You must have talked about that?'

Again, Eva hesitated, and then her shoulders sagged. 'That's the strange thing. When I asked where he lived, he pointed with his finger and said, "Oh, down near the sea". I thought asking him to be more specific would be rude,' she said, inspecting her fingernails.

Margarita let out a long sigh. 'So, now we have even more mysteries to solve.'

They sat without speaking for a few minutes, watching as a man on a bicycle almost collided with a tram. He ended up on the pavement a few yards from where they were sitting. The girls giggled as he shouted, his fist raised as the tram carried on its journey, and then stood shakily, checking to see if anyone had witnessed his undignified fall.

Margarita jolted as Eva grabbed her arm, her other hand flying to her mouth. 'Margarita! I haven't told you my other news!'

Margarita smiled faintly at the excitement on her friend's face, restraining the eye roll that lurked beneath the surface. 'There's more?'

'Well,' said Eva, 'apparently Eulalia told my mother that she feels I'm too old for home-schooling now, that she can't teach me much more.'

Eva frequently complained that she hated having a governess. Aged twelve, Margarita had been forced to leave school, which she had adored, to find a job. She often thought that Eva, who had never had to think about money, was rather ungrateful.

'So, she mentioned the portrait I painted for father's birthday last month and suggested they send me to art school. Mother was dismissive, of course, but father thought it was an excellent idea. I've been offered a place at La Llotja to start the week after next!'

'How wonderful,' said Margarita, struggling to keep her voice level. But Eva kept up her stream of lively chatter until, eventually, Margarita told her she had to go and get changed before starting her shift at the bar. Walking home, she shoved her hands deep in her cardigan pockets, trying to imagine what it would be like to study at the prestigious La Llotja and mix with all those fancy types. While she had no artistic talent, Margarita rarely went a day without reading. How she'd love to have the opportunity to study literature. Life was unfair, she concluded, letting out a sigh at her boring life. And hurried home to change into her waitress uniform.

6

The foreman disappeared inside the office, coming out ten minutes later with a couple of shabby brown overalls slung over his arm.

'These are to be worn at all times on-site, so we know you're ours. They must be kept in a reasonable state, or believe me, you'll hear about it. Start tomorrow at 6.30 am sharp. If you're late, don't bother coming back, *entendido*?'

Kiko and I nodded. After shaking Pichi's hand, the foreman walked away briskly, and we turned to my father expectantly. 'What will we be doing, Pa?' I asked.

'You'll both be on kitchen duty,' said Pichi, chuckling as our faces fell. 'There's a canteen for the workers, which gets hellishly crowded at lunchtime. The Port pays for it, and for many of the men, it's the only food they have all day. You two will be scraping the plates for the washer-uppers.'

'*Joder*, we can't do that. We'll be a laughing stock if anyone finds out we work in the damn kitchen of all places,' I grumbled and glanced at Kiko for support. I was also wondering how these fixed hours would allow me to fit in my work with Tia Rosita. I usually gathered plants early in the morning, when they were at their freshest for infusing. And we always worked until lunchtime, treating the ill who came in a constant stream each day.

But Kiko shrugged. 'I honestly don't care. Anything is better than traipsing all over Poblenou with a cart full of scrap for my dad to sell.'

I lowered my eyes. Kiko was right. It would be a regular wage at the end of every week and wasn't too far from home. Pichi raised his eyebrows pointedly at me, and I felt my face redden slightly. 'Thanks, Pa, thanks for helping us. But *joder,* the bloody kitchen,' I said, shaking my head with a laugh.

We left Pichi chatting with some of his colleagues and began to walk along La Barceloneta towards Somorrostro, watching as hundreds of gulls clamoured around a fishing boat that had just dropped anchor. It was a clear autumn afternoon, and the sun was going down in the orange sky. We ambled, both deep in thought, hardly exchanging a word on the walk home.

After a while, the silence unsettled me. 'What's wrong with you? I thought you were happy about the job?'

With a sigh, Kiko sat down on the seawall and started rolling a cigarette deftly with one hand.

'I can't stop thinking about Eva. I'll never get to see her when we start working. She's only allowed out in the morning or late afternoon,' he explained glumly, his brow furrowed.

'What do you mean, "allowed out"? I thought you said she was nearly eighteen.'

'She's not like us, Santi. We can do whatever we want. No one cares what time we get home or where we go. Most days, my parents throw me out of the house in the morning because there's no space for us all. Even the little ones play outside all day. But Eva has to be accompanied by Eulalia, her governess, every time she leaves the house. When she goes out, it's to have lunch with her parents or go shopping with Eulalia. She has a friend, Margarita, who she meets every couple of weeks. They have to meet secretly, though, because Eva's parents disapprove of their friendship.' He inhaled his cigarette deeply and looked at me, his eyes blazing. 'She's a prisoner in that house, you know?'

Even then, it was clear to me the effect this girl had on my friend. Although I had some misgivings about Kiko's new relationship, it was a relief to see a flicker of the Kiko I loved – proud, loyal and fierce.

'It *is* very odd,' I said, jumping down from the wall. 'We're going to have to find a way for you to see each other, aren't we?'

Kiko followed suit, and we carried on towards home. This was our favourite time of day when the sky darkened on the horizon. We could still see where we were going, but the dusk softened the desolation and gloom surrounding us. Our camp in Somorrostro stretched along the shoreline from the Hospital for Infectious Diseases to Poblenou. We remained unseen, hidden from the rest of the city by the dozens of factories that bellowed filthy smoke along the coast. A dirty secret for those who were either unaware of our existence or simply didn't want to know.

Although it was home, we were old enough now to understand that we didn't live like other people, and whenever we met someone new, we rarely mentioned where we were from. We didn't notice the ingrained dirt on our neighbour's faces and heard only joy in the giggles of the children playing barefoot in the mud. This world was far more real to us than any other we knew.

7

Eva had been spending all her free moments with Kiko for the last few weeks. Margarita had only seen her once since the discovery of the note and her revelation about meeting Kiko. She'd also started her first term at La Llotja, and Margarita was eager to find out how she was enjoying it. Her friend had everything Margarita had ever dreamed of, and to top it all, she was in love, too. It was mean-spirited to begrudge Eva such happiness, and while she felt guilty for thinking such things, it still stung.

Margarita hadn't met Kiko yet, nor had Eva suggested it. She was desperate to be part of their love story, even just a tiny part. It might be unfair of her to resent Eva for spending so much time with Kiko, but Margarita had never felt excluded from Eva's life before, and she felt lonelier than ever. The only bonus to Eva's blossoming relationship with Kiko, providing a much-needed chink of light in her otherwise dull existence, was that Margarita could spend more time reading. Between working at the bakery in the mornings and the bar each night, she immersed herself in books at the Francesca Bonnemaison women's library on the corner of her street.

Margarita found a sense of peace and belonging

within the thick stone walls, the hushed silence a balm to her disordered life. She would spend every hour possible devouring the books that Lurdes, the librarian, put aside for her. She was ploughing her way through Cervantes and Garcia Lorca and had even begun teaching herself English to read Agatha Christie in its original version.

The ongoing tension with her mother and struggle to find money to pay the rent had Margarita picking the painful skin on her hands until they bled. Don Calvet had started coming to the bar each week to find Margarita. She guessed it was because he knew he was more likely to get the rent from her rather than from her old soak of a mother. Margarita could tell Bernat wasn't happy whenever Don Calvet rolled up, but like everyone on the street, he was too wary of the old crook to defend her.

Each time the despised landlord called round, Bernat refused to make eye contact with Margarita, disappearing into the cellar or sweeping the entrance to the bar. He would nod, pour Calvet a whiskey – on the house, of course – growl at Margarita to pay him immediately so he would leave, and quickly shuffle off, muttering under his breath. The atmosphere in the bar was always heavy as Calvet sat in the corner, watching her like a gecko eyeing a mosquito. It was only when he finally stood up to leave that Margarita breathed a sigh of relief.

And each week, she would apologise to Bernat all over again, well aware that it was only because of her that Don Calvet came to the bar.

'It's not your fault, *chiquilla*. I know you're doing your damnedest to keep a roof over your head, but it shouldn't be your responsibility. It's not right,' he sighed, shaking his head. 'You're still a child. That mother of yours wastes all her money on drink when she should be putting it in a savings account for you— ' He paused mid-sentence and licked his lips. 'I mean, she never goes without her drink, does she? She should be spending it on food and paying the damn rent.'

Margarita looked at him. 'What do you mean "putting it in a savings account? What money? She doesn't earn enough money working at the butcher's to save a *céntimo*. Most of it is for her booze, and if there's any leftover, it goes towards the rent.'

Looking shifty, Bernat picked up a tea towel and closely inspected the spotless glasses for invisible smears.

'Bernat?' Margarita tried again, frowning. 'What are you on about?'

'You should ask that grandmother of yours; she'll know more than I do. Rosa knows more than anyone about what goes on around here, especially regarding your mother,' he snapped. 'And for God's sake, don't tell her it came from me! I don't need Rosa Marquez around here, too. It's bad enough that damn Calvet sitting in the corner, eavesdropping on all the customers. Last Friday, Jorge told me he'd seen at least three of my regulars in old Ramon's bar in Calle L'Argenter when Calvet was in here. I'm telling you, Margarita, you better find some other place to pay him because he's losing me business!' he harrumphed before throwing the tea towel at her. 'And finish the damn glasses before you leave.'

Open-mouthed, Margarita stared after him as he began to collect more dirty glasses. Bernat had never spoken to her like that before. She resolved to talk to Yaya as soon as she finished her shift at the bakery tomorrow. She'd take her something tasty for dessert. She finished drying the glasses, occasionally throwing daggers at Bernat, who was cashing up for the day, but he didn't once glance her way.

***

Carmen was sitting at the kitchen table drinking black coffee. It made her stomach heave and gave her heartburn, but Margarita still hadn't arrived home with the milk. She turned the swivel mirror on the scratched kitchen table to the magnified side, avoiding looking at her dirty nails, bitten down to the quick. The other hand held a pair of tweezers which she was using to unsteadily pluck out some stray, black hairs from her top lip and chin. Weeks could go by when the only time she looked at herself was a glance in the mottled mirror above the toilet sink. There was no window in the bathroom, and the weak bulb flattered anything unsightly. But now, in the daylight of this cursed damn mirror, she was dismayed to see how much she'd aged.

In frustration, she shoved the mirror away, almost

spilling the foul black coffee. She'd been so beautiful when she was younger, never in doubt of her beauty. Her mother had repeatedly told her how precious she was, a princess. As she became a teenager, the boys in the neighbourhood ogled her when she passed by, whistles and lewd comments following her wherever she went. She'd brushed them off with the confidence of youth, and it was only now her beauty had faded that she desperately longed to hear those whistles again. These days, people looked through her as if she wasn't there, or worse, looked at her with pity in their eyes.

Carmen thought back to the day her life had changed forever. She'd been crossing Plaza Sant Jaume and was about to step into the path of a horse and cart overflowing with fruit and vegetables. Seconds from being trampled, a pair of strong arms yanked her back. When she turned to give thanks, the greenest eyes she'd ever seen were smiling down at her. And that was the moment Carmen met Paco Perona. He would be the only man she loved for a very long time, and despite saving her that day, he would nearly be the death of her.

Snapping back to the present, Carmen put down her tweezers and sighed deeply. She pulled the mirror back towards her, flipped it over and studied herself, trying to imagine how others must see her. Smoking lines ran from her once plump lips to her nose. Her cheekbones were still prominent, but gone was the rosy glow of porcelain skin, replaced with dark patches and thread veins that radiated out from her nose. Her eyebrows were still beautifully arched, but dark shadows ringed her bloodshot eyes. Her long hair had hung almost to her waist as a child, and her mother would brush it for hours until it shone like a diamond on a dead man's hand. Even when she'd stopped brushing, hefting herself up to see to dinner, Rosa had beamed with pride at her exemplary daughter.

But now, when Carmen's stringy hair wasn't held back by a thin elastic band, it hung flat and greasy, a dull grey from the roots to down past her ears. No longer the luxurious chestnut it had been in her youth. Her fall from grace had been dramatic and utterly crushing. In almost two decades, the need for alcohol had become more important than anything else in her life. She spent hardly any money on food for herself or her daughter. She was also behind on the rent, so a trip to the hairdresser to sort out her roots came way down her list of priorities. And she'd muckied her ticket with her mother, so she couldn't even ask her to tidy up the split ends. Carmen stared at her reflection in the mirror, her chest aching with grief, and she ruminated over how life had gone so spectacularly wrong for the young girl with long, shiny hair and the world at her feet.

8

I was lying on the bed I shared with my twin sisters, eyes wide open, staring at the metal ceiling. I'd arrived home from the port kitchen exhausted and had tried to have forty winks, but the noise from the children playing right outside the window had made sleep impossible.

Kiko and I had arranged to meet at half past seven that evening for a few drinks with a couple of Filipinos from work with whom we'd struck up a friendship. But first, I had to get the rancid stench of greasy food from my body.

Each evening I scrubbed myself from top to toe outside in the communal backyard. All our immediate neighbours used a rusted metal pail to wash in the cramped space. It had no roof except for a strip of corrugated iron which gave it a modicum of privacy. There was only ever cold water, which had to be carried from La Barceloneta and was mainly used for cooking or watering the animals.

My mind drifted back to when Kiko and I were children. We were around three or four when we first went to the fountain in Plaza Brugada with my mother, Merce. She'd encouraged us, amusement tugging at her lips as our tiny bodies struggled with the weight of the plastic carafe, spilling water all the way home until the carafes were almost empty. My mother bathed us each Sunday, popping us in the enormous pail one after the other and ignoring our screams of blue murder as she rinsed each of us down with icy water. Then she'd dump us unceremoniously onto a grubby sheet on the dirty ground to let the air dry our bodies. Since I'd lost my mother, this ritual and many others had died with her.

I rarely allowed myself to think of my mother, but lying there that evening, I remembered the warm, loving arms that had always been open and welcoming after a long day on the streets. As a youngster, I loved nothing more than curling up on her lap while she told me stories about her childhood. Her infectious laugh could be heard all over the camp, and her generosity was renowned.

My parents were distant cousins and had been together since they were young. When my father moved into the house in Somorrostro, he sent for Mama, and they got married the same day she arrived after the long journey from San Sebastian.

She'd died three years ago, mown down on the way to her stall at the market in La Barceloneta by a new-fangled motor car driven by an elderly, myopic man. A wave of sorrow washed over me as I recalled my father telling me when I'd arrived home from a tiring day traipsing the streets with my cart. I remember Kiko holding me up on the long walk to Montjuic cemetery, each step more painful than the last. I wouldn't have made it if it hadn't been for him. Since then, our friendship had become even more solid, and I would do anything for him. But I was still suspicious of this Eva, with her fancy clothes and wealthy parents. I worried we might lose the closeness of a thousand shared adventures, and I prayed Kiko would tread carefully. I feared it might be too late for that. She was all he talked about.

Reluctantly hauling myself out of bed, I got ready to meet Kiko.

***

As we walked up from Somorrostro through Ciutadella park, we kept an eye out for any easy marks. Although we now had legitimate work, neither of us had lost the habit of pickpocketing, a trick we'd learned even before we could ride a bicycle. But that evening, a biting autumn wind was howling up from the sea, and only a handful of people were in the park, mostly young men like us.

We crossed the park, holding our jackets tight across our chests, discussing Kiko's frustrations at not seeing much of Eva and that the governess was always hanging around when they did meet.

'We need to find a place to go. We can't keep meeting in Plaza del Rey forever. I want to be alone with her, to kiss her,' Kiko said, reddening. 'But we have nowhere to go.'

I listened to Kiko, an idea taking shape in my mind. 'What about asking the Filipinos if you could use their apartment?' I suggested.

Kiko considered the suggestion for a moment, pulling at his ear. 'That's not a bad idea, but there are about ten of them sharing, and the damn place is full of Filipinos night and day. I'm not sure how it would work, but I suppose it wouldn't hurt to ask.'

We passed through Plaza Sant Jaume and walked along Calle Ferran, having arranged to meet our friends at Bar Masella on Calle Sant Pau. We were early, so we ordered an absinthe chaser and sat at a table near the door.

'How's your latest obsession going?' asked Kiko, lighting a cigarette.

Tia Rosita and I had been studying the use of Calendula in wound healing, and we'd made some exciting headway. Kiko always showed an interest, but I often suspected he was mocking me with snide comments about witch doctors and magic.

'It's going well,' I told him. 'Although since I started at the port, the only time I have free is evenings and weekends.'

Kiko nodded without comment, so I continued. 'We've been invited to present our findings at the Royal Academy of Medicine in Calle Carme in a couple of months.'

He let out a whistle. 'I didn't realise you and Tia Rosita did anything except play around with plants!' he said. 'What have you discovered, then?'

'Years ago, Tia Rosita used Calendula to heal the

wounds of the soldiers injured in the Civil War. Traditional medicine rejects herbal treatments nowadays, but one of the soldiers she treated successfully is on the board of directors.'

For once, Kiko looked impressed, but before he had time to reply, our drinks arrived. Just as we chinked our glasses, the door to the bar opened, and the Filipinos, Ramil and Datu, entered, their timid faces lighting up when they saw us.

After chatting about our day at work and port gossip, Kiko broached the subject of using their apartment to spend some time with Eva. Nudging each other lecherously, the two boys began speaking ten to the dozen in Filipino, eyeing Kiko and laughing.

After a few minutes, Datu spoke. 'For you, Kiko, I'll speak to the others tonight, but I'm sure it will be alright with them. How do you think we get on when we want to take a woman home?' he said, a lascivious grin on his face.

'There's an annexe behind the kitchen with a mattress on the floor,' Ramil explained, 'where we take our girls. But you'll have to see what slots are available,' he said, chuckling at the look of apprehension on Kiko's face.

I nudged Kiko. 'There's the answer to your problem, *tío*. You can finally see what lies beneath the fancy clothes she wears.'

Kiko scowled as we smirked at him. 'It's not like that. Eva's not like that,' he snapped. 'She's more than a quick fuck on a dirty mattress in a shithole. We love each other.'

With a glare, he swallowed his drink in one, stood up, and left the bar, the door slamming behind him. Shrugging at the Filipinos, I scrambled up after him, regretting my glib words.

'I thought you, of all people, understood my feelings for Eva.' He was stomping heavily towards home, clearly in a foul mood. The misty rain soaked us both.

'I'm sorry, *tío*, it was just a bit of fun,' I panted as I hurried to keep up with him. I couldn't read the emotions of my friend. Maybe I'd underestimated his feelings for this girl.

'She's different, Santi,' Kiko turned to look at me, and the vulnerability I saw in his eyes surprised me. 'She's like nobody I've ever met.'

9

The day after her strange conversation with Bernat, Margarita went to see her grandmother. She'd had a restless night. Each time she'd jerked awake, snippets of the conversation had echoed through her head, and she'd woken unrested and gritty-eyed, determined to find some answers.

She left after her shift at the bakery, taking some fresh bread which was slightly burnt on the bottom – not good enough to sell, but good enough to eat – and made her way through the Barrio Gòtico to Yaya's house in Calle Escudellers.

Yaya lived alone now since Margarita's grandfather, Antonio, had died in the Spanish Civil War in Morocco two months before it ended in 1939. Margarita knew, though, that Yaya hadn't mourned much. She'd grown up on stories that her grandfather was a bit of a loose cannon, prone to gambling and drinking, and with a wandering eye to boot. After his death, life was more settled. Yaya received a paltry military pension and worked cleaning the big apartments in L'Eixample until her chronic back pain worsened, forcing her to retire. She hadn't made a fortune, but it had been enough to cover her basic living costs and ballet lessons for the young Carmen. Margarita loved going to Yaya's house.

The hustle and bustle of Calle Escudellers delighted her, full of hostels, restaurants and the Castilla cinema. After the library, it was her favourite place to pass the time. Whenever Yaya gave her some *céntimos*, she would stay for the double bill on Saturdays, even returning three times to see West Side Story.

But today, she marched purposefully to Yaya's, only slowing down as she passed Las Caracoles to inhale the mouth-watering smell of roasting chicken. Yaya lived over a churreria that made homemade crisps and doughnuts and was nestled between the chemist and Enric's barbers. The buttery sweetness of soft dough frying permeated Yaya's apartment all year round, and whenever Margarita hugged Yaya, she was always comforted by the faint smell of sweet churros. She rang the bell, and Yaya appeared on her balcony within seconds. When she saw Margarita, her face lit up. She took out a set of keys from her pinny and threw them down to Margarita, who caught them deftly with one hand.

Making her way up the dingy stairwell, which was even darker than hers, Margarita pressed the light switch on each floor she reached. She climbed higher and higher until the natural daylight from the overhead glass roof guided her. By the time she reached the top, she was panting. She really must stop smoking. She'd only started because Clara had told her everyone knew women who smoked were more sophisticated, although she didn't feel very elegant when she was coughing like a navvy

54

from the strong cigarettes they pilfered from under the counter at Bernat's bar. The door was already open when she reached the fourth floor, and she went straight in through to the kitchen, where her grandmother was chopping vegetables for a broth. She turned to hug Margarita, kissing her on both cheeks and holding her at arm's length so she could have a good look at her.

'You're getting prettier by the day, Margarita Marquez!' she exclaimed, pinching Margarita's cheek between her finger and thumb. Used to her grandmother's tendency to exaggerate, Margarita batted her grandmother's hands away.

'How are you, Yaya? How's your hip today?' she asked, putting the bread in a cotton bag hanging on the back of the door.

'Oh, you know, *Preciosa*, I'm as strong as a bull. I went to see Doctor Baulies last week, and he told me it wasn't often he saw a sixty-year-old as fit as me. He said I could pass for forty-five, the old charmer!' Yaya replied with a chuckle, then became serious. 'It's when the days are damp that I get a twinge of rheumatism. It'll rain tonight, mark my words. I can feel it.'

Sitting at the dining table half an hour later, Yaya spooned the broth into two bowls. As Margarita tore off a hunk of the fresh bread she'd brought, she felt Yaya's eyes on her.

'So, how's that worthless mother of yours?' Yaya asked, turning her mouth down as if she'd sucked a lemon.

'Well,' said Margarita guardedly, 'that's what I wanted to talk to you about.'

'Oh, *si?* What's she been up to now, then?' Yaya sniffed. 'You won't shock me, Margarita. I've seen just about everything you can imagine with her,' she lamented, crossing her arms under her ample bust and sitting back in the chair.

Margarita hesitated, unsure how to broach such a thorny subject, and nervous about what Yaya would tell her.

'How does Mama get the money to buy her drink? She must spend a fortune in the bodega every day.'

A shadow passed over her grandmother's face. If Margarita hadn't known Yaya so well, she might have imagined it was fear. But Yaya was afraid of no one, especially not Carmen.

Yaya cleared her throat and replied with a slight tremor in her voice. 'Well, she works at Eduardo's, doesn't she? It's not much, but it's enough to keep the wolves from the door, *cariño.*'

Margarita took a deep breath and swallowed. 'Stop treating me like a child, Yaya,' she said, raising her voice. 'Why can't you just be honest with me? All my life, she's lied to me, and now you're doing the same.' She held out her upturned hands and shook her head. 'I've heard the rumours all my life. Can you even imagine how awful that is, Yaya?' she said, her voice trembling. She stood up and grabbed her bag, but despite her rheumatism, her grandmother was still nimble on her

56

feet and stood in front of the door, blocking Margarita's path.

'You're right, *amor mio*. You're old enough to know the truth now. I sometimes forget you're not a little girl anymore. You've had so much to put up with from that mother of yours, and I didn't want to heap more worries on your shoulders.'

'No one ever tells me the truth, Yaya,' said Margarita, slumping back down on the chair, all the tension in her body evaporating. She lifted her eyes to meet her grandmother's. 'Is she a prostitute, Yaya?'

Yaya stared at her, her eyebrows almost disappearing into her hairline. 'Margarita! Of course she isn't. You stay there, and I'll make us a lovely cup of hot chocolate and try and explain what I can,' she said, bustling off into the kitchen to prepare Margarita's favourite drink.

Margarita remained seated, chewing her nails. As much as she despised her unsightly, bitten-down stumps, she couldn't get out of the habit. Glancing around at all the photos in mottled silver frames on the sideboard and along the windowsill, she hoped this was, at long last, the day she found out the truth about her mother. Quite honestly, nothing could be worse than hearing the rumours and speculative tittle-tattle whenever Carmen's name was mentioned. Yaya placed the mugs on the linen coasters she'd painstakingly embroidered despite her painful joints while Margarita gnawed her thumb. Sitting down opposite Margarita, Yaya blew on her hot chocolate and began.

***

After leaving Yaya's house, Margarita wandered along Via Laietana, her steps heavy and her shoulders hunched. She usually window-shopped as she walked, but today she didn't see a thing. Yaya's words were screaming through her head, bringing with them a queasy feeling of unease mingled with a burning hatred for the secrets her mother had been keeping from her.

All the scrimping and saving, hiding money from her mother's grasping, drunken hands. The things Margarita had had to go without for all these years; nice clothes, smart shoes, even food! They would have had enough if Carmen hadn't drunk it all away. Margarita stood staring through a boutique window, longing for the fashionable clothes she'd never be able to own. Her vision blurred as hot tears filled her eyes, and she recalled everything she'd put up with so her mother could feed her sickening habit. Blinking the tears back, she continued her slow walk towards home. She needed to get ready for her shift at the bar that evening, but this knowledge didn't speed up her plodding feet. It felt like she was wading through thick mud. Yaya's words echoed in her mind.

I'd never felt such shame, vida mía, *the day your mother told me Quim, Eduardo's son, had touched her and that she hadn't had her monthly bleeding since. I was horrified, disgusted that a respectable man like Eduardo Diaz had raised such an animal. After the doctor confirmed she was expecting, I took Carmen straight to Eduardo's. When he saw me, Rosa Marquez, in his shop, dragging a red-faced Carmen behind me, he knew. He knew exactly why I was there. I have never forgiven him. I'll never forget how his face turned grey, like cold ashes in the morning.*

It only took us five minutes to thrash out a deal. Eduardo would pay a modest monthly amount into an account at La Caixa bank that I would open that very day. Carmen would continue to work at the butcher's, and Quim would be sent away to his mother's family in the Pyrenees for the foreseeable future. He never came back – disgusting creature.

Did this mean she had a sibling somewhere? Yaya had been vague about the details. Suddenly her stomach dropped into her shoes as it dawned on her that Eduardo the butcher was her grandfather. That had never been one of the rumours. Tears began to threaten again as Margarita stumbled down the street, weaving in and out of the other shoppers before turning left down Calle de la Fontanella in the direction of home. As she passed a dingy dive on the corner, raised voices penetrated her foggy head, and she slowed down.

She would recognize that shrill tone anywhere, no doubt causing trouble after a couple of drinks. She peered through the grimy glass window and made out the silhouette of her mother on her feet, berating some poor soul on the opposite side of the table. Bile rose in Margarita's throat. Of all the people she had to come across at this moment, it had to be her duplicitous mother. She couldn't see who her mother was arguing with, and to be perfectly honest, she didn't care. Probably one of her inebriated friends. Her mother would try to wangle money out of anyone for another drink. With her newfound knowledge of her mother's finances, it sickened her further to see her begging, beguiling, and demanding money from whoever she could.

With a tut, she carried on her way, the corners of her mouth turning down as she hugged her arms around herself. Hopefully, work would take her mind off her shame. The humiliation of finding out she was the result of an unwanted, perhaps forceful encounter pulled at her gut. And, what was more disturbing, she was related to the butcher. She'd known Eduardo all her life, playing in the back with the chickens when she was a child while her mother worked. He'd known she was his granddaughter – had even paid her mother for her silence – how could he live with himself? The idea that he'd known but had chosen not to accept her was almost too much to bear. Her footsteps quickened as she tried to shake off the horror of her new truth.

Her thoughts drifted to Eva, who was having her first romantic date with Kiko. Margarita was happy for her best friend but felt so alone that she wanted to break down in the street and weep. Eva spent every free second with Kiko, and Margarita had no one.

Where was her friend now when she needed her more than ever? Eva was riding a wave of love and happiness. A feeling Margarita was sure she'd never get to feel herself because who in their right mind would love anyone from a family like hers?

Giving her head a shake to clear away the dark thoughts, Margarita returned home, changed her blouse and arrived at work a full hour before her shift began.

10

Sweating heavily, Carmen groaned as she wiped the vomit from her mouth with some scrunched-up toilet paper and pulled the chain. It was the third consecutive morning she'd thrown her guts up as her stomach violently expelled its toxic load. She pushed herself up from the floor on trembling legs, her head still spinning from the amount of cheap brandy she'd drunk the previous night. She couldn't face a coffee today, and after splashing her face with water and pulling back her hair into a stringy ponytail, she left for work.

'Morning, Carmen,' called out Eduardo from the back, the squawk of chickens exacerbating her pounding head.

She hung up her coat and poked her head around the door. 'Morning, sorry I'm a few minutes late,' she said, forcing a smile.

Eduardo peered at her. 'You look worse for wear today, is everything alright?' he said, a look of concern crossing his face.

Carmen knew Eduardo was fond of her, although she doubted he'd be so understanding if he knew about the lie she'd kept up for almost eighteen years. He'd often implied how it pained him to watch from the sidelines as her life spiralled into chaos. Although he couldn't have prevented the direction her life would take, he'd told her on more than one occasion of his remorse for the part his wretched son had played in her undoing.

'I'm fine, Eduardo, *gracias*. I've had some problems with my digestion, but it's nothing a trip to the chemist won't fix,' she replied stiffly.

'Well, make sure you get yourself sorted out sooner rather than later.' He looked at her pointedly. 'How many times have you cut yourself this week, eh? There's more blood from your fingers than from the damn chicken gizzards!' His face softened. 'But promise me if you need help, you'll come to me, *hija*. You know I won't say a word to anyone – all you have to do is ask,' he finished, his cheeks reddening. Eduardo found it difficult to express his feelings to anyone, let alone her, Carmen Garcia. She suspected he was getting soft in his old age, but still, she was grateful for his concern. He was the only person who gave a damn.

Carmen nodded and set about displaying the trays of meat Eduardo had already prepared, feeling the butcher's eyes on her as she worked. Her life was unravelling, and she didn't know how to hold it together anymore. She tried to recall the last time she'd been truly happy.

***

1949

She'd been seeing Paco Perona for a few months. He was

63

exciting, unlike anyone she'd ever met, and she adored him. He made her feel like the most beautiful girl in the world, and she would have done anything he asked. But he was evasive whenever she mentioned his family or asked when he would introduce her to them or where he lived. He had also shown no interest in meeting her mother. It had begun to bother her.

One day, Carmen made the impulsive decision to follow him. She kissed him goodbye at the end of her street and turned to walk home. Glancing over her shoulder, she watched him walk away and then changed direction to run down a narrow alley that would double back to join the street he was now heading down. She followed behind him as he weaved through the congested, narrow streets of the Gothic Quarter, dodging people, animals and motorcycles vying for space.

From his casual comments, she'd been under the impression that Paco lived in La Barceloneta, a working-class neighbourhood of fishermen and port workers. But now, as they veered further away from the city centre, Paco was heading to the left of La Barceloneta towards the sprawling factories that lay along the shoreline, spewing out polluted smoke.

The crowds were thinning now, and he'd probably spot her if he turned. But she'd come this far and wasn't leaving until she found out exactly where he was heading. Angry-looking clouds gathered in the sky, and she shivered. If she were honest, she'd rather Paco discover she was following him than risk walking back alone.

Her mother had often warned her to steer clear of this grimy industrial part of the city. 'Full of oddballs, it is. If they don't murder you, they'll almost certainly rob you! And an innocent young girl like you, Carmen! Well, it doesn't bear thinking about what they'd do if they saw you!' she'd said with a shudder, and it had been enough to deter Carmen from going. Until now.

On each corner, groups of men with dirt-streaked faces warmed their hands over fires blazing in rusty steel drums. They were strangely silent, and the atmosphere was heavy with tension. Every time they passed a group, Paco nodded at them in acknowledgement. Pulling her scarf down over her ears to try and hide her face, Carmen wondered uneasily if he was being polite or if he actually knew these people. As they passed the dark, gloomy factories, the sky came into view again, and she guessed they must be alongside the beach. But instead of a stretch of sand, as she'd expected, it was swamped with a huddle of corrugated iron roofs as far as the eye could see.

Horses and goats were tethered to the buildings. The shrieks of children playing drifted to her ears. The sound of such happiness was at odds with Carmen's first shocking glimpse of Somorrostro. A dull spike of fear travelled up her spine. She'd lost all sense of where she was, so far from the places she was familiar with. So much so that she no longer cared whether Paco would be angry at being followed and let out a panicked shout.

'Paco! Paco, wait for me!'

Paco spun round, a look of horror spreading over his face as the colour drained from his cheeks. He was beside her in a second. Grabbing her arm, he dragged her behind a filthy truck, his eyes flashing as he pushed her to the ground.

'What the hell are you doing here, you stupid bitch?' Without letting her answer, he ran his hands through his hair. 'If anyone sees us, we are both fucking dead.'

All the passion she'd seen in his eyes as they'd kissed goodbye less than an hour earlier had been replaced with fury. Much too late, she realised that following him had been the most foolish thing she could have done. But despite her fear, she tried to brazen it out.

'Well, it's a good job I did follow you, Paco Perona. You're obviously hiding something, or why would you be this mad at me?' She pushed him away from her and tried to stand up, only for Paco to pull her down again, his unyielding grip hurting her wrist.

'I'm going now, Carmen, and I want you to fuck off back home. I mean it. If you're still here in one minute, you'll never see me again,' he growled, his eyes black. He stood over her for a second with a furious snarl on his face and then strode off, his shoulders stiff and his fists clenched. Carmen stared after him as he glanced in all directions and then disappeared from view.

She rubbed the arm he'd grabbed, feeling a bruise already forming, and got to her feet unsteadily. As she walked away, numb with shock, her skin crawled as though she was being watched, but she didn't dare look back.

Carmen made her way home through the dark streets, ignoring the strange men on the corners, no longer afraid. Paco was everything to her. But her curiosity, her stupidity, could have scared him away forever.

***

Now, she placed the last of the horsemeat fillets in the glass display counter and straightened up, unsettled by the memories, stirring up a restlessness she'd been carrying around for a while.

A couple of months ago, she heard on the grapevine that Paco had been hanging around the neighbourhood, asking if anyone knew where to find her. Someone had even given her his address, but she'd known for almost twenty years exactly where he lived. Each time the shop bell rang, her stomach twisted, half expecting to see Paco enter. After learning he was sniffing around, Carmen had been vigilant. She couldn't bear for Paco to see how far she'd fallen. She was a mess, no longer the pretty, free-spirited girl he'd fallen in love with. She disgusted herself, but to see it reflected on Paco's face would kill her.

The door opened, and Carmen plastered a grin on

her face. '*Buenos Dias,* Señora Gisbert. What can I get you today?'

Her feet didn't touch the ground all morning, and her headache had finally eased after a short siesta at lunchtime. The afternoon shift was quiet, and half an hour before closing time, Eduardo told her she could knock off early. Carmen didn't need to be told twice. She grabbed her bag and her jacket and headed towards Cesar's bodega for a carafe of wine. It was all she could afford. Just as she was about to push the door open, a figure appeared from the dark passage where the gigantic casks of wine and ale deliveries were rolled into the cellar.

It was so unexpected that she let out a small scream. And then she found herself looking into Paco's green eyes – eyes that had haunted her dreams for the past two decades.

'Carmen?' he said hesitantly, a far cry from the cocky young man she'd first met in Plaza Sant Jaume all those years ago. 'I've been looking for you for weeks. He reached out his hand towards her, his face solemn. His hair, still thick, flopped over one eye in the same way it always had, taking her back twenty years in a heartbeat.

She couldn't speak. The words stuck in her throat. While her heart screamed to wrap her arms around Paco and never let go, her head, for once in her damn life, told her to wait.

'Well,' she began, the catch in her voice betraying her. 'I haven't been hiding, Paco. If you'd bothered to look for me in the last sixteen years, you would have easily found me.'

He had the grace to look away, a slow flush rising up his tanned neck, as he opened his mouth to reply. But Carmen had found her voice.

'The last time I saw you, you told me you were saving up money for us to elope. You promised. And like an idiot, I believed you.' She tried to swallow down the tears that were thick in her throat. 'I loved you, Paco, and you broke my heart.' Anger bubbled in her gut, and she dug her nails into her palm. 'But I know exactly where *you've* been all these years,' she spat. 'Playing happy families with your wife while I was alone with the lies you told me.'

Paco stared at her, his mouth working, his eyes imploring, but she hadn't finished.

'You took every part of me,' she said, wiping away the hot tears rolling down her face. 'And left me with nothing… except Margarita.'

'How did you find out about Loli?' he asked, unworthy eyes not quite meeting hers.

'It doesn't matter anymore. It was such a long time ago. I've been blind for years, so bitter, destroyed. I've even made a mess of being a mother,' she whispered, her humiliation complete.

Again, Paco held his hand out to her. She looked down at his once familiar, scarred and rough fingers, a dulled gold band on his third finger. The hands that had cupped her face as he'd promised her the world, only to leave her with broken dreams and a problem bigger than any fifteen-year-old should have to face alone.

She shook her head slowly, her eyes finding his. Instead of the disgust she'd feared when he saw how she had changed, there was only tenderness. Something broke inside her.

'Why are you here? Why now? After all this time…'

He rubbed his hand over his eyes, breathing heavily as he looked down at his feet, composing himself for what, Carmen dreaded to think. Then those deep green eyes locked back onto hers.

'Vida mia, I love you. Not one day has passed since the last time I saw you that I haven't thought about you. Haven't loved you. Haven't regretted being so weak.'

He leaned against the wall, his body sliding down until he was sitting on the floor, his head in his hands. Carmen lowered herself beside him, and they sat for a long time in uneasy silence. She hunted in her handbag and opened her purse. Without a word, she handed him a photo of Margarita that Bernat had given her. In it, she was standing behind the bar, grinning widely at the camera, with Bernat at her side.

Paco glanced down at the photo. 'She reminds me of you when we met… she has the same light in her eyes.' He turned to face her, gazing into her as if trying to remove the years of absence.

Her stomach flipped as she looked back at him, the shards of frozen pain in her heart thawing slightly. So much time had passed. It had been the longest time, but it had flashed by in a heartbeat. She'd waited eighteen years to hear these words, but now she'd finally heard them, she didn't know what to do with them. The homecoming, the feeling of being where she'd always been meant to be, didn't come. Instead, any comfort she'd found in his words was quickly chased away by a growing sense of dread. They sat on the cold ground in the shadows of the passage until the sun went down. Carmen was painfully aware that while their legs were almost touching, there was a gaping chasm between them that neither of them had the strength to cross.

11

Margarita was in the back room of the bakery, hauling around hot trays of baguettes, sweating from the heat of the large ovens. She slammed the oven door shut, and as she stood up, stretching her back and blowing her hair off her brow, a familiar voice floated through from the shop.

'I'm here to see Margarita. Is she around?' It was Eva. She'd never dropped in before, even though she lived less than half a mile away. Eva was rarely allowed out alone without Eulalia, so this visit was entirely unexpected. A burst of joy bubbled up inside her, immediately followed by a clenching in her tummy. She hadn't seen Eva for a few weeks, not since she'd found out she was the daughter of Eduardo the butcher's vile son. She was still mortified and wasn't ready to share the news with anyone, not even her best friend.

'Margarita!' barked Montse, her boss, over her shoulder. Margarita jumped up, scurrying quickly into the shop, blinking at the brightness after the gloom of the back room.

'Eva, is everything alright?'

Eva gave her a wide grin and nodded. 'Yes, of course it is! I've come to see you, that's all!'

Margarita sagged with relief and glanced pleadingly

at Montse, who said gruffly, 'Okay, *chata,* take your break, but no more than twenty minutes, alright?'

Margarita nodded. 'Thanks, Montse,' she replied, whipping off her thick white pinafore and emerging from behind the counter into the shop. The girls linked arms and walked down a couple of streets onto Plaza Santa Caterina, busy at this hour with handcarts and vans loading and unloading fresh produce. They found a quiet spot round the side of the market and settled onto a couple of upturned crates.

Leaning close to Eva, Margarita asked bluntly, 'How is everything with you and Kiko?'

Eva filled Margarita in on the visit to the Filipino's apartment, and Margarita was equally horrified and fascinated.

'Did you do the deed?' she asked, biting her lip to suppress an embarrassed giggle.

Eva blushed, her eyes sparkling and replied coyly. 'Yes! He's wonderful, Margarita. So romantic. We've been back twice since then!'

Margarita attempted to stifle a frown. She felt very much out of the loop, and now was as good a time as any to say so. 'Have you met Kiko's family yet, Eva? Has he taken you to his neighbourhood?'

Eva shook her head, a sheepish look shadowing her face. 'No, not yet. It's still very early. We've only known each other for a few months. I wouldn't dream of introducing him to the Doctor and Maria. God, can you imagine?'

Knowing what Eva's mother was like, Margarita gave a half-shrug. 'No, I can't.' She paused for a second. 'But I'm your best friend, Eva. Don't you want me to meet him?' she asked carefully, not wanting to seem too needy but desperate to make her point.

Eva's forehead wrinkled in consternation. 'Of course I do! It's just that I don't seem to have much time nowadays. I'm sorry.'

While her words sounded sincere, Margarita wondered if, deep down, it was a scenario Eva had been avoiding.

'Although, to be honest, Margarita, I have been a bit nervous about you meeting him,' she said, her face solemn, confirming what Margarita had suspected.

Margarita raised her eyebrows. Maybe now she would find out why Eva was keeping him a secret.

'He's a bit...' Her eyes looked skywards as she searched for the right words. 'Rough around the edges. He has a manual job down in the port, and he's not like anyone I've ever met before.'

'What do you mean, "rough round the edges"?' demanded Margarita, alarmed at Eva's confession.

Eva chewed her lip, and her eyes flickered to the left. 'He's a bit scruffy, I suppose. But I don't care. I'm in love with him. I don't give a hoot what anyone thinks,' she said, an uncharacteristic edge to her voice.

'My God!' exclaimed Margarita, horrified. 'You're far too good for some scruffy oik from the port. Ugh,' she said, giving Eva a withering look.

'Margarita! How could you say such a hateful thing?' snapped Eva, her eyes flashing. 'You haven't even met him, and you're already judging him. I *knew* this would happen when I told you. And anyway, who are you to judge?'

Margarita was shocked into silence at her friend's cruel insinuation, and tears stung her eyes.

Eva put her hand on her arm, squeezing gently. 'I'm sorry to be harsh, but you can be such a snob sometimes, Margarita,' she said. 'I often think you care more about everything I have than *I* do. I know you haven't had the opportunities I've had... but without love, nothing else matters.'

Margarita crossed her arms. Eva was willing to throw everything away for a port rat with scruffy clothes. 'I can't believe you think I'm a snob. I know I'm a mess and don't have much, but I want to better myself – that's not being a snob. But you, going from having everything to nothing, that's simply insane,' she said eventually, shaking her head in disbelief.

'You know what it's like to be loved, Margarita. You've been loved all your life. Maybe not by your mother, but by your Yaya. She adores you. The only person who's ever come close to loving me is my governess.' Eva's voice was soft, with an edge of sadness in it that caught Margarita's heart. 'Possessions don't make being unwanted and unloved feel better, Margarita. Things aren't a substitute for love. I wouldn't wish that on my worst enemy.'

In the uncomfortable silence that followed Eva's measured outburst, Margarita covered her face with her hands, processing Eva's words. 'I'm sorry, Eva. I had no idea you felt like this. I shouldn't have said those things about Kiko.'

After a few moments, Eva's smooth hand gently took her rough, calloused one and squeezed it reassuringly. Lifting her eyes to meet Eva's, it struck Margarita that Eva had just taught her a valuable lesson.

They stood up, brushed down their skirts, and began walking back towards the bakery, the tension easing with each step. When they arrived, Margarita hugged Eva, still humbled by her wisdom. She'd always thought she was so street-smart, yet now it felt like Eva was the more mature of the two.

'Oh *Dios*, Margarita! I haven't even told you about La Llotja,' shrieked Eva, grabbing Margarita's arm.

Margarita poked her head around the bakery door and saw no customers. 'Go on then, tell me, but be quick.'

Eva explained how she'd made a couple of new friends. Artie, who was English and Anna, who was from Malaga. She admitted to feeling overwhelmed by everything, how the other students exuded a confidence she knew she didn't have. The three of them had sat together in the canteen, drinking watery coffee and listening to the fascinating conversations echoing all around them, the air heavy with cigarette smoke.

Margarita's heart dipped, emotions she couldn't

decipher vying for her attention. Instead, she pushed them aside, taking Eva's hand. 'I want to share all the good things with you, Eva. I only have bad things happen to me. Nothing ever goes my way, and I want a bit of your happiness.'

Eva's eyes softened as she looked at Margarita. 'Listen, I came to see you because one of my tutors is having an exhibition on Thursday evening at his studio in El Born. Please say you'll come. Anna and Artie will be there, and I know you'll love them! Artie is so sweet, but you'll have to be patient with him because his Spanish isn't great. You'll be able to practise your English with him. And later today, I'm meeting Kiko, so I'll try to convince him to come too. It will be wonderful to have all my friends together at last!'

Margarita picked at her cuticles. 'What will I say to them? We won't have anything in common. And I haven't got anything half-decent to wear, either.' She'd never even been out to a bar other than work.

'You're the funniest, kindest, smartest person I know. You can start a conversation with anyone, and as for clothes, look what I've brought you!' Eva cried, her cheeks flushing. She reached into her handbag and, digging into its depths, pulled something out and handed it to Margarita.

Margarita's heart was racing as she unfolded the most glorious drop waist dress made from a silky material. It was burnt orange, with green and lilac swirls, and Margarita had never seen anything like it. She

77

gasped and turned to Eva. 'Is this for me? Where did it come from? I can't accept this, Eva. It must have cost a fortune!'

Eva beamed from ear to ear. 'Father gave me some money to buy clothes, so Eulalia and I went shopping in Rambla Catalunya. I've never been shopping without mother, so I bought two of everything for both of us.' Gleefully pulling more things out of her bag, she passed them to Margarita, who honestly couldn't remember a time when she hadn't worn second-hand clothes. But despite her pleasure, a small part of her resented the gift, and she still felt like the charity case she'd always been.

'How can I ever repay you, Eva?' she said faintly, her eyes brimming with tears.

'By coming on Thursday and telling everyone you talk to that all the paintings are rubbish and that you could do better like you always do!' she laughed, which set Margarita off and holding each other tightly, they rocked back and forth, howling with delight.

12

Most days, after I finished work at the port, I tried to drop in to see Tia Rosita. It pained me that I hadn't been able to spend much time with her since I'd started work, and I missed her.

One afternoon I called round, and Sofia, Tia Rosita's granddaughter, opened the door. Her face lit up when she saw it was me.

'Santi, come in! *Abuelita*, look who's here,' she called over her shoulder and stepped aside, ushering me in. Tia Rosita was sitting on a stool, bundles of dried plants laid out on the table in front of her. She beamed as I stooped down to kiss her cheek. '*Hijo mío*, we haven't seen you for days! How's the job going?'

'We need the money, Tia Rosita. It's the only reason I'm working there,' I said, sitting down opposite her. 'With Iker in prison, we've got less coming in. Maybe when he gets out, I'll be able to start setting some money aside.'

'You won't need money, *hijo mío*. You'll find your path in other ways,' she said, her gnarled, arthritic fingers separating the plants and putting the flower heads in a bowl.

I shook my head and sighed. 'Not for what I want to do, Tia Rosita. I've told you this before. I'll need more money than I can even imagine to study medicine.'

She glanced at me, her eyes unblinking. 'It will come, Santi. You must be patient a little longer.'

I picked up the knife and began scraping the leaves from the stalks, trying to curb my frustration. Even though I trusted her implicitly, I don't think she truly understood how much of a struggle I faced to follow my dream of being a doctor. I was a nobody from Somorrostro. I'd left school by the time I was eight and had no money or connections to consider attending university.

I'd often hang around the medical faculty in Calle Casanova, soaking up the charged atmosphere as groups of young men and women, not much older than me, hurried from class to class. I would have done almost anything to be one of them. Watching them huddled in groups in the bar opposite, drinking coffee in a cloud of cigarette smoke, I simmered with uncharacteristic resentment, admiring them and envying them at the same time. I eavesdropped on conversations about their favourite professors, the essays that were due, and the work experience they were looking forward to doing. And each time I went, milling among them, it tortured me – this life would never be mine. My birthplace, education, everything, conspired against me, and my heart ached for a life I could never have.

'How's Kiko?' Tia Rosita asked, interrupting my thoughts.

Thankful for the change of subject, I began to tell

her about Paco becoming increasingly morose in recent months and eventually losing his job. She listened, her eyes giving nothing away. I debated whether to mention Kiko's relationship with Eva but decided I shouldn't meddle until Kiko had told his father he was in love with a *paya*.

'What was Paco like when he was young?' I asked. The stories of his pranks had become legends that Kiko and I often talked about.

'Paco Perona has been a scoundrel since he was knee-high to a *grillo*,' she began. 'Even as a boy, he could charm the birds out of the trees and talk his way out of trouble. I remember his parents lived long enough to see him married, but like so many, *hijo,* they died way before their time.' She rubbed her eyes and took a sip from the glass of tea beside her. 'I helped deliver Paco during a storm in the middle of a grim February night. As soon as I swaddled him in a blanket, he kicked me with all of his might, and I knew he'd grow up to be a rascal.' She smiled at the memory. 'He was the youngest of ten children and overindulged by his doting mother. God bless her. It was a shock for her when she fell pregnant with Paco. She was forty-six and didn't think she would have another child, another mouth to feed.' Her hands stilled, and she closed her eyes as if stepping back in time

'When he was a boy, he ran wild all over Montjuic with extended family in every other shack, visiting them on rotation for food, sweets and love. I remember him and Loli playing together when they were both still in nappies, getting up to mischief at every opportunity. I knew, even then, that they were destined to get married and have a family.'

She paused to light her pipe, and the air filled with the earthy aroma of sage. 'It was only when they reached their teens that the mischief became a cause for concern for Loli's parents,' she said. 'They were worried and terrified, in equal measure, that Paco Perona, a handsome charmer, would dishonour their precious daughter. I was summoned to mediate for the two families while they thrashed out the details.'

'Was it what Paco and Loli wanted, Tia Rosita?' I asked, knowing these types of decisions were made differently in gypsy families.

'They didn't have any say in the matter, *hijo mío*. They were simply told they'd be married as soon as they turned fifteen. I remember the wedding day like it was yesterday,' she said with a faraway look. 'It was a hot June day, and Loli looked splendid. She was wearing a knee-length white dress with a short veil and white daisies woven through her long, black hair, and Paco was handsome in a dark grey suit with a black tie.'

Tia Rosita began to cough, and I quickly poured her more of the herbal tincture we brewed each autumn for chest complaints. She'd had a bad chest all through the autumn, and now that winter was setting in, I was worried. She hated any fuss, so I sat down and picked up my knife again.

She took a delicate sip of the tea and continued.

82

'After the wedding, Paco and Loli lived with his parents for two years, but Loli was unhappy. She wanted him all to herself, and she was thrilled when they got the chance to own a shack here in Somorrostro. Loli's Aunt Pepa, whose husband had run off to America on one of those enormous cargo ships that dock in the port, wanted to move back to Montjuic to be with the family. Again, with no discussion, the couple moved into number forty-seven. That was the day when Paco first met your father. They were as thick as thieves from then on, and Loli and your mother, Merce, became the closest of friends.'

'Did Paco sell scrap back in those days?' I asked, the pain of hearing my mother's name still strong.

'No, he sold livestock with his father. He was out from before the sun rose in the sky until nightfall. He was a hard worker back then. Loli kept house and drank coffee with the other young brides from the neighbourhood. They would exchange tips about how to keep the house free of sand, bring up children and please their husbands in bed,' she said with a chuckle. Then her face became grave. 'Poor Loli was desperate to have a child. I gave her potions, encouraged her to eat honey, and only be intimate with Paco under the gypsy moon, but nothing happened for a few years. It did eventually, of course, but by then, everything had changed.'

I was used to her cryptic observations, but something in her voice made me glance up. Her face was impassive, and I knew whatever it was, she would only tell me when she was ready. It wouldn't be long before I

83

found out how Paco's life had changed in the blink of an eye when he'd saved Carmen Garcia from being trampled under the wheels of a horse and cart.

13

Carmen had been an angel when she was a girl, so her mother had always told her. In her eyes, there was nothing Carmen could do wrong. Her mother had never tired of recounting how she had taken her first steps before any of her friends' children and uttered her first words before the other toddlers in the street. Or how she'd never needed any encouragement to get up at celebrations to dance the most graceful movements or sing, her sweet voice bewitching the audience. She had taken people's breath away with her loveliness. And her mother had beamed with pride whenever anyone congratulated her for having such a delightful daughter.

But as Carmen reached her teenage years, her mother's lyrical waxing about her beauty and esteem stopped. The cheerful, talented, and intensely lovable child had become a sullen, headstrong rebel – seemingly overnight. Carmen had watched her mother's pain as she sought solace from the other mothers while they quietly delighted that Carmen Garcia wasn't perfect after all, their fake smiles assuring Rosa that this was how all teenagers behaved.

Seeing Paco outside the bodega had stirred up so many feelings that she'd blotted out, and she was powerless to fend off the memories flooding through her mind.

***

1949

Carmen had been throwing up every morning in the weeks since she'd followed Paco to Somorrostro. At first, she thought it was shock, her unsettled nerves still smarting from the way Paco had spoken to her. But she was appalled when it dawned on her that she'd missed several periods. She had to see him. After hanging around the scrap yard in Poble Nou, she'd eventually run into him. With a curt nod, he'd agreed to meet her at the main entrance to Ciutadella park after she finished work the following day.

As she made her way there, her stomach churned with excitement. Paco had often promised her that they would elope as soon as possible. A baby might bring things forward.

Paco was already there when she arrived, and his face brightened when he spotted her. He walked towards her and pulled her close. 'Hey, what's wrong with that beautiful face of yours, *Preciosa*?'

Relief flooded Carmen's chest as Paco held her in his strong arms, the cruel words he'd said when she'd followed him fading from her mind. Unable to find any words to soften the blow, she came straight out with it.

'I… I think I'm pregnant.' The tiny muscles in Paco's cheek twitched, and Carmen hesitated. 'I haven't had any bleeding for weeks, and I've been sick every morning for days. I… I know it's not part of our plan, but we'll make it work,' she said, cringing at her naïve babbling.

Paco's eyes darted around, and he ran his finger under his grubby collar. Carmen reached out to take his hand but shrank back when he slapped her hand away with a growl, jumped up and stomped away from the bench they were sitting on. Distraught, Carmen burst into tears and dashed after him.

'Pa… Paco, I know it's not the right time, but I love you and want to have our baby.' Her voice dripped with desperation even to her. Paco stopped and turned to face her.

'Carmen, we can't have a child. It's impossible. I haven't even told my family about you, let alone that you're not a *gitana*. I told you it would take a while until we can be together,' he answered, holding his hands out to her as if to placate her. 'Do you know anyone who can help you get rid of the baby? There's a woman on the street next to mine who helps girls out, but we can't go there because someone might see us and ask questions,' he muttered, raking his fingers through his hair in frustration. 'There must be someone who can help you. Think… Maybe your mother knows someone?'

Carmen took a step back. 'But you told me you loved me and wanted to be with me. I don't understand.'

Her gaze hardened. 'Do you honestly expect me to ask my mother how to get rid of her grandchild?'

Paco looked away, his eyes darting everywhere except at Carmen. She laid her hand on his, but he snatched it away and folded his arms.

'I need some time to think about what we can do. Give me a few days to see if I can work something out. Maybe you could tell everyone you've been attacked and raped so that they won't point their finger at me?' he muttered, more to himself than to her.

Carmen nodded, a spark of hope flickering inside her; at least he promised to think about it. 'But please don't ask me to get rid of the baby, Paco. I'll never agree to it.'

As she turned to walk away, Paco caught hold of her arm. *'Lo siento*, Carmen, I'm sorry,' and strode off, leaving her standing alone in the middle of the empty park.

The following week, he was waiting for her one afternoon when she left work. He pulled her down a narrow side street, his face grim. 'Carmen, have you thought about what I said? No one can know I'm the father... you *have* to blame it on someone else. If my family found out about this, they'd send me away. We'd never see each other again.'

Carmen's mind shifted into overdrive. She couldn't lose him, not now. Her throat ached as she looked into his imploring eyes. 'Alright, I'll do it. I promise you,' she said, her voice small.

Paco let out a breath and wrapped his arms around her. '*Te Quiero*, Carmen. When you've had the baby, things will be different. I'll tell my family about you. Prepare them.' He hesitated. 'And we can't be seen together… it will be safer if we don't meet until after the baby is born.'

The tension in her shoulders eased as she clung to him, accepting his conditions without a fight. Ignoring the voice in her head telling her this wouldn't end well.

Over the coming weeks, Carmen racked her brain, trying to think of someone to blame the pregnancy on, until one day at work, she found that the answer to her prayers had been right under her nose all along. Quim Diaz, Eduardo's son, was a couple of years older than her and had been infatuated with Carmen since she'd started working at the butcher's when she was twelve. A sweet, naïve boy, not the sharpest knife in the drawer, Quim was her constant shadow. Every time she turned around, he was gazing at her in adoration. It irritated her no end, but he was harmless, so she hadn't mentioned it to Eduardo, afraid of upsetting the applecart.

After lunch, Eduardo was upstairs having his daily siesta, always from three to four on the dot. Carmen and Quim were downstairs cleaning the counters and bloodstained chopping boards, ready for re-opening at five o'clock. The shop blind was pulled down, and as usual, wherever Carmen went, Quim trailed behind her. She made her way into the back room where pale, plucked carcasses hung from the ceiling, and the chickens yet to be slaughtered, scratched quietly in their crowded pen.

Turning to face Quim with a simpering smile, Carmen took his hand and led him to the back of the building where the slaughtering took place. In the stink of dead flesh and to the sound of soft clucking, she began to kiss him, pressing herself up against him. She kissed him as if her life depended on it, which, in fairness, it did. Sighing and giggling, she swallowed her revulsion as he slobbered all over her. When poor, sweet Quim finally shuddered in her arms, she smirked inwardly when she saw the wetness spreading over the front of his firmly zipped-up trousers.

Telling her mother that she suspected she was pregnant after being molested by Quim Diaz shamed Carmen to her very core. She saw the pain cut like a knife through her mother's heart and, later, the ravaged grief on her face when the pregnancy was confirmed. But after the initial shock, her mother had softened. As the bump became increasingly difficult to hide, Carmen fretted about what the neighbours would think, but her mother scolded her. 'People will always judge you for something, *hija*. If I hear one word said against my grandchild, there'll be hell to pay.' And she'd been true to her word, fighting off the gossiping neighbours like a lioness protecting her cub. Each time they went out, her mother had brushed off the knowing stares and disparaging slights, her head held high, daring anyone to criticise Carmen. And when Margarita was born, no one was prouder than Rosa Marquez.

14

Thursday evening came around quickly, and Margarita's hands trembled as she tried on the clothes Eva had given her. She would never forget wearing cast-offs donated by the wealthy residents of Sarriá to the Santa Maria del Mar church.

She'd decided to wear the orange dress with some shiny, black kitten heels she'd bought at the market earlier in the day. She washed from head to toe at the sink, enjoying the feeling of being completely clean. She'd even attempted to paint her nails in a glorious orange polish that matched perfectly with the dress. She quelled the pinch of guilt at pocketing it from a make-up stall near where she'd bought the shoes. She hadn't been able to afford both.

As she slipped her feet into the new shoes and smoothed down her dress, Margarita glanced down at herself, overwhelmed by the transformation. The dress fitted her perfectly, and the softness of the silk next to her skin was unlike anything she'd ever felt before. She'd never looked so magnificent in all her life. Tears threatened to smudge the bold Kohl lines around her eyes, which made her look like a young doe, and she breathed deeply until the emotion had passed.

Montse, from the bakery, had insisted that she

borrow some perfume. Margarita dabbed it on her wrists and behind her ears as instructed, and put her house keys into a black sequinned clutch bag, also lent to her by Montse.

It was only half past five, but Margarita couldn't wait any longer and set off on the five-minute walk to the cathedral. She'd arranged to meet Eva and her friends there at six o'clock, from where they would walk down to the studio in Calle Banys Vells.

The trembling in her fingers had turned to full-blown panic, and her stomach churned uncomfortably at the thought of socialising with the kind of people Eva now mixed with.

She came out onto the street and glanced nervously up and down, dreading bumping into her mother. Aside from an interrogation about where the new clothes had come from, Margarita knew her mother would no doubt find something derogatory to say about her appearance. After so many years of being belittled, Margarita was determined that no one, especially not her mother, would spoil this special occasion.

Setting off down the street, holding the clutch bag to her chest like a protective shield, Margarita dodged the swarms of shoppers. She teetered along the cobbles, unused to walking in heels and tried to keep to the flat edges of the narrow streets, her gaze aimed low. She couldn't help but notice, though, the appreciative looks she was getting. A couple of wolf whistles rang out, and her heart beat faster as she suppressed a nervous giggle.

Margarita, the ugly duckling with shabby clothes and a strange smell, had turned into a swan.

As she walked along Avenida Francesc Cambó near the Santa Caterina market, a shout came from behind her. Her heart sank as she spotted Clara Artola and the twins, Berta and Blanca – none of whom she'd seen hide nor hair of for weeks – approaching. As they came closer, she could see their mouths were agape like fish mouthing for air.

'Margarita! Blanca thought it was you,' puffed Clara, her round face shiny with perspiration, 'but I said it never was! How could it be Margarita looking so lovely?'

Blood rushed to Margarita's cheeks at the backhanded compliment, a sense of *déjà vu* taking her back to the school playground, and the other children poking fun at her with their cruel jibes about her scruffy appearance.

'Where are you off to dressed like that?' demanded Blanca, as nosey as ever.

Margarita heard the sneer in her voice and saw the smirk on her face, but this time, instead of shrinking away, she straightened her back, put one hand on her hip and turned to face Clara. 'Why wouldn't it be me, Clara Artola?' she demanded, trying to disguise the tremor in her voice.

Clara stared at Margarita, a look of wide-eyed astonishment on her face. 'I ... I've never seen you look so nice, so smart, that's all...'

Turning next to Blanca, Margarita looked her up and down with a scornful gaze. 'And where I'm going has absolutely nothing to do with any of you. Especially not *you*, Blanca, you bloody busybody.'

Looking at the three of them now with new clarity, their blouses spotless and their shoes shining, Margarita could see how their spite made them ugly. Everything they said was accompanied by snide put-downs and unkind barbs to crush the confidence of their intended victim. Well, no more. She shifted her weight to the other foot, leaning towards Clara and raising her finger. 'All these years, I thought you were my friend, Clara. But actually, you're as stupid as you always say the twins are.' Inwardly, her confidence billowed further as the twins' glared at Clara, who had bowed her head, her cheeks flushing. Buoyed by the shift in power, she raised her chin. 'Stay out of my way, all of you. And Berta and Blanca, before you think about running to your father telling him I've been mean to you to get me sacked, I'll tell him Berta had sex with Miguel Perillo on the sofa while Bernat was downstairs working in the bar.'

Now Blanca and Clara gaped in horror at Berta, who began to bluster her innocence. But Margarita continued, 'And I heard it straight from the horse's mouth, Berta, so don't try to deny it.'

Leaving the three girls speechless, Margarita stalked off, her arms no longer folded over her chest but swinging at her sides. A carefree smile brought out the glow in her eyes. Why had she allowed them to look down their noses at her for so long?

Two minutes later, she was waiting on the cathedral steps. With only a thin cardigan over her dress, Margarita shivered in the shadow cast by the imposing building. She skimmed the throng for Eva, but there were so many people milling around the Plaza that it was impossible to spot her. Dozens of cars were parked around the bottom of the steps. Margarita watched as they reversed out, only to be filled immediately with much horn-honking by those waiting to park. People weaved in and out of the cars, paying no attention to the irate shouts of the drivers. It was chaotic, a welcome distraction for Margarita. Her elation at standing up to the girls quickly turned back into nerves.

Turning to look over towards Calle dels Arcs, the direction she knew Eva would be coming from, she noticed two boys around the same age as her standing a few feet to her left. Both were smoking cigarettes and talking animatedly, and their conversation was punctuated with laughter. They were very handsome, with thick, dark hair curling fashionably over their collars. The shorter boy had striking eyes, strangely feline, and Margarita could tell they were a brilliant shade of green even from a distance. As she studied the pair more closely, she noticed that neither of the boys' slightly flared trousers was very clean, and their black ankle boots were covered in dust. But there was something was compelling about them. Margarita had never seen anyone else remotely like them, and she

95

couldn't help but stare. Most boys she knew were like Miguel, harmless but dull-witted, and behaved like silly children. It was impossible to have a serious conversation through their wisecracks and smutty innuendoes. They certainly didn't exude the relaxed confidence of these two boys.

She hadn't realised she was staring so overtly until she noticed the taller boy, who had a beard, was smiling right at her, and their eyes locked. With a jolt in her stomach, her face burned, and she quickly lowered her eyes, embarrassed at being caught gawping.

When she dared to look up again, the boys were craning their necks, pointing at something in the other direction. She followed their gaze to see Eva coming into view, trailed by another girl Margarita didn't recognise.

Taking a deep breath, Margarita began to make her way towards her friend. But before she could reach her, the boy with green eyes ran down the steps, swooped Eva up in his arms, and spun her around, kissing her. Margarita froze. Was this Kiko? As the boy put Eva down, Margarita saw Eva's eyes blazing with love. Laughing, the boy with the beard kissed Eva on each cheek and pulled her into a hug.

When Eva saw Margarita standing there, she shrieked, her face flushing with delight. 'Margarita! You're here. Come and meet everyone!'

Margarita smiled shyly at all the faces that had turned in her direction and made her way over.

'Everyone, this is Margarita, my very best friend!'

said Eva, putting her arm around Margarita's shoulder. Swallowing her nerves, Margarita stuck out her hand to the boy beside Eva. But instead, he pulled her into a hug.

'I'm Kiko,' he grinned. 'We meet at last.' Something about his familiarity with her made Margarita instantly at ease, and she leaned into him. 'It's lovely to meet you.'

He turned to the boy with the beard. 'And this is Santi.'

The boy was staring at her, his eyes penetrating hers. Margarita's face grew hot again, and as he bent down to kiss her, his lips felt cool on her cheek, and his beard tickled her face

Before she had time to wonder about the bubble in her belly, Eva's voice interrupted. 'And this is Anna.' The other girl, Anna, was tall and graceful, her messy dark chestnut hair worn half up and held in place with a silver clip. She wore large silver hoops in her ears and had an array of bangles on her wrists. Anna beamed at Margarita, kissing her on each cheek. Beside her, Margarita felt small and plain. She envied Anna's confidence.

With the introductions over, the awkwardness Margarita had been feeling melted away.

'Artie is meeting us at the studio,' Eva informed them. 'He's having some problems with the landlady at the hostel where he's staying. She does his washing, and some items have gone missing. I mean, the poor thing hasn't got many clothes to start with, but he swears he saw the landlady's son wearing one of his tee shirts,' she said, laughing. 'He'll be along later, hopefully.'

They walked through the side streets towards the studio on Calle Banys Vells in the Born neighbourhood. Anna led the way, her jewellery jingling and jangling as she moved self-assuredly through the scores of people out for an evening stroll or doing their shopping. Eva and Kiko walked behind her, their bodies close and their fingers entwined. Margarita found herself walking alongside Santi. She was oddly tongue-tied, and the conversation was a bit stilted. But as they neared the studio, Margarita began to relax. Santi made her giggle as he began imitating how Eva and Kiko walked and touched each other, just like she'd seen the entertainers do on Las Ramblas.

Finally, they arrived at some heavy, arched wooden doors which were open, the chatter of voices and raucous laughter inside spilling out onto the street. Santi held out his arm for Margarita to enter. As she took in the enormous paintings hung by chains from the ceiling and illuminated by the light of dozens of candles, Margarita felt like she was stepping into another world.

15

The girl in front of me looked so young. There was a fragility about her that I found intriguing, yet at the same time, she looked as though she'd seen the world. She wore a striking orange dress, and her dark hair was pinned up in a beehive. My heart quickened as I watched her eyes darting around, worrying at her perfectly full bottom lip.

I tried not to stare, but our eyes met for a moment, and I smiled. She quickly looked away, and my thumping heart faltered. I wondered if she was waiting for her boyfriend.

I was taken aback when Eva, released from yet another of Kiko's passionate embraces, called out. 'Margarita! Come and meet everyone!' And the girl, with a timid smile, came down the steps towards us, tripping slightly on the final step.

She seemed nervous, and when I kissed her cheek in greeting, it felt warm on my lips, the scent of apples on her skin. We found ourselves walking along together. At first, the silence was awkward, and I wracked my brain for something interesting to talk about, but I was tongue-tied. When I started to imitate Eva and Kiko, copying their smooching, Margarita relaxed, throwing her head back and laughing the most contagious laugh I'd ever heard. It fell on my ears like the sound of waves rippling up the shoreline on a still evening in Somorrostro, and my pulse, as well as my loins, quickened at the sight of her smooth throat as she laughed.

As we'd walked along Calle Princesa, it took every ounce of restraint I possessed not to keep turning to her or take her hand in mine. Even in the following years, I don't think she ever really understood that I fell in love with her the second I laid eyes on her. From that night on, I couldn't imagine spending the rest of my life without ever having kissed her or a future without her in it. And each time I saw her from then on, it was like that first day all over again. She was like a fish in the desert among all those artists and bohemians as much as I was. But with each glass of cheap red wine, her laugh became louder, and she chatted to everyone with a confidence she hadn't shown on the cathedral steps.

Margarita's beauty wasn't so much on the outside, and she didn't stand out in the crowd. She was neither tall nor short, her hair was mousey, and her features weren't extraordinary. But something about her glowed, something I couldn't quite put my finger on. Or was I the only one who saw the light within her? I believe I was meant to meet her that night, that she was destined to be the one I gave my heart to. And forever after, the hand of love remained tightly clasped. Every day of my life since that night, she has been on my mind and in my heart, even in the smallest ways. It was the beginning of a lifetime of loving her.

I've always wondered since, if Artie, e*l guiri* – the foreigner – hadn't made an appearance at the exhibition, whether everything would have turned out differently for Margarita and me.

16

However much she thought about it, and from whatever angle, Carmen was sure that having Paco Perona back in her life would lead to no good. She needed to thrash out her feelings about the whole situation and share her worries with someone. But she'd driven away all her friends with her drinking, even the treacherous ones who'd secretly enjoyed watching the fiasco of her life.

So many years had passed since she'd last seen Paco, yet he was still the one she saw when she closed her eyes each night. Even when she was three sheets to the wind, his face was as clear as day to her.

After the incident outside Cesar's bodega, Carmen had reluctantly arranged to meet Paco for a drink in a bar on Calle de la Fontanelle, where she was confident no one she knew would see them. She was anxious as she made her way there. Standing at the bar entrance, she spotted Paco sitting at one of only a handful of tables, a bottle of beer in his hand, and her mind drifted.

***

1950

Life with a newborn was bittersweet. Carmen fell in

love with Margarita the second she was placed in her arms. Much to her mother's chagrin, she spent hours gazing at her daughter.

'You should be napping while she's asleep, *hija*. Your milk will dry up if you don't rest.'

But Carmen didn't want to miss a second of her child's life. Excitement triumphed over exhaustion as she imagined introducing Margarita to Paco. Too scared to return to Somorrostro, she could only wait patiently until he came to see her.

One day, when Margarita was three months old, Carmen left the baby with her mother to go and get a long overdue haircut. Making the most of the peace and quiet before she had to go home for Margarita's next feed, Carmen spent a leisurely hour sitting on a bench in Plaza Real. She was flicking through a magazine when a shadow loomed over her. It was Paco, grinning widely.

'Paco!' she cried, leaping into his outstretched arms. She giggled as he picked her up and swung her off her feet, kissing her hungrily.

'*Guapa, guapíssima,* I've missed you, Carmen,' he laughed, taking her face in his hands and wiping away her tears of joy with the filthy cuff of his jacket. In an instant, the distress she'd felt at not seeing him for almost a year evaporated.

'Paco, wait here! I'll go home and get Margarita. You can finally meet her,' she said, her eyes shining at the thought of him seeing their adorable daughter for the first time.

'I can't stay long, *amor mio*. I'm sorry,' he replied, looking sheepish.

Carmen's heart sank. 'Are you still angry with me, Paco? Don't you want to meet your daughter?'

'Of course I want to meet her, *vida mia*. But what if someone I know sees me holding a baby? What would I say? I'll see her soon.'

It wasn't the answer Carmen wanted to hear, but she said nothing. He needed more time. Over the following months, they picked up exactly where they'd left off before Carmen had fallen pregnant. They went dancing and drinking in the bars of the Eixample district, where Paco could be sure he wouldn't be recognised. They rented rooms by the hour in El Raval, and Carmen prayed that with time, Paco would change his mind and tell his parents about her and the baby. Until then, she would wait for him for as long as it took.

Or at least until the unimaginable happened when Margarita was nearing her first birthday. Carmen's secret was discovered.

The day her mother caught her kissing Paco in the entrance to the cinema was as terrible, if not more so, as the day she came home pregnant. As soon as her mother clapped eyes on Paco, Carmen saw the judgement in her eyes, the stark assumption that this boy wasn't like them.

After dragging Carmen home, kicking and screaming, her mother had locked her in their apartment and stormed off to collect Margarita, who was being watched by Conchi in the churreria downstairs.

In the space of the few minutes it took her mother to pick up the baby, Carmen went berserk. She pulled out all her clothes from the wardrobe and stuffed them into a plastic sack, crying ugly, hysterical tears of rage. She even broke one of her mother's best porcelain plates that hung on the wall – a tiny rebellion that soothed her angry soul.

When young Margarita saw her mother in such a state, she immediately burst into tears, clinging to her grandmother, who was formidable in her anger.

'Is this how you want your child to see you? Is it, madam? And kissing a good-for-nothing layabout in the street where all and sundry could see you? He's a damn *gitano*! I can tell a mile off, and I don't need a bloody crystal ball! *Madre de Dios*, you're playing with fire, and you will not do it under my roof, Señorita,' she snorted furiously. 'And while you're packing, you can damn well pack for Margarita, too, because you will not leave your child behind for any man, *gitano* or otherwise.'

Carmen burst into tears, and there was no talking to her until she calmed down hours later. 'I love him, Mama,' she said defiantly. 'I know he's a *gitano,* but it doesn't make a scrap of difference to how I feel about him.'

'Have you met his family yet?' her mother asked, her lip curled in disdain.

Carmen shook her head. 'He told me his parents would never agree to him marrying someone outside their community. He's waiting until he has enough money for us to elope.' Her gut twisted with discomfort as she watched the pity spread across her mother's face.

'Well, you're not the first, and you certainly won't be the last to fall for the charms of a sweet-talking gypsy, believe you me,' muttered her mother, with a shiver.

But Carmen was powerless to resist the pull to be with Paco, and she continued to meet him whenever she could, leaving Margarita with her mother. On the occasions her mother refused to babysit, Carmen would climb down from the balcony, risking life and limb to spend even half an hour with him. He was all she thought about, and she would do anything to be with him.

***

Watching Paco now across the smoke-filled bar, an older, fatter, watered-down version of the man she'd known, tears stung her eyes. She entered the bar, feeling his eyes on her as she walked to the counter to order a beer. He was half out of his chair, clumsily pulling out a chair for her by the time she got to the table. His face was flushed, and an eagerness, a haunted desperation, wavered in his eyes.

She sat down and lowered her gaze, feeling the tension between them like a guitar string thrumming in discord.

The waiter placed a glass of beer in front of Carmen without a word and went back behind the bar. Paco reached for her hand, but she flinched. All she'd been able to think about for years had been the burn of his skin touching hers. Now she couldn't bear for him to touch her. What had changed? She lifted her eyes, taking in the recognisable yet jarringly alien features of his face. His eyes appraised her, the same lust in them that would have turned her legs to jelly in the past. But now, resentment swirled in her gut. The memory of the last time she'd seen him was still raw, painfully etched into her mind, even now. The all-consuming agony which had filled her body from that moment on, snatching away any kind of relationship she could have had with her daughter.

'Paco,' she began, 'it's been so long... I don't even know what to say to you,' she said, her eyes filling with hot tears. 'Did you think I would fall into your arms after so many years of absolutely nothing?' Looking at him across the table was akin to waking up from a long sleep, one that had lasted almost seventeen years. She pushed her chair back and got to her feet. Resting her hands on the table, she glared down at him and asked him again. 'Tell me honestly, Paco, did you think I would simply forgive you after all this time?'

Paco had the grace to look ashamed. 'I'm sorry, Carmen... I loved you, but how could I have left Loli? I'm older now, though, not the frightened kid I was back then. You have to believe me.'

'I believe you, Paco. I believe you loved me.' Carmen paused, her throat tight. 'But it wasn't enough.'

He took a drink from his bottle of beer, and Carmen

sank back down onto the chair, her anger spent. 'I need time to think about how Margarita will react. My poor child deserves so much more than I've given her.' She lifted her eyes heavenwards as if an uncaring God had any hope of healing her shattered life as the weight of all the years of estrangement from her child slammed down on her. '… and my mother, I can imagine what she'll say about it.' She shook her head, frowning. 'I'm so angry, Paco. It frightens me sometimes how bitter I've become.'

They drank their beer without speaking, lost in the memories of what they would never feel again.

17

Margarita turned to find Santi at her side.

'Would you like some more wine?' he asked, brandishing a bottle. She nodded, embarrassed at being caught with her mouth full of *Escalivada*.

In a quiet moment, she'd wandered over to a table at the back of the studio, plates of tempting tapas vying for space. Ravenous and more than a little tipsy from the wine she had drunk, Margarita helped herself to slivers of mouth-watering, oily, roasted red peppers.

She hastily wiped her hands on her napkin and dabbed her mouth. As Santi poured the drink, his hand trembled slightly, mirroring her own slight sense of displacement. She smiled a 'Thank you' at him and took a sip of the warm, sour wine, wincing as it went down. Thanks to her mother's excesses, she'd never really drunk before, but she had to admit it had taken the edge off her fears of fitting in.

Santi was glancing around, his leg tapping in time with the music. He was looking everywhere except at her, and she suddenly felt shy. They stood in awkward silence for a while.

Eventually, unable to bear the silence, she tapped him hesitantly on the arm. 'What do you think of the exhibition? Some of the paintings are huge, aren't they?'

she asked, nodding towards a painting that stretched from floor to ceiling close to where they stood. At the same time, Santi blurted out, 'Are you an artist, too?'

He grinned at her, his dark eyes meeting hers, and she returned the smile, flustered under his intense gaze. He turned to stub out his cigarette in the ashtray on the table and repeated his question.

'No!' Margarita said with a laugh, shaking her head. 'I haven't got an artistic bone in my body, although, to be honest,' she whispered, looking around to check no one was in earshot, 'I'm sure I could do something similar to the paintings I've seen tonight. A child could have done some of them.'

Santi chuckled, and Margarita noticed his beautiful full lips and straight, white teeth hidden by his beard. The warmth of his breath as he reached behind her to grab the bottle of wine to top up their glasses made her shiver, goosebumps prickling on her neck

'What about you? Are you interested in art?'

'No, not at all. I've never stepped foot in a place like this before,' he admitted. He looked at her and arched an eyebrow. 'In fact, I've never seen so many oddballs in my life.'

Margarita nodded in agreement and looked around. *He was right...* She'd thought these kinds of people only existed in the books and magazines she read at the library. She'd been staggered when she'd read Henry Miller, but now she felt like she'd stepped into one of his novels. In her world, life revolved around the bakery, the bar and her lonely existence at home. There wasn't much time or money left for flashy clothes and the kinds of excesses that the people at this exhibition seemed to take for granted. She'd stepped back from one of the paintings as if she'd been slapped when she saw the price. She felt so unworldly, so small, among such sparkling personalities and obscene wealth, and wondered where she would ever fit in. The only place she felt like she truly belonged was sitting at her favourite desk in the library, lost in a fictional world. But tonight wasn't fiction, and she was overawed.

She turned back to Santi, glad he was there and that he, too, seemed like a fish out of water. She smiled at him again, a warm glow filling her tummy as he returned it. Feeling the urge to keep the smile on his face, she began to tell him about her so-called friends, Clara, Berta and Blanca. He roared with laughter at Margarita's parting shot about Berta sleeping with Miguel. She'd never had a conversation with a man like this before, relishing the ease with which they conversed, making him laugh and watching his reactions to her little story.

'What do you do in your spare time? Have you got any interests?' she asked, genuinely curious. Most of the boys from her neighbourhood hung around the Plaza, either smoking and drinking or playing football.

'Erm, I'm quite interested in health and medicine,' he answered, scratching his beard.

'Oh,' said Margarita, 'how fascinating.' A sudden flash of what looked like regret passed over his face, and

Margarita, feeling the heat in her cheeks, could have kicked herself. 'I'm sorry for being so nosey. My grandmother always tells me off for asking too many questions,' she stammered, her cheeks warm.

Santi grinned and topped up their glasses. 'No, please, it's me who should apologise. I'm not used to people being interested in me.' He took a large gulp of wine. 'I want to be a doctor, but right now it seems like an impossible dream.'

Margarita could empathise; she, too, yearned for something more. 'Well, maybe you could get a scholarship. The lady at my library always tells me I should further my studies, but I wouldn't know where to start,' she said with a half-smile. 'And to be honest, people like me don't get the same opportunities as people like Eva.'

The air cooled as Santi's shoulders sagged. 'People like me don't, either, Margarita.'

There was an awkward silence. Margarita felt like she couldn't breathe, whether from the hot, smoky studio or because of the grim look on Santi's face she wasn't sure. 'Shall we go outside and get some fresh air? It's stuffy in here.'

He brightened. 'Great idea! Come on,' he said and led the way to the entrance.

On their way out, they passed Eva and Kiko with their arms around each other, chatting to Eva's tutor. Margarita tapped Eva on the arm. 'We're going outside to get some air,' and Eva grinned, nodding. Kiko whispered something into Eva's ear and followed her and Santi outside. It was the first time Margarita had spoken to him, aside from the quick introduction at the cathedral earlier, and she felt a fizzle of apprehension.

'Eva talks about you all the time, Margarita,' said Kiko, his eyes crinkling in a smile.

'Does she? When I see her, she *never* stops talking about you!' laughed Margarita, his disarming words taking the edge off her nerves. I'm glad we've met at last. I was beginning to think she'd made you up to make me envious.'

'Tell me about it, Margarita!' laughed Santi. 'I hardly see Kiko anymore except on our way to and from work.'

Margarita smiled at Santi and turned to Kiko. 'I'm thrilled for you both, though. She told me you followed her home one day, which is very romantic! The next step will be meeting her awful parents.'

He grimaced. 'She's told me all about them, and from what I can gather, she's had a rough time.'

Margarita shivered. 'Ughhh, her mother is a cold shrew. Did Eva tell you that they have no idea we've been friends since we were girls?'

'Yes,' replied Kiko. 'She said the only support she has is from you and Eulalia and now her friends from La Llotja. What do you think of them?' he asked.

'I've only met Anna,' said Margarita. 'I don't think the other has arrived yet. Have you met him?'

'Truth be told, I have no idea. I've been introduced to

so many people tonight that I've lost track of who's who,' he said with a laugh, shaking his head. 'But it's been a blast spending time with Eva. We've never been out together like a proper couple,' he said, with a hint of pride in his voice.

Margarita watched how Kiko's eyes lit up when he talked about Eva. Would she ever meet a man who felt the same way about her? She turned to Santi, who was chuckling at his lovesick friend. 'So, do you two live close to each other? Or were you at school together?'

Santi nodded. 'Yes, Kiko lives down the street from me. We've been friends since before we could walk, according to our mothers,' he said, looking fondly at Kiko.

'Where do you live?' she asked. The boys glanced at each other, and Kiko began to gnaw on his bottom lip, his eyes fixed on the ground.

Santi, scratching his chin, replied quickly. 'Down near Poblenou. Do you know the neighbourhood?'

'Not really. Montse, from the bakery where I work, lives in Sant Marti, but I've never been there. What's it like?'

She caught the look between Santi and Kiko. What had she said?

Kiko spoke. 'Well, it's alright, I suppose – not as nice as round here.'

Margarita's eyebrows shot up. The Born district wasn't as bad as some areas in the city, like the Raval, but she wouldn't say it was nice. His answer only served to make her even more curious to know precisely where they were from.

Suddenly, a shout came from one of the apartments above the studio. '*Calla, Joder!* Some of us have to be up early in the morning! The wife has been giving me earache about the racket for the last hour.'

The three of them looked up to see a man on his balcony about to hurl a bucket of water down on them. Kiko held up his hands placatingly. 'Sorry, *tío*. We're going back in now,' he said, backing up against the wooden doors. They managed to open them and get inside just as the water cascaded down, missing them by inches. As they came in, roaring with laughter, Eva spotted them and waved, weaving her way through the buzzing crowd towards them.

'Oh, you're here at last,' she said cheerily. 'I was just about to come outside, but I got waylaid by some dullard droning on about how he's related to Gaudi, and I couldn't get away. Did I miss anything exciting?'

Margarita caught Santi and Kiko's eye, and they all burst out laughing again. Eva looked at them and smiled. Margarita knew her friend had been on edge about introducing her to Kiko, anxious they wouldn't get on. But the truth was, Margarita thought Kiko was incredibly charming, even if he wasn't very forthcoming about where he lived. And there was no denying that he was utterly smitten with Eva.

'Come on, Santi, let's go and get some more drinks for the girls before all the freeloaders finish it off,' said

Kiko and disappeared into the haze of cigarette smoke.

The following few hours flew by in a haze of chatter, smoke, wine and laughter. Margarita found herself squeezed in next to Santi, and they exchanged more stories about their lives. She listened, fascinated, as he told her about the healing he did with an elderly neighbour. When he asked about her family, she avoided any mention of her mother, instead regaling him with anecdotes about Yaya. Margarita had never had so much fun. On her way back from the ladies, she squeezed back through the crowd, unsteady on her feet. She returned to where she'd left Eva, Kiko and Santi, only to find they'd disappeared. She was gazing around, trying to spot them in the knot of people, when a shriek rang out from the vicinity of the door.

'Artie! You're here at last!'

Surrounded by Eva, Anna, and a few other students was a giant of a man, his thick, long blonde hair tied back in a messy ponytail. He was wearing the widest flared jeans Margarita had ever seen and a tight t-shirt with the name of a rock band she'd vaguely heard of. The man hugged Eva and shook Kiko's hand, slapping him on the back with a huge grin. He shook hands with Santi and then picked up Anna, making her squeal as he swung her around before putting her down and planting a kiss on her cheek.

'Margarita! Come and meet Artie!' called Anna, catching sight of her.

Artie turned to look at Margarita, his smile dying as

116

he stared at her.

Eva dragged him over to where Margarita was standing. 'This is Artie, my friend from La Llotja, the one from England,' she grinned, 'and Artie, this is Margarita, my best friend in the world.'

Margarita stuck out her hand to shake it, but the man brought her hand up to his lips and kissed it, his warm breath making her shiver. No one had ever done such a thing, and she was startled into silence, heat rushing to her cheeks. The crowd swallowed the others, leaving her alone with him, his hand wrapped around hers. Almost fearfully, Margarita raised her eyes to look at his face. He was staring down at her, pale blue eyes fixed on hers, and her face grew even hotter under his gaze. Clearing her throat nervously, she spoke. 'Eva said you're from England. How did you end up here?'

'I'm not sure,' he said, his voice a husky drawl. 'I was in Paris but felt compelled to come to Barcelona. Until this moment, I thought I was here to improve my fine art skills,' he said, 'but that would be a lie.'

Margarita was puzzled, struggling to understand his heavily accented and slightly formal Spanish in the buzz of background noise. 'Oh?' she said, edging closer to him.

He bent down so his face was level with hers, and the chatter of rowdy voices faded into nothing. Margarita stood taller, her heart pounding as Artie traced a finger down her cheek. Before she knew what was happening, he gently cupped her face with rough hands and pressed his mouth to her lips.

She melted into him, her mind racing as the kiss became more passionate. She didn't recognise herself! Where was the Margarita who worked from dawn until dusk every day? Who was this alluring woman that had this effect on men? She knew she was more than a little drunk but threw caution to the wind and threw her arms around Artie.

***

The following morning, Margarita woke up, her tongue stuck to the roof of her mouth, the brightness of the early morning sun shining through her eyelids and making her head throb. She stretched her aching body, and, in a flash, everything from the previous evening came back to her. As her eyes opened in horror, an arm slid around her waist and began stroking her hip. She turned to see Artie watching her, a lazy smile on his lips.

'Good morning, beautiful,' he said, pulling her close.

Without the wine to make her bold, she stiffened. 'Artie, I … I …' but he put his finger on her lips and began kissing her shoulder. She trembled as his tongue flicked over her skin and gave a moan of pleasure. His hand tightened on the back of her head, but Margarita drew back. 'I'm sorry, I can't. I have to be at the bakery at seven o'clock. I think I'm already late.'

A flicker of disappointment flared in his eyes. 'No

worries,' he said, reaching over to the nightstand for a cigarette. 'I'm sure we'll see each other around.'

Margarita's heart plummeted. How gauche he must think she was, running away like a scared fawn. 'I... I had a wonderful time last night,' she stammered, pulling the sheet over her body.

Artie looked crestfallen for a second, and then his face brightened. 'So did I,' he said, tugging at the sheet. But Margarita tightened her grip on it.

'I can't get enough of you,' Artie said, rolling out of bed with a groan.

Margarita lowered her eyes. She'd never seen a naked man, and her body tingled at the vague memory of the things they'd done last night. Artie tossed Margarita her knickers, and she struggled into them as quickly as possible, her cheeks burning. He untangled the creased orange dress from the heap of clothes on the floor, and she pulled it over her head, cringing as she felt his eyes on her. She grabbed her bag and slipped on her shoes, wincing at the blisters she hadn't noticed last night.

'Have you got a telephone?' asked Artie. 'So we can arrange to meet.'

'No, but I work in the bakery on the corner of Calle Sant Pere,' replied Margarita, reluctant to tell him where she lived. One look at her mother would scupper any budding relationship.

'Great, I'll drop by in the next few days,' replied Artie, drawing her in for one last kiss.

She ran down the grimy stairwell of Artie's hostel

and onto Gran Via, near the university. She had almost no recollection of walking back there last night. As she dashed home to change before work, Margarita couldn't stop smiling. At long last, she had met someone who desired her. No longer the same girl who had waited on the cathedral steps just hours earlier, Margarita floated home. Her dream of a handsome, wealthy man from Sarriá with a stylish apartment and communal gardens had now been replaced by dreams of the dashing Englishman with paint flecks in his long hair and a twinkle in his blue eyes

18

On the way home from work the following evening, I listened with half an ear as Kiko talked about his fears. 'Mama is getting suspicious,' he said. 'She keeps asking me where I'm off to, and I hate lying to her.'

We sat down on the breakwater, and Kiko took out some bottles of beer he'd slipped into his bag from the kitchen pantry. He flicked them open with his penknife and passed one to me before continuing. 'I overheard her and my dad talking the other night. She was chewing his ear, saying that every time I leave the house, I look like I'm going to a wedding or a funeral!'

I smirked, although it was true. We usually wore the same things in our day-to-day life until they fell apart at the seams. Kiko had pawned a necklace given to him by his parents as a communion present so he could buy a smart bespoke suit from El Barco, which had been ready within six hours. I'd always wanted a suit, but I had nothing to pawn, and my father would have given me hell. We needed every penny.

'So, what did Paco say, then?'

'He told her to stop wittering on about it, that I'd tell them when I was ready,' replied Kiko and took a long drink from the bottle. 'Eva's always asking me where I live or which school I went to. I'm running out of excuses. Last week I met her to have a coffee. She was going on about it so much that I couldn't handle it, and I left her sitting there alone. Stupid, I know,' he said, scratching the adhesive label on the bottle.

'When are you planning to tell your parents, then?' I'd already told him several times that I thought they would be furious when they found out he was dating a *paya*. Even though I could see Eva was perfect for Kiko, I knew this wouldn't cut much ice with Paco and Loli if she wasn't a *gitana*.

'I don't know… I'm scared of what they`ll say,' he said, staring out into the distance.

'You're damned if you do and damned if you don't. If you tell her where you're from, she'll probably dump you; if she doesn't, when your parents find out, they'll make you dump her!' I was trying to lighten the mood, but as soon as the words came out of my mouth, I knew they were too close to his deepest fears.

Kiko glowered at me. 'Thanks a lot, *tío*. I wasn't asking for your opinion.'

'Ah, come on, Kiko, you know I'm only joking. Where's your sense of humour?'

Kiko shook his head, his mouth set in a grim line. 'But you're not joking, are you? You're right. It probably will pan out like that. I don't know what to do.'

If I started seeing a *paya*, no one would bat an eye. It wouldn't be remarked upon because I wasn't a *gitano*. While we'd both been brought up in the same place with the same values, unlike me, it was taken as given that

Kiko would marry into another gypsy family.

A damp mist was coming up from the sea, making us shiver in the gloomy dusk. We carried on walking, the flickering lights of home getting closer. Kiko nudged me. 'So, what about Margarita, eh?'

The impact of meeting Margarita had been so profound that I was desperate to share with Kiko the effect it had had on me. But I knew it was futile; she'd chosen another. Shaking my head, I gave a non-committal shrug.

Artie. Tall, charismatic, full of energy and vitality, and so much more sophisticated than a man from a slum. From the moment he'd arrived, he'd commanded all Margarita's attention for the rest of the evening, cutting her off from the rest of our group. Monopolising her. I could see she was a little tipsy, perhaps not used to drinking wine like that. But in the end, she'd willingly kissed him, with an enthusiasm that couldn't be faked.

I stood abruptly, trying to forget what had happened, but it was impossible.

As we had returned with the drinks, I came to a sudden halt, and Kiko had almost crashed into my back. Artie was all over Margarita. My heart had shattered into a thousand tiny pieces and when Kiko handed a drink to Eva, he looked at me curiously.

Now, his voice interrupted my thoughts.

'Do you think we should ask your Pa how he thinks they'll react? I mean, he knows my father better than almost anyone,' he asked, his face earnest as I caught up with his rapid change of subject.

I nodded, pushing away the choking feeling in my chest. 'That's not a bad idea. He should be home now. Come on, let's go and see what he says.'

As soon as we came to the end of the alley, we were immediately surrounded by children begging us for cigarettes. We knew if we didn't give them a few to share, they'd hound us all the way home. Cheering, they danced off, no doubt heading down to the beach to practice their smoking style. We'd done the same thing when we were their age, and catching each other's eye, we grinned at the memory. Opening the door, the smell of garlic-infused mussels greeted us, and my mouth watered. My father was sitting in his underpants and vest, trimming his nails with a penknife over the open fire, and one of my sisters was laying the table for supper.

'*Chicos*! How are you? How was the kitchen today?' he asked, a glint of humour in his eyes. We shook his hand, and I headed straight to the back to wash my face. Coming back into the room, I caught the end of my father's words and came to a halt.

'...he was like a bear with a sore arse this morning, Kiko. Do you know what's bothering him?'

'Not really, Pichi. We went to an art exhibition last night.'

There was a loud guffaw from my father. 'An art exhibition? What on earth would you two be doing at an art exhibition?'

I heard Kiko clear his throat and wondered if he was going to say anything about what had happened last night. My father laughed so much that he began coughing, hacking up some mucus. The fire hissed as he spat it out, and I heard his lighter click as he lit a cigarette. I walked back in and asked them what they were laughing about.

'Ah, nothing, *hijo*,' said my father, winking at Kiko, who shrugged.

I grabbed some clean clothes from the back of a chair and pulled them on – there was no room for privacy or modesty – and sat at the table next to Kiko. Kiko spoke. 'I've been telling your Pa that while I'm grateful for the job, I've felt a bit trapped.'

It was the first I'd heard, and I was perplexed. I wouldn't say I liked it either. I knew my dreams of studying medicine would only become more of a reality by earning a steady wage instead of collecting scrap. 'But, *tío,* would you rather be trudging around the streets collecting rubbish all day?'

'No, of course I wouldn't, but I haven't got time for other things anymore,' he said, disgruntled.

'Ayy, be careful, *chico*. You don't want to end up like that father of yours, do you?' my father reproached. 'Paco's had some good opportunities in his lifetime, and half of them he's thrown down the drain.'

I caught Kiko's eye, and he nodded towards my father. 'Pa, can we take you for a nightcap at Manolo's when we've finished supper?' I asked.

125

If Pichi was surprised, he didn't show it and nodded. 'Okay, *chicos.*'

We finished eating, helped the girls take the dirty plates out into the backyard to wash, and then the three of us set off on the two-minute walk to Manolo's bar. We walked in comfortable silence, calling out greetings to neighbours. On the corner by the bar, we paused to watch an impromptu performance by Rosario and her cousin Antoñita, who everyone called La Singla. Each time I saw them dance, they took my breath away. La Singla was a runt of a girl who had been born almost completely deaf. She'd learned to dance flamenco from the vibrations in her feet. She rarely walked, running everywhere as if she had the wind behind her and always went barefoot, even in winter. The only time I saw her wearing shoes was when she was dancing. Her tiny feet would stomp *zapateados,* beginning slowly and getting faster and faster until they reached a crescendo of movement. As her hands clapped *palmas,* the ragged girl became a true *Duende,* a spirit of flamenco, her eyes blazing with emotion. She danced with such passion that grown men were often moved to tears.

Kiko and I loved La Singla as if she were our younger sister. She sometimes followed us almost to Las Ramblas, but each time we turned to tell her to go back, she would snicker at us in her strange high-pitched voice, darting away before we could catch her.

As I watched her now, my heart almost burst with pride. All of us in the camp hoped Antoñita would be as famous and successful as Carmen Amaya, the world's most talented Flamenco dancer, born, like us, in Somorrostro. Kiko, my father and I were hypnotised until the performance finished as suddenly as it had begun, and the two girls ran off clapping and giggling. That night all the usual regulars were in the bar watching football on the only television in the neighbourhood, which was hooked up to a generator. My father ordered three beers, and we went and sat outside the bar at the plastic table customarily reserved for card games.

'So, what do I owe this pleasure to then, *chicos*?' he said, an inquisitive look on his rugged face

'Kiko's got a dilemma, Pa. I thought you might be able to help him,' I said. I wasn't used to speaking about such things with my father and squirmed in my seat. I forced myself to sit still and signalled to Kiko to take over.

Kiko put his hands on the table in front of him. 'Pichi, you've known my parents for years, haven't you?' he said, and Pichi nodded, his face solemn. 'Well, I've met someone, a girl, and I need some advice.'

Pichi chuckled. 'I reckon this is a talk you should have with your father, *chaval*. I haven't had much experience with this sort of thing. My older boys never came to me with women troubles,' he said, winking.

'Pichi, promise you won't say a word? If he finds out from someone else, he'll probably skin me alive,' said Kiko, his tone urgent.

'Come on then, spit it out. What's bothering you?'

my father urged, flicking me a quizzical glance.

'Her name is Eva,' said Kiko, his face flushing in the dim light from the bar, as he began to tell my father the same story that he'd told me weeks earlier. 'She's beautiful, isn't she, Santi?' he said, his eyes bright as he turned to me.

I nodded and took one of my father's cigarettes from the packet in front of him on the table.

'I'm sensing a "but",' said Pichi, also lighting up a cigarette and taking a slug of the beer Manolo had just set down on the wonky table.

'Yes', said Kiko, looking over his shoulder to check Manolo had gone back inside. 'Eva isn't a *gitana*, Pichi... she's a *paya.*'

I cringed inwardly, expecting my father to object immediately. But he didn't. Instead, his eyes widened. 'Well, I have to say I wasn't expecting that, Kiko. And I can guess why you're telling me first, not your parents.'

'I don't know what to do. They'll be furious and stop me from seeing her. What if they make me marry someone else?' said Kiko, his face strained. 'If they don't accept her, I swear, I'll leave home,' he said, his eyes flashing.

'Steady on, *fiera*, you don't know how they'll react,' said Pichi, putting his hand on Kiko's arm. 'But you're right. I've known your parents since the day they came to live here, a good few years before you were born. We've had our ups and downs over the years, and I know as well as anyone that Paco can be a useless layabout a

128

lot of the time. But one thing he is, Kiko, and that's fair. He's cocked up more times than I've had hot dinners. So, whatever you tell him, whether he likes it or not, he'll consider it fairly.' He paused to drink some more beer and light up another cigarette. 'Although I don't think it's Paco you should worry about. I think you'll get more grief from your mother if I'm honest. Loli has always been very moral about such things. I remember when one of her sisters, Rosario, married a French *payo*. Loli was horrified and wouldn't speak to her for years. She went to the wedding, of course, your mother loves a good wedding, but she didn't speak to the bride or groom once, not one word. It was impressive. Talk to your father, *chico*. I think he'll understand.'

Sitting back in his chair, he shouted for more beers for the three of us. I was puzzled. I hadn't expected such a pragmatic response, and I could see Kiko hadn't either. We raised our bottles in a toast, and the subject was closed.

19

Margarita glanced around her, enthralled by the groups of young people milling around the Plaza del Sol. So used to the conflicts and skirmishes of La Ribera and the Old Town, the village-like feel of Gràcia was a revelation. The atmosphere was unlike anywhere in the city Margarita had ever been, peaceful yet charged with bonhomie and excitement. She and Eva were sitting at a table outside the Café del Sol. They hadn't seen each other since the exhibition, and Margarita was bursting to tell her friend about Artie. Eva had suggested catching the metro up to Gràcia, an adventure for Margarita, who could count on her fingers the number of times she'd travelled on the underground.

Margarita knew she'd had more life experiences than Eva, not all good, but she'd certainly had much more freedom than Eva. Now, though, their roles were reversed, and she smiled as she saw how Eva puffed up with pride as she introduced Margarita to this exciting new world. When their drinks arrived, Margarita took a deep breath and brought up the subject of Artie, the blood rushing to her face as she told Eva about the night they'd spent together.

'Margarita Marquez,' Eva exclaimed. 'You dark horse! Although I can't say I'm shocked. You were glued to each other all night at the exhibition. Tell me everything!'

'I've hardly even kissed anyone, let alone… you know,' Margarita giggled, her face hot. 'We couldn't keep our hands off each other.'

'Well, I'd *never* kissed anyone until I met Kiko!' Eva said, grinning. 'And we're the same, although I must say, I'm getting fed up with going to the Filipinos' apartment all the time,' she said, which set Margarita off again.

'Seriously though, Eva, do you think he likes me?

Eva fiddled with her bracelet. 'I'm sure he does, although I saw him yesterday, and he didn't mention anything. I'll tell you what, I'll organise another night out for all of us, and you can ask him yourself.'

Disappointment flooded through Margarita. Did it mean he wasn't interested if he hadn't asked Eva about her? 'Do you think I should have waited? What if he thinks I was just a one-night stand? I couldn't bear it,' said Margarita, looking to Eva for guidance.

'No, I don't think he's like that. He's a big flirt, but I've never heard him talking about any girls he's been with.'

Eva's words reassured Margarita. She sat back in her chair and sighed. Perhaps he did like her after all, although it had been more than a week since the exhibition, and he'd yet to come and see her at the bakery. Feeling a tap on her arm, Margarita turned to Eva, who was leaning in close, her eyes glowing expectantly.

'What did you think of Kiko, Margarita? I've been dying to know! Don't you think he's wonderful?' she swooned, not giving Margarita a chance to reply to her first question.

Margarita had known it would be one of the first things Eva would ask her, and she'd considered her answer carefully beforehand. 'He's lovely, Eva, obviously head over heels for you,' she said, the note of caution in her voice making Eva raise her brow. Margarita sensed how important her approval was to Eva. 'He's very charming, isn't he? she said truthfully. 'And he's so handsome, Eva. I can see why you've fallen for him.' She fiddled with her hairgrip, not wanting to upset Eva again by mentioning her misgivings about Kiko and Santi, but it had been bothering her. 'Did you ever find out where he lives, Eva?' she asked.

Eva's shoulders immediately tensed. 'Oh, not this again!' she said, scowling.

It was mean of Margarita to burst Eva's bubble, and she took hold of her friend's hand. 'I'm sorry to put a dampener on things. But I don't understand why they were so reluctant to say.'

Eva nodded, her eyes downcast. 'It's me who should apologise, Margarita. To be honest, you're only saying what I've been thinking for a while.' She poured a second glass from the jug of sangria they'd ordered and took a sip. After a moment's hesitation, she continued. 'He's also quite bad-tempered sometimes, Margarita. Last week, we were having a coffee near Plaza Molina, and I asked him which school he went to. I swear he nearly snapped my head off. Then he got up and left me sitting alone at the bar like an idiot! I waited for ages, but he didn't come back, so I went back to the academy. I was so upset.'

Margarita's eyes widened. 'Have you seen him since? What did he say?' she asked.

'Well, that's the strange thing. Whenever he gets in a mood, he's completely back to normal by the next time we meet,' mused Eva, shrugging.

'Santi said they lived near Poblenou. Montse told me it's quite a pleasant area, mainly fishing families and working-class people. A bit like where I live.'

They sat in silence for a while until Margarita spoke. 'Shall we follow them one night?'

She was only half-serious, but Eva immediately exclaimed. 'Oh no, I wouldn't dare! I don't even know how to get there, do you?'

Margarita shrugged. 'Well, they never take the metro, do they? So it can't be too far away.'

Eva shook her head. 'I don't care how near or far it is, Margarita, I'm not going to follow them, and that's that,' she said, clamming up.

Margarita changed the subject and they finished their drinks, speaking no more about either Artie or Kiko. As they headed back to Fontana metro station, dodging pedestrians, they glanced in the shops that were closing up for the night. A busy tram crawled past, full to bursting with people on their way home from work. Although they didn't mention following the boys again, a seed had been planted in Margarita's mind. She didn't know it then, of course, and would never have believed that before long, she would be following in the very same footsteps her mother, Carmen Garcia, had taken years earlier.

20

'I'm afraid if you continue drinking to excess, Señora Garcia, you will cause permanent liver damage and, quite possibly, premature death,' said the solemn-looking doctor from behind his desk. Carmen's hands trembled from either nervousness or a lack of alcohol – she wasn't sure which. She'd missed so many days of work with gastritis that, in the end, Eduardo had made her an appointment with his doctor. They'd done a barrage of tests, and the prognosis was bleak.

She called in at the pharmacy to collect the doctor's prescription before limping numbly home. What had started as a way to mask her pain had now become a threat to her life. It had been sixteen years since Carmen had even attempted to function without a drink, and it had passed in the blink of an eye. Her daughter was an adult, her mother was a stranger, and she, herself, a pitiful shell of a woman. The doctor had instructed her to take one pill three times a day. He warned her that she would be violently ill if she drank and almost certainly have to be admitted to hospital. It was the wake-up call she needed. No one was able to save her, not her mother, not her daughter, and not Paco.

Despite constant nausea and wretched stomach cramps, Carmen was undeterred. She couldn't remember being too ill to take even a sip of alcohol; a small paradoxical victory, but a victory in her mind, nevertheless.

The return of Paco had acted as the catalyst for change, knocking her life completely off-kilter. More than at any other time before, the need to keep a clear head to tackle everything going on in her life was paramount. When she told Eduardo about the test results, he ordered her to take a few weeks off work. He insisted that she could return with reduced hours only when she was feeling better and assured her that her wages would remain the same. Her guilt at conniving him all these years stabbed her conscience, but she wasn't in a position to tell him the truth. Others needed to know the truth before Eduardo.

Margarita was in and out at all hours of the day, and it was only now that Carmen was at home she'd begun to notice. Usually, Margarita was the one who tried to keep their lives on the straight and narrow, doing the shopping, keeping the apartment reasonably tidy and chivvying Carmen for the rent. She would even regularly turn her mother on her side at night so she didn't choke on her vomit. How ironic it was that now that Carmen was trying her hardest to keep herself in check, Margarita was nowhere to be seen.

As she lay in bed, while her body relaxed, her mind raced, flickering recollections of things that had happened during those missing years coming back to her as she regained her sobriety. With the chaos in her mind beginning to clear, Carmen could pinpoint the very moment she'd finally lost the will to carry on. The day when something inside her had broken, and coldness had settled in the place where her heart used to be.

***

1950

After rekindling her relationship with Paco when Margarita was just months old, she was ecstatic. She hoped that this time they would be able to make it work and become the family she'd dreamed of, despite her mother's disapproval. They'd even talked about having more children. But after a whirlwind six months of drinking and dancing, making love whenever they had the chance, Paco Perona disappeared again. Carmen blamed her mother for scaring him away. Day after day, she waited for him to contact her, dropping in frequently at all their usual haunts. But the days turned into weeks and then months.

She lost interest in the baby and stopped eating, at which point her mother threatened to take her to see the doctor. But however much Carmen tried to get on with her life, without Paco, it had lost all meaning. He was her life, her everything. It was the baby's fault he had left her. She should have got rid of it just as Paco had suggested, but now it was too late. Each time Margarita cried or needed feeding, Carmen's resentment grew, and she withdrew from the child completely.

After four long months of waiting, Paco still hadn't reappeared. She needed to see him, to find out when, or if, he was coming back to her. But the memory of his anger when she'd followed him home was still vivid in her mind. After weeks of procrastination, the desire to see Paco outweighed her fear, and she decided to return to Somorrostro. The walk towards Somorrostro the second time around was far less intimidating. This time she relished each step that took her closer to Paco. The factories billowed out choking smoke from sooty brick chimneys, but occasionally she caught a glimpse of the sparkling cerulean sea between the shadowy warehouses.

She immediately recognised the place where Paco had shouted at her. It was the entrance to a long alley full of debris and bits of scrap metal, leading to the shacks beyond on the beach. Household rubbish and bottles, most of which were broken, were scattered around haphazardly, and an elderly man was poking at some hemp sacks with a metal bar. She wasn't brave enough to go down the alley and instead found a spot across the road in the doorway of a boarded-up factory. There was no one around, so she settled down to wait. When the sun was high in the sky, a stream of people began arriving, most pushing handcarts like the ones she'd seen in the market. Several old women skilfully manoeuvred the heavy-looking carts, yet none of the men milling around offered to help. Carmen tried to imagine her

138

mother pulling a cart from La Barceloneta or even further and shook her head with a tut.

More people arrived, turning the area into a busy hive of activity and noise. Young men on horseback with carts attached to the back, or straw panniers over the horses' rumps, filled to the brim with junk. People called out greetings to each other, some friendly and others vulgar, punctuated by raucous laughter. Carmen had some trouble understanding a lot of what they were saying. It was almost like a different language, still Spanish, but with many words she didn't recognise. Most of the women, even the young girls, wore long skirts and sturdy ankle boots, and apart from the occasional widow dressed head to toe in black, their clothes were a brilliant jumble of bright colours and prints. With only a few exceptions, the women's hair was long and jet-black, either pinned back in the nape of their neck or plaited. Many wore headscarves to protect themselves from the burning sun.

Although her hiding place wasn't in direct sunlight, Carmen began to sweat. Her hand was smeared with dirt when she wiped her forehead. The dust from the factories and the dirt track had left a layer of grime all over her clothes, and she knew her mother wouldn't pass up the opportunity to say something about it. There was a lull in the comings and goings in the alley for a couple of hours, and her eyes closed as she sat on the hard, dusty ground. The heat of the day and an empty stomach made her drowsy, and she napped for a while.

Raised voices disturbed her sleep, and she struggled to her feet to see what the commotion was about. Peeking out from her hiding place, she saw two women, one petite with a tiny waist and the other taller, thicker around the middle, with strong-looking arms. They were yelling at each other, hands on their hips and gesticulating wildly. From what Carmen could tell, they were arguing about a valuable ring that had gone missing from the petite woman's kitchen immediately after the tall woman had popped in to borrow some cooking oil. A group of spectators surrounded the two women, jostling and heckling, clamouring to give their opinions on who had likely taken the ring.

Fascinated, Carmen held her breath, watching in admiration as the petite woman stood her ground, even when her hefty adversary began to push her backwards. The woman's eyes glowered as she resisted the advances. She was breathtaking and had something about her that Carmen couldn't pinpoint. More onlookers had begun to gather, clapping them on. Even the children running in and around the crowd hollered encouragement until a loud shout reverberated from the alley. The two women and their supporters turned around and immediately simmered down. Carmen shielded her eyes from the blazing sun to see a tiny old woman emerging from the alley, flanked by two men, flat caps pulled low over their faces. When the ancient woman came into view, Carmen drew a sharp breath. She'd never seen anyone as tiny or as old. She was unhealthily thin, the deep creases on her face visible even from a distance. Her fine, white hair was held tightly in a bun that poked out from under a black headscarf. Her bright clothes hung huge on her child-like frame, and she was barefoot despite rocks and shards of glass littering the ground. Even from her place across the road, Carmen felt the presence this woman possessed, a commanding strength emanating from her, as the crowd melted into respectful silence.

The old woman stood between the warring pair, speaking to each of them in a voice too low for Carmen to hear. Several onlookers began to drift off now the show was winding down, and Carmen could see the old woman more clearly. She spoke firmly but calmly, with a hand on each woman's arm. They nodded, appearing to accept what she was telling them without rancour or hostility.

With the drama calming in front of her, Carmen allowed her eyes to wander over to the men who had accompanied the ancient matriarch. Her heart almost stopped beating. Standing a short distance back, leaning on a van, was none other than Paco, his hands stuffed in his trouser pocket, shirt sleeves rolled up to the elbows, and a cigarette dangling from his lips. She pressed herself into the doorway, unable to take her eyes off him. He looked as handsome as ever, and his hair was longer than the last time she'd seen him. At the sight of his firm, toned arms, Carmen shivered at the memory of those same arms around her, holding her close.

141

After all these months, here he was, and all she could think about was how she longed to run her fingers through his hair. He was talking intently to the other man, who looked around the same age, their heads close together, shooting concerned glances at the women. Carmen's gaze flicked back and forth between Paco and the women. As Paco eventually approached the huddle, she hardly dared to breathe. A weight smothered her. It was the sweetest torture to watch the man she loved with her whole being walk over to the petite woman and gently take her by the hand.

She knew that look he gave the beautiful woman before they turned away. And there was no mistaking how the woman gazed up at Paco, her dark eyes full of love. Silent tears rolled down Carmen's cheeks, cutting through the dust on her dirty face. She didn't move for hours. Her tears had left white stripes down her dusty face, and her heart had turned to stone. The sun was going down in the sky, yet still she stood in the same place, her legs paralysed. Perhaps she knew, on an unconscious level, that leaving here would spell the end.

As she stood shivering, her eyes never left the entrance to the alley. She stayed, frozen to the spot until something rustled beside her. She turned to find the tiny old woman she'd seen earlier standing by her side, her bright eyes locking with Carmen's. The sight of the old woman didn't faze her. Quite the contrary. She'd prayed that if she stood here long enough, someone would feel her pain and come to help her.

The old woman's eyes creased, and her face softened in the dusky light of the sky. She took Carmen's cold, stiff hands in hers.

'This is the second time in my life I have seen you, *hija mía*,' said the old woman, her tone warm and gentle. 'And both times, I have seen Paco Perona break your heart right before my eyes.'

Carmen searched the old woman's face. 'Is he married? Was that his wife?' she croaked, her voice trembling.

The old woman nodded. 'She is, *hija mia,* and has been for many years. They have been together since they were no more than children. He's young and foolish, but he'll never leave Loli.' Her tiny, claw-like hand was strong as she squeezed Carmen's hand. 'I'm sorry you had to find out like this*, hija mia*. Paco loves you, but it will be a long time before he realises just how much. He may or may not come back to you one day, but don't spend your life waiting for him.'

Carmen stared at the woman, her chest pounding. 'He loves me? And one day he might come back to me?' she whispered, her voice hoarse from the hours of silence but with a spark of hope so bright it almost brought tears to the old woman's eyes.

She cupped Carmen's face in her wrinkled hands. 'You must live your life, *hija mía*, as well and as marvellously as you can. If your paths cross again one day, you may have another chance to love each other.' The old woman let go of Carmen's face. 'Leave now and never come back to this place. Don't waste your precious life on Paco Perona. He won't be worth it in the end. I'll keep you in my thoughts, always.'

Carmen stepped closer and kissed the old woman's cheek, her leathery-looking skin surprisingly soft. 'Thank you,' she said, her eyes full of tears. *'Cómo se llama usted?'*

'They call me Tia Rosita,' the old woman replied, touching her face where Carmen had kissed it.

'I'll never forget you, Tia Rosita,' said Carmen. Although her heart screamed not to turn and leave, she could see she no longer had a reason to stay.

As the old lady watched Carmen walk away that night, she knew without a doubt that the girl would struggle to make it on her own. She shook her head as she thought of Paco and poor Loli, hoodwinked without even realising. She turned to walk back down the alley, cursing the pain of a broken heart and hoping the *paya* would value her worth instead of waiting for Paco Perona.

When Carmen finally arrived home, disoriented and numb, her mother was standing at the door with a scowl on her face and Margarita in her arms.

'Where on earth have you been? Look at the state of you,' she said, holding out the toddler towards Carmen. 'I've missed evening mass.'

Unshed tears almost choked Carmen as she tried to hold her daughter in her arms, but she found being near the child too painful. She thrust the screaming baby

144

back into her mother's arms, hardly noticing the look of contempt her mother gave her as she refused to comfort Margarita. Ignoring her mother's questions, she shut herself in her room, her daughter's screams piercing her heart. In the following weeks, her child's demands were more than she could bear. Even the sound of Margarita crying was enough to trigger her anxiety. She began slipping out at night to hang out in the Plaza with the other teenagers, desperate to shrug off the weight of responsibility. Her mother pleaded with her, berated her, and shamed her, but Carmen was lost. As she tried to drink away the pain, all she did was hurt those she loved and herself more than anyone.

***

Now, Carmen took a sip of water from the cracked glass on her bedside table and sank back into her pillows with a sigh. She remembered every word spoken by Tia Rosita that terrible day. She'd taken the words so literally that she'd become blind and deaf to her daughter, her mother, her life and herself. How could she have been such a fool? The memories of those wasted years pained her, and she was ashamed. She so desperately wanted a second chance at life but feared that she'd left it too late.

21

It had been several weeks since Margarita had spent the night with Artie. She daydreamed endlessly about the handsome Englishman, recalling the heat of his kisses and the touch of his strong hands roaming all over her body. Thinking about that night made her blush with lust and shame. She'd never been intimate with a man. Of course, she'd had flirtations with boys, but only kisses and fumbles, and certainly not with anyone as worldly as Artie. Margarita didn't know his age, but she suspected he was quite a few years older than her. Some days she wanted to burst with happiness, while others were plagued by self-doubt and dejection. Why hadn't he contacted her? Had she scared him away with her lack of experience, her naivety?

At the bakery, Montse had reprimanded her countless times for dilly-dallying while taking the baguettes out of the oven, complaining they'd have a job to sell such crunchy bread. But it all went in one ear and out of the other for Margarita.

In the end, fed up with Margarita's despondency and her incessant need to know if Artie had asked after her, Eva had snapped that no good would come from waiting around and pining for him. Though Margarita was irked that Eva refused to quiz Artie, she knew her friend was right. One evening, she agreed to go to the cinema with Eva and Kiko as a distraction. When they arrived at the Palacio Balaña, Margarita was surprised to see Kiko chatting with Santi in the entrance. As Kiko and Eva hugged, Margarita fell back into the easy banter she had shared with Santi at the exhibition. She'd been so wrapped up in Artie that night that she'd forgotten how interesting Santi was to talk to and how much they had in common. After the movie, they walked back through the Raval, crossed Las Ramblas, and stopped for a quick drink in a bar on Calle Ferran before parting ways.

As they waved the boys off, Margarita turned to Eva excitedly. 'Now's our chance, Eva. Let's follow them and see where they go!' Eva hesitated, but Margarita insisted. 'Don't you want to know? If we don't do it now, we might not have another opportunity.'

Eva nodded, her mouth set in a tight line, and they hurried to keep the boys in their sight. They trailed behind, hiding in the throng of people on the street and crossed the busy Via Laietana. Margarita could see Eva was getting increasingly uncomfortable as they headed down towards La Barceloneta, and she reached out for her hand. The crowds were thinning out now the early evening rush was over. At this time, most people were heading home to have supper. It was easier to keep tabs on the boys, but there was also more likelihood they would be spotted if either turned around.

Eva tugged on her hand, and when Margarita turned,

Eva's face was white, tears threatening to fall. She pulled Margarita into the doorway of the Maritime Museum. 'I want to go back, please.'

Margarita swallowed her impatience. 'I think we're nearly there now. I can see the factories up ahead. Come on, Eva, we might as well carry on a bit further. What have we got to lose?'

'I don't like being so underhand, Margarita. It's not me,' Eva pleaded. 'If Kiko finds out, he'll be livid and won't trust me ever again,' she said, wiping away her tears.

More gently, Margarita tried to reassure Eva. 'How will they find out? It's almost dark now. They won't see us.'

'Okay, we'll go on a bit more, but I swear, Margarita, you'll be on your own if it's much further,' snapped Eva.

The boys came to a standstill and looked out towards the sea, the tips of their cigarettes glowing brightly in the dark sky. Low tones of conversation, punctuated by barks of laughter, drifted over the sand. They finished their cigarettes and started walking again, with their hands in their pockets and their heads down. A teenager on a rusty, old-fashioned bicycle cycled alongside them, and the boys greeted him with a pat on the back, shaking his hand. They chatted for several minutes, roaring with laughter at something the boy on the bicycle said, and then raised their hands in farewell as the boy continued on his way.

When the boy had cycled past the girls, Margarita turned to Eva. 'I didn't like the look of him, did you?' Eva shook her head, her forehead creasing.

'I remember when I was a child, my father used to take me to the summer fair in Plaza Lesseps every year. That boy reminded me of the boys who worked on the Ferris wheel and the carousel. My father always put the fear of God into me, warning me to stay close to him and not talk to strangers. He said they were all *gitanos* and would kidnap girls like me the first chance they got.' She turned to face Margarita, her eyes wide. 'Do you think he was a *gitano*?'

Margarita pulled a face and shrugged. 'I don't know. I'm not sure what *gitanos* look like, to be honest. Miguel Perillo reckons his family are *gitanos*. He told me his dad was a blacksmith for the family horses, but he had a falling-out with his parents and left to open their hardware shop. Miguel said once you leave the clan, you're dead to them. But I know what you mean, Eva.'

Without warning, Kiko and Santi suddenly vanished from view. Margarita stopped dead and clutched Eva's arm. 'Where the hell have they gone?' she whispered, turning to Eva, who shrugged.

Bawdy laughter and shouts came from up ahead, alerting them to a group of men walking towards them. They crouched behind an abandoned car jacked up with no wheels and held hands tightly. Margarita was beginning to regret her impulsiveness and suppressed a shiver. What a stupid idea it had been to follow the boys.

149

But then, just like Kiko and Santi, the men also disappeared, their voices becoming fainter the further away they got. The two girls came out from behind the car.

'Eva, look. There's an alley, can you see it?' whispered Margarita, pointing to a shadowy wall next to a pile of what looked to be building debris.

'Yes. I can hear the sea. It must lead to the beach.' Slowly, they inched closer. They heard the distant melody of music and occasional shouts and laughter, and the smell of smoke was overpowering.

Eva snatched her hand away from Margarita and turned to leave. 'I've had enough now. You can go, but I'm staying here,' she said, her voice edged with panic, and made her way back to the safe place behind the car.

Margarita let her go. They'd come this far, and she couldn't stop now. Intent on discovering what the boys were hiding, she began to creep down the alley. As she neared the end, a surge of adrenalin pushed her towards the flickering of what seemed to be a hundred burning fires, illuminating a vast expanse of metal roofs. She knew exactly what this place was. She'd often heard the men in the bar talking about the horrors that took place here. Hadn't Yaya and even her mother, who usually couldn't care less where Margarita went, warned her never to come here? Despite her racing heart, she couldn't tear her eyes away from the sight in front of her, morbid curiosity stronger than fear.

Children played in the darkness, their faces lit up in

150

the firelight. Men sat on crates or on the floor, watching the children, while women passed around bowls of food. Margarita had never seen anything like it. Taking a final look towards the beach, her eyes smarting from the smoke, she made her way back up the alley to the road, wondering if Eva had put two and two together. Or would she have to break the news that Somorrostro – hell on earth – was where Kiko Perona lived?

They made their way home in tense silence. When Margarita explained that Kiko and Santi lived in Somorrostro, Eva frowned. 'What's Somorrostro?'

It hadn't occurred to Margarita that Eva wouldn't know about the infamous *barracas,* but she had been sheltered in her small world from the reality of life. Margarita had once overheard her mother and Yaya Rosa talking about "that dreadful place". At the time, she'd wondered why Yaya had appeared so riled, and out of curiosity, she'd asked where this place was and why it was so terrible. But her grandmother had clamped her lips together immediately, frowning at Margarita, and her mother had gazed into the distance, a wistful expression on her face. 'It's nowhere you'll ever need to go, Margarita,' her mother had warned enigmatically before disappearing into the kitchen to wash the dishes.

Of course, in the interim years, she'd heard its name dropped into conversations in the bar and learned about the terrible conditions suffered by its inhabitants. Still, talk of *gitanos* always made her nervous. Yaya had repeatedly warned her as far back as she could remember that all *gitanos* – bar none – were villains. They would steal her very soul if she so much as glanced their way.

Since then, Margarita had worried she might not recognise a *gitano* and unknowingly speak to one while they stole her soul. What did they even look like? Of course, the Perillos were rumoured to be *gitanos*, but they were a respectable family, even Miquel, albeit a simpleton. And Santi, too, she realised, astounded. She'd liked him immediately. They'd laughed and talked for hours on the night of the exhibition. He was so genial and kind. Aside from Eva, he was one of the first people she'd met who shared her love of books. Before Artie arrived that night, it was all they'd talked about. He'd even taught her how to dance, swinging her around as they walked down the Ramblas after leaving the cinema. She'd squealed with delight as he'd instructed her to put her feet on top of his, and they'd swirled up and down, clapped on by a group of pensioners sitting at a restaurant terrace. As Eva and Kiko walked on ahead, Eva's head resting on Kiko's shoulder, they'd turned to watch Margarita as she danced past, her hair flying out behind her.

Remembering this, as she and Eva walked home, Margarita was troubled. Was it because the boys hadn't been honest about where they lived or because she'd believed such cruel lies about the *gitanos* for so many years, flesh and blood like her? Sweet and caring Santi, whose smile had greeted her like an old friend when they'd seen each other earlier.

It was late by the time they reached Plaza Catalunya after the long, silent walk home from Somorrostro. Eva was still deathly white, so they went to sit on their favourite bench, and Margarita broke the news. At a loss for how to sweeten the truth, she was blunt. 'Well, it's where the *gitanos* live, I think,' she said, glancing sideways at Eva, who was staring into the distance, her eyes unfocused. Without warning, Eva's lip began to tremble, and the tears finally began to fall.

'Why didn't he tell me? I love him so much. I don't think he even knows me. If he truly did, he would know that I'd love him no matter who he was or where he was from.'

Eva looked at her for an answer, but Margarita had no words left to offer her. All she could do was hold Eva, stroking her hair as she cried. When the tears dried up, Margarita walked her home and promised they would get to the bottom of this. 'I'm sorry, Eva, it's all my fault. None of this would have happened if I hadn't pressured you into following them. What a foolish idea it was,' she said, cursing her stupidity.

They hugged each other tightly. 'I don't blame you, Margarita. I blame Kiko. I'm so cross with him,' sniffed Eva. 'He should have told me the truth, no matter how afraid he was of my reaction. But it doesn't change a thing, though. I still love him.'

22

The days had dragged on for Margarita after the extraordinary revelations about Kiko and Santi. She'd heard nothing from Eva since they'd followed the boys. She'd been round to her house a few times, whistling up at the window like she always did, but the lights had been off, and there had been no signs of life, which was odd. Especially with Christmas, their favourite time of year, approaching. Every year Margarita and Eva arranged weeks in advance to visit the Santa Lucia market to admire the Christmas decorations. She was worried and mystified in equal measure. Perhaps Eva had confronted Kiko about living in Somorrostro, and they'd quarrelled? There was nothing Margarita could do except wait until she got in touch.

She was also despondent that Artie hadn't contacted her. It had been weeks since they'd spent the night together, and her mood was sombre, loneliness gnawing at her insides.

***

One evening, Margarita arrived home from her shift at the bar. She was looking forward to having a milky coffee, accompanied by some leftover cinnamon rolls from the bakery, before bed. But when she opened the door, she was startled to see her mother sitting on the sofa, a magazine on her lap. 'Oh, hello. What are you doing here?'

Her mother glanced up. 'Why shouldn't I be?' she asked, her lips tight.

'If you've been here all night, you could have at least done the dishes from lunchtime,' Margarita said, eyeing the dirty plates on the dining table. What was more bewildering was that her mother appeared to be stone-cold sober, which bothered Margarita more than her shenanigans when she was drunk.

Her mother frowned. 'Actually, I haven't been feeling very well for the last few weeks.'

'Well, it's hardly taxing, taking a few plates into the kitchen,' Margarita said, picking up the plates and dumping them onto the kitchen sideboard with a clatter. Truthfully, she was so used to coming home to an empty house that she couldn't care less if her mother was there or not. And because she was sober, there would be no opportunity to take any money from her purse. So no, she wasn't glad. Her mother *had* been looking a bit peaky for a few weeks, more so than usual, but Margarita found it difficult to give a damn. She left the plates soaking in water and retreated to her room, muttering a sharp 'Night' in her mother's direction.

The following morning, Margarita walked down to Santa Maria del Mar and waited opposite the entrance for Yaya to finish Mass.

'*Cariño*!' exclaimed Yaya when she eventually came out, dressed in her Sunday best. 'How are you? Are you coming for lunch?'

'No, I have to work in the bar at lunchtime,' replied Margarita. 'I thought I could walk you back home.' She tucked her arm into Yaya's, and they set off.

'Yaya, I wanted to talk to you about something,' she began. 'Mama was at home last night when I arrived. Completely sober.' Beside her, Yaya stiffened.

'Oh, *Nuestra Señora*,' she sighed, her eyes narrowing with mistrust. 'What does she want? She only behaves well when she wants something. Mark my words, Margarita, she'll soon be asking you for money, and before you know it, she'll be in a drunken heap at the entrance to the market. Did I ever tell you about the time she was arrested after she passed out in the *Correos* post office?'

Margarita had heard the story many times, but Yaya carried on without waiting for an answer.

'I was mortified when the police brought her back! Ten o'clock in the morning, and they just dumped her outside the churreria, as bold as you like. I looked down from the balcony to see what all the commotion was about, and there she was, her skirt up around her middle and sick down the front of her jumper.' She genuflected, shaking her head at the memory, and Margarita stifled a giggle.

But she had indeed been expecting her mother to ask her for money any day. And when she did, Margarita would tell her that she knew everything about the deal she'd made with Eduardo the butcher, her grandfather no less. Then she would tell her mother she could whistle for any money. If she wanted to drown in a sea of alcohol, it wasn't Margarita's problem. She'd also considered threatening to go and live with Yaya. That would make her mother sit up a bit.

They reached the end of Yaya's street, and Margarita hugged her grandmother, promising she would drop in again soon. She pulled her jacket tight against the frosty December morning as she walked back towards the bar, and her mind drifted to Artie. The mystery of her mother's volte-face was now overtaken by the memory of the night they'd spent together. He was all she could think about.

23

A couple of days after we'd spoken to my father, Kiko plucked up the courage to tell his father and invited him to go for a nightcap. It was an unusually humid night, overly warm for this time of the year, and we were glad of the fresh breeze coming up from the shore.

'What's up with your father?' I asked Kiko in a low voice as I watched Paco's tense back ahead of me while we walked in single file down a narrow street that led to Manolo's bar.

'He and Mama have been arguing almost every day for weeks. She's been nagging him to find another job.'

We ordered drinks from the bar, beers for us and a double whisky for Paco. When Manolo brought our drinks to the table, Paco downed his with a grimace and immediately ordered another. Kiko and I glanced at each other, and he hesitated for a second before lighting up a cigarette. The minutes dragged out as he exhaled a long stream of smoke, clearing his throat and fiddling with the cuff of his shirt. He cleared his throat again, shifting in his seat.

'Papa, I need to tell you something... but it's so big, I don't know where to start.' He inhaled deeply on his cigarette, and I knew he was at the point of no return.

Paco raised his eyebrows but didn't speak. Kiko

continued, 'I'm in love, Papa. I'm in love with the most beautiful girl you've ever seen.'

Paco's face brightened. 'That's wonderful, *hijo mio*! Why on earth were you worried about telling me?'

Kiko locked eyes with Paco, and he spoke almost inaudibly. 'She's a *paya*. Eva is a *paya*.' He paused, taking a deep breath. 'And I don't care what anyone thinks. I'm going to marry her.'

I observed the exchange, holding my breath for the explosion I was sure was coming. But Paco's shoulders slumped, and he gave Kiko a look I didn't understand before rubbing his chin. Then he turned his gaze towards the sea, letting out a long breath.

Kiko glanced at me, and I shrugged. 'Papa, please... say something.'

'Wait, *hijo,* give me a moment,' mumbled Paco, his hand over his mouth. When his shoulders began to shake, and silent tears glided down his cheeks, Kiko looked as shocked as I was. For a while, we sat without moving, each of us in our own world. Worlds that had, without our knowing at the time, changed forever when Kiko uttered the word *'paya'*. Kiko had his head in his hands. Paco's weeping ceased, and he became unnaturally still, his gaze again tethered to the ocean. My leg twitched with the desire to run off into the night and leave the two of them with their pain and awkward silence. But how could I leave my friend?

At last, Paco stirred, knocking back his whisky as if it were liquid courage.

'*Hijo mío, te quiero mucho,*' he said, his voice breaking. 'I'm proud of you. Thank God you've inherited your determination and pride from your mother. She's always fought for what she believes in. Even when she was wrong, she battled with courage and grace. You've gone against everything we've raised you to be, and I feel nothing but respect for you, *hijo.*' He paused and laid his hand on Kiko's arm. 'I wish I'd had the same backbone as you when I was younger,' he said, his eyes not quite meeting Kiko's. 'You've told me your truth without fearing the consequences, and I'd like to tell you my truth, too. It could help you. Remember, I may be your father, but I'm only human, weak, and I don't want to disappoint you... ever.'

My father had vaguely implied that Paco skated on thin ice with Loli, yet as a father, there was no one better. But this was at odds with what Kiko had shared with me – that he'd always sensed a remoteness in his father. There in body but his spirit often elsewhere. Watching Kiko, his eyes wide and uncomprehending, I shared his fear that his father would admit something which would change their relationship forever.

'When I was a few years older than you are, I, too, met someone. Her name was Carmen, and like your Eva, she was a *paya.*'

Kiko's face was white in the moonlight, and I saw a muscle twitch under his eye.

'I loved her. I would have sold my soul to the devil to be with her – but I was married to your mother.' Paco

160

pressed his knuckle over his lip, the shame of betraying Loli etched on his face, the fear of being judged by his son tangible.

'You were in love with a *paya*?' whispered Kiko.

Paco nodded his head, his eyes lowered. 'Yes, I was…'

'But what about Mama?' asked Kiko. His world was spinning off its axis, and I wanted to reach out and touch him, but I was afraid he'd crumble.

'I've loved your mother since I was a boy, *hijo mío,* and that has never changed. She was my first love. When I met Carmen, all I could think about was hurting your mother, terrified of the family's disapproval. I loved them both. But back then, I was spineless. I didn't fight for a new life. I stayed in the one that had been chosen for me. If I'd been half the man you are, I would have followed my heart.'

Kiko's face twisted. 'How could you betray mama?

Paco couldn't meet Kiko's eyes. 'I'll never forgive myself, *hijo.* It'll haunt me until the day I die. In the end, I realised your mother meant more to me than anyone. We were blessed with you the year after that.'
Kiko glowered, studying his clenched knuckles. 'Did mama ever suspect anything?'

'No, never,' said Paco. 'Whatever you think of me, *hijo,* I love your mother.'

Kiko fiddled with a box of matches, striking one after another. 'Do you regret staying?'

Paco reached over and patted Kiko's arm

awkwardly. 'Never. Not for one moment, *hijo,* you have to believe me.'

The fight went out of Kiko. His shoulders drooped, and he gave a slight nod. Paco leaned back on the breakwater, and the colour returned to his face as if all the tension had dissolved, the burden of a lifetime's secret lifted in an instant. 'Tell me about Eva, *chiquillo.*'

Kiko looked out at the reflection of the moon on the calm sea, his face softening. 'She's not perfect, Papa, but she's the closest thing to perfection I've ever seen.'

'How did you meet her? Where is she from?'

Kiko explained about following her up Las Ramblas, to where she lived on the corner of Calle Pelayo. Paco's eyes narrowed as he listened. Maybe he was wondering, as I had, why a girl from such a well-to-do family would be interested in Kiko, a *gitano* from Somorrostro.

'Does she know you're a *gitano*?' asked Paco.

Kiko shook his head. 'No, not yet. I've been worrying about it,' he confessed. 'How can I tell her? As soon as I do, she'll probably run a mile.'

Paco looked at Kiko, and I was surprised to see a look of empathy on his face. 'The one thing I've learned in the last twenty years is that love doesn't care about money, class, or where you live. You don't choose love. It chooses you. And if you look after love, it will take your hand and never let you go.'

I'd never seen this side of Paco, and I suspected it was the first time Kiko had ever heard his father lay himself so bare. His admission made me think of Margarita. I desperately wanted to ask Paco how it felt to be consumed by another person. When would loving her from afar hurt less? But how could I ask him when I hadn't even told Kiko my feelings towards her? I dug my nails into my palms and bit my lips to stop myself from pouring out my deepest fears.

Kiko spoke. 'Did you ever tell anyone about Carmen?

Paco cleared his throat. 'Yes, *hijo*. Like you, I told my best friend.'

He turned to me as if seeing me for the first time. 'Your father is a decent man, Santi. He's been there for me for more than half my lifetime. He told me to walk away from Carmen, to look after my family, and not to follow my heart. He warned me that the risk of losing my family was too high a price to pay, and he was right. But there were times when I resented him, hated him for telling me to stay. I hope you and Kiko will always be there for each other.' His eyes turned back to Kiko. 'We need to think about what we'll tell your mother.'

We ordered more drinks and sat for a while, listening to Paco reminisce and share stories with us. I was glad for Kiko, relieved his secret was finally out in the open. It was only when we were getting ready to leave that, out of the corner of my eye, I saw a pair of wise, beady eyes that I knew so well, watching us from a distance. I blinked once, and they were gone.

24

Margarita was in the kitchen at the bar, gutting some cod for the lunchtime rush, which was always busier after the New Year celebrations. The damn knife was blunt, making the hateful task even more complicated, and she stabbed at the fish in frustration. After an unsuccessful search for the sharpener, she went through to the bar, up to her elbows in silvery scales. 'Bernat, I'm making a complete hash of the fish. Where's the—?'

Ten sets of eyes swivelled in her direction, and the room fell silent. With a frown, she marched over to confront Bernat. 'What's going on? Have I missed something?'

Bernat shook his head. 'Nothing's going on here,' he said, holding his hands up in front of him, a sheepish look on his face. As Margarita opened her mouth to respond, the bell tinkled as the door to the street opened. Irritably, she glanced over her shoulder. Her eyes widened, and she took a step back. The object of her musings for the past few weeks had materialised in front of her. And all she could do for a moment was open and close her mouth like the fish she'd been gutting moments earlier. Her heart thumped in her ears, heat flooding her cheeks and sending a tingle through her body. Embarrassed, she glanced at the customers scattered around the room who were eyeing them with interest and lowered her voice.

'Artie? Er, hello,' she said. *Dios,* he was handsome. Today, the thick hair she'd spent that night running her hands through and hadn't stopped thinking about was loose. She couldn't stop staring at it cascading down his back. Had he been speaking to her? She had no idea. She'd just been staring at him like a *burra* while he attempted to talk to her in broken Spanish. Oh, and those eyes. She'd forgotten how dreamy they were. Like pools of… of what she didn't know, but they reminded her of something romantic she'd read about a French actor in a magazine at the library. She became horribly aware of what a mess she looked with fish scales hardening on her hands and arms, her unwashed hair held back by a rubber band. 'It's wonderful to see you,' said Artie with a grin, closing the door behind him.

Holding onto the back of a chair to stop her from bolting back into the kitchen, she plastered a smile on her face. 'Yes, it's lovely,' she said faintly, trying to keep her arms out of sight

'I'd forgotten how pretty you were,' he smiled, letting his eyes trail up and down her body. 'I was asking this lot if they'd seen you today,' he said, nodding his head towards the men, who were now watching the exchange with amusement. 'But, curiously enough, none of them had. I only came back because I couldn't find my metro ticket, and I thought I might have dropped it here.'

Margarita glared at all the customers with

narrowed eyes and then turned to Bernat. 'That was rude of you,' she said, her hands on her hips.

Bernat, looking shamefaced at being caught out, began to bluster. 'Well, you've already invited trouble in through the door with that damn Calvet, so how am I supposed to know who *this* one is?' he muttered and busied himself cleaning the already gleaming pumps. The show had ended. The men turned back in their seats, and the hum of chatter returned to normal. Suddenly aware of the intense aroma of fish coming from her, Margarita cringed. 'Please excuse me. I need to wash my hands. Go and sit at that table,' she said, pointing to a quiet corner. 'I'll be back in two ticks.'

Hurrying through to the back, Margarita couldn't believe she was awake and gave herself a good hard pinch to check she wasn't dreaming. After all this time, she'd thought Artie had forgotten her and moved on to another, more exciting and sophisticated girl. That he'd bothered to come and find her – well, it must mean she meant something to him. She quickly dumped the fish back into the prep boxes to finish later. Then she scrubbed her hands and splashed cold water on her face. After rubbing rosehip oil into her hands and impulsively on her neck to camouflage the stink, she smoothed down her hair. She took a deep breath and returned to the bar, her hands shaking and a beam on her face.

Artie was sitting with one leg casually hooked over his knee. The easy charm and bravado of their first meeting was even more pronounced in the confines of the bar, and her insides fluttered.

'Would you like a drink?' she asked, worrying she had turned slightly breathless and was bordering on gushing at him.

'Yes, I'll have a beer, thank you.'

Did he just wink at her? Rubbing her sweaty palms on her skirt, Margarita quickly turned, ignoring a glare from Bernat. She flicked the lid off a bottle of beer for Artie and poured herself a glass of water, tutting as she spilt some down her skirt. Her face felt hot enough to cook the fish stew on. She prayed she wasn't sweating and discreetly patted her top lip. Scuttling back to the table, she sat down opposite Artie. As he gazed at her, she sat on her hands so she wouldn't be tempted to start biting her nails or fiddling with her hair.

Artie's lips curved upwards in the same lazy smile that had captivated her at the exhibition. He cleared his throat and leaned forward to look deeply into her eyes. 'I couldn't remember the name of the street you said the bakery was on, so in the end, I had to ask Eva.'

Margarita's stomach fizzed when Artie's leg brushed against hers under the table. 'How is Eva? I haven't seen her since before Christmas.'

Artie sat back in his chair, playing with one of the beer mats on the table. 'She was away for a few weeks. Her grandmother died, and the funeral was in Madrid. That's why I didn't come to find you until now,' he said and took a long drink of his beer.

Margarita knew Eva wasn't close with any of her

extended family, and it wouldn't have been an enjoyable trip for her. 'Oh, thank goodness she's alright. I've been worried about her.'

Lighting up a cigarette, Artie offered Margarita one, but she shook her head. She was already sailing close to the wind with Bernat as it was, sitting here when she was supposed to be working.

'I dropped into the bakery earlier and was interrogated by a woman called Montse,' he said with another wink.

'Oh dear, she's terribly nosey. What did she say?' 'Well, she was a bit abrupt at first. But then I explained that I was a bit sweet on you and wanted to ask you out for dinner one evening.'

Margarita swallowed a giggle, her stomach doing somersaults as Artie leaned in towards her again and beckoned her to come closer. She could smell the beer on his breath and feel the heat of his body. A sudden urge to run her hands up his thighs had her pushing herself back again as he continued.

'Although once she learned I was English, she treated me like I was the Prince of Edinburgh himself and gave me a bag of chocolate croissants on the house.' His face became serious. 'So will you come, then?'

Margarita chewed her lip. He was here. All these weeks, she'd been dreaming about him, and here he was asking her out. In a heartbeat, she replied. 'I'd love to go for dinner with you, thank you.' For a second, she wondered if she'd been too eager, but nothing like this had ever happened to her, and she didn't know the rules of the game.

Artie's eyes lit up and beamed at her. 'Well, that's the icing on the cake!'

'What do you mean, the icing on the cake?' He'd translated it literally, and she had no idea what it meant.

'It means this has been a great week! One of my paintings has been accepted for an exhibition in a top gallery in Calle Valencia. I've also found a new place to stay. And now you've agreed to have dinner with me!' He leaned towards her again, stroking her cheek softly with his index finger.

Margarita hardly heard his words. She was so enthralled by the handsome Englishman, the feel of him touching her again, that she could barely form a thought, let alone string a sentence together.

Artie gazed at her, his eyes tracking from her eyes to her mouth and back again, causing her to lick her lips involuntarily. 'Margarita, I've been dying to see you again,' he said finally, taking hold of her hand, his voice deep and so quiet that she had to shuffle her chair closer to hear him. 'I haven't stopped thinking about you since the night we spent together. It was magical. You're special.'

'Really?' she stammered, her cheeks hot. 'I thought I must have imagined you. I'm glad you came looking for me.'

Hearing a loud cough from the bar, they turned to see Bernat scowling at them.

'That fish won't cut itself and jump in the *cazuela* to cook, Margarita,' he said gruffly.

She stood up and turned back to Artie. 'You know where to find me now, don't you?' she said, her heart pounding as Artie lifted her hand and gently kissed it. 'I'll drop in tomorrow, Margarita,' he whispered and left the bar.

As the door closed behind him, she marched to the bar, where Bernat was drying some glasses, looking shifty. 'I wish you'd stop meddling in my business, Bernat.'

'It's my bar, Margarita, and I can do what the hell I want,' he sniped at her with a tut. But nothing could dampen her happiness, and she floated back to the kitchen to resume the fish gutting.

The next day, Margarita did her hair more carefully than usual and put on a touch of makeup, just in case Artie had meant it when he'd said he would come back to see her. Sure enough, he arrived around seven o'clock and perched at the end of the bar. They were busy that evening. Barça was playing, and the men huddled around the new TV Bernat had recently installed on the wall, rightly claiming it would bring in the punters. Every time there was a match, it was impossible to move in the smoky, cramped bar, and Margarita had to squeeze through the crush of bodies, her hands full of tapas dishes and empty glasses. She didn't have much time to speak to Artie but felt his eyes following her all evening, which made her flustered. Bernat had chided her several times for mooning over *el Inglés*. The match finished, and the customers left the bar in dribs and drabs until only a couple of regulars remained, eking out their drinks and grumbling about the nagging they knew would be waiting for them back home.

Bernat nodded at Margarita and told her she could knock off for the night when she'd emptied the overflowing ashtrays. Artie winked at Bernat, who gave him a disapproving scowl. She finished the ashtrays and nipped into the back to dust herself down, glad to see her makeup hadn't sweated off after the busy shift. Chewing a sprig of parsley from the kitchen, she checked her teeth in the mirror and, with a shiver of anticipation, went back out to the bar.

Artie was paying his bill, which Margarita noticed was a bit on the high side. She narrowed her eyes at Bernat, who had the grace to look sheepish.

Artie laughed. 'I worked in a bar in Gracia for a few months, so I know exactly what I should be paying. But I'd pay triple this amount to spend time with you.'

Margarita felt her face flush, Bernat and his money-grubbing antics forgotten. Artie held the door open for her, and as they walked down the narrow street, he took her hand. She was oblivious to the drunks singing on the corner after the Barça win that evening, so absorbed was she in the handsome English man, enthralled as he described his hometown. How the air was pure and clean, how much he yearned for the rugged coastline and the endless beaches, about the green hills which rose into majestic mountains, how he missed the silence. Margarita asked about his family. He turned to her, and grinned, and her heart did a strange somersault. 'I miss them,' he said. 'They're good people. I'd love you to meet them one day.'

'Oh yes!' she said, overwhelmed that he would even think about this so soon. 'I've never even been outside Barcelona. Except when I went with Yaya on the train to Tarragona for her aunt's funeral: But it wasn't the most enjoyable day out,' she giggled, and Artie laughed along with her. As they neared her building, she took out her keys. Artie touched her arm, and she turned to face him, hoping he couldn't hear her heart hammering in her chest. He leaned forward to kiss her, and she melted into him, feeling even more desire than she had when they'd spent the night together. It felt like a dream she didn't want to wake up from. But it was real, and she was in heaven. Margarita was the one to pull away. Worried one of the neighbours would see her, or *que Dios no le permita,* her mother would arrive, and she would die of embarrassment, she told him she had to go. They arranged to meet up the following Sunday for a walk and maybe have lunch. Then they kissed one last time.

She danced up the stairs, her heart singing. How would she get through the next few days until she saw Artie again? Never before had Margarita Marquez felt so special, and she was determined to hold on to this feeling as tightly as she could.

25

Sunday morning finally arrived, and Margarita was delirious at the prospect of seeing Artie again for their date.

The night before, she'd looked through the clothes Eva had given her and picked out a daring black and white striped skirt that came above her knees and a soft pink jumper which flattered her curves. She stuck her head out of the balcony door and sniffed. The sky was cloudless, but there was a nip in the air. She pulled on some tan tights, praying they weren't laddered and spent several minutes twisting around to check before she was satisfied they were presentable. After putting on a touch of makeup, her palms clammy with nerves, Margarita crept out before her mother stirred. If Carmen saw her dolled up, she would immediately be suspicious and Margarita was terrified she'd find out and ruin things with Artie.

When she reached the corner, he was already waiting, dressed in the same jeans he always seemed to wear and a light blue shirt with the sleeves rolled up, despite the crisp morning. He pulled her into a tight embrace and whispered into her hair, 'You look spectacular, Margarita. I know it's only been a few days, but it feels like an eternity since I saw you.'

She giggled as they kissed but pulled him down the street, fearful of being spotted by nosy neighbours. They meandered through the quiet Sunday morning streets, and Margarita pointed out places of interest. When they passed the library, she paused. 'This is probably my favourite place in the whole world.' But Artie merely nodded, continuing down the street without a word. Margarita stared after him. Maybe he hadn't entirely understood her – his Spanish wasn't very fluent – and she hurried to catch him up.

As they walked through Plaza de Sant Felip Neri, she told him this was where she used to meet Eva to play when they were young. 'We had to hide our friendship. Well, we still do.'

'That's ridiculous. Why on earth do you have to hide it?' replied Artie, glancing sideways at her, a look of amusement on his face.

Margarita's toes curled, and she shrugged. 'Eva's mother can be ruthless,' she said lightly, not wanting anything to mar this wonderful day. But Artie had already begun to wander off, distracted by the octagonal fountain in the centre of the square. Margarita trailed after him, hurt by his lack of interest.

They called in a bar in Plaza del Pi for a *cafe con leche* and some pastries, enjoying the morning sun on their faces while they watched the nuns entering the basilica. Then, hand in hand, they continued walking along Calle Portaferrissa. When they reached the end of the street on the corner of Las Ramblas, Margarita stopped by the water fountain. The exquisite mosaic-tiled backdrop was the work of Juan Baptista Guivernau, a cousin of Yaya's. All the family were very proud of the fountain, and her grandmother was a genius at dropping it into even the most fleeting conversations. Apart from Eva, Margarita had never shown anyone her tiny piece of family history. Artie paid much more attention, intrigued by the exquisite detail of the tiles. Margarita promised him they would go and visit cousin Juan in his studio in Calle Ticia one day.

As they crossed Las Ramblas, Margarita admired the unusual baroque style of the Palacio de la Virreina, but Artie declared it to be quite dull and nothing compared to Gaudi's modernist style.

'I don't know much about Gaudi,' she said. 'I used to go to Parc Guell with Yaya on Sundays, and I've been past the Sagrada Familia a few times on the bus.'

Artie arched an eyebrow. 'But you know La Pedrera, right? And Casa Batllo?

Mortified, Margarita couldn't meet Artie's eyes. 'Not really. I mean, I … I've heard of them,' she said in a small voice.

'Well, we'll have to remedy that, won't we? Don't worry. I shall take you on a tour another day,' Artie said with a shake of his head.

While the weight of her ignorance crushed her, a tiny part of her seethed. How dare he belittle her? This was her city, yet here was Artie promising to show her Gaudi's work. She vowed to herself to read up on Gaudi and well-known other artists. They could have a serious debate about the things he loved, and she could impress him with her observations. Steering the conversation away from her lack of culture, Margarita put her arm through Artie's. 'Where were you before you came here?'

'Oh, it's a long story,' he grinned. 'Come on, let's go and rest our feet for a while, and I'll tell you.' He ushered her over to sit on the row of chairs for rent at the side of Las Ramblas. The elderly man in charge came over to take their money, and Artie, his arm resting on Margarita's shoulders, began to talk.

After completing his art degree at Goldsmiths, he'd travelled to Paris, where he continued to work on his techniques. It had been a disappointment, though. He'd only mixed with fellow British artists and felt stifled and uninspired, surrounded by grey buildings and even greyer people. Some of the people he'd met were realists like him, but most clung to the pretentious belief that they would find the holy grail on the rainy Parisian streets; that is, if they could see it for all the dog shit. He hadn't been able to take to the language either. As much as he'd tried, he'd felt like a slow-witted interloper, unable to join in discussions with anyone other than the tedious group of English speakers he'd found himself stuck with. 'Eventually, I became so disillusioned with the city that I got up one day and decided to hitch a ride with some other artists headed for Morocco.'

Margarita listened, charmed by his story. How

176

wonderful it must be to wake up one day and decide to go live in another place, another country. But she also felt a shiver of alarm at his words. What if he upped and left Barcelona when he became bored? She couldn't bear the idea of never seeing him again.

'Travelling down through France was an eye-opener for me. I couldn't believe I'd wasted so much time in Paris! The vibrant tones of the countryside and the quaint villages we passed through in Provence, then later those stark, majestic Pyrenees…' A nostalgic look came over Artie's face. 'It ignited something in me, something I hadn't felt in years, a passion, a sense of purpose.'

'I've never seen the Pyrenees,' Margarita said, unable to imagine how mountains could inspire someone to such a degree. Then again, Yaya often spoke about her pilgrimage to Montserrat and how she'd wished for a child as she'd lit a candle for the Catalan virgin. She'd been pregnant with Carmen two weeks later and had always claimed it was the magical mountain's doing.

If he'd heard her remark, he didn't reply and carried on with his story. 'And then, driving down the coast was amazing. The Mediterranean was sparkling, and the people were friendly everywhere we stopped. I loved the expressive voices, even though I didn't have a clue what they were saying,' he said with a grin.

'How did you learn Spanish so quickly?' asked Margarita. 'I enjoy reading in English, but I never have the chance to practice speaking. Maybe you could teach me?'

'When I arrived, I worked in a bar near the Plaza del Sol. I was thrown in at the deep end, so I had to learn quickly, he said, then laughed. 'I'd be delighted to practise English with you. Then you'll be able to speak to my family when I take you home with me.'

Margarita shivered in delight. 'Didn't you care about starting again from scratch?' she asked, gazing at him. Her admiration for Artie had grown as she'd listened to his story, and she was overawed by how much more experienced he was than her. She tried to ignore the scornful, niggling voice inside that asked why he'd be interested in her.

'No,' he replied, stroking his chin. 'I don't think I've found my niche yet. And if I hadn't come here, I wouldn't have met you.' He took her hand and brought it to his lips, and Margarita almost swooned. God, he was wonderful.

'I'm glad you hated Paris so much,' she said, stroking his paint-stained hand. 'I would never dare do what you've done,' she said. 'To come to a strange place without friends or family. Weren't you lonely?'

'No, as soon as I arrived, I met some great, like-minded people, unlike the pompous lot from Paris. I can't wait to introduce you to my good friend, Herman. He's a photographer.' Reaching into his bag, he pulled out a camera, explaining that Herman had insisted Artie take it as a gift. Margarita was fascinated. She'd never touched a camera before, and he showed her how to use it. Worried she'd drop it, she passed it

178

carefully back to Artie, who then spent ten minutes taking pictures of Margarita. She was embarrassed at first but soon became more confident, posing for the camera.

'I've never heard of anyone called Artie before,' she said as he put away the camera.

'It's short for Arthur, nothing mysterious,' he replied with a grin.

'Oh, I thought it was something to do with you being an artist,' she said, deflated. He must think she was an idiot.

'There are so many Arthurs, and I wanted to be a bit different.'

'Is Eva taking the same classes as you at La Llotja?' Margarita asked, a prickle of envy for all the opportunities she would never have jabbing at her insides. What did she have to offer this man sitting beside her?

'Yes, she is. She's extremely talented,' said Artie. 'She was the first person I spoke to on our first day. And she was also the first Spanish woman I'd seen with red hair. She told me she was adopted and wondered if her biological parents were from Scotland. My grandparents were Scottish. I told her we could be related.'

'Poor Eva, she had a sad childhood,' said Margarita. 'I mean, I don't get on well with my mother, but at least I've got my grandmother,' she said, playing down how much this bothered her, worried she might frighten him off.

179

'How old are you, Margarita?' The abrupt change of subject made her hesitate. Did he think she was just a kid with all her silly questions?

She straightened her back. 'I'm nearly eighteen. What about you?' she asked, feeling rather impertinent. Yaya had always told her it was rude to ask someone their age.

'I was twenty-eight last month,' Artie replied, and Margarita's pulse quickened. More than ten years older than her. Yaya would be scandalised.

'How long have you worked at that bar?' he asked, kissing her fingers again.

Her eyes closed for a second, these new sensations making her stomach tingle. She dragged herself back into the present. 'Since I was thirteen.'

Artie's eyes widened. 'Really? I suppose I've been lucky. My father was an accountant in a bank, and my mother didn't work.''

Frowning, she asked, 'So you've never had a job, then?'

Artie shrugged, nonplussed. 'No, not as such. I worked in the bar when I arrived here, but that's about it. My parents pay for everything. I send them a telegram when I'm running low, and they wire a transfer to me.' He stretched his legs out, smothering a yawn. 'Like most parents, I expect.'

His candour unsettled Margarita. He was a grown man, yet still financially dependent on his parents and quite unabashed. 'Well, my mother isn't like most parents. I can't imagine what it must be like to never worry about money,' she said, crossing her arms. 'If I didn't work, I suppose we'd have to live with Yaya, although that would be impossible – she and Mama don't get along.' She lowered her eyes, wishing she could talk about her family as openly as he spoke about his.

Artie lifted her chin gently and looked at her intently. 'I can't wait to meet your Yaya and even your mother,' he laughed. The mood lightened, and they stood up and carried on with their walk.

26

After a fitful sleep, I woke up early on Sunday morning with my sisters' restless legs and arms poking me in the back. Unable to drift back to sleep, I clambered over the little ones and crept out into the backyard to wash. Kiko and I had arranged to go for a stroll in the city centre. I splashed freezing water over my face, buzzing with excitement.

I went back inside the house, rifled through a pile of clean clothes folded neatly on a chair in the corner of the kitchen, and pulled out a worn but clean shirt belonging to one of my brothers. My father was fast asleep, snoring in his armchair. I tiptoed past him and closed the front door carefully on my way out. I still had a short while to wait for Kiko, so I dropped in to see Tia Rosita. She was always up before sunrise. She answered the door, blinking in the bright morning sunshine. Her weathered face was pale, her eyes dull, and wispy tendrils of white hair were escaping from her bun.

'Santi, *hijo mío*,' she said. 'Come through. I've just brewed some coffee.'

I followed her into the main room. Her back was hunched, and she moved like she was in pain. 'Sit down, Tia Rosita. I'll get the coffee.' For once, she didn't argue. Bringing the pot and two cups, I poured the strong black coffee and passed one to Tia Rosita.

She sipped it gratefully and smiled at me. 'Where are you off to, all dressed up like a show pony?' she asked, her eyes creasing up.

'Kiko and I are going into town. We haven't been for ages, not since he...' I stopped, mentally kicking myself.

She stared at me for a moment. 'Since what, *hijo*?'

I tried to backpedal. 'I mean, since the weather has begun to get warmer. I don't think we've been since before Christmas.'

She squinted at me. 'You're a terrible fibber, Santi Calaf. I'm old, not daft.'

My face grew hot. I wasn't used to lying to Tia Rosita. She was the most important person in my life, even more than my father.

'Ach, *hijo,* take that look off your face. I know all about Kiko and the *paya,* have done for months now.'

I shouldn't have underestimated Tia Rosita. She always knew everything that was going on. 'So do you know about Paco, then?' I asked, predicting the answer before the question was even out of my mouth.

Tia Rosita nodded, her brow creasing. 'I do indeed. It's a burden that has weighed heavily on my mind for almost twenty years, *hijo*. And lately, I feel...' She reached for her coffee and took a drink.

'How do you feel?' I prompted her gently.

She shook her head. 'Like everything is coming full circle. Changes. Changes everywhere.'

Despite the smile she gave me, there was sorrow in her eyes. My heart dropped. I was afraid for her, for me, for all of us.

'Go on, *hijo,* get away with you! Go for your day out with Kiko. Pick me up some rosemary from the vendors behind La Boqueria, but make sure you get a fair price. Be sure to tell them it's for me, won't you?' I nodded. It was pointless asking her to expand on her worries, and I would be late if I didn't get a move on. I stood up, but she caught my hand, pulling me close. 'It won't be forever, *hijo*, this pain in your heart, I promise you.'

I frowned as I bent down to hug her, feeling a tremor pass through her tiny body. 'I'll come round with the rosemary later, Tia Rosita.'

I raced to the alley where we'd arranged to meet, but Kiko wasn't there yet. I sat down on a pile of bricks and put on my tie, smoothing my hair back off my face. Dressing in our smartest clothes and escaping the dirt and chaos of Somorrostro, even if only for a few hours, was a welcome respite for us, and we treasured days like this. Things had been tense at home recently. My brother, Iker, would be released from prison in a few weeks, and we were all on tenterhooks. Trouble followed Iker like an evil pied piper, and he wallowed in the misery he caused. My father wouldn't admit it, but whenever Iker's name was mentioned, I saw a flash of fear and disappointment in his eyes.

My thoughts were interrupted by the sound of

184

footsteps, and Kiko appeared around the corner, a scowl on his face.

'Hey, *Qué pasa, tío*?' I greeted him, wondering what had upset him so early in the morning.

'Paco's coming with us,' he said. 'He's getting dressed now. He said he'll be along in a few minutes.'

'Is that what the long face is for?' I asked, surprised. Kiko enjoyed his father's company even more so since they'd opened up to one another.

'No, it'll be good to have him come along. His mood is still very low. Maybe a day out will cheer him up,' he answered, patting down his pockets for a box of matches.

I passed him my lighter, and he lit his cigarette with a deep sigh. 'So, what's wrong then?' I repeated.

His shoulders slumped as he looked at me. 'The girls followed us, Santi. They followed us home the night we went to the cinema.'

'What do you mean, they followed us? What are you on about?'

'Eva and Margarita followed us back to Somorrostro. She arrived back from Madrid a couple of weeks ago and was as mad as hell. I had to tell her everything.'

I raised my eyebrows, and my heart sank. I wouldn't stand a chance with Margarita now she knew I was from Somorrostro. 'What did she say? Has she ditched you?' I knew my words were insensitive, and it was unlike me to be intentionally harsh.

He stared askance at me. 'No. She was upset I hadn't

told her the truth, but she doesn't care where I'm from. She said nothing would make her love me any less.'

His face had lost the anguished look of the last few months, and despite my irritation towards him, I was glad things were out in the open. If Eva could accept Kiko, then maybe Margarita would agree to go out with me when I finally plucked up the courage to ask her.

Interrupting my thoughts, Kiko spoke. 'Can you believe they came here at night on their own? I told her it was a foolish thing to do. There are all sorts of villains.'

I chuckled at the irony of his words, and Kiko, his frown turning into a smile, joined in. 'Anyway, what's rattled your cage?' he said, and once more, I felt ashamed of my earlier reaction. It was the perfect moment to tell him about Margarita, but as I opened my mouth, there was a shout.

'Hey, *chicos*! What a marvellous day for a stroll!' It was Paco, dressed up to the nines in his funeral suit, his hair slicked back and a wide grin on his face. My confession would have to wait a while longer.

The three of us set off in high spirits. We walked past La Barceloneta until we reached the bottom of Las Ramblas, meandering past the artists setting up their easels for the day and pausing to admire the caricatures. Groups of people milled around, and even though it was only mid-morning, the sun was already warm. We left Las Ramblas and made a detour to Bar Pastis on Calle Santa Monica. The owner, Joaquin, didn't encourage *gitanos* in the bar, but he'd known Paco since their

186

teenage days when they frequented Bodega Ca Rosita in the Paralelo neighbourhood. Paco was a chancer and a crook, but he wasn't a troublemaker, and Joaquin always had time for him. We stayed for a glass of Pastis and a couple of beers, and once our thirst was quenched, we carried on up Las Ramblas.

It was heaving with well-to-do couples and families parading up and down, groups of youngsters on every corner. Still, however tempting, we'd made a solemn promise to refrain from skulduggery today. It was a rare outing for us, and we didn't want anything to ruin it. I noticed Kiko becoming distracted as we neared the top of the long avenue, perhaps at the possibility of bumping into Eva. But before we went any further, I mentioned Tia Rosita had asked me to take back some rosemary. None of us from Somorrostro shopped in the La Boqueria market itself. It was too expensive. But on Sunday mornings, a few individual stallholders set up in Plaza Sant Josep, and it was possible to negotiate a fair price. I haggled with the seller for a few minutes, telling him it was for Tia Rosita. His face mellowed, and he accepted my offer. While the seller was wrapping the herbs up in newspaper, Paco disappeared into a bar, saying he'd spotted an old friend and would catch up with us. I put the parcel inside my jacket, and Kiko and I ambled along Calle del Carmen, bringing us back out on Las Ramblas.

But just as we were about to cross the road, Kiko suddenly let out a shout. 'Hey, Margarita! Artie! *Qué tal*?'

My heart almost jumped out of my chest, my lips tingling from a rush of adrenalin as I spotted Margarita and him, e*l guiri*. His arm was draped lightly over Margarita's shoulder, and out of nowhere, white-hot jealousy consumed me. I put my hands behind my back so no one would see my fists curled in fury.

'Artie, *amigo!* And Margarita, *guapísima*! What a coincidence!' exclaimed Kiko, looking thrilled. He turned to me, smiling, and steered me over to where they were standing. How could he not see my discomfort?

Margarita was glowing, her eyes shining as she kissed Kiko on both cheeks. When she saw me, her smile was broad. 'Santi, how wonderful to see you again!' She was in my arms for only seconds, but it felt like a lifetime. I inhaled the smell of her hair, and time stopped.

'You remember Artie from the exhibition, don't you?' she said, dragging me back to the present, and I found myself face to face with him. I tried to smile, but my jaw clenched as if it had been wired shut, and I was sure the smile came out as a snarl. Artie smiled confidently and held his hand out to me with a friendly nod. I shook his hand, but my eyes didn't meet his. I feared he'd tell Margarita of the contempt he'd seen in them.

'Hey, *chicos*, what's going on here?' puffed Paco, finally catching up.

'Papa, come and meet Eva's friends,' Kiko said, stepping aside to introduce Margarita and Artie to his father.

Paco stopped dead, rooted to the spot, his eyes unblinking as he stared at the couple. I glanced over at Margarita, and she, too, was standing stock-still. Something tangible passed between them as if they knew each other. I caught Kiko's eye, and his forehead wrinkled.

'Papa?' he said, his voice hesitant, but still Paco didn't speak. The silence stretched on uncomfortably as we stood like statues. I couldn't think of a thing to say to break the tension.

Eventually, giving Kiko a worried look, *el guiri* urged Margarita away, gently holding her arm. She didn't say a word or even look at me as she walked blindly past. After they'd disappeared from view, I turned back to Kiko, and he flashed me a worried look. 'I think he's in shock.'

I was ashamed to say I couldn't have cared less. Seeing the Englishman with his hands all over Margarita had knocked me for six. Behind me, Kiko guided a dazed-looking Paco to the nearest bar for a stiff brandy, and I followed them, my legs trembling. 'What was all that about, Papa?' Kiko asked when we were seated in a quiet corner of the bar.

'What do you mean?' Paco glowered, loosening his tie. 'I thought I knew her from somewhere, *hijo*. It was one of those – what do you call them?' He raised his eyes to the ceiling. 'You know, when you think you know someone, that's all it was.'

'Yes, I know what you mean, Papa, but it was both of you. Margarita looked like she'd seen a ghost. Do you know her?'

But instead of replying, Paco knocked back his drink in one, dropped a handful of coins on the table, and staggered outside, his face white despite the brandy. Open-mouthed, we watched him leave.

'What's going on?' Kiko said.

I shook my head. 'No idea, but they recognised each other.' We ordered a couple of beers and sat silently, smoking one cigarette after another. I cracked my knuckles, the tension from earlier returning. 'You didn't tell me Margarita was seeing the artist,' I said, trying to keep my tone neutral. 'Did you know?'

'Yeah,' he replied, his tone blithe. 'Eva mentioned it last week. It had completely slipped my mind.' His eyes narrowed as he looked at me. 'Why? Does it bother you?'

'No, of course not. I just think he's a bit of a jerk,' I said lightly, hoping Kiko didn't notice the loathing in my voice.

'Apparently, she's head over heels for him, and the feeling's mutual from what Eva told me.'

My insides turned to water, and I bit the inside of my cheek so hard I immediately tasted the metallic sting of blood. Kiko had no idea how I felt about her, which was my own stupid fault – I should have made it clear that I liked her the night we met instead of standing in the shadows and letting the silver-tongued foreigner take her from right under my nose.

We finished our drinks, settled the bill, and set off to search for Paco, our faces grim. The day that had started with such promise ended up being a day I would never forget. For all the wrong reasons. As we made our way home, I remembered the bunch of rosemary I'd bought for Tia Rosita. I'd left it on the table in the bar, and I could have kicked myself. We eventually came across Paco sitting on the wall at the top of the alley to Somorrostro. His face was still ashen, and the grey tinge of his skin matched the streaks in his hair. When he saw us approaching, he tried to smile, but instead, he grimaced, and despite the cool afternoon breeze, he was sweating profusely.

'Papa, are you alright?' asked Kiko, putting his hand on Paco's shoulder.

'Yes, yes, *hijo*, I'm fine. I walked back here too quickly,' he said, but when he stood up to walk, he winced, putting his hand to his chest. Kiko shot me a fearful look, and we lowered Paco back into his sitting place.

'It's these damn twinges I've been having. All those years of pulling the scrap cart have played havoc with me,' he said. 'It's nothing, Kiko, and I don't want to hear another word about it,' he said, his lips pressed together, a frown on his face. 'And don't mention it to your mother either, or I'll never hear the end of it.'

We walked back home, our steps slow and measured. As we reached Tia Rosita's house, she was sitting outside, accompanied by Sofia. She was watching us, an unfathomable expression on her face, and I felt a shiver of apprehension ran down my spine.

She called out in greeting. *'Hola chicos, Qué tal?'* We came to a standstill, and I bent down to hug her. 'I'm sorry, Tia Rosita, I left the rosemary in a bar.'

She waved me away with her hand. 'Don't worry, *chico.'* She eyed Paco. 'How are you today? You look like you have the weight of the world on your shoulders, *hijo mío.'*

'Oh, just the aches and pains of getting older, Tia Rosita,' Paco shrugged, smiling tightly. 'And these two have dragged me halfway around the city today.'

Her eyes narrowed. 'Kiko, you make sure your father rests today. I'll send Sofia around later with a potion to cleanse your spirit, Paco. It's in chaos. You need to be strong for those you love,' she said.

Her cryptic words made my pulse quicken, and I glanced at her, catching her eye. She shook her head, and I wondered if it was in some way connected to what had happened earlier when Paco had met Margarita. Paco thanked her, and we went on our way, but I felt her eyes following us as we walked down the street.

27

Margarita was only vaguely aware as Artie steered her away from the group, her legs stiff with tension, her eyes unseeing. The shock had frozen her on the spot, and she'd felt the blood draining from her face.

Moments before, standing only yards in front of her, was a man she'd never forgotten. The man from the market that Yaya had sworn at – the man with hair like a raven's feathers. Faced with him today, though, whilst basking in the happiness of her special date with Artie, her first instinct had been to turn and run. But Artie had taken hold of her hand and squeezed it reassuringly. She'd blinked as if waking from a dream and tried to swallow, but her throat was as dry as dust. How did this man know Yaya? How was it possible? The man, who Kiko had introduced as his father, Paco, had stared at her, his face grey, and she knew she hadn't imagined the flash of recognition in his eyes. She'd heard Kiko say, "Papa?" but neither she nor the man could drag their gaze away.

After walking in silence for several minutes, Artie stopped and turned Margarita to face him. 'What happened back there? Do you know Kiko's father?' he asked, curious eyes drilling into hers.

She shook her head, searching for the words to

explain. 'I'm not sure. I… I remember seeing him when I was with Yaya one day, years ago, when I was a child.' She paused and looked into the distance, her brow wrinkling. 'How would Yaya know him, though?' Something was whirring in the back of her mind, the pieces of a complicated puzzle struggling to fit together. The note! The note she'd found in Carmen's handbag months *before, El Paco, Barracas, 47.* Was it referring to Kiko's father, Paco? Was this something to do with her mother? Her visceral reaction to the man had some significance, but she felt ridiculous admitting it to Artie. 'I think he's connected to my mother somehow. I need to speak to Yaya. Will you come with me, Artie? I want to go right now.'

He raised his eyebrows. 'Of course.'

They made their way to Calle Escudellers, each step taking Margarita closer to hopefully finding an answer about Kiko's father. She was desperate to know why the man had been equally shocked when he'd seen her. Did it mean he'd recognised her, too? But that was impossible. She'd been a child that day in the market, half-hidden behind Yaya's back, and had changed beyond recognition. He, on the other hand, was almost the same, although his black hair was now flecked with grey. Her romantic day with Artie was forgotten as they reached Yaya's, the smell of churros thick in the air. She rang the bell, and after a minute, Yaya's face appeared above them, looking taken aback to see Margarita with a man down on the street.

'*Estas bien, cariño?*' she shouted, visibly relaxing as Margarita waved at her.

'Yes, I'm fine, Yaya. Throw the keys down!' Despite the flutter of unease in her belly, Margarita smiled to herself when she saw Yaya smoothing down her hair as she bustled back inside, her vanity, as always, getting the better of her. After the shock of seeing the man from the market, Margarita hadn't thought through the effect that introducing her to Artie would have on her grandmother, but any awkwardness at bringing Artie to Yaya's house passed quickly

Yaya greeted him using the voice she used when she spoke to anyone in authority, usually her doctor or the priest, and Artie kissed her hand, causing Yaya to titter girlishly.

Margarita groaned inwardly, rolling her eyes.

'So where are you from, *chico*?' Yaya asked, her cheeks pink from all the attention. She nodded politely as he told her all about his hometown in England.

Margarita knew what was coming next. Whenever anyone mentioned distant places, Yaya felt obliged to mention the only time she'd been on holiday.

'Well, the furthest I've ever been was on my honeymoon with my late husband, Margarita's grandfather, Antonio. We went on the train to Lloret de Mar for four days.' She smiled, a nostalgic look on her face. Margarita stole a glance at Artie, and he winked at her.

'It was quite the fashionable destination back in the

195

day. I remember we stayed at the Hotel Costa Brava, which was very well to do.' Then Yaya's face dropped. 'We were having a lovely time until I ate a bad mussel and had to spend most of the time in the room. I thought Antonio should have stayed by my side instead of going out day and night without me. It caused a terrible argument, the first one we'd ever had,' she concluded, frowning at the memory.

Artie jumped in at that point, regaling Yaya with tales of his adventures in Paris, and before long, he had her eating out of the palm of his hand. Margarita was thrilled to see the two of them getting along until she remembered the reason for their visit, and her insides twisted with dread. After the niceties were over and she'd prepared a second pot of coffee, Margarita couldn't wait any longer and cleared her throat. 'Yaya,' she began, her voice strained. 'I need to talk to you about something.'

Yaya took a sip of coffee. 'Of course, *cariño,* what is it?'

Margarita took a deep breath. 'It's something that happened a long time ago. I… I remember bumping into a man in the market, and you swore at him, telling him never to return. He had jet-black hair and a gold tooth. You were rude to him.'

Yaya's face had lost all its colour, and she stared at Margarita with unblinking eyes.

'Who was he?' Margarita asked, growing more confident. Yaya was indeed rattled.

'Margarita! I barely remember what I had for lunch yesterday, so don't expect me to be able to recall years back,' she snorted. 'And how could you ask such a thing when we have a guest?' she said, jerking her head towards Artie.

'Please, Yaya, I know you know the man I'm talking about because I remember you and Mama quarrelling later the same day.'

A look of horror passed over Yaya's face, and Margarita could tell she was stalling. It made her more determined to get to the bottom of the mystery.

'*Vida mía,* I don't know what on earth you're talking about, but I promise I'll have a think and see if I can recall any such event,' sniffed Yaya, sitting back in her chair, hands clasped on her lap.

Knowing how stubborn her grandmother was, Margarita reluctantly let the topic drop for now. But it was clear she was hiding something.

Yaya stood up and busied herself clearing away the cups, and Artie jumped up to help her. Margarita remained seated, chewing the skin around her thumb – maybe she should talk to her mother about it.

'Would you like to stay for lunch, *chicos*? asked Yaya coming back into the lounge followed by Artie.

Margarita glanced at him and was surprised when he shook his head.

'Actually, Margarita, I've booked a table at 7 Portes for two o'clock, and if we don't leave now, we won't make it.'

Both Yaya and Margarita gasped. It was the type of place they'd only ever dreamed about going to, and Margarita was suddenly self-conscious about her appearance.

Yaya must have been thinking along the same lines. 'Excuse us for a moment, Artie,' she said, shooing Margarita towards the bedroom. Five minutes later, they were ready. Margarita's hair was stiff with hairspray, her cheeks dusted with powder.

'Off you go, then,' said Yaya, smiling. She turned to Artie. 'You must come for lunch one day. Maybe next weekend?'

'I'd be delighted, Señora Marquez,' he said, catching Margarita's eye and grinning.

Despite the strange occurrence with Kiko's father, Margarita was excited as they made their way to the restaurant. Approaching the restaurant's emblematic arches, she was suddenly anxious that she'd make a fool of herself, and gulped back her nerves, trying to stand taller. Artie gave their name to the Maître d', and an elderly waiter appeared. His eyes flickered over them and with pursed lips as he showed them to their table. Margarita's cheeks felt hot as the waiter held out her chair and unused to such formality, she sat down with an unladylike thud and stared in dismay at the assortment of complicated cutlery. Fortunately, Artie was busy hooking his bag over the back of the chair and didn't appear to notice her lack of grace. She took a deep breath and took the menu the waiter passed her. They perused the specialities and finally agreed on a *Paella de pescado con Langosta* for two and some *vino blanco de la casa.*

'Artie,' whispered Margarita after the old waiter had poured their wine. 'It's terribly expensive. Did you see the price of the paella?'

'Don't give it a second thought, Margarita. I've had some excellent news this week,' he said, his eyes lighting up. 'I think I mentioned it briefly when I came to the bar. A colleague of Eva's father from the hospital needed someone to look after his apartment for a few months while he's working as a locum in Sevilla. Lady Luck is smiling down on me at the moment!' he grinned. 'I'm moving in a couple of weeks. I'll be saving a fortune now that I don't have to pay for the dreadful hostel anymore.'

'How wonderful,' exclaimed Margarita, her imagination revving into overdrive. They'd have some privacy at last. Catching herself drifting off, Margarita snapped back into the conversation. 'Where is the apartment?'

'It's a penthouse on Calle Pau Claris. You won't believe your eyes when you see it!'

She probably would. When Margarita was a girl, Yaya had cleaned for a family in the same part of L'Eixample. When Margarita didn't have school, she'd often tagged along rather than stay with her mother. She loved exploring the spacious apartment, with its high ceilings and beautiful handmade glazed ceramic floor tiles.

'And you should see my room,' he continued. 'The bed's got a silk canopy over it! I've never seen anything like it. The balcony doors in the lounge open out onto a huge terrace. You can hardly hear the traffic from the street because it's full of plants to deaden the noise. I'll be able to have some great parties there,' he said, winking at her.

The food came, and Artie took the opportunity to ask the waiter if he'd ever served any of the famous artists reputed to dine here, particularly the celebrated Salvador Dali. The waiter nodded regally, his face solemn. 'Yes, indeed I have. Señor Dali was here several weeks ago.' When Artie asked him for an interesting anecdote, the waiter grimaced. 'I could never comment on our valued clientele, Señor.' He turned to Margarita, his mouth pinched. 'Would you like some *alioli* with your paella, Señorita?'

As the waiter glided away, Artie's eyes followed him with a flicker of irritation, and he tutted. Turning back to Margarita, he recounted how he'd searched high and low for Dali when he'd visited Figueres.

'When did you visit Figueres?' Margarita asked.

'We passed through on our way down from France,' he replied, gulping down the cold white wine and making a start on his paella.

'I'd love to go to all these places you talk about,' she said, stealing a glance at which knife and fork Artie had picked up.

'You'd love the Costa Brava. I'll ask Herman if I

can borrow his car one day, and we can have a drive up,' and began to explain about the time he visited Cadaqués.

Margarita was beside herself with excitement. She didn't know anyone who even *had* a car, never mind going on a trip to the coast. The food was delicious, and they ate until they were fit to burst. After they'd finished their coffee and Artie had paid the bill, they wandered hand in hand down towards La Barceloneta. Margarita began to tell Artie how she and Eva had discovered Kiko and Santi lived in Somorrostro, but he had never heard of the place. She tried to describe it based on the hearsay she'd heard over the years, and Artie agreed that it sounded dire.

'I should invite them all over for dinner one evening, although did you notice how Santi looked at me earlier? I've only met him once at the exhibition, and we hardly spoke, so I don't know what that was all about.'

Margarita smiled tightly. 'No, I was far too distracted by Kiko's father. How did he look at you?' Artie shrugged his shoulders. 'Like he wanted to kill me,' he said, with a grin, his pale blue eyes crinkling at the corners.

She frowned. He must have imagined it. Santi was sweet, and he'd been the perfect gentleman on the few occasions she'd seen him. Recalling the fateful encounter earlier made the anxious knot in her stomach twist once again, and she shook her head as if to banish the memory. Artie accompanied her home, and they spoke no more about what had happened. On the doorstep, he pulled Margarita close and, in between kisses, murmured that it had been the best day of his life.

28

Carmen had reached a decision. It was time to face her mother. One afternoon after she finished work, she made her way to her once-happy childhood home. She'd brought along some *chuletas de cordero*, knowing how partial her mother was to Eduardo's lamb chops.

A full minute after she'd rung the bell, her mother's curt voice came down from above. 'To what do I owe this pleasure, then?'

'Mama, please. I haven't come to argue. Look, I've brought you some *chuletas de cordero*, so throw the keys down before the neighbours start gawping.'

Her mother glanced surreptitiously to check if any neighbours were around and, satisfied no one was watching, dropped the keys into Carmen's outstretched hands. Even from the street, she could hear her mother muttering about an attack of heartburn as she shuffled back inside.

Wheezing, Carmen reached the front door to the apartment and walked in to find her mother in the kitchen, warming up the coffee pot on the stovetop. She held out the bag of lamb chops like a sacrificial peace offering, and her mother took it without a word, her lips pursed. Carmen dropped her handbag on the sofa and sank down next to it. The whole place was just as she remembered, not a cushion out of place and the silverware sparkling on the sideboard. She understood why Margarita preferred to come here rather than stay at their apartment in Calle Sant Pere. Even with the presence of her overbearing mother, it was comfortable and homely. She let out a sigh as she allowed her body to soften back onto the cushions. Her eyes flickered over the dozen or so photos on display of her as a child, alongside a few of Margarita, including some recent ones she'd never seen before. Her heart swelled with unaccustomed pride as she gazed at a photo of her daughter laughing with her head thrown back – there was no doubt she was Paco's. Her eyes were drawn back to the photos of herself as a teenager, and she felt a pinch of anguish once again at the loss of her beauty and vitality. How young she'd been when she had Margarita. How would she have coped had Margarita come home pregnant and unmarried at fifteen? A newfound respect for her mother stirred inside her.

Her mother came out of the kitchen with a sour expression on her face and placed the coffee pot down on the table with a bang. 'What do you want, Carmen? Money? What mess do you need me to get you out of this time?'

Carmen sighed, and pulled out a chair. This was going to be more difficult than she'd anticipated. 'I wanted to see you, Mama. Do I need a reason?'

'You haven't willingly popped round to see me in sixteen years, Carmen, so don't play the innocent with me.

Has something happened to Margarita?' She lowered herself into her armchair with a grunt.

'Margarita is fine. At least, I think she is. We're like ships in the night,' she said, immediately realising this had been the wrong thing to say.

'Well, whose fault is that then?' snapped her mother with narrowed eyes. 'She's no doubt had a bellyful of your antics, like everyone else. She's old enough to understand the rumours now. Old enough to see her mother is nothing but a common drunk. You're no better than the girls who hang around the Raval, except they get paid for it!'

Carmen recoiled at her mother's words. She was guilty of every wrong that could be thrown at her, but that particular insult cut her to the bone. There was nothing to gain from trying to defend herself, and her mother was only just warming up.

'I raised you to be a good girl, Carmen, respectful and loving. When I see how you've dragged Margarita up, my heart breaks for her.' She searched up her sleeve for a tissue and dabbed her eyes and nose. 'She came to me a while back. The poor child has spent her whole life listening to malicious gossip about who her father could be, and she's fed up to her back teeth.'

Carmen opened her mouth to speak, but her mother held up her hand.

'She begged me to tell her the truth. Said she was sick of being treated like a child – and she's right.' Her mother paused, her eyes resting on the framed photos of

Margarita on the sideboard as she breathed deeply. Quietly, composure taking over again, she looked Carmen straight in the eye. 'So I told her the truth. She knows her father is Quim Diaz.'

Blood pounded in Carmen's ears, and her throat constricted. Margarita knew about Quim, yet she hadn't said a word. It highlighted how fractured their relationship had become. 'What did she say, Mama?' she croaked, reaching for a cigarette and striking the match with a shaking hand.

'What do you think she said?' Her mother glared at her. 'She was devastated we'd kept it from her, stunned that Eduardo is her grandfather but has never acknowledged her.' She went to fetch an ashtray and sat back down. Her eyes met Carmen's. 'And before you ask, I have no idea if she's planning to confront either you or Eduardo,' she said, her shoulders sagging, her anger seemingly spent.

'She hasn't said a word,' said Carmen. 'She doesn't even talk to me anymore.'

'Well, what do you expect, *hija*? She's had to bring herself up, with only me to turn to. You've never been there for her,' said her mother, her tone now despondent rather than accusing.

'I've made such a mess of everything, Mama. I've been trying to stop drinking. I haven't touched a drop for three weeks.' Her mother's eyes softened, and Carmen took a sharp breath. 'I'm tired of fighting with you … I've missed you.'

It was a release to say those words and finally admit that she needed her mother after so many years adrift. It was the only time she'd reached out to her since Margarita was a baby, and the shock on her mother's face was tinged with scepticism.

Reaching across the table, her mother patted Carmen gently on the arm. 'Well, you're here now, aren't you?'

At her mother's touch, the years of pent-up emotions surged from deep within her, and Carmen burst into tears, holding out her arms to her mother. Cautiously, her mother pulled her into a wooden embrace. As Carmen sobbed, her mother's grip tightened, and she stroked her daughter's hair just as she'd done when Carmen was a child. They stayed like that for a long time. When Carmen had no more tears left, she sat back in the chair and said the words she knew her mother had never expected to hear.

'I'm sorry for everything I've put you through, Mama. I'm sorry I've been such a disappointment to you. Everything you've done for me, all the times you tried to protect me from myself, was because you loved me. I understand now.' She lifted her eyes, searching her mother's face. 'Can you forgive me?'

Her mother nodded, taking Carmen's hand. '*Cariño,* for more years than I can remember, I haven't liked you very much. Watching how you've left Margarita to fend for herself has been tough. You've made a fool of yourself with the drink, and you've disgraced me time and time again. I don't think I'll ever forget. But you're my only child, Carmen. How could I ever stop loving you?'

These were the words Carmen needed to hear. The angst and the altercations had worn her out over the years, and finally, she saw the tiniest glimmer of hope for their future. The ticking of her mother's precious cuckoo clock echoed between them as they sipped the strong coffee. Until her mother broke the silence.

'Have you met Margarita's new fellow, then? I must say, I was very impressed. What a delightful young man, even with that long hair, although I suppose it's all the rage these days, isn't it?'

'Margarita has a boyfriend?' Carmen said, dismay twisting in her gut. She knew nothing about her daughter's life, and although it was evident that she had no one to blame but herself, it still hurt. When was the last time she'd spoken to Margarita in a loving tone, shown any interest in what she was doing in her life, or who her friends were? All she did was snap at her and berate her for simply existing.

'She certainly has, *hija*. Besotted with him, she is! He's from England and is very charming. He even kissed my hand, can you believe it?' she chuckled, her cheeks pink. 'I must have looked a state, though. I was cleaning the toilet when they came.'

'Oh, so they dropped in without warning?' asked Carmen, surprised. An introduction to a *novio* was usually more formal, requiring an invitation to afternoon tea, at the very least.

Her mother squirmed in her seat, looking cagey. 'Er, no, she said they were passing and came round to say hello,' she said, her eyes not quite reaching Carmen's.

Detecting an undertone in her mother's voice, Carmen frowned. 'Mama, this is a new start for us. From now on, we must try and be honest with each other. I don't want to ever go back to lying to you.' The hypocrisy of her words niggled, but she didn't think her mother could cope with the truth right now. Or was it that she wasn't ready to reveal her ugly secret?

'I'm telling you the truth! They popped in on their way to lunch – you'll never guess where they were going,' her mother said, with a gleam in her eye. '7 Portes! I told Margarita he's a keeper.' She reached over to the dresser and took one of the framed photos Carmen had noticed earlier. 'They came for lunch last week, and he brought me some photos he'd taken of our Margarita. Look.'

As her mother handed her the photograph, Carmen exhaled, the tension leaving her limbs. It felt good to share things with her mother after so many years out in the cold. 'Tell me everything,' Carmen said, her heart finally beginning to thaw.

If anyone had peered through the window that evening, they would have seen an ordinary mother and daughter, chatting and laughing until nightfall.

29

I sensed the change that was happening around us. One evening after supper, I was sitting with my father outside the front door. We often took a couple of chairs out onto the street on muggy nights, the cooling sea breeze a welcome relief after the cloying heat inside the house. I hadn't had the opportunity, or the courage, if truth be told, to talk to him about Paco's revelations.

'Pa,' I said, hesitating slightly. 'Have you spoken to Paco recently?'

My father raised his eyebrows. 'No, why? What's he been up to now?'

I cleared my throat. 'Kiko told him about Eva, you know, the *paya.*'

'And how did he take it, *hijo*?'

'Surprisingly well,' I answered, nodding my head in greeting at a passing neighbour. I lowered my voice. 'He told us about Carmen, the woman he met years ago. Did you know her, Pa? Paco said you were the only person he told.'

With a sigh, my father fished a packet of cigarettes from his trouser pocket and offered me one. Inhaling deeply, he spoke. '*Si, hijo*, I knew all about her. I remember him coming to me when Loli had just found out she was pregnant with Kiko – he was in a state,' said

Pichi, rubbing his jaw. 'I thought he was coming to tell me she'd had another miscarriage, but no, he'd been having some bother with Carmen. She'd followed him here one day, and he was worried it was getting too close for comfort.'

I shifted slightly, biting my lip. Eva and Margarita had done the same.

My father continued. 'I told him to get rid of her. No one was worth risking his marriage for, and with Kiko on the way, it was madness.' He scratched the back of his neck, looking uncomfortable, and I sensed there was something he wasn't telling me.

'Did you meet her?'

'No, *chico*, I didn't want to get involved. Your mother would have killed me if she'd found out. Loli was her best friend.'

We sat in silence for a few moments. I was thinking about my mother, and when I saw my father's eyes glaze over, I knew he was thinking of her, too. He flicked his cigarette into the street.

'But I remember the day your mother and Loli fell out over that damn missing ring,' he said, his eyes narrowing as if trying to recall something pertinent.

Although I hadn't even been born when it happened, I'd heard the story of their legendary fight many times.

'It's a strange thing, Santi, and I've never told another living soul this before...' he paused, deep lines furrowing his forehead.

I leaned closer, perspiration coating my skin from

the humid evening air or something else. I wasn't sure.

'I remember Paco and I had run to fetch Tia Rosita. She was the only one who could have sorted them out that day. They were screaming like banshees. There was no way Paco or I would get in the middle of them.' His eyes took on a faraway look before glancing around to check for eavesdroppers. 'We could hear the shouting, even from the other end of the alley. Tia Rosita marched over and put herself between them, and sure enough, after a good talking to, they calmed down.' He turned to face me. 'But I think I saw her… Carmen. Tia Rosita was talking to Loli and your mother, and I spotted something out of the corner of my eye. A girl was watching the drama from inside a doorway across the road. She was so pretty,' he said, and I saw his face flush in the moonlight. 'Don't get me wrong, *hijo*, your mother was the only woman for me. But even from a distance, I could see the shock on the girl's face when she spotted Paco standing next to me. It couldn't have been anyone else.' He rubbed his hand over his face, shaking his head slightly. 'I should have told Paco, but he seemed to have forgotten about her by then, and he and Loli were in a better place.'

I shrugged. 'To be honest, I think I'd have done the same thing in your shoes.'

'Well, it's too late now, *hijo*. It was a long time ago, and I reckon Paco did the right thing. Though I don't doubt this situation with Kiko and Eva will have stirred up some old feelings for him.'

'Did Paco tell you about what happened when he met one of Eva's friends last week?' I asked, curious to know what he made of Paco's strange behaviour.

Pichi frowned and shook his head. I told him the story, and when I'd finished, a muscle in his cheek twitched, but he didn't say a word. For some reason, I hesitated to press him any further. After several minutes of silence, I asked him if he'd heard any more about the recent rumours on everyone's lips. The word on the grapevine that Somorrostro was to be destroyed had been gathering momentum, but as yet, we'd had no official news. I'd grown up hearing these rumours, false hopes that always came to nothing, but that year, 1966, our lives would be turned upside down. The dictator, General Franco, had been advised that the slums were a blight on Spain's reputation and that all slum-dwellers must be rehoused. It was purely for aesthetic reasons that we were to be moved, not humane, but still, we thought our luck was on the up.

'No,' he replied. 'Tia Rosita has organised a committee to take our concerns to the *ayuntamiento.* You should come with us, *hijo,* and take some positive action.'

I said I would, feeling as if everything was perfectly placed to unsettle me.

***

A few days later, a group of us traipsed to the *ayuntamiento,* the town hall, in Plaza Sant Jaume. But when we arrived, we were met with hostility and not permitted to even cross the threshold. The police arrived, and warning us not to return, they escorted us away from the Plaza towards Via Laietana as if we were no more than common criminals. A scuffle broke out when one policeman purposely tripped Tia Rosita, causing her to stumble to the ground, her leg twisting awkwardly. When she cried out in pain, I turned to see the policeman towering over her with his baton poised. Several of us ran back, pushing the policeman out of the way to reach her. A whistle blew, and police officers surrounded us. Tia Rosita remained gracious through all their threats and insults, but I was deeply troubled as I helped her to her feet. Until that moment, I'd never truly felt the injustice and bigotry of those in power against the people of Somorrostro. The elders in the group were neither surprised nor shocked, but I was humiliated, enraged that we were dismissed in such a cold-hearted way. It made me question everything I'd ever aspired to be.

We would discover our fate sooner rather than later, and everything would change for us.

30

Margarita, Artie, Eva and Kiko had spent the day together at the fairground on Tibidabo. As they took the bus from Plaza Catalunya, Margarita stared out of the window, recalling the same trip she'd made with Yaya all those years earlier. But she didn't notice the modern apartment blocks or the lush green spaces this time. Everything she had ever wanted was sitting right beside her, his hand resting on her shoulder. After so much loneliness in her life, she couldn't believe a man like Artie could have feelings for a girl like her.

The bus arrived in Sant Gervasi, and they took the cable car up to the fairground. As they came out of the station, Margarita had the most peculiar sensation when she gazed up at the statue of Santiago, the patron Saint of Spain, who watched over the whole of Barcelona. She'd only ever seen the statue from down in the city, where the figure looked enormous with his outstretched arms. But up close, they'd all agreed it was an optical illusion, and the statue was disappointingly small.

They'd been on several dates as a foursome over the past few weeks, and she and Eva were delighted the boys got along so well. She was overcome with a sense that she'd finally found what she'd been searching for all her life.

On the way back down to the city, Margarita sighed with contentment. It had been a wonderful day, filled with laughter, but it was far from over. Artie had invited them all to have dinner at his new apartment. She shivered with anticipation. It would be the first time they would be properly alone, away from the grubby hostel with its thin walls and squeaky bedframe. They arrived at the elegant building and crammed into the caged lift to take them up to the penthouse. Margarita felt the heat of Artie's body, the gentle pressure of his hand snaking around her waist, and thought she would die of longing. She bit her lip and, catching Eva's eye, tried not to giggle. Artie unlocked the door to the apartment, and Margarita gasped. It was beautiful, even more so than the place Yaya had cleaned, and her mouth dropped open as she took in the opulent decor and chandeliers.

Eva nodded appreciatively. 'Oh, this is lovely, Artie,' she trilled, flinging her jacket over the back of an elegant chaise longue, seemingly underwhelmed.

When Kiko entered behind Eva, Margarita saw that his reaction was even more incredulous than hers. He stopped, frozen to the spot as his eyes roamed the entrance hall. It was almost the size of her whole apartment in Calle Sant Pere, so she could only imagine how it compared to his home in Somorrostro. Artie led them through to the living room, and Margarita marvelled at the beautiful paintings on the walls, the heavy-draped curtains, and the grand fireplace. Looking dazed, Kiko followed Artie to the kitchen to prepare

216

supper, and Margarita settled down on the sofa next to Eva. 'Can you believe this place?' she whispered. 'It's like how I imagine the inside of a royal palace to be.'

Eva smiled without comment and kicked her shoes off.

'Is your house like this?' asked Margarita.

Eva flushed. 'I suppose it is, but it's not the place or the things inside it that make a home. It's the people, the love. I wouldn't care where I was as long as I was with Kiko.'

Margarita nodded. A few months ago, Eva's observation would have grated on her – it was such an easy, throwaway thing to say when you didn't live in a dump. But now she saw the truth of Eva's words. She thought of Yaya, who lived in a tiny apartment and didn't have a bean. Her home was full of love, welcoming, a haven. Had Margarita really been so blind? A wave of shame washed over her as she recalled her arrogance at discovering the boys lived in Somorrostro. Eva lived in a luxury that Margarita would never experience, yet never once had she made Margarita feel inferior or less of a person. She shuffled closer to Eva and rested her head on Eva's shoulder. 'Can you remember when we were in the hospital?'

Eva nodded, her eyes creasing. 'Yes. You were the wildest person I'd ever met. The nurses were always scolding us for jumping on the beds and disturbing all the other patients. I'd never had so much fun in my life before then,' she recalled, her words tinged with sadness.

They were nine years old when they'd met in the hospital. Eva had been suffering from a severe bout of measles, and Margarita was recovering from whooping cough. They'd played with each other's hair and pored for hours over Eva's comics. Even then, Margarita recalled feeling envious of her new friend. 'Do you remember the day your mother caught us fast asleep on my bed?'

'Oh, yes!' Eva said, her eyes widening in mock horror. 'I remember the nurses shaking their heads at each other as she tried to pull us apart, but we clung to each other even tighter. She was furious.'

Although Margarita hadn't had comics and fruit on her bedside table like Eva, at least Yaya had visited her regularly, lavishing her with love and kisses. Even her mother had dropped by a few times. When the day came for Margarita to be discharged, with much angst and tears, they had vowed to stay friends by any means possible. Aided and abetted by Eulalia, Eva's governess, they'd managed to meet to play for a few carefree hours each month, their friendship a secret from Eva's mother.

'I don't know what I'd do without you,' said Margarita, as Eva played with her hair like they'd done when they were girls.

Laughter rang out from the kitchen. Artie came through the door, holding a platter of *jamón ibérico* and *chorizo* aloft his head. Kiko followed with a basket of bread and tomatoes and a couple of bottles under his arm.

218

Sitting on the floor on soft rugs with a low wooden table between them, they toasted the bread on the fire Kiko had lit in the marble fireplace. Margarita felt like she was in a dream, and a sidelong glance at Kiko told her he was feeling the same. They ate ripe green olives infused with cloves of garlic and smooth, creamy *Tetilla* cheese, washed down with some sparkling wine Artie had found in a bodega in Gràcia.

'The owner told me it's almost impossible to get hold of and they were the only ones who stocked it in all the city,' he informed them with a look of pride on his face.

Margarita burst out laughing. 'And you fell for it?' She covered her mouth with her hand, giving Artie a gentle look to soften the impact of her laughter. 'You can get Txakoli in any bar or bodega from here up to the Basque country where it's made!'

Next to her, Kiko guffawed loudly, his shoulders shaking.

'I bought a whole damn crate!' Artie said with a bark of laughter and went to get more bottles to open. When it was very late, Eva and Kiko began to yawn. She and Artie saw them to the door, promising to plan another supper soon.

They cleared away the plates, and Artie put some coffee on the stove. As they waited for it to brew, their kisses became more passionate, and Margarita was dizzy with longing. When the coffee was ready, they added some Cognac and took their cups outside onto the balcony. It was a clear night, and the sky was full of stars. The statue of Santiago illuminated high on the Collserola hills, and they marvelled that they'd been standing in its shadow only hours earlier.

There was a shift in the mood. Artie turned to her, taking her face in his hands. 'I'm falling in love with you, Margarita. I thought I'd been in love in the past, but nothing comes close to how I feel about you.'

Overcome by his words, Margarita's eyes blurred with tears. 'I feel the same, Artie, I really do.'

Taking her by the hand, Artie led her to his bedroom. He lit the sconces attached to the wall on each side of the bed, soft shadows transforming the austere room. The air between them crackled, and Artie took a step towards her. His arms slid around her, and as his kisses became more passionate, Margarita lost herself in him, never wanting this night to end.

When Artie finally fell asleep, Margarita lay beside him, and her heart rate slowed. A surge of jealousy flared in her heart as she imagined him with another woman. She'd never experienced this feeling and wondered if this was what love did to a person. But before long, exhaustion overcame her, and with her arms tightly wrapped around Artie, she drifted off into the soundest sleep she'd ever had.

31

The front doorbell rang. 'Drat it, Margarita, you're always forgetting your key,' Carmen grumbled as she buzzed her in. She waited at the open apartment door, and heard the click of heels echoing hesitantly up the stairwell. That wasn't Margarita. She squinted through the dusk-shrouded railings as a pretty, beautifully-dressed girl came huffing up the last flight of stairs.

'*Hola*?' Carmen said. 'Who are you looking for, *reina*?'

The girl smiled shyly at Carmen, her white teeth bright in the gloom. 'Hello. Are you Señora Garcia, Margarita's mother?' the girl asked politely.

Carmen's eyes widened. 'I know who you are! You're Eva, aren't you?' she said, opening her arms in greeting. 'She's talked about you so much over the years that I feel I already know you. How could it be anyone else with such glorious hair?' Carmen was thrilled to meet her daughter's friend but caught the look of caution that crossed Eva's face. Margarita had no doubt filled her in over the years about Carmen's failings as a mother, so she couldn't blame the girl for her trepidation. She ushered her into the living room. 'Margarita isn't here at the moment. She's on the suppertime shift at the bar today. Come and sit down for a moment.'

'I don't want to trouble you, Señora Garcia. I'm sure you must have things to do.'

'Please call me Carmen,' she said. 'Señora makes me feel so old. At least have a drink before you leave?'

Eva hesitated for a second and then smiled. 'Thank you, it's very kind of you.'

Carmen pulled out a chair for Eva and hurried into the kitchen to warm up the coffee she'd made earlier in the afternoon. Realising she hadn't asked what Eva would like to drink, she rushed back out of the kitchen. 'Would you prefer coffee or fresh lemonade?' She wasn't used to having company or even being sociable, at least not without a strong drink to settle her nerves.

'Coffee would be great,' replied Eva.

When she returned to the room carrying a tray, Eva was sitting back in her chair, and Carmen beamed. 'It's wonderful to meet you,' she said, placing the coffee pot and two tiny cups on the table and sitting opposite Eva.

Eva's smile reached her eyes. 'It is! I don't know why Margarita hasn't introduced us before now.'

'Well, I think I probably know the answer to that,' Carmen said, rubbing her temple, 'but it's a subject for another day.' Eva nodded and lowered her gaze, leading her to wonder again how much Margarita had told her friend. Composing herself, she poured the coffee. 'How are your studies at La Llotja going? Margarita mentioned it briefly. But if I ask her too many questions about anything, she tells me to mind my own business,' she added with a wry grin, passing the sugar bowl to Eva.

Carmen listened for half an hour, enchanted, as Eva explained about her course. 'I would have loved to study dance, but I had to start working at the butcher's to help make ends meet at home,' she mused. 'And then I fell pregnant with Margarita. After that, well, then everything changed.'

Eva nodded. 'It must have been difficult for you.' Carmen glanced at her, expecting to see scorn in Eva's eyes, but saw only kindness. She'd always assumed people looked down on her and derided her. But perhaps the truth was she'd never given anyone a chance to get close to her. Pushing people away had seemed easier and would save heartache down the road. 'It was, yes. I was nothing but a child when I had Margarita,' she sighed. 'I can't travel back in time and change the past... but I'm determined to change the future. Neither my mother nor Margarita thinks I can turn things around,' she added.

An awkward silence followed, and Carmen could have kicked herself for being so frank. She'd only known the girl for five minutes.

Clasping her hands together on the table, Eva lifted her eyes to meet Carmen's. 'I popped round today to speak to Margarita about something that happened weeks ago. Did she mention anything to you?'

'No,' replied Carmen, sitting up straighter in her chair.

'Well, she and Artie were walking down Las Ramblas.' Eva stopped, and her cheeks flushed. 'Oh, erm, Artie is Margarita's boyfriend.'

Carmen gave her a tight smile. 'It's alright. Her grandmother told me all about him.'

Eva continued, 'Anyway, the pair bumped into *my* boyfriend and his father.'

'You have a boyfriend, too?' asked Carmen. 'Have you known him for long?'

'Almost six months now,' replied Eva, her eyes lighting up.

Carmen clapped her hands together. 'How lovely! What's his name?'

Eva smiled shyly. 'Kiko,' she replied, blushing again. It briefly crossed Carmen's mind that she and Margarita had never once shared such moments.

Eva carried on with her story. 'So, Kiko greeted Artie, but when he turned to introduce them, Margarita and Kiko's father were standing in a trance, staring at each other as if they knew each other. Artie managed to drag Margarita away, but then she insisted on going straight to her grandmother's, convinced she'd know who he was. And Kiko's father stomped off in a rage.' Eva paused and glanced at Carmen as if unsure whether to continue.

Carmen's heart was almost beating out of her chest. She dug her nails into the palms of her hands, trying to keep her face inscrutable and nodded at Eva to carry on.

'Artie said Margarita was agitated and was convinced she'd seen this man when she was a child shopping in the market with her grandmother. She remembers them arguing. But her grandmother said she

224

had no recollection of the man and no idea what Margarita was talking about. Artie was quite concerned about Margarita because she was so unnerved,' shrugged Eva. 'It was very bizarre. So, I wondered if Margarita had any more news about it.'

Carmen stood up and went over to a chest of drawers, taking out a packet of cigarettes. As she struck the match, her hand trembled. Inhaling deeply, Carmen looked searchingly at Eva. 'What's Kiko's father's name?'

32

Margarita had finished working at the bakery for the day. She'd arranged to meet Artie for lunch and spend the rest of the day with him. Her feelings were growing stronger each time they met, and she was obsessed with him. Just as she'd finished applying her mascara, the bakery doorbell tinkled, and she heard Montse gush, 'Artie, how nice to see you again.'

Margarita hurried into the shop. 'Hi,' she said brightly, and he turned to face her. He was so handsome. A jolt of excitement shot through her. She caught his arm and propelled him outside, calling goodbye over her shoulder to Montse. 'Ugh, she was about to start grilling you,' Margarita laughed. He leaned down to kiss her, and she pressed herself into him, her arms reaching up around his neck to pull him closer. Then, realising she'd lost herself in the moment, she took a step back and glanced around. There was nobody she knew in sight.

'You're so beautiful. You drive me crazy. Let's skip lunch and go back to my place.' He grinned and took her hand in his. Margarita felt blood rush to her cheeks and placed her other hand at her throat, lost for words. Was sex all he was interested in?

He nudged her, his smile broadening before he winked. 'Well, I suppose we can go and have some lunch first.' His grasp tightened around her hand. 'Come on, let's go. I've reserved a table at an amazing restaurant in Gràcia. You'll love it.'

They made their way up to Plaza Catalunya and ran down the steps to the metro, hand in hand. As they went down to the platform, they were met with the warm, dusty, metallic air that Artie told her was the same on all the undergrounds he'd ever travelled. Waiting for the next train to arrive, they kissed, oblivious to the other passengers, and they only pulled apart when the train came rumbling into the station.

Artie knew the narrow streets of Gràcia well, and as Margarita trailed by his side, he told her about the restaurant on Calle Sant Joaquim. It crossed her mind that she probably wasn't the first girl Artie had brought here, but she batted the thought away, not wanting to spoil the date before it had even started.

Once they were seated and the waiter had taken their order, Artie took her hand, raising goosebumps on her arm as he gently stroked the inside of her wrist. 'I haven't stopped thinking about you since last week,' he whispered, his voice husky. Margarita tingled at the memory of the night they'd spent together at his apartment. Before she could react, the waiter bustled up to their table with tiny plates of *patatas bravas*, octopus and anchovies. He returned with the wine, proudly presenting their finest bottle of Priorat, which Artie tasted, declaring it delicious.

Margarita busied herself rubbing garlic and

tomatoes on the crunchy, toasted bread, hoping he wouldn't ask her what she thought of the wine. She felt so inexperienced and unsophisticated in this lovely restaurant with the expensive wine.

He poured her a glass, pressing his leg against hers as he leaned towards her, which brought on another spasm of shivers up her spine. 'We should go to see the vineyard. The Priorat region is only a couple of hours from here. Maybe we could go next weekend?'

Margarita nodded, taking a delicate sip of wine. Part of her was tempted to remind Artie that he'd said the same thing about going to the Costa Brava, but she didn't want him to think her rude or ungracious. He must have forgotten, so she smiled, dismissing her doubts. Artie was much more than she'd ever dreamed of. Experienced, well-travelled and talented. She was grateful to him for showing her a different side to life.

He raised his glass. 'To our future, Margarita, to a whole lifetime together!' Raising her glass to his, Margarita could hardly believe her luck.

'To us,' she whispered, unable to remember her life before she met Artie. He was like the air she breathed, imperceptible but essential, and she felt blessed.

33

Biting her lip, Eva cleared her throat. 'His father's name is Paco,' she said, twisting the ring on her finger. Carmen felt like she was underwater, desperately trying to reach the surface but flailing, unable to breathe as she was dragged back down into the murky blackness below. When she spoke, her voice sounded like it was someone else's. 'And Kiko is from Somorrostro, *verdad*?'

'Yes,' replied Eva, her brow furrowed. 'His mother is called Loli.'

Sitting down heavily on the chair, Carmen closed her eyes and covered her face with her hands. She sat without moving a muscle, her heart racing as she fought nausea. After a few moments, she felt Eva's gentle touch on her arm.

'Carmen, do you know them?' asked Eva in a whisper.

Carmen's eyes blurred with tears. 'Yes, I do. It's Perona. His surname is Perona, isn't it?' Eva nodded. How was it possible Margarita had recognised Paco? She'd been no more than five years old that day at the market. And Paco had only seen the young Margarita briefly – she was a young woman now, nothing like the child from the market. Her mind raced, trying to make sense of how he'd known her. Then it came to her – the photo she'd shown Paco months ago. Carmen looked at Eva and saw the confusion in the girl's eyes, yet she had no idea how to explain the web of deceit and lies she and Paco had created. In the silence that followed, Carmen agonised over whether to tell Eva the truth. Maybe she could help her make sense of everything. But she barely knew the poor girl. It wasn't fair to involve her in this mess. So many people were going to be hurt when the truth was revealed. Her mother, her daughter, all these years of deception on top of what she'd already put them through with her drinking. How would she confess to Eduardo that his son, Quim, had been an innocent victim of her deceit all along? And why was everything crumbling around her just as she'd finally decided to change her path and make peace with her mother? She had no idea how to put it right. Something suddenly struck her. 'How old is Kiko?'

Eva's brow wrinkled. 'Well, he's eighteen now. He had his birthday in January.'

Carmen's heart plummeted. 'I need to tell you something, Eva, but you must promise not to breathe a word to either Kiko or Margarita until I've spoken to Paco, *me prometas*?'

'Er... yes,' faltered Eva, her eyes wide. 'Yes, I promise.'

Carmen closed her eyes and took a deep breath. 'Paco Perona... is... Margarita's father. Kiko and Margarita are half-brother and sister. Kiko would have been around four months old when Margarita was born.'

Eva stared at Carmen, the colour draining from her face. After a few moments of stunned silence, she found her voice. 'What? Paco is Margarita's father?' she whispered, putting her hand on her chest. *'Díos mio,* did he force you?'

Carmen reached out to take her hand. 'No, no, it wasn't like that,' she said, feeling Eva relax. 'I... I was in love with him,' she whispered.

'But how did you meet him?'

Fresh tears filled Carmen's eyes. 'He saved my life. And then he broke my heart.'

Eva rested her elbows on the table. 'What will you do now?'

Carmen shook her head. 'I have no idea. But please promise me, whatever happens, never let this come between you and Margarita. I know you've been there for my daughter many times when I wasn't, and I'll always be grateful to you. I've let her down all her life, and I fear there'll be no way back for us after this. She'll need you more than ever when she finds out who her father is.'

'How will you break this to her?' Eva asked, her lip trembling. 'And how on earth will I be able to behave normally around the two of them until they know the truth?'

Carmen stroked Eva's hand, smooth and pale against her own, weathered and calloused, and clasped it tightly. 'I'm sorry you've had to find out like this. You're the only person who knows the whole truth, and

231

I hate putting you in such a difficult situation.' Carmen took a deep breath. 'First, I need to tell my mother everything, and then I'll ask her to help me break it to Margarita.'

'What about Kiko? Who will tell him?'

Carmen shrugged. 'I'll talk to Paco and warn him the truth is out. It's time for Kiko and Margarita to know everything. He needs to talk to his son.'

Holding hands, the two women sat in heavy silence until darkness fell. When Eva eventually got up to leave, they hugged each other tightly, bound by a secret soon to be revealed.

34

I was making my way home – mentally exhausted – after spending another evening with Tia Rosita. We'd been preparing for the talk we were giving at the Academy of Medicine in a few days. I was anxious to be taken seriously by the eminent men who could have such an impact on my future. Determined to put on our finest performance, we worked tirelessly night after night to prepare our notes and think of every possible question we might be asked. After the debacle at the town hall, it crossed my mind that we'd be treated as second-class citizens again. But despite my fears, I was grateful for the opportunity to share our findings, knowing it could help with my dream to be a doctor.

I hadn't seen Kiko much outside work, and even less so in the past week. He'd called in sick to the port and had been staying at Eva's apartment. Her parents had gone to Seville to visit family, and I envied him living like a king for a few days. I also knew he'd been on several double dates with Margarita and *el guiri,* which had been difficult to bear. Keeping busy with Tia Rosita was a much-needed distraction.

'Hey, Santi!'

I turned to see Kiko. As he came closer, he looked different, but I couldn't put my finger on why.

'*Qué tal*? What are you up to?' I said, shaking hands with him.

'I'm off to look for my dad' His smile was replaced with a frown. 'I've just spoken to Mama; apparently, he's been acting strangely all week. She said he's spent most of the time in bed.'

It *was* out of character. 'Shall I come with you?' I asked. Kiko nodded. We began to walk down to the shore and turned right towards La Barceloneta, and it suddenly struck me why he looked different. I'd never seen the smart clothes he was wearing, and his hair was styled as if it had been cut by a barber instead of by his mother. He seemed cleaner somehow. 'How was your week with Eva, then?' I asked, giving him a sidelong glance.

Kiko grinned. 'We didn't see daylight all week. Eva was worried the neighbours would see us, so we had to stay holed up inside! You wouldn't believe the size of her apartment, *tío*, it's even bigger than the place Artie is staying. It's immense,' he said, spreading his arms out wide. 'I swear, Santi, there was a bath with taps that you turn, and hot water comes out. It was like being in the sea on a hot day, but better.'

I raised my eyebrows, tensing at the mention of Artie. But he was right. I couldn't imagine it. The old drum we used to wash was filled with cold water, and removing the dirt from our bodies completely was impossible.

Kiko continued. 'And all the lights turn on and off at the flick of a switch. Eva's bedroom alone is twice the size of both our houses put together, and there are rugs on every floor.' He paused, and a sudden look of despair crossed his face. 'It's not fair. I'll never be able to give Eva the sort of life she's used to, never in a million years.'

'But she loves you. She knows where you live now, and she's *chosen* to be with you,' I said, not even trying to hide my frustration. He didn't look at me. Perhaps he sensed my patience was running thin with his constant, unfounded doubts. Before I could add anything, Kiko tugged my arm, pointing to where the newly-paved *Paseo Maritimo* ended and Somorrostro began. It was Paco, sitting staring out to sea, a cigarette between his lips.

'Hey, Papa, *¿Qué haces?*'

Paco looked up, startled when Kiko shouted out from the edge of the camp and got to his feet stiffly and walked over to where we were standing.

'*Qué pasa, hijo?*' he said, patting his son's shoulder affectionately, then turned to me, holding out his hand.

I shook it. 'How are you, Paco?' but he just shrugged.

'Mama said you've been unbearable this week. What's up with you?' asked Kiko.

Paco let out a long sigh. 'All I can think about is what a shambles I've made of my life,' he said, rubbing the nape of his neck. 'I'll be honest, this business with you and Eva has brought a lot of things back for me, but I suppose it's to be expected. I'll be okay, *chicos.*' He looked anything but okay.

Beside me, Kiko stiffened. 'Have you thought about how we'll tell Mama about Eva?'

'I've hardly given it a thought, *hijo*,' said Paco, crossing his arms. 'She's not going to be best pleased, but the world is different now. She'll have to accept it.'

I don't think Kiko really heard the edge in his father's voice or fully understood the pain I saw in him that day. Paco seemed overwhelmed, crying out to be heard, but all Kiko did was punch him blithely on the arm.

'Come on, Papa, let's go and see if Pichi is around and go to Manolo's for a beer. It'll stop you from overthinking things.'

I saw Paco close his eyes for a second and felt his desperation as if it were my own. We rounded the corner to see a huddle of neighbours standing outside my house, shouts of laughter and excited chatter echoing down the street. I caught sight of my father, his mouth set in a grim line, and my heart dropped as I saw a flash of copper hair in the centre of the group. It was my brother, Iker, home from his stint in prison. Back to cause bother. Throughout my life, he'd bullied me relentlessly, inflicting physical pain at any opportunity, and I hated him. Whenever I mentioned my work with Tia Rosita, he belittled me and called her an old witch. Once, he even threatened to burn her at the stake, laughing when my father told him that was enough.

All the sycophants surrounding him now, slapping

236

his back and pumping his hand, hated him, too, but keeping on his good side was imperative. Even Paco, who had known us all our lives and never uttered a harsh word about anyone, despised my brother. Although he would never say as much out of respect for my father.

My father sidled over, his face downcast. 'He's back,' he said in a low voice. 'God only knows what new tricks he's learned inside this time.'

When Iker spotted us watching him, he said something to his cronies, who all looked over and laughed. Breaking away from the group, Iker swaggered towards us, his dark, hooded eyes glinting. We shook hands with him, and I cringed as he pulled me into a half hug, his grip tightening painfully on the top of my arm. He turned to Kiko with an arrogant smirk, but Kiko was braver than me and stared him out. The seconds passed until Iker sneered, spun on his heel and was swept off by his gang of so-called friends.

We all breathed a sigh of relief as he disappeared around the corner, and Kiko turned to me. 'What was all that about?'

I shrugged. 'No idea, *tío*. Stay away from him, though. I don't trust him.'

I caught my father and Paco exchanging worried looks; like me, they were wary of Iker.

'Come on, I think we all need a drink,' I suggested, desperate to relieve the tension.

Kiko nodded. 'Yes, come on, Papa, Pichi, let's go and have a game of dominoes. The loser can pay for the

237

drinks,' he laughed, but not before I'd seen a shadow of fear in his eyes.

Much, much later, all of us would remember this day. We spent a couple of carefree hours playing dominoes, ribbing each other, and raising our glasses to toast something different with every round. We would look back on this night as the last peaceful time before the secrets of the past caught up with us and set off a chain of events that would change our destiny.

35

After Eva had left, promising not to say a word to anyone, Carmen sat quietly for a long time. The only sound came from the hiss of cigarettes as she drew the smoke deep into her lungs, one after another. She wanted time to stand still so she wouldn't have to face the truth. After weeks of abstinence, it was clear she had drunk to numb herself, drowning the agony of the past into oblivion. As the clouds in her mind cleared, it was time to tell her mother and daughter the truth. But her heart quailed at the thought. She'd seen nothing of Paco since they'd met in the bar a few months ago. Rather than elation at his sudden, brief return and sweet words of love, she'd felt only disappointment, let down by the man she had spent so many years aching for. He wasn't the man she had thought he was. He was weak. He'd cast aside not only her but his daughter, his flesh and blood, leaving Carmen stumbling through the years, pining for something that had only existed in her mind.

Finding out Kiko was only four months older than Margarita was the ultimate betrayal. Paco had been with her, promising her the world, while his wife was pregnant with Kiko. She remembered how much she'd needed him when Margarita was born. All the times he'd promised her that they would be together as soon as he had enough money. Everything he'd said had been a lie, and now he thought he could come back, almost twenty years later, declaring his love for her and wanting to be a family with them! She applauded his audacity, but how could she ever trust Paco Perona? He'd abandoned her and their child. How was that love? How had that *ever* been love?

She had to tell Margarita as soon as possible, but her mother deserved to hear the truth before anyone else. Afraid her courage would desert her, Carmen grabbed her coat and handbag and ran through the dark, empty streets, the gravity of the situation snapping at her heels. She breathed through her nose, composing herself and rang the bell. Her mother's startled face appeared over the balcony, and without a word, she threw the keys down.

When Carmen reached the top of the stairs, her mother was waiting, with rollers in her hair and wringing her hands. 'What is it, *cariño?* It's late, what's happened? Is it Margarita?'

'No, Mama, let's go in. I need to talk to you. Let's make some *chocolate caliente* to warm me up,' said Carmen, keeping her tone light to mask the terror inside her. She closed the door behind her and followed her mother inside.

As she sat on the sofa opposite her mother's armchair, Carmen's hands gripped the warm mug of hot chocolate. 'Mama,' she began, unable to meet her mother's eye. 'I've wanted to tell you something for a long time, but I've never known where to begin.' She hesitated and glanced up.

Her mother's eyes drilled into hers, her face inscrutable. 'At the beginning, *hija mia*, start at the beginning.'

Carmen took a deep breath. 'Do you remember Paco Perona, Mama?'

Her mother paled, her shoulders tensing. 'Him again? When will you ever stop, Carmen? It's been almost twenty years,' she said, rubbing her temple.

'Please, Mama, hear me out,' she said, her heart hammering.

Her mother sat back in her armchair and crossed her arms with an exasperated sigh.

'I know you think I met Paco after Margarita was born, but I didn't. I met him before,' she said carefully, placing her mug on the coffee table, her hand trembling.

Her mother's brow furrowed. 'So you already knew him before that terror, Quim Diaz, took advantage of you, then?

Carmen nodded.

'I'm surprised the gypsy didn't go around there and sort him out,' her mother said, her eyes full of contempt.

Carmen pinched her forehead, shooting her mother a look. Her mother clamped her lips together, fishing a tissue from her pinafore pocket to wipe her top lip.

'Please, Mama, don't make this any harder than it is,' said Carmen, knowing she should spit it out, just like ripping off a plaster.

But before she could speak, her mother's eyes narrowed, and she grunted, her tone spiteful. 'Did he leave you then, eh? When you got pregnant with someone else's child? It's a wonder he took you back after she was born.'

Swallowing, Carmen closed her eyes. 'Quim Diaz isn't Margarita's father, Mama... Paco is.' The truth was out, and she felt light-headed. She opened her eyes and glanced at her mother. She'd expected a roar of anger or a cry of horror, but her mother's pale face crumpled, and she began to weep. The minutes passed slowly as Carmen waited for her mother to speak.

'Why didn't you tell me the truth?' her mother asked eventually, twisting the damp handkerchief between her fingers.

'I'm sorry, Mama,' she whispered. 'I didn't know what I was doing. I was desperate. I thought he would marry me, but he said I had to get rid of the baby. I told you it was Quim Diaz so I could keep Margarita.' The pity in her mother's eyes crushed Carmen, but it was time to tell her everything. She began the story of how she'd met Paco when she was fourteen, not sixteen. How she'd fallen in love with him, believed all the things he'd told her, how he promised her they would elope when he'd earned enough money and that he'd sworn to love her and take care of her always.

Wiping her eyes with the damp handkerchief, her mother sniffed. 'Never believe anything a *gitano* promises you, my girl. Didn't I always tell you that?'

As Carmen looked at her mother, she felt a lone tear trickle down her cheek.

'And another thing,' continued her mother, 'that poor Quim Diaz may have been a bit simple, but he didn't have a malicious bone in his body. No one has ever seen him again since then. How could you do such a wicked thing? And as for the *gitano*, I tell you if I ever see him again, I'll rip him from limb to limb.'

'I loved him. I knew what I was doing,' said Carmen, but her mother glared at her. 'And what about Eduardo? All the money you've swindled from him over the years!' Her mother put her hand to her forehead. 'You've led us all a merry dance, *hija mia.*'

Carmen bowed her head. 'I... I'm sorry.'

But her mother hadn't finished. 'I don't understand why you've treated Margarita the way you have. She didn't ask to be born. When she was a baby, you adored her, treated her like a little doll.' She glowered at Carmen, her eyes full of contempt. 'All those times you left her with me to meet the gypsy... and then after, off drinking in the plaza and up to all sorts with God only knows who.' Her mother slumped in her chair, seemingly spent from so much emotion, anger and disgust. She shook her head at her daughter. 'You ought to be ashamed of yourself for hurting so many lives.'

Carmen's eyes met her mother's. 'I am, Mama, terribly. You must hate me.'

Her mother's head snapped up. 'Hate you? So many times, you've almost driven me half-mad, my girl, with your antics and lack of love and warmth for Margarita. You've humiliated me, coming home drunk in the back of a police van and always out gallivanting. I've been at my wit's end, Carmen, but I love you more than you'll ever know.' Her mother paused, her face grim. 'Oh Carmen, what does all this mean for Margarita, the child of a *gitano?* What will we tell her?'

They sat at the table for a long time, each with their thoughts, wondering how nearly twenty years had passed in the blink of an eye and wishing they could turn back time and change the past.

36

Margarita had left Artie's house early that morning, her mood low. The end-of-term exhibition at La Llotja was coming up in a few weeks, and Eva had come round first thing to go through all the details with Artie. Margarita had felt in the way and had made an excuse to leave, but instead of going home, she headed to the library.

'Morning', called out Lurdes as Margarita came through the door. 'The Agatha Christie you ordered has arrived.' She rifled through a pile of books on the desk and passed one to Margarita.

'Thank you! I've been looking forward to getting my hands on a copy of this for ages.' Making herself comfortable in her favourite chair near the window, she opened the book. But after reading the first page three times, she snapped it shut. It was impossible to concentrate.

Margarita and Artie had been spending more and more time together in recent weeks. They'd explored the city together, discovering new places to eat and making love in every room of Artie's apartment. She'd spent hours posing for him, half-naked, as he hurried to finish the painting of her in time to show at his exhibition. Hour after hour, she'd sat, gazing at him as he worked, her self-confidence growing daily. Being charming seemed to be in his nature, and Artie did it as naturally and easily as breathing. The inhibitions she'd initially felt had all but disappeared, and she had even started to believe him when he told her she was beautiful.

'Margarita, we're closing up for the day.' Margarita snapped out of her fantasising as Lurdes appeared at her side. She'd been sitting there daydreaming for hours. She gathered her things together with a long sigh and left the deserted library. Although she wasn't supposed to be working that evening, when she passed by the bar, she popped in to ask Bernat if she could do a shift tonight instead of tomorrow. She'd been crying off work – feigning illness – as often as she dared to spend more time with Artie, which had caused ructions with Bernat.

After some grumbling, he agreed, and Margarita headed home to change clothes before she started. When she walked through the door, her mother was sitting at the table, a cigarette in her hand as always. Margarita's jaw dropped when she spotted Yaya sitting opposite her. If that wasn't astonishing enough, they appeared to be perfectly calm and comfortable in each other's company, both smiling warmly at her.

'Well, this is unexpected, Mama, Yaya? Has something happened? Has someone died?'

Yaya frowned at her. 'Don't be facetious, Margarita. It's very unbecoming.'

Her mother smiled gently at Margarita, who suddenly felt like she'd walked into the wrong apartment. It even looked cleaner. Something was going on, and she wasn't sure if she wanted to know what it was. 'I can't stop and chat. I have to be at the bar in fifteen minutes, and I need to have a wash and get changed,' she said, heading towards her bedroom.

'*Espera,* Margarita, we need to talk to you. Come and sit down,' said Yaya, her resolute tone stopping Margarita in her tracks.

'This is important, *hija*. Bernat will manage fine without you,' said her mother, her eyes not quite meeting Margarita's.

Margarita sat down and began chewing her nails, a habit she'd been trying to break since she'd met Artie. 'Is one of you going to tell me what this is all about?' she said, sitting back in the chair with her arms folded tightly across her chest.

Yaya opened her mouth to speak, but her mother placed her hand gently on her arm. 'It's alright, Mama,' she said and turned back to Margarita. After taking a deep breath, she began to speak. 'There are some things you should know, Margarita. Yaya told me you met Kiko's father recently and thought you recognised him from when you were a child?'

Margarita gave a slight nod, a stab of anxiety in her gut. Was she finally about to find out how he was connected to her family?

'Well, you were right. You *did* see him one day when you were at the market with Yaya, who was very rude to him. She didn't like him because years earlier

I... I'd been in love with him. Yaya thought he was bad news.'

Margarita stared at her mother, unable to believe what she was hearing. She'd been in love with Kiko's father? Before she could say anything, her mother held up her hand.

'It's difficult for me to talk about. I've lied to Yaya for a long time, and she, without knowing, has lied to you. It's me who caused this mess, so please don't blame her.' She closed her eyes for a second before she spoke, a tremor in her voice. 'Kiko's father, Paco, is ... is your father.' Her mother paused, locking eyes with Margarita. 'We loved each—.'

Margarita jumped up, sending her chair clattering to the floor and turned to her grandmother. 'This isn't true! Yaya, tell me it's not true. You've always said my mother was a liar and a drunk and to take anything she says with a big pinch of salt. Tell me she's lying,' she shouted, banging her fist on the table with each word.

Yaya tried to take her hand, but Margarita snatched it away as if she'd been burned. 'Don't touch me, Yaya. You're as bad as she is,' Margarita screamed, inches away from Yaya's face. Turning to her mother, she snarled, 'You're a lying old drunk, Carmen Garcia. You don't care about me. You've *never* cared about me, so don't tell me I was born out of *love*,' she spat, 'with a fucking *gitano* from Somorrostro.' Unable to look at the pair of them any longer, Margarita ran into her room and slammed the door.

She fell onto the bed and curled up in a tight ball, too shocked to cry. So many thoughts were spinning around her head. Paco was her father. Paco and her mother had been in love. And, *Dios mío,* that meant she and Kiko were brother and sister. She was half *gitana*! She didn't know what to do, trapped in her room. Why hadn't she run out of the front door and back to Artie, who would have held her in his arms and made this all go away? She couldn't face going back through the lounge and seeing her treacherous, shameful excuse for a mother. And her duplicitous grandmother, always so quick to judge. It was clear they'd been cut from the same cloth.

She put her hands over her ears to drown out the excruciating truth that was threatening to engulf her and banged her hands on the sides of her head to banish her mother's lies. But all it did was bring hot tears to her eyes. She lay there until the room became dark, listening to the neighbours voices through the open balcony doors, the clink of cutlery and plates being set at tables. Ordinary sounds, everyday sounds, but not loud enough to drown out the noise in her head.

37

Things had been tricky at home since the return of Iker. I'd tried to spend as much time out of the house as possible, and so far, I had avoided being alone with him. My father, though, had told me Iker was even worse than before. He'd been hanging around with a notorious gang from Sant Adrià de Besòs, and rumours were rife that he'd become heavily involved in their drug running. I felt a stab of guilt at not being there to support my father, but the truth was Iker terrified me.

When I wasn't at work or Tia Rosita's, I spent a lot of time at Kiko's house. Loli had been my mother's best friend. She knew what a devil Iker was and told me their door was always open. One evening, Loli went to stay with her sister in Montjuic and took the younger children with her. Kiko invited me for a late supper, telling me that Paco still hadn't snapped out of his lethargy and that if anything, he was becoming more melancholy with each passing day.

When I arrived, the aroma of frying onions was thick in the air, not entirely disguising the smell of the goats tied up at the side of the house. Kiko was putting the finishing touches to a *tortilla*, and Paco was nowhere to be seen. I raised my eyebrows at Kiko, who jerked his head towards the bedroom.

'He's been in bed all afternoon. I'm hoping the smell of this will tempt him out.'

I set some plates on the table and took knives and forks from the chipped jug on the shelf above the gas ring. We sat down, and just as Kiko put a piece of omelette on my plate, Paco shuffled out of the other room. His clothes were crumpled, and he had several days' worth of stubble on his ordinarily clean-shaven face. He nodded at us without a word and bent down with a grunt to take a bottle of beer from a crate on the floor. As we ate, Kiko and I made idle conversation, but Paco remained silent, shovelling food into his mouth as if he were starving. After we'd finished, Kiko took the plates out to the back to let them soak, leaving Paco and me alone. He leaned back in his chair next to the fire and belched loudly, wincing. The dizzy spell he'd had the day we'd seen Margarita in Las Ramblas was on my mind and looking at him now, his face was still the same shade of grey as it had been that day.

'Are you alright, Paco?' I asked, my voice low.

'*Si, hijo.*' He nodded, but I could tell he wasn't. He rubbed his arm, his eyes skittering towards the back door. 'Not a word to Kiko, I mean it, Santi. He's been fussing around me like an old woman.' Paco paused. 'I keep getting these shooting pains right here,' he said, pointing towards his chest.

I reached out to touch his forehead. He was burning up. I poured him a glass of water from the jug on the table, and he gulped it down. He asked me to pour him another just as Kiko came back inside, whistling.

Paco glanced over at me and narrowed his eyes with a shake of his head. I lit up a cigarette, feeling torn. Kiko had a right to know his father was ill, but I couldn't bring myself to betray Paco. I resolved to mention it to Tia Rosita – she'd already given Paco a potion – but I would let her know it wasn't working. There was a gentle tap on the door, and from under the table, the dogs began to growl. Paco stood up and went to answer it, and after less than a minute, he returned, his face deathly pale.

'*Chicos*, I need to go out for a while,' he said and disappeared without even stopping to get his jacket.

'What was that all about?' I asked, alarmed by Paco's sudden departure.

Kiko's gaze followed his father, and he shrugged. 'He's up to something,' he said, scowling as he poured some cognac into our coffees. 'He's been secretive for months now.'

We sat nursing our drinks in awkward silence. Couldn't Kiko see something strange was happening? Something was bothering Paco, yet Kiko didn't appear to be concerned. I closed my eyes for a second, and when I opened them, he was glaring at me, his brow furrowed. 'What is it?'

This should have been when I shared my worries about his father's health with him, but I hesitated. 'Nothing, nothing at all.'

38

Carmen and her mother stared open-mouthed as Margarita ran from the room. Her sobs sounded through the thin walls in the heavy silence that followed, and although it was the reaction Carmen had expected, her daughter's words had cut deep. Her mother wrapped her arms around her, pulling her in close, and Carmen inhaled the familiar, reassuring smell, unchanged even after so many years.

'I'm devastated for her, I won't lie,' said her mother softly. 'But I'm proud of you, owning up to your lies, telling your terrible truth to the one person who needed to hear it. But she's hurt right now, *hija*.'

Carmen sat back in her chair. 'For so many years, I've been a sorry excuse for a mother. Why should I expect her to understand or forgive me?' She searched her mother's face for an answer, but all Carmen saw was pity in her eyes. After Margarita had been in her room for a long time and showed no signs of coming out, Carmen stood up wearily and put on her coat.

'Where are you going now, *hija mia*?' asked her mother. 'You should be here when she comes out.'

Carmen picked up her cigarettes and matches and put them in her coat pocket. 'Now that she knows the truth, I have to speak to Paco.'

Her mother's eyes widened as Carmen pulled on her coat. 'How do you know where to find him? It's getting late now. Please don't tell me you're going to go to that place alone?'

With a sigh, Carmen kissed the top of her mother's head. 'I'll be fine, Mama. No one will hurt me. No one can ever hurt me again after tonight,' and quietly closed the door behind her as she left. She took the same route she'd taken years earlier, but this time, she felt no fear. She strode towards the camp, unaware of the fine drizzle that soaked her to the bone. It didn't take her long to reach the alley that led down to the camp, but she hesitated when she got there. Rushing into Somorrostro alone, an outsider, a *paya*, would be foolhardy. They would know she didn't belong there the minute she stepped foot in the place, which could be risky.

She crept behind a pile of rubble and breathed deeply to calm herself down, wondering how she could get a message to Paco to tell him she was there. She fumbled for her cigarettes and struck a match. As she held it up to her mouth to light the cigarette, she let out a cry. Peering around the side of the carriage, she saw a pair of wide-set, unblinking eyes staring straight at her. She swallowed down a scream and asked, a tremor in her voice. 'Who are you? What do you want?'

The eyes creased in a smile, and a musical, velvet voice whispered back. 'Come with me, *paya*, you'll be safe with me,' and the sweetest-looking woman that Carmen had ever seen came out from behind the old trap

254

and took her gently by the hand. As strange as it was, Carmen instinctively knew she would be safe and hurried behind her. Instead of heading down the alley, they followed a winding track with sparse, scrubby bushes on either side and sand underfoot. They eventually came out on a quiet stretch of beach, the distant camp visible by the occasional glow of flickering lights.

'*Espera aqui, paya.* I'll tell him you're here, don't leave.'

Carmen panted, trying to catch her breath. 'Who are you, and how do you know who I want to see?'

With a giggle, she replied. 'My name is Sofia. I'm Tia Rosita's granddaughter. She told me you'd be coming soon and that I must be waiting for you when you did. I've been at the alley for the last three nights. We thought you'd never get here.'

Leaving Carmen open-mouthed, she danced off noiselessly into the darkness. Carmen was oddly calm. A voice in her head screamed that it was a trick and she could be in danger, but her heart said she was safe here and everything would be alright. She had never forgotten the old woman, Tia Rosita, and knew she could trust her with her life. Waiting in the darkness, she felt stronger and better prepared for coming face to face with Paco. Her breathing had returned to normal, and the gentle lapping of the tide coming up the beach soothed her nerves. Telling her mother and Margarita the truth about Paco had set her free, sparking something inside her, something she hadn't felt since she was a child. It was hope. Hope that everything would be alright – all that remained to be done was this one last thing.

In the distance, hurried footsteps drew closer. Carmen tensed, hearing Paco's voice. '*Coño,* where the hell are we going, Sofia?' he said, gasping for air.

Taking a deep breath, Carmen emerged from the shadows. 'Hello, Paco. I need to talk to you.'

Paco's head shot around, shock and fear mixed with happiness flashing across his face. Sofia melted away into the blackness, and Carmen stood face-to-face with him. Swallowing back her emotions, she stared at him for seconds that felt like hours and felt a rush of hot tears. 'I've told Margarita you're her father, Paco. She knows now. The truth is out.'

Paco opened his mouth to speak, but Carmen held up her hand. 'I only came here tonight to let you know, so you can tell Kiko about his half-sister before he finds out from someone else. When I leave here, I never want to set eyes on you again,' she said, her heart breaking. Not for herself but for this pathetic shell of a man standing before her, so far removed from the strong, fearless man she'd seen all these years in her dreams.

Paco didn't say a word, just stared at her in bewilderment. Had he honestly been expecting her to say she couldn't live without him, that they could finally be together as a family? Looking into his eyes, she witnessed the precise moment the penny finally dropped for Paco Perona. His face darkened, and he gave a low growl. 'No, Carmen. I've never stopped loving you.

Didn't I come to find you and admit I was wrong to leave you alone with the baby? I don't believe you never want to see me again. You love me. I know you do,' he said, taking a step towards her.

Carmen raised her hands to keep him from coming any closer. Trying to keep the bitterness out of her voice, the time for blame long gone, she spoke quietly. 'You don't deserve my love, or Margarita's for that matter, but she'll have to decide for herself. Nor do you deserve the years I've wasted loving and waiting for you. When I leave here tonight, I'll finally be free.'

She turned to leave, but Paco grabbed her by the arm. 'Carmen, *vida mia*, believe me, if you go now, you'll spend the rest of your life regretting it, just as I've done. Lying to you was the biggest mistake I've ever made, and because of it, I've missed seeing Margarita grow up. You're not the only one who's suffered. Haven't I also wasted years loving you?' His voice had become self-pitying, wheedling. 'And what will I tell Kiko? He'll tell Loli, and I'll lose everything. Please, *amor*, don't do this. It's only ever been you.'

Carmen brushed him away and, standing up straight, looked him right in the eye. 'You've only ever loved yourself, Paco. You've disrespected Loli and forsaken Margarita and me. And you have the gall to tell me you're afraid to lose everything?' she said, angry with her younger self for believing his lies. '*Qué te vaya muy bonita,* Paco. Thank you for giving me the most precious gift – my daughter. I can only pray she'll forgive me one day for not being the mother I should have been. I don't blame you, Paco. I was a fool.' She turned, her spirit soaring with bittersweet joy unlike anything she'd ever felt. Nobody could hurt her again; she was fearless. She felt his eyes burning into her back as she walked away, and she shivered. But she didn't look back.

**

Margarita stayed in her room, troubled and angry. She'd never considered herself a snob, although recently, she'd realised she could be quite judgemental. Perhaps she took after Yaya more than she'd thought. How arrogant she had been when they'd followed the boys home and seen where they lived. And now she was connected to the place she'd judged so superciliously.

How would she be able to face Kiko again, knowing they were related? What would it mean for her and Eva's friendship? So many questions were spinning around in her head, making her dizzy. She curled up on the bed and lay there until she fell into a disturbed sleep, the shimmering lights of Somorrostro shining brightly in her dreams. The clock on her chest of drawers showed it was well after midnight when she awoke, sweating from her awful dreams, the sheets twisted and damp. She'd been running down the alley towards Somorrostro, a cawing conspiracy of ravens attacking her, trying to peck her eyes out. She shook her head as if to banish the sound of the birds and shivered in disgust. Desperate for the toilet, she tiptoed past Yaya, fast asleep on the sofa with her mouth open, snoring softly, and peeked into her mother's room. It was empty. She'd heard the front door open and close a short time after she'd locked herself in her room and had assumed it was Yaya leaving. Margarita had been determined to stay in her room, starve herself, if need be, to punish her mother, but now she felt a prickle of alarm. Where had she gone, and why wasn't she back? What if she had a relapse and ended up drinking?

Even so, the thought of being here when her shameless mother returned was too much to contemplate. But where could she go? To Artie's house? She cringed in shame as she imagined what he would say. How would he feel about her when he found out she was half gypsy? No, the only person who would understand was Eva. She dragged a brush half-heartedly through her tangled hair, brushed her teeth and slipped out of the apartment dressed in the same clothes she'd fallen asleep in. Hurrying through the quiet streets, oblivious to the drunks weaving their way home, Margarita arrived at a deserted Plaza Catalunya.

All the lights were off in Eva's apartment. Picking up a handful of small stones, Margarita began throwing them up at Eva's bedroom window. She missed several times and breathed deeply through her nose to calm herself. The next shot hit the window and sounded deafening in the silence. She stepped into the shadows until she heard the creak of a window opening. There was a whistle from above, and Eva was peering down when Margarita stepped out under the street light.

'Margarita, it's the middle of the night,' she whispered loudly. 'Hang on. I'll come down.'

Margarita waited outside, gnawing her nails as she paced.

Eva came out, rubbing her sleepy eyes. 'What is it?' she asked, stifling a yawn.

Margarita couldn't hold back her tears any longer. Eva took her by the arm, leading her to sit on a bench across the road. She rubbed Margarita's back, her face etched with concern. 'Shhh, it's okay now.'

Shuddering through her tears, Margarita spoke. 'You won't believe what I've found out.' Her head sank into her hands. She felt Eva's gentle touch on her back and sniffed. 'It's my father, Eva. I know who he is after all these years. I finally know his name.' Margarita lifted her head and turned to face Eva, who was biting her lip. She took a deep breath. 'It's Paco Perona…Kiko's father, Paco. Kiko is my brother.'

But to Margarita's surprise, Eva didn't look at all shocked. Her eyes flickered to the side, and her face flushed in the dim light of the streetlamp.

'Eva?' said Margarita, with a growing sense of disbelief. 'Did you know?'

Eva's shoulders slumped. She sat back on the bench and turned to Margarita, her mouth set in a grim line. 'Yes, I did,' she said, her eyes not quite meeting

Margarita's. 'I stopped by your house to see you but you were at work.'

Margarita's mind was whirring, her gut churning. How could her mother have told Eva before her?

Eva spoke in a rush. 'Artie told me how upset you'd been when you met Kiko's father, and I was worried about you. I mentioned it to your mother, and it just slipped out. You have to believe me.' Her eyes filled with tears as she met Margarita's glare. 'Your mother was kind, nothing like I'd always imagined her to be.'

Clenching her fists, Margarita was speechless. All those years, her mother had made her life hell, and now, Eva was singing her praises after meeting her once. 'So why did she tell *you* before she told me?' Margarita demanded. 'And why didn't you tell *me*? Some friend you turned out to be.'

Eva shifted on the bench. 'It wasn't like that, I promise. I told your mother about Kiko, and somehow, she put two and two together. It was such a shock for her, Margarita, it really was. She was heartbroken when she realised Kiko's mother was pregnant with Kiko at the same time as she was pregnant with you. Please don't blame me. I can't bear it.' Pulling a handkerchief from her pocket, Eva mopped at her puffy eyes with shaky hands.

For the first time since her mother had revealed her shameful secret, the anger in Margarita's heart subsided and was replaced with a jolt of pity towards her friend for being burdened with keeping her mother's dirty secret. 'When did you find out?' she asked, reaching out a tentative hand to Eva.

'Last week. I felt terrible yesterday morning when I saw you at Artie's apartment. I wanted to tell you, but I'd promised your mother I wouldn't say a word. I've been half expecting you to turn up here, but not in the middle of the night,' said Eva, her lips turning up into the beginning of a smile as she gripped Margarita's hand.

'I'm sorry for taking it out on you,' replied Margarita. 'When my mother told me, I was horrified. I still am. I can't believe it, can you?'

Beside her, Eva shook her head. 'No, I can't. How do you think Kiko will take it?'

Margarita shook her head and shrugged. 'I have no idea. What if he hates me when he finds out the truth, Eva? I mean, his father cheated on his mother with mine. It's a lot to forgive, isn't it?'

'Well, it's not your fault, and it's not your mother's fault either. She was just a girl,' said Eva, crossing her arms. 'If anyone is to blame, it's Paco. He should have known better.'

'Do you think Kiko knows?' said Margarita.

Eva's eyes widened. 'No, he wouldn't keep something like that from me.'

'I wonder if Paco will tell him,' said Margarita, rolling her head from side to side to ease the tension in her neck.

'I don't know, but I hope he does. I don't want to

keep any secrets from Kiko. Listen, I've left a note for Eulalia, telling her there's an emergency, and I have to stay with you tonight. Let's go to your house, and we can work out what to do,' said Eva, standing up and hauling Margarita to her feet.

Margarita sighed with relief. Eva always knew what to do. Making their way to the old town, arms linked tightly, Eva gave Margarita a gentle nudge and had a faint smile on her lips. 'When Kiko and I get married, we'll be sisters just like we've always dreamed of being.' As they passed the Palau de la Música, the old doorman tipped his hat at them, *'Buenos Noches, Señoritas'*. The tension of the last few hours dissipated and the girls started giggling. Margarita dared to imagine the future with a father and a half-brother.

She squeezed Eva's hand and smiled wryly. *'Dios mío,* Eva, we're going to be sisters.'

***

Bright light crept through the gaps in the closed window shutters, piercing Margarita's eyes. She blinked, trying to clear the fog in her mind. She and Eva were curled up to each other, huddled under the thin blanket, as they'd done when they were young girls in the Hospital de Niños. They'd talked into the early hours until Eva had fallen asleep.

'Eva.' Margarita gently shook her friend's shoulder, smiling as Eva stirred and stretched like a cat, yawning widely. 'Morning, sleepy.'

'Morning,' said Eva. 'What time is it?'

'Time you left. You don't want your father to be cross with Eulalia.'

'Yes, you're right. I should get moving.'

Margarita ushered Eva towards the bathroom while she tidied up the sitting area a little. When they arrived last night, there had still been no sign of her mother. Yaya had stirred as they crept past, but she'd rolled over and begun to snore almost immediately. Now she was gone, and only the imprint of her body remained on the sofa, the blanket she'd thrown over herself folded neatly. Margarita felt a pang in her chest as she recalled the harsh words she'd hurled at her beloved grandmother.

'I'll come back later this evening,' Eva promised as Margarita saw her to the door. 'Go and see Artie. He's a good man; he won't judge you. And he's head over heels for you.'

Margarita hugged Eva. 'I'll get changed and leave right away.' But as she closed the door, she shivered. Artie meant so much to her; she prayed it wouldn't scare him off. She put on some clean clothes and did her best to make her hair presentable, pinching her cheeks to get some colour in them. Fifteen minutes later, she was heading up Calle Pau Claris towards Artie's apartment, the warm sun on her face lifting her spirits. When she arrived, Pedro, the concierge, beamed at her. 'Ah, Señorita Margarita, good to see you. How can I help you?'

'I'm here to see Artie. Is he in?' She smiled warmly back at him. Pedro hadn't batted an eye when Margarita left first thing in the morning on more than one occasion.

His smile faltered, and he licked his lips. 'Erm, no, he's not here. He's gone. I thought you'd know. Back to England.'

'Wh…what?' Margarita's mouth grew dry, blood whooshing in her ears. 'When did he leave?'

Pedro scratched his chin and glanced to the side. 'Yesterday, about an hour after Señorita Eva had left, after lunch. A telegram arrived for him saying there'd been a family emergency and he had to leave immediately.'

Margarita's legs began to tremble, and she clutched Pedro's arm to stop herself from falling. He gently led her to the sofa that adorned the hallway. 'Don't move. I'll get you a glass of water.'

Her mind was racing. So much had happened since she'd last been here. Was it only twenty-four hours ago? Pedro returned with the water, and she gulped it down greedily, hoping it would clear the muddle in her head. She pleaded with him to let her go and check the apartment, and though he told her it was more than his job was worth, he reluctantly agreed.

Margarita rushed past him the moment he opened the door and raced from room to room, calling Artie's name. All his possessions were gone. Everything, except his exhibition piece. Paint brushes were scattered on the old sheet he used to protect the tiled floors, and his set of oils was sitting next to the painting of her, which was propped up against the wood-panelled wall. She stood in the middle of the room staring at the image of herself as Artie had seen her, and her heart ached. A gentle hand on her shoulder snapped her out of her trance, and she turned to see Pedro staring at her with compassion in his eyes. 'Come on, *hija mia*, let's get you out of here.' Margarita allowed him to guide her to the lift and out onto the street. She thanked him, and he patted her arm. If she'd turned around, she would have seen Pedro rubbing his chin, wondering if he'd been right to lie to the girl. The part about the telegram had been true, but if he'd told her the whole truth – that the Englishman had girls coming and going to and from his apartment at all hours of the night and day – he wouldn't have been able to live with himself. Poor girl. He had a daughter the same age. Sighing, he shook his head and headed back into the building.

As Margarita walked home, the stinging pain in her heart was almost too much to bear. She didn't notice the jostle of people passing her or the whistle of a policeman directing traffic. She walked blindly on autopilot until she reached the Old Town. A single thought reverberated around her head – so many dreadful things were happening to her at once. She must be cursed.

39

A docker's strike had been called at the port. Two workers had died in an accident caused by alleged negligence, and the canteen had closed mid-morning until further notice. As Kiko and I strolled home, the sun was high in the sky, and it was a treat being outside in the middle of the day, like being on holiday. We stopped for a beer at La Cova Fumada in La Barceloneta and found two free stools at the busy bar. It was usually quiet at this time of day, but we recognised a few port workers who had the same idea as us.

'I'm sick and tired of this job, Kiko,' I admitted, taking a long gulp of ice-cold beer. I lit a cigarette and passed the packet to Kiko.

He took one out, glancing sideways at me. 'Yeah, me too, but what else can we do?' He paused to strike a match and light up his cigarette. 'How did the presentation you gave with Tia Rosita go, by the way?'

I was surprised that he'd even remembered. 'Better than we could have hoped. I was nervous, but you should have seen Tia Rosita. She stood there in front of thirty of the top medics in the city and told them that her method was superior to anything they used. She had them eating out of the palm of her hand by the end of the presentation.'

'That's great,' Kiko replied, nodding. 'Well done.'

I sensed his distraction and clamped my mouth shut. 'How are things with you and Eva?' I asked instead, signalling to the bartender to pour me another beer.

Kiko immediately brightened, his face breaking into a wide grin. 'I've never felt like this about anyone in my life,' he said. 'Since I stayed at her house when her parents were away, it's been hell. I want to be with her all the time. I want to ask her to marry me.' As quickly as it came, his smile disappeared. 'Why does she want to be with me when she can live like a princess with her parents? I'll never be able to give her anything close to what she has now,' he glowered, 'and if I'm afraid to tell *my* mother, imagine what *her* parents would say.' He took a long drink of beer and banged his glass down on the bar, receiving an irate look from the bartender.

I tried to keep my voice even. 'Maybe just loving someone is enough? Maybe *you*, Kiko, are enough for her.'

Kiko shrugged, stubbing his cigarette out savagely in the ashtray in front of us. '*Dios* only knows what will happen.'

'How's Margarita? I haven't seen her for ages,' I said, hoping he couldn't hear the hunger in my voice. 'Still with Artie. I haven't seen them for a couple of weeks. He's even talking about taking her to meet his parents,' he laughed, and I wanted to punch the smile off his face.

'Great,' I said, my voice flat. But he didn't notice.

We finished our drinks, paid and began walking towards Somorrostro. As the sun warmed my face, my bad mood ebbed away with each step. We entered the camp, enjoying the silence before the evening rush hour began, and walked past the bar where Manolo was cleaning the table and chairs. 'How's that father of yours today, Kiko? I bet his head was hurting this morning,' he called out with a guffaw.

Kiko frowned. 'What time did he go home?'

Scratching his head, Manolo replied. 'Well, he was one of the last to leave, so I suppose it must have been well after two o'clock.'

Kiko turned to me, frowning. 'That's strange. I didn't hear him come home. When he's had a skinful, we always know about it because he wakes the dogs.'

'He probably passed out on the beach and fell asleep,' I said, trying to keep my voice even. 'Let's go and see if he's back home.' My mind was in overdrive, my heart hammering in my chest as a bad feeling clenched in my gut and wouldn't go away, no matter how many deep breaths I tried to take. I had known something was wrong with him, yet I'd done nothing. How could I even think about studying to become a doctor? Throwing away all the knowledge Tia Rosita had carefully instilled in me all these years. Failing to act when faced with such clear signs of illness. And for someone who I cared about so much. Kiko's family were my family, and I'd let them down.

The guilt gnawing at my insides spurred me to stride

after Kiko. We searched all over the house, around the back and even under the tarpaulin where the dogs slept, but Paco was nowhere to be seen.

We were about to go back out to check the beach when there was a bang on the door. Kiko threw it open and gave a sharp intake of breath. With a jolt of dismay, I saw Iker, one arm resting above his head on the doorframe, the customary sneer on his face, and before he could see me, I ducked behind the door. Even the sight of him through the crack in the door made me shudder.

'What do you want, *tío*?' Kiko said, a slight tremor in his voice, although I could see he was determined not to show any fear in front of my bullying brother.

'I'm looking for Santi. He's needed at home,' said Iker, his voice hostile.

Kiko stood tall. 'I've not seen him since this morning.'

After a pause, Iker spoke. 'How's your little *paya*, Perona? I've heard she's well-off, a real beauty, too. What's she doing with a runt like you?' he goaded, throwing back his head with a cackle to reveal stumpy, black teeth. 'She likes a bit of rough, does she? The *payos* don't satisfy her, is that it?'

I saw Kiko's knuckles turn white and wouldn't have blamed him if he'd smashed Iker's rotten teeth out of his head. But Kiko smirked. '*Si*, that's right, Calaf. She chose a good one, didn't she? Not an ugly *cabrón* like you.'

As Iker came closer, Kiko stepped back an inch, a

grimace on his face. 'I'm watching you, Perona… and if you see that poncey brother of mine, tell him to get his arse back home,' Iker snarled.

Kiko squared up to him. 'And I'm watching you. We're *all* fucking watching you. One wrong move will mean the end for you here.'

Iker smirked and spat on the ground, narrowly missing Kiko's foot, and strode away. Kiko slammed the door shut and turned to me. He rubbed his chin with a trembling hand. '*Madre mía*, I nearly pissed myself.'

'He's crazy. Try and stay out of his way.'

'I will, don't worry,' he replied, although we both knew it rarely ended well once Iker got fixated on something or someone.

We resumed our search for Paco, but after an hour of looking high and low with no success, we returned to the bar. Kiko addressed the men sitting outside.

'We can't find my dad. No one has seen him since he left here last night. Can some of you help us search for him?'

Everyone immediately sprang into action, running off in different directions. Kiko sat down heavily on a stool, his shoulders slumped, and I didn't know what to say. Instead, I entered the bar and asked Manolo to pour me a brandy. He thrust the whole bottle at me, and I took a gulp before taking it out to give to Kiko. We sat in silence, passing the bottle back and forth and smoking one cigarette after another for what felt like an eternity. Suddenly, shouts sounded in the distance, too far away to make out the words but near enough to hear the panic in the voices. Kiko got to his feet, his hands on the sides of his head.

I squinted in the direction of the shouts. Tia Rosita, followed by Sofia, came into view, walking towards us as if in slow motion. I couldn't see what was behind them at first, but as they got closer, my body froze. It was the men from the bar carrying Paco's lifeless body.

From beside me came a howl of anguish. Kiko fell to his knees, the palms of his hands pressed into his eyes, and I crouched down, my arm supporting him. I felt his pain. The loss of a parent is the deepest.

Tia Rosita knelt on the dirty ground beside us and laid her hand on Kiko's arm. In a whisper, she spoke. '*Niño mio*. It was his time. He knew it was the end and didn't want to be at home for you to find him. Sofia brought him to me in the early hours, but it was too late for me to help him. It was his heart. I promise you he felt no pain. He's at peace now.' She stroked his head gently, then stood up and disappeared through the crowd of silent spectators surrounding us. I don't think he'd understood her words. He was staring at nothing, his eyes unfocused. I stood up, my legs numb, as Kiko turned to face his father's body lying next to him in the dirt. With a roar of grief, he crawled over to Paco and stared down at his father's slate-grey face, the spider veins on his cheeks like rivers of blood even more pronounced in the stillness of death.

40

After Margarita left Artie's apartment, she didn't know what to do. Loath to go home and face her mother and wary of going to Yaya's after the hurtful things she'd screamed at her, she decided to go to the library. There, the peaceful silence washed over her, and her body relaxed. But it didn't soothe her troubled thoughts of Artie. She'd known he was too good to be true all along, but it hadn't stopped her from falling for him and believing his lies. Because that's what it had been all along, and she was sick of being lied to. She sat there for hours, torn between heartbreak and anger, fear and betrayal, shedding more tears than she'd cried in her entire life. What had she missed? Every word Artie had uttered the final night they were together, every look he'd given her, each touch played on a loop in her mind. But she came up with nothing. All she remembered was his laughter, the way he'd gazed at her, his soft caresses as they'd made love. His sleepy smile when he opened his eyes the following day – their last morning. She must have done something wrong. Or maybe it had all been a sham from the start. He was just a red-blooded foreign man wanting a fling with a local girl to pass the time.

When Margarita finally stood up to leave, her body was stiff, her eyes puffy and bloodshot. She hobbled home, her chest tight, waves of nausea causing painful spasms in her gut. When she walked through the door, her mother was sitting at the table, the tip of her cigarette glowing in the dusky light.

'Margarita?' she said, the lines on her forehead more pronounced than ever as her eyes met Margarita's.

Something twisted in Margarita's stomach, and without thinking, she threw herself into her mother's arms. 'Mama,' she whispered, unable to hold back her tears for a moment longer. Her mother wrapped her arms around her. She couldn't recall a time when she felt protected and safe in her mother's embrace. Until now. Her heart was beating in time with her mother's, and Margarita clung to her, crying for herself, for everything she'd had and lost. She felt as though she'd been scooped hollow.

Her mother held her, crooning softly and rocking her. When the bout of emotion had been spent, Margarita dropped into a chair. Her mother knelt before her, gently brushing the damp hair from her eyes. 'I'm sorry you had to find out about Paco like that, *cariño*'.

Blinking, Margarita tilted her head and stared at her mother. 'No, it's not Paco … It's … He's gone, Mama, Artie…' said Margarita, the pain of saying his name out loud crushing her.

'Yaya told me about Artie. Have you had a fallout?'

'You don't understand, Mama, he's gone,' Margarita sobbed. 'He's taken all his belongings and just disappeared, as if… as if he were never here.'

'He'll be back,' her mother shushed, patting her arm as if to reassure her. 'Everything will be alright, *cariño.*'

Trying to slow down her erratic breathing, Margarita took a shuddering breath. The thumping of her heart was shredding her nerves. 'Do you think so, Mama?' she said, eager for any words of hope. But a shadow passed over her mother's face.

Her mother paused for a moment. 'Promise me you won't sit around and wait for him as I did with Paco, *hija mia.* Please don't let whatever this is ruin your life.'

In the stillness of the library, it had been easy to put herself in her mother's shoes. To feel an inkling of the pain her mother had experienced when Paco had abandoned her. Now, she was beginning to see that her mother had spent the last twenty years alone and lonely, grieving for a love she could never have. 'Mama, I love him so much it hurts,' she whispered, her face crumpling again.

Stroking Margarita's cheek, her mother said, 'I know you do, *hija*, I know.'

In light of what she'd learned about Artie today, Margarita allowed a softening for her mother. It had been a long time coming and in the direst of circumstances, but a shared experience finally united them. As the night drew in, they laughed together and cried even more. And the reasons her mother had never told anyone the truth about her father became clearer to Margarita. Instead of the downtrodden, drunken woman she'd only ever known, Margarita caught a glimpse of the young Carmen, the girl in the photographs on Yaya's sideboard. The one with beautiful long hair and shining eyes. Her heart ached for that young woman who had wasted years pining for a man she couldn't have, who'd never really wanted her.

'I don't deserve your support or forgiveness, *hija*,' said her mother, cupping Margarita's face. 'I was lost for such a long time. I was too cowardly to tell you or your grandmother the truth. No better than Paco, really.'

'But I know now, Mama,' replied Margarita, 'and that's enough.'

41

Watching Kiko kneeling on the ground cradling his father's head in his arms, is one of my saddest memories. I've seen many horrors throughout my lifetime, but the hopelessness on Kiko's face, the torment in his eyes, was tangible. I put my hand out to touch his arm but then snatched it back, worried it might be dangerous, like waking someone from sleepwalking.

The arrival of Loli, La Bati and the rest of the Perona children, hastened along by the wives of those who'd gone to look for Paco, jolted us out of the bleak silence. Strong arms held the youngsters back while Loli threw herself onto her husband's body, wailing in shock.

Kiko blinked slowly, roused from his inertia and began to rock his mother in his arms, who in turn was rocking Paco, a monstrous domino effect. I cried for Kiko, for Loli and for my father. My pain was always for the living, never the dead.

In a paradoxical twist of fate, the same day Paco Perona left Somorrostro forever was the day we had an official visit from the Department of Urban Planning. They confirmed the camp would be destroyed and all its inhabitants re-housed over the next few months. It was what we'd fought for. And though we rejoiced – silently out of respect for the Perona family – a part of me was terrified by how quickly our lives were being turned upside down. I desperately wanted to return to the seemingly carefree days of only weeks earlier.

I knew all I could do for Kiko was fetch Eva. I didn't stop to consider the consequences of Loli finding out about her. I did what I thought he would want. Shaken and swallowing back endless tears, I hurried to the top of the Ramblas and entered the building where I knew Eva lived. The doorman's stern face softened when I explained I had some bad news to deliver. He told me to wait while he went upstairs to let Eva know, and I prayed neither of her parents answered the door. I caught sight of myself in the ornate mirror hanging in the entrance. I looked as dishevelled and distraught as I felt and tried to brush the mud off my trousers and flatten my hair. Urgent footsteps echoed in the silence, and Eva flew down the stairs, her face petrified.

'Santi! What's happened?' she cried, grabbing my arm. 'Is it Kiko?' Her blue eyes threatened to spill the tears already pooling, and her lip trembled.

I shook my head. 'No, no, Kiko's fine... it's his father, Paco. He's dead.'

She put her hand over her mouth. 'Oh no, how terrible. How's Kiko?'

'He's not good. I thought he might need you. It's been such a shock to him, to us all.'

Her eyes glistened with tears. 'Poor Kiko, I'll get my coat and tell Eulalia I'm going out.'

As we made our way back to Somorrostro, I told her

Paco had had a heart attack, and she listened without comment, biting at her lip. I was startled when, halfway back to camp, she tugged my arm.

'Santi, can we stop for a moment?'

'I'm sorry, I'll slow down.'

But she shook her head. 'It's not that. I need to tell you something. Something about Paco.'

I glanced at her. Her breathing was shallow, and she was wringing her hands. 'What is it?' I asked, taking her trembling hands in mine.

'It's Paco,' she said, clutching my hand. 'He's – was – Margarita's father.'

I blinked and looked away, wondering if I'd misheard what she said, but when I turned back, her eyes bore into mine, and she nodded.

'It's true. Her mother told her yesterday evening. Margarita came to tell me in the middle of the night, and I stayed with her.' She paused, her shoulders drooping. 'She's devastated.'

My mind was spinning, connecting what I already knew with what Eva had told me. I sat down on the wall next to her, fumbling for my cigarettes, just as the final piece of the jigsaw clicked into place. 'Is Margarita's mother, Carmen, the *paya* Paco told Kiko and me about?'

With a nod, Eva replied. 'Kiko mentioned it, but I never dreamed it would be Margarita's mother. I mean, why would I?' She paused, her lips pressed together in a tight line. 'Has Kiko said anything about it to you?'

279

'Nothing at all,' I said, my mind buzzing. If he knew something so big, he would have told me.

Eva shot me a worried glance. 'Do you think we should tell him?'

I rubbed my chin. 'I don't know.' We sat in heavy silence, and as I processed the news, I wondered what it meant for Kiko and Margarita, for Loli and Margarita's mother. And what would happen with Margarita and *el guiri*? Would their relationship survive the fact she was half *gitana*? I had a feeling it would make her even more bewitching to the unconventional English man. We trudged back to camp in silence, and when we reached the alley, Eva tensed as the sea of metal roofs came into view. Taking a deep breath, she gripped my hand.

The gentle hum of the waves coming up the beach was audible that day as the neighbours paid their hushed respects to Paco. Several voices called out to me, offering condolences and prayers.

Eva turned to me with a frown. 'What are they saying? Don't they speak Spanish?'

'It's *Caló*,' I replied. 'The language of their ancestors.'

As we neared Kiko's house, I tried to see the camp through Eva's eyes, imagining how shocking it must be for her. It wasn't just the mud underfoot but the barefoot children dressed in filthy rags that ran alongside us as we walked. Their excited whispers were silenced by the women standing in the doorways of the flimsy, makeshift homes. As we passed, the women gawped openly at the well-dressed girl by my side, her silky auburn hair shining like fire in the late afternoon sunlight. When we reached the Perona house, I guided her through the door. As my eyes became accustomed to the darkness, I saw several heads turn in our direction. Paco was laid on a low table along one wall, covered with a blanket up to his shoulders. Loli lay half draped over his body, weeping wretchedly. Beside me, Eva trembled, and I squeezed her hand. A subdued exclamation came from the other side of the room as Kiko spotted us standing in the doorway. In two long strides, he was beside us, burying his head in Eva's shoulder and sobbing. From the corner of my eye, I saw Loli stand up, her swollen face grim as she watched Kiko and Eva. She cleared her throat, and Kiko and Eva broke apart. A shadow of fear crossed Kiko's face, but in a second, he straightened up.

'I'm sorry, Mama, I should have introduced you straight away. This is Eva, Eva Sanchez. She's my *novia*,' he said, his eyes not meeting his mother's.

Stony-faced, Loli held out her hand. *'Encantada.* Kiko hasn't mentioned he had a girlfriend, although I suspected he'd met someone. Now I see why he hasn't told me. You're a *paya, verdad*?'

Eva nodded, clearly uncomfortable under Loli's disapproving gaze. In a whisper, she replied. 'I'm so very sorry for your loss, *Señora* Loli. Kiko has told me what a wonderful man his father was. If there is any way I can help, I will.'

Kiko stroked her hand gently as Loli sniffed, gave a

curt nod, and returned to take her place at her husband's side.

It was a long evening and night. We took turns sitting beside Paco's body while neighbours and friends came to pay their respects until dawn rose.

***

Later that morning, Paco's body was carried through the alley to the road and loaded onto a carriage pulled by two black horses. We followed behind it in a slow procession towards Montjuic cemetery, Paco's final resting place. Kiko led the solemn cortege, holding up his mother as she stumbled blindly, her cries heart-wrenching.

When the service ended, we returned to Somorrostro, a muted group of mourners remembering Paco. My thoughts were jumbled, my fond memories of him at odds with the news he'd fathered a child with another woman. Despite the sorrow, the day passed smoothly, full of tributes and anecdotes, dancing, music, tears and lots of drinking. Eva stayed close to either Kiko or me, shrinking back whenever someone wanted to touch her clothes or feel her hair. As the funeral celebration was coming to an end, Tia Rosita approached us.

She raised her eyebrows at Kiko. 'You haven't introduced me to your friend,' she admonished and took Eva's hands.

As she leaned down to kiss her on both cheeks, Tia

Rosita gripped Eva's arm with her bony hand, and I heard her whisper. '*Bienvenido, hija mia. Por fin*'

Eva smiled at Tia Rosita, but as the old woman turned to leave, I could see Eva was unnerved. It had been a long night and day for all of us, and I was overtired. But even so, something about Tia Rosita's words spooked me. It wouldn't be long before I found out why.

42

Margarita woke up gritty-eyed after a restless night spent once more mulling over the last time she'd seen Artie, desperately looking for clues that he was about to leave. She was desperate to tell Eva what had happened, but she hadn't seen her since she'd discovered Paco was her father a couple of days ago. She hauled herself out of bed and went into the kitchen, where her mother was making a pot of coffee. 'I feel awful this morning, Mama. Can you go to the bakery and let Montse know I can't work today?'

Her mother returned ten minutes later and, much to Margarita's surprise, announced she'd taken the day off, too. 'I don't want to leave you alone today, Margarita, not after everything that's happened,' she said, her face reddening. Margarita raised an eyebrow, but her mother crossed her arms. 'I know you probably want to be on your own, but this is our new start. And to be honest, I think you might need me to be with you today. Almost as much as I need to be with you.'

Margarita smiled, grateful something positive had come from the devastating events of the last couple of days. She refilled her cup from the percolator sitting on the stovetop and poured one for her mother.

With a heavy sigh, her mother lit up a cigarette. 'I

wonder if Paco has told Kiko,' she mused, rubbing her chin as she stared into the distance.

Margarita sat down opposite her and took a sip of coffee. 'Do you think Paco will want to meet me, Mama?' she asked.

Taking a deep drag of her cigarette, her mother exhaled slowly. 'I should think so. He says he's remorseful about not being in your life, and I believe him. He was a coward then, though. Even now, I'm not sure he'll be able to bring himself to tell Kiko you're his sister.' She paused, her eyes glazing over.

The prospect of meeting Paco terrified Margarita, yet she also had a sense of somehow feeling more whole than before. Her anger had melted into sorrow at all they'd lost, so much time wasted. She shivered and gripped the warm cup with both hands.

***

The shrill ring of the doorbell resounded in the silence, making them both jump. Carmen stood up with a frown. Who could be calling so early in the morning? She pressed the buzzer to let them in. Margarita glanced at her, her eyes bright with hope, and Carmen silently cursed the Englishman. With her hands on her hips, she scowled, peering over the rusted railing into the darkness below. The tread on the stairs was soft, and as Carmen's eyes adjusted to the gloom, she was surprised to see Eva.

'Eva! It's early for a visit, is everything alright?' she

asked, her eyes taking in the dishevelled girl. The last time Carmen saw her, Eva had been groomed to perfection, her clothes immaculate and her hair smooth. Now, she had dark circles under her eyes, and her pale skin was grey.

'*Hola,*' said Eva, her breathing heavy. 'I came as soon as I could. I… I've got some awful news, Carmen.'

A sudden coldness hit Carmen at her very core, and her knees buckled as she took a step backwards. Eva gripped her arm, her face troubled, but Carmen pushed her away, unable to bear the pity in the girl's eyes. 'It's Paco, isn't it?'

Eva lowered her eyes. 'Yes. I'm so sorry. He died two days ago, and it was his funeral yesterday.'

The door creaked behind them. Carmen snapped her head around to see Margarita standing in the doorway, looking confused.

'Whose funeral?' she asked, her eyes wide, stepping towards her mother.

As if roused from a deep sleep, Carmen snapped into action and herded both girls back inside.

In the living room, Margarita repeated the question. 'Whose funeral, Mama?'

'Sit down, Margarita,' said Carmen, her voice gentle but firm. Margarita sat down and crossed her arms. Carmen took a deep breath and faltered for a second. 'It's… it's Paco,' she said. 'He's gone.'

Margarita tilted her head. 'What do you mean "he's gone"? Where's he gone?' She looked at Eva, but Eva didn't look up, so she turned back to her mother. 'Mama?'

'I'm sorry, *hija,*' Carmen said, her eyes locked on Margarita. 'He's dead.'

Without blinking, Margarita stared at her, her chest rising and falling as if she were having trouble breathing. She reached out and took Carmen's hand. 'Are you alright, Mama?' asked Margarita.

The distress in her eyes twisted like a knife in Carmen's gut. Fate had snatched away her daughter's chance to know her father, but Margarita's only concern was for her mother. After everything Margarita had been through and the things Carmen had put her through, seeing this side of her daughter, her sweet nature, only served to intensify the guilt and shame Carmen felt. Bringing Margarita's hand up to her face, she began to weep, the pent-up tears of the last few days erupting. She clung to Margarita, stroking her hair and inhaling her sweet scent as eighteen years of love poured out of her. 'I'm so sorry,' she said. 'For everything.'

'How did he die?' asked Margarita, wiping her nose on the back of her hand.

Eva, silent until now, passed a crumpled handkerchief to Margarita. 'They think it was his heart. He was with an old woman called Tia Rosita when he passed. Santi told me she's a healer, but not even she was able to save him.'

A shiver passed through Carmen as she remembered the old woman, her wrinkled face still bright in her mind's eye. Even now, after all these years, the memory of her compassion was undimmed. 'I saw him,' Carmen whispered, 'the night he died.' Unsure she'd said the words aloud, Carmen glanced at Margarita, who was staring at her and cracking her knuckles, a habit that always set Carmen's teeth on edge.

'You went to Somorrostro? Why?'

Carmen explained how they'd met several times recently, and Paco had claimed he wanted to leave his wife to make a fresh start with her and Margarita.

'After all these years of nothing?' said Margarita, her tone hardening. 'What did you say, Mama?'

'In the end, I didn't believe him. I think I finally saw how flawed he truly was,' said Carmen. 'The only reason I went was to tell him that you knew the truth and that it was time for him to be honest with Kiko.' Her eyes blurred with tears again. 'I told him I never wanted to set eyes on him again. But I didn't mean I wanted him dead.' She paused, her hands clenching and unclenching in her lap. 'And you deserve so much better, too, Margarita, than this English drifter who's done a disappearing act just like Paco did.'

After a deathly silence, Margarita burst out sobbing.

Eva looked at them both, baffled. 'What? Artie's gone?' she said, her mouth falling open.

'Si, he's scarpered, Eva. Margarita's been to his apartment, and the doorman said he left on Monday. He said he had to go back to England and he's taken all his belongings, except his painting.'

Eva shook her head. 'No!' she cried, reaching out to Margarita. 'I was there with him that morning, Margarita! He never said a thing to me, I swear.'

The two girls held each other, and Carmen was grateful her daughter had Eva in her life. Carmen had never had a close friend, not since she was a child anyway. It had been a long few days, draining for all three of them. As she stood up, her spine cracked, and her legs were heavy. Leaving the girls comforting each other, she headed into the kitchen to warm up some more coffee.

43

'He's left?'

'Yes, a couple of weeks ago,' said Eva, sipping her coffee.

'Does she know why?' I asked, forcing myself to breathe slowly. Inside, my heart was racing, my mind whirring with questions, and I prayed he'd gone back to wherever he'd come from.

Eva shook her head and explained what Margarita had discovered.

It was Sunday, two weeks after Paco's death. Kiko, Eva and I were having a late breakfast at Bar Tropezón, just off Via Laietana. Eva had been staying with Margarita for the last few weeks. After Paco's funeral, she'd told her parents about Kiko, and predictably they'd been outraged, even threatening to involve the police. But Eva had stood her ground and calmly informed them that she would leave immediately. And that's what she'd done. It meant she couldn't continue at La Llotja after her first year, as her father had refused to pay any more fees, but she was adamant that she didn't care.

'I knew he was a piece of shit from the minute I met him. I'm glad he's gone,' I replied, unashamed of my bias, but Eva rebuked me.

'Margarita is devastated. I've never seen her so sad,'

she said, frowning at me.

But knowing she was suffering was unbearable and further heightened my animosity towards Artie. Changing the subject, I turned to Kiko. 'How's your mother bearing up?'

Kiko sighed. 'Better than I expected, to be honest. She's too busy fretting about what the neighbours will think of me being in love with a *paya*,' he said, his mouth twitching as he glanced at Eva.

I'd witnessed Loli's outrage on several occasions. 'What will the neighbours say, Kiko?' she'd muttered. 'My firstborn marrying a *paya*.' She'd looked at me, her hands upturned. 'What do you think of all this, Santi?'

Fearful of incurring her wrath by saying that I thought Kiko and Eva were an ideal match, I'd shrugged. Her shoulders had slumped as she'd sat down at the table. 'Your father would be turning in his grave if he knew what you were up to.' Kiko and I had exchanged a guilty glance, bound by Paco's dirty secret.

'Is there any more news about the demolition, Santi?' asked Eva as she stirred more sugar into her coffee.

'I'm still not sure of the exact date. I went to the town hall with my father last week to put his name down for one of the new flats in La Mina.'

A cousin of Loli's from Montjuic had been re-housed in one of the purpose-built *gitano* blocks, which had been knocked up in record time. She'd boasted to

Loli that her two-bedroom flat had running water and electricity, luxuries we'd only ever dreamed about. And Loli, in turn, had told my father.

Kiko laughed. 'Mama has asked Santi to take her to the town hall, too. She doesn't trust me.'

I didn't mind. Loli had always treated me like a son. She'd been a loyal wife and mother and hadn't deserved to be deceived by a rascal like Paco. Keeping the secret that Paco had taken with him to his grave had been weighing heavily on my mind. Eva and I had decided to wait until the initial rawness had passed before telling Kiko he had a half-sister. But playing God didn't sit easily with me.

44

Carmen was shopping with her mother. They'd been to La Boqueria to buy her mother's favourite hake, some artichokes and a bag of lentils. As they walked back to her mother's house, Carmen suggested stopping for a drink in Plaza Real.

Her mother raised her eyebrow. 'I thought you'd finished with all that?'

Carmen rolled her eyes. 'I meant for a Bitter Kas, Mama, not a whisky on the rocks!'

Her mother laughed. 'Come on, then. It's my treat.'

They found a table on the terrace of Bar Glacier and sat down, grateful to be out of the sun. A waiter took their order, and they settled back in their seats. Carmen sneaked a glance at her mother. They hadn't done anything like this since she was a teenager.

Her mother caught Carmen staring and gave her a rueful smile. 'I've missed you, *hija mia*,' she said, cheeks flushing.

'So have I, Mama,' said Carmen.

The waiter reappeared with their drinks and placed two bottles of Bitter Kas, two glasses and a bowl of peanuts on the table. Carmen poured out their drinks and handed a glass to her mother.

'Cheers, Mama. Here's to me and you and

Margarita.' They chinked glasses and sipped at their drinks in comfortable silence, watching the passers-by.

'How have things been for you, then, you know, with the drinking?' asked her mother, patting her top lip with a handkerchief.

'I won't lie, Mama. It's the worst and the best thing I've ever done.'

Looking pensive, her mother smoothed her skirt. 'Is it still there... the urge?'

Carmen nodded. 'Yes. But I can't ever go back to how I was. It consumed me day and night. Wishing my life away until it was time to go to the bodega for my first drink of the day.'

'You silly thing. You should have come to me sooner,' said her mother, shaking her head softly. 'I wouldn't have turned you away.'

'I know, Mama,' replied Carmen, biting her lip. Tears threatened to overcome her. She swallowed, frightened that if she started, she wouldn't be able to stop. 'Everything is more intense. Happiness, sadness, disappointment – alcohol doesn't mask my emotions anymore.' She paused to sip her drink and fished out her cigarettes and a box of matches from her handbag. She lit one and inhaled deeply. 'Every day, it astounds me that life is so – so lifelike. I couldn't have done it before, Mama, not without you and Margarita supporting me. Whenever I think I need a drink, I remind myself of the years I've lost, the years we've all lost, and the urge fades.' Carmen inhaled, blew her cheeks out and then released the air. Her doctor had encouraged her to voice her feelings about her struggles, but shame engulfed her like a mountain mist whenever she did.

Her mother reached out for Carmen's hand. 'I'm proud of you for turning your life around, *cariño.*'

Carmen swirled the ice around in her glass, playing for time. 'I've had some news, Mama… about Paco.' Her mother's mouth pursed, but Carmen ploughed on. 'He died two weeks ago. From a sudden heart attack.'

Her mother's eyes widened, and she shook her head. 'That's a terrible shame. How old was he?'

Stubbing out her cigarette in the ashtray, Carmen said, 'He was five years older than me, so not even forty.'

'That's no age,' her mother tutted, crossing her arms. 'How do you feel about it?'

'Sad,' said Carmen, catching the moue of disapproval on her mother's face. 'Not in the way you think, but sad that Margarita will never have the chance to know him. Although she says she couldn't care less.' She shrugged. 'I wish it hadn't come between you and me. I was so young, wasn't I? If only I could go back and give myself a bloody shake.'

'You were a madam, Carmen. You wouldn't have listened to anyone.' Her mother sighed. 'Before you met him, you were the sweetest daughter I could have wished for,' she said, her eyes glazing over. 'And after, it was like a light fizzled out in you.'

An elderly man dressed in a grubby suit, held

together with safety pins and toes poking out of the holes in his worn shoes, approached their table, holding out his cap. *'Un céntimo para un café?'* he asked, his deep-set eyes squinting out from under bushy white eyebrows. Her mother rummaged in her purse and gave the man a couple of pesetas. He smiled and bowed deeply before disappearing into the bar.

'Poor bugger,' said her mother. 'Although he's a damn sight luckier than Paco Perona.' She leaned her elbows on the table. 'After all the trouble he caused you, *hija*, I think it's safe to say he got the comeuppance he deserved, didn't he?'

Carmen swallowed back the lump in her throat. Her mother wasn't wrong. Immature foolishness was one thing, but Carmen's youthful folly had turned out to have far-reaching consequences.

Her mother continued. 'Margarita told me her half-brother is walking out with Eva. What a coincidence, eh? At least he's not a stranger. I still can't believe our Margarita is half *gitana*. But she was always a lovely little dancer. I thought she'd taken after you, but it must have been from her father's side.'

Carmen laughed, glancing at the other tables to see if anyone was eavesdropping. 'Mama, you can't say that.'

'Why not? Her mother sniffed, draining the last of her Bitter Kas. 'Anyway, next time I go to Mass, I'll say an extra Hail Mary for Paco, although he's probably roasting in hell right now.'

Knowing how much her mother had despised Paco,

this offer was more than Carmen could have hoped. Leaving some coins for their drinks on the table, they gathered up their shopping bags and made their way home.

45

The visit to the housing office was a success. Loli was interviewed by an owlish administrative clerk, who had been moved by her plight and promised she would arrange a time for Loli to view one of the available flats. We came back out into Plaza Sant Jaume, shielding our eyes from the bright spring sunshine, thankful that Loli wouldn't be facing homelessness. Our relief was palpable, our step lighter.

As we approached Via Laietana, Kiko nudged me. 'I haven't seen Eva for a couple of days. I think I'll call round to see her. Are you coming?'

Until now, Kiko hadn't visited Eva at Margarita's. I panicked as I imagined him coming face-to-face with Carmen and Margarita. After kissing us both, Loli turned right, heading back to Somorrostro. Kiko and I turned left and made our way through the twisting, narrow streets of the old town. My heart began to race as we got closer to where Margarita lived. Despite my anxiety about finally revealing the truth to Kiko about his father, my stomach churned with anticipation. I hadn't seen Margarita since *el guiri* had vanished. As we rounded the corner of Calle Sant Pere, I took a deep breath, all too aware that the next hour would be challenging. Kiko pressed the bell, and we waited silently until the door buzzed. He took the lead, and I trailed behind as we headed up the old stone steps. Eva was hanging over the railings as we came up and rushed straight into Kiko's outstretched arms.

A timid voice came from the open door. 'Santi, how wonderful to see you,' and there she was. I smiled and kissed her on both cheeks, trying to stop myself from holding her too close.

'Hello, Margarita, you look well,' I said, cringing at my formality.

She opened the door wider to let me in. 'Come in and meet my mother.'

My stomach lurched as I followed her inside, my eyes taking everything in. It was more than we had in Somorrostro, but I could see Margarita and her mother didn't have much. Margarita's mother stood up when she saw me, holding out her hand, and I shook it, noticing the deep creases around her eyes. But despite her fading looks, I caught a glimpse of the girl Paco had described. Her eyes were flecked with gold and sparkled with kindness. The way she looked at me hinted she understood my fear, and her eyes reassured me that everything would be alright. Margarita had told us more than once that her mother was a harridan, and her empathy surprised me.

Carmen looked over my shoulder as Eva and Kiko came in, their arms wrapped around each other, and her eyes softened.

Beside me, Margarita cleared her throat. 'Mama, this is Kiko, Eva's *novio*,' she said with a slight quiver in her voice.

Carmen gave Kiko a weak smile as she gripped his hand. '*Encantada.* I was sorry to hear about your father, Kiko. It must have been a terrible shock for you. Please sit down,' she said, pulling a chair out for him. 'Margarita, will you bring some more coffee?'

I stole a glance at Eva and Margarita. Their faces bore the same strained expression as mine. They disappeared into the kitchen, and I sat next to Kiko at the dining table. Carmen was fiddling with a gold chain around her neck, the only outward sign she was anxious. She offered us a cigarette, and we both took one, grateful to have something to occupy our hands. The girls came back in, Margarita carrying a tray with a pot of coffee and five cups and Eva behind her, wafting her hand through the haze of heavy smoke. Margarita passed everyone a coffee, and there was an awkward hush apart from the sound of sipping. I saw Eva glance over at Carmen, and next to me, Kiko shifted in his chair, a puzzled expression on his face as he, too, caught the look that passed between them.

'I knew your father, Kiko, a long time ago,' said Carmen, her voice low. 'I saw him the night he died.' Kiko stared at her, his eyes wide. After an uncomfortable silence, he spoke. 'How did you know my father, Señora Garcia? And why were you with him the night he died?' he asked, the look of surprise turning into one of suspicion and his jaw clenched.

I put my hand on his shoulder, but he shook it off,

300

scowling. 'Can someone tell me what's going on?'

Eva took his hand. 'Kiko, listen to what Carmen has to say.'

At that moment, I saw the realisation on Kiko's face as he made the connection between his father and Carmen, the *paya*. He smouldered, cracking his fingers and glowering at Carmen without speaking for so long that she twitched with discomfort. 'You're *that* Carmen, aren't you? He told me all about you,' Kiko said, and his face hardened.

Si, cariño, soy yo,' she whispered, lifting her chin. 'He betrayed me, too, Kiko. I didn't know he was married to your mother. When I found out, I never saw him again.'

Kiko's shoulders sagged, and he shook his head. After endless minutes of silence, he finally spoke. 'Even though he's gone, I'm not sure I'll ever be able to forgive him.' His hand curled into a fist, and his knuckles stretched white. 'Every time I look at my mother, I'm ashamed of what he did. I can't get past it.'

Carmen nodded and paused for a beat. 'But your father died before he could tell you the whole truth.'

'What truth?' asked Kiko, his face pale.

I held my breath and turned to Margarita, who was grasping Eva's hand, her eyes round with fear. I had no idea how Kiko would react.

'Your father is also Margarita's father.'

***

Watching Kiko freeze as he grasped the significance of her mother's words, Margarita was overcome with emotion. She, too, had felt the same confusion, anger and betrayal she saw now on Kiko's face. But she'd never had a father. She wouldn't miss Paco because she'd never known him. How must Kiko feel? Faced with the fact that not only had his father betrayed his mother, he had also fathered a child with another woman. Her father, their father. Any anger she'd felt towards her mother had subsided and was now solely for Paco. For abandoning her and her mother. For breaking his son's heart. In the heavy silence, Kiko stared at her mother without blinking, his gaze unfocused. Eva squeezed her hand. Thank God she and Santi were here.

Her mother spoke, her voice gentle. 'I'm sorry you had to hear it from me. Your father was too afraid to tell you.'

Kiko swallowed. 'He had so many opportunities to tell me in those last few months, but he didn't.' His voice was thick with emotion. 'I don't understand why he didn't tell me.'

'I think that's what killed him, said her mother. He couldn't live with lying to you anymore – yet he couldn't tell you the truth either. You and your brothers and sisters were everything to him, and he would never have left you. It broke his heart in the end.' Her mother's face was grave.

Margarita's throat tightened as Kiko turned to look at

her, his green eyes damp with tears. Brushing them away with his threadbare sleeve, he stood up and walked around the table to where she was sitting. She stood up on unsteady legs and fell into his embrace. They stood holding each other for a long time without speaking. When they finally pulled apart, Margarita turned to look over at her mother. She was holding her head in her hands, and tears streamed through her fingers. In two steps, Margarita was by her side. It was a day for forgiveness and acceptance – a new start for them all.

From behind her, she heard Eva whisper. 'I'd never noticed until this moment how alike they are.'

Margarita turned around and caught Santi's eye. With a jolt, her pulse quickened under the sheer intensity of his gaze, and she saw something in it she couldn't make sense of, almost as if she was seeing him for the first time. Dragging her eyes away from him, she pressed her head back into her mother's shoulder.

46

One morning several weeks later, Margarita woke up at dawn. She'd lain awake most of the night, tangled up in the sheets, too hot one minute and cold the next. When she finally fell asleep, her dreams were vivid. She saw Artie in the distance, but when he turned around, it was Santi, holding out his arms to her. As he held her, she looked over his shoulder to see Artie glaring at her with a cruel smirk.

In the past few weeks, she'd been to all the places Artie had talked about, but no one had seen or heard from him. Eva had tried to reassure her that Artie wouldn't have left without a compelling reason, but Margarita refused to consider it. He had left her, and it was her fault. She hadn't been exciting or pretty enough to keep him. Her mother and Eva were losing patience with her, but she couldn't shake off the crushing feeling of inadequacy. She had thought he felt the same way about her.

She dragged herself out of bed, her body heavy, and a pain thumping behind her eyes. She couldn't face a coffee and instead sipped a glass of water before leaving for the bakery. Montse's endless chatter got on her nerves. She busied herself in the kitchen, loading and unloading hot trays of freshly-baked bread and croissants, but the smell of the pillowy-soft dough, which normally made her mouth water made her want to heave. She tried to distract herself, popping the still-warm bread in baskets to take out into the shop, when spots swam in front of her eyes, making her light-headed. She sucked deep breaths through her mouth, pressing her forehead against the cool refrigerator door. After a few moments, the dizziness passed as suddenly as it had come on. By the time she arrived home for lunch, her head was aching relentlessly, the queasy churning in her stomach even more pronounced than earlier. Her mother was in the kitchen frying onions and garlic and turned to greet her with a smile, only for Margarita to run to the bathroom. Her stomach emptied itself pitifully, given she'd not eaten anything all day. When she came out, her mother was sitting at the table, a cigarette in her hand and a worried expression on her face.

'What is it, Margarita? Have you been sick?'

Margarita nodded and flopped onto the sofa, her stomach clenching with spasms. 'It must have been something I ate. Yesterday I polished off all the unsold apple tarts. It's probably that,' she muttered, lying as still as she could, one hand resting on her forehead.

Her mother frowned. 'When did you last have your monthlies?' She leaned forwards to stub out her cigarette in the ashtray before reaching for another.

Margarita froze. 'I'm not sure… I… I can't remember.' Her hand was clammy as she covered her face. The clock ticking on the sideboard seemed unnaturally loud in the silence as she tried to recall when it had been. After a few moments, she raised her eyes to look at her mother. 'Oh no, Mama. It was before Christmas.

With a grim look on her face, her mother pulled on her jacket. 'I think we need a trip to the doctor's surgery, don't we?' she said, and left the apartment.

Margarita sat frozen in horror, terrified. Everything was falling around her, and she wasn't sure how much more she could take. For the last few weeks, her breasts had been heavy. The pinny she wore in the bakery was slightly tighter, but she'd dismissed it, putting it down to comfort eating in the weeks since Artie disappeared. After what felt like forever, her mother arrived home, her face pinched and drawn as she sat down at the table. 'Five o'clock on Thursday,' she said, taking Margarita's hand.

'He told me it would be safe,' said Margarita, her cheeks on fire. 'What will I do if he never comes back?'

'Come here, *cariño.*' Her mother gathered her into her arms. 'Everything will be alright.'

She allowed her mother to hold her, batting away the irony that if she was pregnant, history would be repeating itself.

***

A week later, Margarita and her mother left the doctor's surgery. A pregnancy test had confirmed she was around ten weeks pregnant. Although she'd tried to prepare herself for the result, she still reached for her mother's arm, letting her steer her home. Neither spoke, but her mother's gentle hand squeeze reassured her she wasn't alone. They would deal with this together. When they arrived home, Eva was sitting at the table sketching for her final exams the following month, deep in concentration. She glanced up when they entered and took in Margarita's distressed face. Catching a flash of sympathy in Eva's eyes, Margarita burst into tears and ran to her room, almost banging the door off its hinges. She lay on the bed and cried for herself, her baby, and the man who had turned out to be just like her father for hours until her body was cold and stiff, her eyes itchy and dry. She didn't deserve the comfort of a warm blanket. Even though her throat ached with thirst and her stomach begged to be filled with food, Margarita remained immobile, staring at a stain on the wall that looked like a little horse. Curious that she'd never noticed it before.

There was a soft tap on the door. It was Yaya who popped her head in. '*Hola, vida mia,* come on. Let's get you a hot drink and something to eat,' she said gently.

Margarita shook her head numbly, but Yaya sat on the edge of her bed, making the springs creak.

'I won't take no for an answer, *cariño*,' she said, stroking Margarita's messy hair off her face. 'You have a precious life inside you now, and you must look after it.'

Slowly, Margarita pulled herself up to a sitting position and put her arms around her grandmother, inhaling the comforting smell of churros. It was real. She was expecting a baby. Yet no one was angry with her, and nothing terrible had happened. She felt love and acceptance as she sat beside her grandmother, cradled against her chest. A tiny shiver of hope trembled inside her. Having a baby wouldn't spell the end for her. She may have turned out like her mother, but she knew without a doubt that this child would be the most loved in the world. Instead of feeling resentment every time she saw its face, as her mother had done throughout Margarita's life, she vowed to cherish every moment.

***

Carmen, her mother, Margarita and Eva sat late into the night, thrashing out potential pitfalls. They agreed that while the situation wasn't ideal, if Margarita wanted to keep the child, they would all pitch in and help. Typically candid, her mother had made her view of Artie very clear.

'I can't deny it. He took me in completely with his beautiful manners and silky smile,' she muttered. After shooting Carmen a terse look, she turned to Margarita. 'I remember I told your mother the same thing years ago, *cariño*. You're not the first, and you certainly won't be the last to fall for someone from the wrong side of the tracks.'

The following day, Carmen told Eduardo about Margarita's pregnancy. While he'd never taken much interest in Margarita, he'd always provided for her, and she knew he'd help out now. He went into the back of the shop and returned, pressing a cheque into Carmen's hand. She was momentarily lost for words when she saw the amount he'd made it out for.

'It'll be my great-grandchild, Carmen. Please let me do this for Margarita,' he said, his face flushing. She had a twinge of guilt about deceiving him, but things would be tight with a new born baby. As long as Eduardo never found out, they would all be winners. No one could deny Carmen was making excellent progress with her continued sobriety and new outlook on life, especially her newfound skills as a mother. But she was still the street-smart girl of old, hustling and hoodwinking whenever and wherever necessary.

She tucked the cheque away carefully, ready to be deposited in the bank account they would open the next day for Margarita, and had a momentary sense of déjà vu as she recalled her mother doing the same for her eighteen years earlier. Carmen could only pray a new baby would be the making of Margarita and not the downfall it had been for her.

47

Early one Monday morning, Carmen nipped into the butcher's to tell Eduardo she had to see the doctor and wouldn't be in until after lunch. His face was a picture, and tight-lipped, he nodded. Carmen hid a smirk. He hated talking about anything he deemed "women's problems".

She'd accompanied Margarita several times to Artie's apartment to see if there was any news, but each time, when Pedro, the concierge, shook his head, the disappointment on Margarita's face had been too much for Carmen to bear. An all too painful reminder of the day she'd watched Paco gaze lovingly into his wife's eyes, and inside, she raged at both Paco and Artie. But last week, Pedro had informed them that the owner, Señor Carvajal, would be arriving at the weekend.

After a leisurely breakfast, she and Margarita set off towards Plaza Urquinaona, crossed the busy junction and strolled up Calle Pau Claris. It was a pleasant walk, a respite from the Old Town's dark, fuggy streets. Here, the avenues were wide and lined by plane trees that provided dappled shade from the warm spring sun. Carmen's apprehension at meeting the mysterious Señor Carvajal increased as they neared the apartment block. She was glad she pinned back her hair this morning and made herself look presentable. She'd always been ill at ease around anyone she considered superior to her. Wealth had always intimidated Carmen, unlike her mother, who made friends without difficulty, regardless of social status. Even before she met him, Carmen had predicted that Señor Carvajal, with his fancy apartment and distinguished career, would be a pompous arse. Beside her, Margarita's shoulders were rigid, and she was chewing the inside of her cheek. Carmen caught her eye, and slipped her arm through her daughter's, giving it a gentle squeeze. She patted Margarita's hand. 'Try not to worry, *cariño*. I'm sure Señor Carvajal will help us unravel the mystery of Artie's disappearance.'

As they reached the entrance, Pedro was standing outside on the pavement, smoking a cigar. He waved when he saw them. 'Ah, Señora Garcia and Señorita Margarita! Señor Carvajal arrived home on Saturday and was informed of the situation. He's expecting you.'

Thanking him, Carmen took the lead, propelling Margarita towards the ornate lift. Margarita swallowed as it creaked its way up to the penthouse apartment, dabbing away her ever-present tears. Carmen gave her back a reassuring rub.

Rapping the gold knocker with more force than was necessary, Carmen braced herself, her mouth dry. From the inside, a dog began yapping. The door opened to reveal a giant of a man, his thick, greying hair curling in messy waves over his collar and round tortoiseshell glasses perched on his head. He wore fashionable flared jeans and a striped tank top over a white t-shirt, and his feet were bare. Before Carmen could speak, a tiny poodle ran out of the apartment, running in and out of their legs and jumping up at Margarita.

'*Trufa!*' the man yelled. 'Inside, now!' The dog obeyed, and the man scratched his ear. 'Sorry about that,' he said, his eyes creasing into a smile.

Carmen, her cheeks on fire, was frozen to the spot. A sharp dig from Margarita startled her, and she cleared her throat. 'Señor Carvajal?'

Opening the door wider, the man nodded. 'That's me.'

Carmen couldn't ever remember being so tongue-tied. She'd expected someone older, an imperious braggart who would look down his nose at them. She certainly hadn't anticipated the man standing before her with eyes the colour of molasses as he gazed down at her. 'Ermm, Pedro said you were expecting us. I... I'm Carmen Garcia, and this is my daughter, Margarita, Artie's *novia,*' she said, her words coming out in a rush.

Señor Carvajal stuck his hand out, and Carmen shook it, praying he wouldn't notice her sticky palms.

'*Encantado,* Señora García,' he said, his gaze lingering on Carmen for a second before he turned to shake Margarita's hand. 'I recognise you!'

Margarita gave him a weak smile as he stepped back to let them in. 'Come in, come in,' he said, 'Please excuse the mess. I've been working away for several months. I have a lot to sort out.'

Leading them into the living room, Carmen smothered a gasp. She could have fit her whole apartment in this room alone. Her eyes darted around the room, taking in the lacquered furniture and the chandeliers that hung from the high ceiling, sparkling in the sunlight that poured in through the open balcony doors. She gazed in wonder at the colourful explosion of art hanging on the walls.

Once again, Margarita nudged her. 'Mama, keep moving,' she hissed with a frown.

Señor Carvajal gave a slight cough. '*Bueno*, I'll make some coffee for us all. Please make yourselves comfortable,' he said, pointing at a sofa and chairs outside on the terrace.

As soon as he was out of view, Margarita turned to her. 'It's spectacular, isn't it?'

Carmen looked around. 'I've never seen anything like it. I bet those chandeliers are a killer to clean.'

'Señor Carvajal seems very pleasant, doesn't he?' said Margarita, touching the leaves of an orange tree.

Heat flooded Carmen's cheeks, and she fiddled with her hair grip. 'Look at this wonderful view,' she said, desperate to distract Margarita's attention.

'This is where we spent most of our time, Mama,' said Margarita, slumping down on a large sofa, a catch in her voice.

Sitting down beside her, Carmen took Margarita's hand. 'Oh, *cariño*, being here must be difficult for you.'

Margarita nodded. 'I miss him so much,' she said,

tears pooling in her eyes. 'What if something awful has happened to him, Mama?'

Biting back her thoughts of Artie, Carmen pulled Margarita close. 'Let's wait and see what Señor Carvajal says.'

With a rattle of china, he reappeared. 'Call me Oscar, please, Señora García! Señor Carvajal reminds me of my father,' he said, a grin lighting up his face as he set down a tray on the table.

Flustered, Carmen replied. 'Then you must call me Carmen, Oscar,' she said, her heart speeding up as she said his name.

He poured the coffee. 'I must say I'm glad to be back in Barcelona. The heat in Sevilla is blistering. I'm looking forward to resuming my evening stroll down Paseo de Gràcia after work. I can't tell you how much I've missed it.'

Carmen smiled politely and took a sip of her coffee.

'I can sit for hours in Plaza Catalunya, people-watching,' he said.

Thank Christ he didn't venture as far down as Plaza Santa Caterina, thought Carmen, recalling the drunken states she used to get into. She turned to Margarita. 'Why don't you explain a little about Artie to Oscar, *cariño*?' Carmen's shoulders relaxed as Margarita began to talk about Artie's disappearance. Closing her eyes for a second, she took a deep breath. The fragrant scent of jasmine reminded her of the potted plants her mother kept on her tiny balcony.

'So, you've heard nothing for months?' Oscar said, snapping Carmen back into the present.

'No, not a thing,' said Margarita. 'He took everything, except his painting.'

Oscar shook his head. 'It's very odd indeed.' His face became grave. 'The apartment was in a state when I arrived home. The balcony door had been left ajar, and one of those damn green parrots had got in. Made an awful mess, a stink, as you can imagine,' he muttered, sniffing the air as if to check for the lingering smell of dead parrot.

Carmen clapped her hand over her mouth. 'Oh no, I'm so sorry. We'll pay for any damage.'

But Oscar's eyes creased in amusement. 'You'll do no such thing,' he said. 'I've got some professional cleaners coming in tomorrow. The place has needed a thorough clean for a while, so the parrot did me a favour!' He turned back to Margarita. 'Did you say he had an urgent telegram?'

Margarita nodded. 'Yes. Pedro said that when he passed it on, Artie left almost immediately. He even missed his first-year exhibition at La Llotja.'

'Ahhh, La Llotja. It makes sense now.' He looked at Margarita closely and then turned to Carmen. 'Have you seen the paintings?'

'No,' she said, her cheeks heating up again under the intensity of Oscar's gaze.

'Come this way,' he said, jumping out of his seat. 'Margarita, I expect you know what I'm talking about, don't you?'

Margarita's face was downcast. 'Yes, I do.' They entered another breathtakingly elegant room, and Carmen stopped in her tracks. A life-sized portrait of Margarita was propped up against the wall, on top of a sheet protecting the floor, rags and dried-out tubes of paint still scattered around it. It captured Margarita in such a way that Carmen hardly recognised her daughter. Her usual unruly, shoulder-length nondescript hair was soft and shiny, curling down over a smooth, unblemished, white shoulder. Every detail of her face was exquisite. The freckle under her eye, the imperceptible bend of her nose to the left. And the gilded flecks in her eyes that Yaya always told Margarita were real gold, a gift from God to only the luckiest. As she gazed at the painting, her eyes filled up. Oscar passed her a handkerchief, and she blew her nose, embarrassed by her outburst. 'I'm sorry,' she said, her throat tight. 'It's been a difficult few months since he left. It's the not knowing that's been difficult for Margarita.'

Beside her, Margarita was biting her lip, trying not to cry. Oscar's concerned gaze flicked between them.

'I'm sorry, I didn't mean to upset you,' he said, gently taking Carmen's elbow and guiding her back outside to the terrace, leaving Margarita staring at the painting. As he poured some more coffee, Oscar spoke. 'I couldn't help but notice she's pregnant. Has the boy left her in the lurch?'

'We didn't find out about the baby until after he'd

316

gone, so it can't be the reason he disappeared.' Carmen took a sip of strong coffee and placed her cup on the table with a sigh. 'I don't know what's going to become of her.'

'Leave it with me, and I'll arrange an appointment with an excellent obstetrician, a colleague of mine from Hospital Sant Pau.'

'Oh, no, that's not necessary, but thank you,' Carmen replied. She would have bitten his hand off in any other situation, but she didn't want him to feel pity for her or Margarita.

'I'd like to help,' he said, his kind eyes watching her. 'Helping people is what I do.'

Carmen's heart thumped in her chest, and after a beat, she nodded. 'Thank you.'

Margarita returned to the balcony, her mouth set in a grim line, her eyes red, and they sat in silence until Oscar spoke. 'Here's what I suggest we do, Margarita. I'll put the painting in storage and then report his disappearance to the authorities. They can contact his family in England.'

The weight of the past few months lifted from Carmen's shoulders. She caught Margarita's eye and saw the same palpable relief on her daughter's face. 'You'll never know how much this means to us,' Carmen said, humbled by his generosity.

Oscar crossed and uncrossed his legs, looking pleased. 'It's my pleasure, really.'

They finished their drinks, chatting about his stay in

Sevilla. He told them about a medical scholarship he was helping to set up in his department at Hospital Sant Pau and his plans to travel to France the following summer.

As Carmen listened to Oscar's rich voice, a warm glow spread through her body, and she hung onto his every word. Margarita chimed in now and then with a question, but Carmen's eyes hardly left Oscar's face.

Much later, after more coffee and mouth-watering butter biscuits from Seville, Margarita stretched her back, and Carmen felt a tap on her arm. 'Mama, I have to start work in an hour.'

A pang of disappointment shot through Carmen. There would be no reason to return to Oscar's apartment again. She fiddled with her bag and stood up. 'Yes, we've already taken up too much of your time. Thank you for everything.'

'It's been a pleasure to meet both of you. You must give me your address so Dr Blanco's secretary can get in touch about the appointment,' said Oscar, picking up the dog who'd fallen asleep on Margarita's lap. As he led them to the enormous hallway, Margarita gave Carmen a puzzled look.

'Oscar has offered to put you in touch with one of his colleagues. An obstetrician,' explained Carmen.

Margarita's cheeks turned pink. 'Th…thank you so much,' she stammered.

Oscar beamed at them and swung his gaze towards Carmen. He hesitated. 'Yes, a pleasure indeed. Here, write down your address on this,' he said, pointing at a notebook on a black lacquered table next to the front door. Carmen jotted down their address, trying to still the tremor in her hand, and straightened up. Oscar opened the door and turned to Margarita, but instead of shaking her hand, he enveloped her in a hug, once more apologising for not having more information to give her about Artie. Then he turned to Carmen and leaned closer, his lips brushing her cheek. His earthy scent, the scratch of his stubble on her skin, made the hairs on Carmen's arms rise, and a shiver ran down her spine. As she followed Margarita to the lift, she felt his eyes on her until the ornate door closed behind her with a clang, and they slowly descended.

It was a very different walk back down to the old town. Never had she been so unsettled in all her life. It had been an eternity since she'd felt the flutter of attraction in her stomach, and it made her giddy. When they passed the hairdressing salon on the corner of Calle Bou de Sant Pere, Carmen impulsively called in to make an appointment to have her hair cut and coloured the very next day.

48

Tia Rosita and I were walking in Collserola. We'd taken the tram from Avenida Tibidabo into the forest to collect St John's Wort for Tia Rosita's favourite infusion. As we meandered, I told her the news about Kiko and Margarita being half-siblings. She nodded without speaking throughout the whole story.

'Did you know, Tia Rosita?' I asked, unnerved by her silence.

She turned to face me, leaning heavily on the walking cane she used more and more often. *'Hijo mio,* I was there when Paco ripped the *paya's* heart to shreds. She was nothing but a child, and it shattered her,' she said, her eyes glazed. 'I knew Paco all his life. I helped bring him into the world and I adored him – but I could never forgive him for how he treated the *paya.'*

I'd never seen Tia Rosita afraid or unsure. But now, as she looked at me, her eyes misted, and a tear trickled down her crepey cheek.

'I could have saved him, Santi,' she whispered. 'I could have helped him that night when he came to me.'

My scalp prickled. She had dedicated her life to helping the sick, curing the hopeless cases who sought her out when all other treatments had failed. She would never give up on anyone. 'What do you mean, you could have saved him?' I asked, struggling to keep my voice even.

Tia Rosita lowered her eyes. 'I couldn't watch the misery that followed Paco around any longer. He hadn't learned from his errors, *hijo mio*.' She paused and took a deep, shaky breath. 'And he never would have.' With a wince, she shifted position. 'Paco Perona only cared about himself. If he'd lived, he would never have been the father Margarita needed. He would have hurt her the same way he hurt all those close to him.' She lifted her eyes to meet mine. 'I did it for you.'

I was lost for words. My legs trembled, and I sank onto the long grass, reaching for my cigarettes.

Gripping her stick, Tia Rosita lowered herself beside me and put her hand on my arm. But I flicked it away. 'She deserved to know him, Tia Rosita,' I snapped. 'You've taken that chance away from her – And what do you mean, you did it for me?'

'*Hijo mio*, you're in love with her,' she said, her voice even. 'And she's in love with you. She just doesn't know it yet.' I was about to speak, but she held up her hand. 'Right now, she thinks she's in love with the Englishman. It'll be a while until she realises true love was right under her nose all along. Margarita would never have been strong enough to be rejected by Paco and believe me, he would have broken her heart. I couldn't let that happen.'

While I was reeling at her words about leaving Paco to die, my insides surged with joy at her prediction about Margarita. I clung to it like a drowning man.

***

Back home, Tia Rosita was resting in her armchair, exhausted after the trip and, I suspected, her revelations. I was heating some water on the gas ring to make us tea when there was a tap at the door. It creaked open, and Kiko appeared, followed by Eva.

'Kiko! Eva!' exclaimed Tia Rosita, her face brightening when she saw them. 'Come and sit down. We're having some tea. Will you join us?' She beamed at them through the haze of burning sage swirling from the wooden pipe in her hand.

I went to boil more water, thinking how naturally Eva had fitted in among us as if she'd lived here all her life. I was still in awe of everything she'd given up to be with Kiko.

'*Cómo estás, chico?*' Tía Rosita asked Kiko gently.

Still numb from his father's loss, Kiko gave a standard answer. 'I'm fine.'

Tia Rosita's eyes narrowed. '*Ayy, hijo mio,* when anyone asks me how I am, I tell them that my bones are tired. That I'm thankful for the herbs I found in Collserola or that my heart aches for all the suffering I see around me. I tell them the truth, Kiko. None of those fancy new houses everyone's talking about will ever mean anything without the truth. Is that why you're here, *niño,* to find the truth?'

Kiko nodded, his gaze fixed on the old woman as she sucked on her pipe, her rheumy eyes gazing into the distance.

'I can't tell you your truth, Kiko, because it's right here,' she said, leaning closer to Kiko and pointing to his chest. 'In your heart... but I *can* tell you that you will live a long and happy life with Eva. Your father wasn't strong enough to choose the life you've chosen, but he's always with you and will always protect you.'

Kiko's view of Paco had been tainted since his death, and he'd badly needed to hear those words from the last person to see his father alive. Gratitude glowed like fire in his eyes.

Tia Rosita's face became solemn. 'But Margarita will need all of you very shortly. You must keep your head when faced with danger.' She looked over to where I was standing. 'Be vigilant.'

Kiko glanced at me and turned back to Tia Rosita. 'What kind of danger?'

'Someone wishes you harm, *niño mio*. You must protect those you love,' she replied, her face inscrutable.

The threat Iker had made to Kiko flashed through my mind, but I dismissed it. While Iker was a bully, he also knew how well thought of Kiko was by everyone in camp. I didn't think he'd dare try to harm him.

Tia Rosita drew on her pipe for a moment, and we waited for her to continue. After a minute, she held out her bony hands to Kiko. 'I will never leave Somorrostro. My time here is almost at an end, but I have one last thing left to do. Come and see me again when the fires of Sant Juan burn on the twenty-third of June, and I will tell you everything.'

Her words made the fine hairs on the back of my neck stand up. She still had so much to teach me, and the thought of losing her tore at my heart. Kiko squeezed her hand and promised he would come. Like me, he knew better than to ask her why. The sound of the old kettle whistling broke the tension in the cramped room. When I'd prepared the tea, we sat around the table chatting about the upcoming demolition and the rehousing situation.

Kiko and Eva planned to stay with one of Kiko's cousins in Gràcia until they could find a place of their own to rent. Eva had found a teaching position at a secondary school, which would give her plenty of time to dedicate to her art.

I was refilling everyone's glass with tea when Eva put her hand over her mouth. 'Kiko!' she exclaimed. 'We haven't told them the news about Margarita.'

My hand trembled so suddenly that I thought I might drop the pot. I set it down on the table, wincing as a splash of boiling water hit my arm. I don't think Kiko or Eva noticed, but I could feel Tia Rosita's eyes on me from across the table.

'She's pregnant! She was appalled when she first found out, but now she's thrilled, said Eva, looking round at us all, her eyes dancing in the candlelight.

A wave of nausea swept over me, and I swallowed

hard, my heart hammering in my chest. I flicked a glance at Tia Rosita, and her eyes bored into mine as though she was telling me to stay calm. I closed my eyes for a second and took a deep breath.

'What wonderful news! Kiko, you'll be an uncle,' said Tia Rosita, her tone light. 'Does this mean the Englishman is back?'

Kiko shook his head. 'No, Margarita still hasn't heard a thing. She's crushed, but the baby has given her something positive to focus on.'

Tia Rosita smiled. 'I expect it will give her mother, *la paya*, another chance at life.'

Kiko had no idea that Tia Rosita knew about Carmen and his father. Raising his eyebrows, he shot me a look. But the news that Margarita was carrying *el guiri's* child had hit me like a punch to the stomach, and all I could offer him was a non-committal shrug. Kiko and Eva listened in astonishment as Tia Rosita gave them a potted version of her side of events. It gave me time to gather the thoughts swirling around my head. Did this mean Margarita would wait for him? What if he never came back? It took me all my self-restraint not to run to Margarita and promise I would always be there for her. I was certain that if I ever crossed paths with Artie, I would kill him.

49

Margarita was resting in bed, her legs propped up with Yaya's rolled-up blanket to ease the swelling. Being on her feet every day at the bakery was taking its toll. She'd already told Bernat she wouldn't be able to work for the foreseeable future, and although his eyes had widened, he hadn't asked her why.

She groaned, swallowing back a wave of nausea and reached for the glass on the floor next to the bed. It was empty. With a tut, she hoisted herself out of bed and pulled on her dressing gown. Smoke swirled from a cigarette still lit in the ashtray, and Margarita gagged. It turned her stomach. 'Mama?' she called out, filling a glass of water from the kitchen tap.

The bathroom door opened, and out came her mother. '*Cariño*, do you feel a bit better after your nap?' she asked, bustling into the living room and stubbing out the burnt-down butt.

Margarita sat down at the table opposite her mother. 'Slightly. I haven't got any energy today,' she said, yawning. 'I'm supposed to be meeting Eva and Kiko for a stroll, although the damn swelling in my legs is getting unbearable.'

Her mother gave her a fond look. 'It'll soon be over, and my grandchild will finally be here. I think it's going

326

to be a girl,' she said. 'You're carrying it all on your hips like I did with you.'

Margarita shuddered. 'Don't remind me, Mama. Every time I think about it, I start panicking. Does it really hurt?'

'Once you have your baby in your arms, all the pain disappears just like that,' said her mother, clicking her fingers. She stood up. 'I'll make us some coffee. It might perk you up a bit.' She returned to the living room, set down the tray, and passed a cup to Margarita. 'Anyway, tell me, will that lovely friend of Kiko's be there tonight? What a gentleman he is – and so very handsome.'

Margarita couldn't disagree. Her heart quickened whenever she thought about the last time she'd seen Santi – the day they'd told Kiko that he was her brother. But as soon as these thoughts came into her head, she batted them away, too afraid to listen to the voice in her head taunting her, telling her no one would want her now, unmarried and with a baby on the way. Her child would be her focus, and she would ensure nothing and no one got in the way of that.

Her mother's voice cut into her thoughts. 'So what time are you meeting them?'

'At seven,' said Margarita, glancing at the clock on the sideboard. It was a quarter past six. 'Are you going out tonight, Mama?'

Her mother shook her head. 'Well, not unless you class popping round to your grandmother's for a natter as going out,' she said.

Margarita reached for her mother's hand across the table. 'You're doing so well, Mama. I'm proud of you, and I know Yaya is, too.'

Her mother flapped her hand at Margarita, her face pink. 'Go on, shoo, or you'll be late.'

Half an hour later, after a quick wash and change of clothes, Margarita flopped down onto a bench on the corner of Portal de l'Angel, out of breath from the ten-minute walk.

'Margarita!'

She turned to see Eva approaching her, hand in hand with Kiko. Lagging slightly behind was Santi. Margarita's heart thumped. It was the first time she'd seen him since she'd found out about the baby. After hugging Eva and Kiko, she turned to greet Santi.

'Hello again, Margarita!' he said, clearing his throat. 'You look wonderful. Pregnancy suits you.' His eyes creased into a smile as he kissed her on both cheeks.

He was even more handsome than she remembered, and she shook herself. Being pregnant was playing havoc with her hormones. At once, Eva and Kiko began to bombard her with baby-related questions. Grateful for the diversion, Margarita regaled them with her latest symptoms as the four of them strolled along the street towards Plaza Urquinaona and sat down on an outside terrace. Over beers for the boys and milkshakes for the girls, talk turned to the demolition of Somorrostro.

'When are you moving into the new apartment, Santi?' asked Margarita.

'Probably in the next few weeks. I think my father is dragging his heels a bit,' he said. 'Somorrostro is all he's known since he was a boy. Although he's thrilled that Loli and the kids will be neighbours.' He took a sip of his beer. 'But there are so many new rules for us. There's a strict occupancy policy to prevent overcrowding, which is good because it means there's no room for my older brothers.'

Margarita caught the look that passed between Santi and Kiko. She'd heard about Santi's nasty brother from Eva and changed the subject. 'What about you, Santi? Are you looking forward to moving?'

Santi's face darkened. 'Yes and no. I'm worried about Tia Rosita.'

'Yes, Eva mentioned that she doesn't want to leave the camp.'

'I'm sure she'll change her mind. But she's very stubborn,' he said with a tight smile, his discomfort tangible.

Margarita turned to Kiko and Eva. 'When are you two moving to Gràcia?'

'Next month,' said Eva, her eyes shining. 'I can't wait! Kiko's cousin, Juani, has cleared out her basement for us. We're painting it at the weekend. You can come and help us.' She grinned and patted Margarita's belly. 'Although if this one grows anymore, you won't be able to touch your toes, never mind paint a wall!'

Margarita slapped Eva's hand away, laughing. 'Don't be so rude. I'm not that big!'

329

They finished their drinks and walked back towards Las Ramblas. As they reached the corner of Calle Pelayo, close to where Eva had lived with her parents, Margarita stopped suddenly and blinked twice. Across the road, her mother was sitting outside Bar Zurich, dressed in her best skirt and blouse!

'What's the matter? Are you alright?' asked Eva, tapping her on the arm.

'Look, Eva. It's Mama over there,' she said, pointing. Eva and the boys all turned to look just as a man approached the table, kissed her mother on both cheeks, and sat opposite her. 'No!' said Margarita, unable to believe her eyes. 'It's Señor Carvajal! The man whose apartment Artie was staying in.'

'They look very cosy,' said Kiko, winking at Margarita.

She frowned at him. 'Oh my, what is she thinking?' Margarita grabbed Eva's sleeve. 'Come on, before she catches us gawping at them.'

Santi took Margarita's arm. 'I don't think they'd notice if the waiter were stark naked, to be honest!'

As they walked away, Margarita glanced back over her shoulder, only to see Señor Carvajal reach out and take her mother's hand. *Dios,* this was all they needed. Shaking her head, she set off walking beside Santi. His fingers rested lightly on her forearm, and Margarita shivered, her pulse quickening. By the time they reached Calle Portaferrissa, all thoughts of her mother and Oscar Carvajal had disappeared from her mind.

50

The demolition began before many of us had even left. We were woken up one morning by the din of crunching metal and splintering wood reverberating through the camp, the stench of diesel strong in the air. The diggers had arrived, driven by faceless men. Destroying our homes meant nothing to them except a paycheque at the end of the week.

Kiko and I met at the entrance to the alleyway, as we did every morning to walk to the port together. Fear gripped my heart as we watched the enormous excavators begin flattening the homes nearest La Barceloneta, which crumbled to dust metres from where we stood. One by one, the neighbours came out to see what was happening, watching in grim silence as all the memories, the love and the laughter absorbed over the years by the bricks and wood were crushed to nothing. It was sobering to know our homes would soon suffer the same fate. We'd lived in conditions that weren't fit for animals, let alone humans, but Somorrostro was *ours,* and we had made the best of what little we had.

The machines carried on for days, dust and debris choking those of us who had yet to leave. We felt like rats abandoning a sinking ship, trying to escape the jaws of the advancing enemy diggers. My family left two days before the Peronas. My father and I loaded our possessions into the back of my father's dilapidated Sava van, apprehensive yet excited at the prospect of having a proper roof over our heads. As a mark of respect, everyone came out to bid farewell to us. We drove off, waving at the dwindling number of neighbours, but there was a shout. My father checked in the mirror, and I turned to see Sofia running alongside the van. My father slammed on the brakes, and I scrambled out.

'Tia Rosita wants to see you before you leave. I thought I'd missed you,' she panted. I grabbed her hand and we made our way to Tia Rosita's. 'She's still refusing to come to La Mina,' Sofia told me, her dark eyes flashing, 'and it's almost Sant Juan, the final day for moving. What can we do, Santi?'

Each time I'd seen Tia Rosita in the past few weeks, she'd insisted I take some of her tools and base potions for safekeeping, claiming she was anxious the roof would collapse from the vibrations caused by the demolition. I shook my head. 'I don't know. Every time I mention it, she says she'll never leave here.'

'I know she looks feeble, but she's as fit as a butcher's dog,' said Sofia with a sigh.

I'd often thought the same, but the more Tia Rosita had taught me, the less I believed in miracles, in magic, in our ability to change the natural order. I struggled to believe in the afterlife, in reincarnation. Nature was brutal and relentless, and we would never outrun the passing of time. All we could do was pray that our time was free of pain and suffering and help those who couldn't help themselves. I realised this was the most meaningful lesson she had taught me.

Rounding the corner, the old woman was leaning against her doorway, looking frail and wizened. When she saw us approaching, she turned to go inside. Sofia ushered me into the gloomy interior, and the door closed behind her with a loud creak in the silent street.

'Were you leaving without saying goodbye, *hijo*? Her words were stern, but her eyes danced with amusement. With a weary groan, she sat down on her stool and began filling her pipe.

'I'll be back in a couple of days to help Kiko and Loli. I was planning to come and see you then. And anyway, I'll see you when you and Sofia come to La Mina.'

She shook her head, eyes on the pipe she was filling with sage. 'How many times must I tell you I will never leave Somorrostro?'

My stomach clenched. Yes, she'd said it several times, but I'd brushed it off as sentimentality, fear of change. 'You have the new apartment to go to with Sofia. I've even promised to help with the move the week after next,' I said, tempering my panic.

There was a short silence, only broken by the sizzle of burning sage as she lit her pipe. She leaned forward, and her milky eyes drilled into mine. 'Don't be sad for me, *hijo*. My life has been longer than I could ever have imagined when I was your age.' She paused as if to catch her breath. 'You've been like a son to me, Santi, and I'm as proud of you as any mother could be.'

I put my hand up to interrupt her. But she silenced me with a glance, holding her palm up and nodding at me to take it before continuing.

'You have the same gift of healing as I do, but unlike me, you will succeed more than you ever dreamed possible. Never doubt you will be the best in your field, and I will always be with you, *hijo*, watching your journey.'

I squeezed her hand. 'I'll see you in a few days when we come back to help Kiko, and we still have to celebrate Sant Juan,' I said, my voice breaking.

Her bird-like eyes fixed on me, and she nodded. 'Go now. Your father will be impatient to get going,' she said, flapping her hand to dismiss me. I pressed my lips to her soft white hair and left.

As I got into the van, my father glanced at me. If he noticed my eyes were red, he didn't say a word. When we arrived at La Mina, we immediately spotted old neighbours passing by. Children played hopscotch in the wide, pedestrianised streets, and my father honked the horn in greeting. It almost felt like home. But there were many faces we didn't recognise, watching us with narrowed eyes as we carried our meagre possessions up the endless flights of vertiginous stairs, the new lifts already out of order. When we'd finished, we ventured out to familiarise ourselves with the neighbourhood, buying staples from the supermarket five minutes away.

It was as close to luxury as we'd ever come, with shiny fruit and vegetables and shelves full of things we'd never seen before. After lugging our haul back to the apartment, we carefully placed everything in the electric refrigerator the council had provided, in awe of such modern technology.

We finished arranging every last thing and sat down at our old table, incongruous in the bright living room, with the dirt of Somorrostro forever ingrained into the wood. Claustrophobia threatened to suffocate me so high up within these four walls. 'Pa, shall we go down to the bar on the corner and see if anyone we know is there?'

My father's face lit up, and he nodded. 'That's not a bad idea, *hijo*.' As we walked towards the bar, he turned to me. 'I've been trying to put my finger on what's wrong with me.' he said, gazing around at the concrete blocks surrounding us. 'I can't taste the salt of the sea.'

He cleared his throat and started walking again, his eyes dulled with a sadness that hadn't been there before.

51

'Off out again, Mama?' Margarita was lying on the sofa, trying to ease her aching back after a busy day in the bakery. Her mother was fiddling with her hair in the swivel mirror and gave a non-committal 'Hmm,' and her cheeks coloured. The downtrodden woman from months earlier was now glowing with contentment. Her face had filled out since she'd given up drinking, and the vertical lines between her eyes were less pronounced. Her lank hair had been cut into a shorter, flicked-up bob which she took very seriously, putting rollers in her hair even just to go to work. She'd bought some material from the market, and Yaya had run her up some new skirts, blouses and dresses.

'So where are you off to, then?'

'I'm nipping round to your grandmother's again,' said her mother. Margarita began to giggle, and her mother glared at her. 'What's so funny?'

'Mama, you're not going to Yaya's. I saw her yesterday, and she told me she hasn't seen you for days!' Even the tips of her mother's ears had turned red as she concentrated on her reflection in the mirror.

'I know you've been meeting Señor Carvajal. You don't have to hide it from everyone,' said Margarita, grinning as her mother turned to her, her mouth hanging open. 'I've known for weeks. I've been waiting for you to tell me.'

'I suppose I didn't think anything would come of it,' said her mother, her shoulders sagging. 'I mean, with my history, I keep expecting him to tell me it's all been a mistake.'

Margarita took her mother's hand. 'Mama, I saw how he looked at you the day we met him.'

Her mother's face softened. 'He's wonderful. I've never been treated like a lady before. I feel like I've won the *quiniela*.' With a sigh, she shot Margarita a rueful look. 'First Paco, and then all those years pickling myself with alcohol and neglecting you. But this – with Oscar – I've never felt anything like it.'

This unfamiliar, softer version of her mother was a revelation. 'How did you even meet him again?' asked Margarita.

Her mother chuckled and bit her lip. 'I strolled up and down Paseo de Gràcia every evening until I bumped into him! He told me he'd walked past our house countless times trying to spot me.'

Margarita laughed, but something niggled at her. 'I don't imagine you'll be inviting him up here to have a nightcap, will you?' Although the apartment was much more comfortable than before, it was a far cry from Señor Carvajal's place.

Carmen's eyes dulled for a second. 'You know, Margarita, I've told him about my drinking, about everything,' she said, her eyes lowered. 'He says none of it matters, nothing.' She brightened. 'He keeps asking me if I've told you yet. Says he'd like to take both of us out to lunch.'

I'm happy for you, Mama,' said Margarita. 'You've been alone for so many years. It's about time something good happened to you.'

Her mother's eyes sparkled. 'I can't wait for you to get to know him. Before we met him that day when we were looking for Artie, I imagined he'd be very well-to-do. But you'd never believe it, Margarita, he was born on the street next to your grandmother's!' At the mention of Artie, Margarita froze, a pang of regret twisting in her gut. She rubbed her expanding stomach.

'Oh, I'm sorry, *cariño,*' said her mother, watching her.

'It's not your fault, Mama,' said Margarita, with a lump in her throat. 'Sometimes I remember how special he made me feel, how loved.' She closed her eyes for a second. 'But then I feel dirty, used. I despise him for leaving.'

Her mother came round the table and crouched down in front of her. 'You're beautiful, and you have the biggest heart of anyone I know,' she said, gazing at Margarita. 'After the way I treated you, you've never once thrown it back in my face.'

'What will I tell my child when it asks who its father is?'

Her mother straightened up. 'We'll deal with that when it happens, *hija,* together, as a family.'

52

When I woke up on the 23rd of June 1966, my insides were churning. In a few hours, I would be back in Somorrostro with my family, friends, and Margarita.

Kiko had told me she was excited about spending time with us, meeting his family and friends, and seeing where her father had lived. We'd exchanged a knowing look. Margarita had no real idea of the hardships we had endured.

My father and I arrived in the late afternoon. We heaved the crates of beer and wine that we'd purchased earlier in La Mina into an old supermarket trolley abandoned at the end of the alley. As word of the party had spread, many of the recently moved families returned for the final time, and an air of excitement rippled through the camp. Groups of children ran wild, shrieking with delight at being reunited again and quickly slipping back into the freedom their new neighbourhoods didn't allow. Music floated on the balmy air, the strum of guitars and singing welcoming the revellers as they arrived. The dancing began even before the sun had set.

As we dragged the trolley down the alley, our arrival was met with cheers, and like long-lost friends, we greeted everyone with handshakes and slaps on the back. I searched for Kiko and found him lighting a fire to cook the meat. Loli was laying out a lavish buffet on long wooden tables, humming to herself.

'Hey, Santi, *amigo,* you're here at last!' he called out, his face smudged with dirt from the fire. 'Will you take over? I haven't had time for a wash, and the girls will be here any minute.'

I nodded, taking the iron glove he'd been using to add wood to the burning pyre, and grinned as he ran off, eager to look his best. I was happy for him; he and Eva were made for one another. Loli stood for a moment, stretching her back, a tea towel in her hand.

'Ayy, he's crazy about the *paya.* I've never seen him so happy, even after this terrible year.' She let out a contented sigh. 'It's good to be back, isn't it, Santi?' I wasn't sure how to answer. This place had been Loli's whole life, and she knew no other. Her children had been born here, and her husband had died here. It had been the only place I'd ever known, too. But I'd been dreaming of leaving since I was a boy – how could I tell her I was glad it was being demolished? That being razed to the ground was the only way to cleanse the horror and suffering of living here.

I put my arm around her shoulder. 'It is, Loli, just this one last time. It's good to be home.' She beamed at me and carried on wiping the plates.

Kiko returned after a quarter of an hour, his hair swept back into a quiff and his face scrubbed. He'd changed into his smartest trousers and rolled up the sleeves of his white shirt.

'Are the girls here yet?' he asked, an expectant look on his face.

'No, not yet,' I said, and a shadow passed over his face. He checked Loli was out of earshot and lowered his voice. 'What if my mother takes one look at Margarita and works out the truth? I couldn't bear for her to suffer anymore.'

It wasn't the first time we'd talked about this. Kiko and Margarita were startlingly similar. While Margarita's features were softer and Kiko's more angular, both arched their eyebrows in the same way when they were sceptical, and when they were amused their lopsided grins were almost identical.

'She won't. She has no reason to think anything other than Margarita is a friend of Eva's,' I said, but Kiko didn't look convinced. Leaving him to help Loli put the finishing touches to the table, I drifted back towards Manolo's bar, which now stood empty. Manolo had relocated to La Mina, where he was doing a roaring trade in his new bar, which he'd named Bar Somorrostro. The crates of beer we'd brought and a vast supply of spirits were lined up along the bar wall, and already a crowd was gathering. My father was snapping the lids off the bottles with his old penknife, and animated chatter filled the air. It was too early for me to have a drink, and we had a long night ahead, so I made a detour down to the beach, where the fire was almost ready for lighting. I caught a glimpse of Tia Rosita. She'd been given the comfiest chair – positioned with the clearest view of the bonfire – and a table at her side for her bottle and pipe. My heart softened as I got closer, and I noted the serene expression on her face as Rosario placed cushions around her. Her bare feet had left tiny imprints in the sand, and I wanted to sweep her up in my arms, protect her from danger and keep her safe.

As if sensing me, she looked up, a flicker of relief in her eyes. 'Santi, *hijo*, you're finally here,' she said, her voice gruff with emotion.

I kissed the top of her head and crouched beside her. 'Look at you with the best seat in the house,' I laughed and accepted a small cup of coffee from Sofia.

We sat in silence, and I stole a glance at her. Although her face was impassive, her lip trembled slightly. She turned and fixed me with her gaze. 'I'm ready, *hijo,*' she whispered.

My blood froze. 'What do you mean? Ready for what?'

'For tonight,' she said, sucking in a breath. 'For the final *Revetlla*, the last night in Somorrostro.'

With a heavy heart, I took her bony, translucent hand in mine, the slow pulse of her tired veins reminding me that our time was running out.

53

Margarita and Eva walked along the *Paseo Maritimo* towards Somorrostro, carrying the *croquetas* that Yaya had made for them to take to the party and some *Coca de Llardons* from the bakery.

'I can't believe I'm finally going to Somorrostro,' said Margarita, threading her arm through Eva's. 'Tell me about Tia Rosita again.' She'd heard so much about the old woman from Santi and the strange thing she'd said to Eva.

'You'll see her yourself in less than half an hour. You're so impatient!' said Eva, laughing. 'Anyway, how are things with your mother and Oscar? She's been acting like a dog with two tails.'

Margarita laughed. 'I've honestly never seen her like this. She's a completely different person, and Oscar adores her.' She grimaced as the baby kicked and rubbed her belly protectively. 'I've been thinking a lot about her being so young when she fell pregnant with me,' she said, shaking her head. 'She must have been terrified.'

Eva nodded. 'Eulalia still laid out my clothes until last year. And I wasn't allowed out on my own. I can't imagine how your mother must have felt.' She looked at Margarita. 'Are *you* afraid?'

They'd reached La Barceloneta but still had a way

to walk. Margarita wiped the sweat off her brow and sank onto a bench to rest. She was still having frequent bouts of nausea, and the muggy summer evening was taking its toll. 'Yes, I am. Do you think he'll ever come back?' She still found it difficult to say his name out loud, torn between hating him and worrying about him.

Eva gazed out at the sea. 'He told me so many times how much he was in love with you – and I believed him.'

Margarita's chest tightened. 'That makes it even worse,' she said, her voice wobbling. 'Whenever I despise him for leaving, I feel guilty in case something terrible has happened.'

Eva took hold of Margarita's hand. 'Don't upset yourself again, Margarita,' her tone was stern, but her eyes creased into a smile. 'We'll have a marvellous night celebrating *La Revetlla*. The first of many we'll be able to spend together!'

Margarita swallowed the lump in her throat and smiled as Eva hauled her up from the bench.

54

Ten miles out of the city near the airport at El Prat de Llobregat, was Sant Cosme, one of the newly-constructed housing estates for the *gitanos*. It was where the three older Calaf boys had gone to live a couple of months earlier after their father had told them there would be no room at the new place. They'd found an unoccupied apartment, broken the locks on the door, and had been living there rent-free and in relative comfort ever since. All three had been in trouble over the years, frequently embroiled in sticky situations, and although they'd spent plenty of time in prison, even *they* were astonished at the tension in the neighbourhood. Drunken brawls broke out most nights, violent fights between rival *gitano* clans, and the three boys kept to themselves for the most part. But in recent weeks, Iker had been disappearing at all hours, refusing to tell his brothers where he'd been or what he'd been doing. They weren't stupid, though, and whenever Iker arrived home dead-eyed and shaking, they shook their heads in disgust. Heroin had never been Iker's drug of choice before now, but in this tiny urban enclave, it was available on every street corner. They'd argued with him and taken away his money, but nothing had deterred him, and he'd begun stealing anything he could get his hands on to feed his habit.

Their father had unwittingly mentioned the Sant Juan party at Somorrostro within earshot of the boys, and they'd decided to swing by. People's guards were always down when music and dancing were involved, and they would use it to their advantage.

Waiting for Iker to return from yet another bender, the two brothers contemplated leaving without him. But they knew if they left him alone, he'd sell everything they owned, even the mattresses they slept on. Such was his desperation. They headed downstairs to wait for him in an old Citroen they'd borrowed from an elderly neighbour from Somorrostro to move to Sant Cosme, and which they had no intention of returning. Enraged yells came from the bar on the main street, and the boys hunkered down behind the van as the angry voices got closer. The last thing they wanted was to catch the attention of anyone from the reviled Vargas clan – the area's main drug suppliers – who ruled the neighbourhood with intimidation and violence. Finally, after a long wait, they heard the slow shuffle of feet, and Iker came into view, a pitiful sight, track marks visible on his bruised and bloodied arms. With a low whistle, they beckoned him over, bundled him into the van, and set off on the twenty-minute drive to Somorrostro.

55

I was helping to put the finishing touches to the bonfire when I heard Kiko calling my name. I came up the beach, and my heart began to thump. Margarita and Eva had arrived. Kiko was swinging Eva around while Margarita stood quietly apart from them, nibbling on her lip, one hand covering her stomach. I'd never seen her look more beautiful. Her cheeks were flushed, and she'd filled out since the last time I saw her. A pale blue smock was straining over her neat bump, and a matching silk scarf held back her glossy hair.

Their arrival had drawn a swarm of high-spirited children, who surrounded the trio, giggling as Kiko planted a kiss on Eva's lips. When Margarita saw me approaching, her eyes lit up and she waved.

'Santi! How are you?' she asked, slightly breathless.

I pulled her close and pecked her on both cheeks, breathing in her clean smell. 'You look wonderful, Margarita,' I said, holding her at arm's length.

She reddened under my gaze and rubbed her belly. 'Oh, I feel like a whale. It's quite uncomfortable. By the end of the day, my legs are double their size,' she said with a grin. Her eyes darted towards the children reaching out to touch her dress, and I shooed them away. As they ran off howling with glee, she turned to me, her face serious. 'I'm so anxious about meeting Kiko's mother.'

'Everything will be fine.' I reassured her, praying I was right.

Kiko put Eva down, and they walked over to where we were standing. He pulled Margarita into a tight hug. 'Welcome to Somorrostro, *hermana pequeña*!' he whispered in her ear, his eyes twinkling.

'I feel sick with nerves,' she said, but Kiko shook his head.

'Enjoy tonight, Margarita. It may be the last fun you have before this one is born,' he said, pointing to her bump.

She rolled her eyes. 'Yes, Eva said much the same to me on the way here.'

The ground was uneven, pitted with rocks and debris, and I feared she'd trip and harm herself or the baby. I took her bag and held out my arm for her. As we walked down towards the bonfire, she tightened her grip on my arm, and her eyes widened as we walked past the remaining houses. The camp looked even more appalling now most of it had been pulled down. The air was thick with dust, and piles of rubble were dotted around. I squeezed Margarita's arm, and she turned to me.

'Thank you, Santi,' she said, holding my gaze. Before I could reply, there was a shout.

'*Chicos*! Come and get some drinks. We're about to light the fire!' It was my father. When he saw Margarita, his eyes widened, and he did a double-take.

'Pa, this is Margarita,' I said, then turned to Margarita. 'This is my father, Pichi.'

She stuck out her hand and gasped in surprise as my father embraced her. 'Margarita, welcome to Somorrostro,' he said, his eyes glistening.

'Thank you,' she said shyly.

My father took hold of Margarita's other arm, and we went to find somewhere to sit. Loli was seated next to Tia Rosita, deep in conversation, and they glanced up as we approached. As Kiko introduced Margarita to his mother, I held my breath, but Loli just smiled, gave Margarita a friendly kiss on both cheeks, and bustled off to check the children hadn't pilfered anything from the buffet. Margarita exhaled in relief, and I squeezed her hand. Sometimes people don't see what's right under their noses, and although it was for the best on this occasion, I still felt sad for Loli. But no good would come from dwelling on it. She hadn't recognised Margarita, and what she didn't know couldn't hurt her.

There was a chesty cough beside me, and I turned to see Tia Rosita struggling to her feet, her face pinched with pain. 'Tia Rosita, where are you going?' I asked, taking her hand.

She was staring at Margarita, her eyes bright in her pale, sunken face. She held out a knotty hand towards Margarita. I put my hand on the small of Margarita's back, feeling the heat of her body through her dress. 'Margarita, this is Tia Rosita.'

'*Hija mia,* I've waited a long time to meet you,' said Tia Rosita, smiling. 'I see in you the same spark your father possessed. God rest his soul. It's been a long time coming, but you're here now.' Her eyes shone as Margarita bent down to kiss her. Tia Rosita shot me a knowing look and settled back in her chair with a grunt.

56

Margarita's chest thumped as she bent down to kiss the old woman. The guitars, the mouth-watering smell of roasting meat, and people stroking her hair and shaking her hand. It was overwhelming. But as her lips grazed Tia Rosita's papery cheek, a feeling of peace settled over her. She straightened up, thankful that no one had recognised her and reached for Santi's hand again. His presence was like a balm in this strange environment, grounding her.

'*Chicos*! I've got us some chairs,' shouted Kiko from behind them, and he and Eva appeared, each carrying two plastic chairs.

Margarita sank down. '*Dios*, I feel like I've climbed Tibidabo,' she said, tugging her dress over her knees.

Kiko grinned at her. 'I told you everything would be alright, didn't I?'

Margarita returned his smile. 'You did. Everyone is so welcoming. But seriously, Kiko, I'm about to die of thirst very soon.'

'What do you want to drink?'

Margarita asked for water, and Eva wanted cider. Eva pulled her chair closer to Margarita's as the boys disappeared into the crowd. 'What did Tia Rosita say to you?'

'That she'd waited a long time to meet me. It's like she knows everything,' Margarita said, glancing over to where the old woman was sitting. She was clapping along to the music, engrossed as she watched a huddle of women dancing on a raised wooden stage. Leaning in close to Eva, Margarita lowered her voice. 'The people are so friendly, but this place is awful. I've never seen so much mud. These are my best shoes.' Her pumps were coated in dust, and dirty specks had splattered up her calves.

'It'll wash off,' replied Eva in a defensive tone. 'It wasn't always so grim. When I first came here the day Paco died, all the houses were still standing.'

Margarita looked around. There were hardly any houses remaining now, just heaps of debris as far as the eye could see. The area they were sitting in had been cleared, though, and Margarita slipped off her pumps, the sand cool on her feet. 'Santi is a sweetheart, isn't he?' she said. 'Doesn't he have a girlfriend?'

Eva's head swivelled. 'Margarita Marquez, you're blushing!'

'Don't be silly.' Margarita pressed her hand to her cheek. 'What I meant was that he's so lovely. He must have a girlfriend.'

'Kiko told me Santi is more interested in plants than girls,' said Eva, with a bark of laughter. Before Margarita could reply, the boys returned. Kiko carried the glasses and a couple of bottles, and Santi balanced a tray overflowing with food from the buffet. Sipping her sparkling water, Margarita snuck a glance at Santi. He was very handsome. Unlike Kiko, whose hands were covered in scars and tiny nicks, Santi's were smooth and slender. He caught her watching him, and his mouth turned up in a soft smile. Heat rushed to her face once again, and she looked away.

The sun was setting on the horizon, the pink sky darkening. A voice called out, *'Feliz Verbena!'* As the smell of petrol and cherrywood pervaded the warm night air, everyone around her began to cheer. The fire crackled, and the flames turned into a thundering blaze instantaneously. Margarita reached out to take Eva's hand as a glimmer of hope for the future flickered inside her. She had never felt more alive.

57

Cries of delight rang out from the children who skipped around the fire, undeterred by the sparks spluttering and popping at them. Toasts were made, the chink of bottles barely discernible over the roar of the bonfire. The volume of the music increased, and some of the women began to dance, tapping and stamping their feet on the cobbled-together wooden stage which had been placed on top of the powdery sand. Staccato shouts, *'Olé, asi se baila!'* from the men clapping in rhythm with the guitars. The younger girls crept shyly onto the stage to join their mothers and aunts, emboldened by the encouragement from the audience.

A sudden gasp of excitement rippled through the crowd. La Singla had arrived with her grandparents to bid farewell to the place where she'd learned to dance flamenco. That night, she danced as she had never danced before, twirling and flicking her long, red skirt. The graceful *florea* movements of her hands were at odds with the intensity of her tapping feet, which moved faster and faster as the audience cheered her on. Through the dance, she told the story of Somorrostro, Montjuic and all the other *gitano* slums, lamenting the pain and suffering, the despair of living in abject poverty.

Eva and Margarita clapped along in time to the

music as La Singla danced. While the performance entranced them, they didn't understand the story of the *gitanos*. And though one of them was engaged to a *gitano*, and the other was his half-sister, the daughter of a pure-blood *gitano*, they probably never would.

***

Scores more people had arrived since the fire was lit. Over much rejoicing and excitement, roars of laughter and singing, no one noticed the arrival of the three Calaf boys who stayed hidden in the shadows.

On the journey from Sant Cosme, Iker had sat quietly in the backseat, his head lolling on the headrest, half-conscious. As they'd been parking up at the end of the alley, there was a rustle of plastic, and a sharp sniff as Iker snorted something up his nose. His brothers had shaken their heads, muttering their disapproval, but had also conceded it might be a blessing. It was when Iker ran out of drugs that he became problematic, and they didn't want any trouble tonight. They wanted to be in and out, taking as much as they could find as quickly as possible. While everyone was at the party, their homes almost empty and unprotected, the three brothers crept around the houses, searching for anything of value. But there was nothing left worth stealing.

As the night progressed, Iker became more unpredictable, growling in frustration as they left each house empty-handed. His brothers were increasingly uneasy about drawing attention to themselves, well aware that the inhabitants of Somorrostro had no time or patience for the Calaf brothers. They knew there would be trouble if they were caught red-handed. Dragging Iker by the arm, the brothers began to make their way back to the car. But Iker had had enough. With a roar, he punched one brother, knocking him out cold. Spotting a twisted metal bar in the dirt, he picked it up, brandishing it at the other brother, who had raised his hands to defend himself. But Iker was too far gone. In a perfect storm of drugs and rage, he brought down the bar with such force that his brother's head shattered, spraying blood all over Iker's face and upper body. As his brother crumpled to the ground, Iker smirked, a cocktail of adrenalin, drugs and alcohol burning through his veins. He was unstoppable, enraged, and he had scores to settle.

58

As La Singla came off the stage to shouts and applause with tears of emotion pouring down her face, I turned to Margarita. Her brow was shiny with sweat, and she was fanning her face with her hand. 'Shall we get another drink and find somewhere quiet to sit for a while?' I asked, concerned this was all too much for her. She nodded gratefully, and I guided her away from the heat of the bonfire, grabbing a jug of water and two mugs from a table. Margarita linked her arm through mine. 'All of this, the people, the noise, the dancing…' she paused as if taking it all in. 'I've never seen anything like it. I'm so ashamed of myself – part of me was dreading tonight, meeting your friends and family, Kiko's family – but everyone has been so welcoming.'

She didn't have to explain to me how a lifetime of rumours about the *gitanos* could colour people's views, stirring fears and deepening divisions. We strolled along the water's edge, the gentle waves cooling our bare feet. When we were far enough away from the music, I unbuttoned my shirt with fumbling fingers and laid it down on the sand so Margarita wouldn't ruin her dress. I caught her eyes running down my body before she averted her gaze and my pulse quickened. I helped lower her to the ground, and as she shifted to get more comfortable, I poured us some water. Passing her a chipped mug, I held up mine in a toast. 'Happy *Verbena*, Margarita. I'm glad you're here.'

Our eyes locked, and she swallowed. 'So am I,' she said, her voice no more than a whisper, and turned her gaze to the black sea. 'You've always been so kind to me, Santi.'

My heart drummed in my chest – this was finally the moment to tell her how I felt about her. But it was shattered as the voices of my father and Kiko singing a duet reached our ears, their off-key drunken warbling provoking howls of amusement and boos from the crowd. Margarita's face cracked with a giggle, and I joined in, the tension from moments earlier evaporating as we laughed. I leaned back on the sand, propped up on my elbow, and gazed up at the dark midsummer night sky, full of stars. Beside me, Margarita lay back and inhaled deeply as if she were about to speak. Instead, she sighed and turned her head towards me.

'I'm frightened,' she said, a tear rolling down her face and trickling into her hairline.

I pushed her hair off her forehead, my fingers aching to stroke her face. 'Don't be afraid, Margarita. You're not alone.'

'I know I have people supporting me,' she said, stabbing at the sand with her hand. 'But the one person who should be here has disappeared.'

Jealousy flared in me, and I turned away so she wouldn't see my face. 'Have you heard anything from

358

him?' I asked, struggling to keep the venom out of my voice.

She shook her head and pushed herself into a sitting position. 'No. I don't think I'll ever see him again. I can't explain why, but I feel it strongly, right here,' she said, pressing her hand on her chest. 'And to be honest, Santi, I don't think I'd even want to see him. How could I ever trust him after this?'

Without waiting to hear any more, the words tumbled from deep within me. 'I've loved you since the first moment I saw you on the cathedral steps, Margarita... I'll look after you and the baby.' I paused for a second as her eyes widened but ploughed on. 'I know you were in love with him and that you don't care for me in the same way. But I will always love you. And I'll be here when you're ready to love again.'

She sat without moving, her eyes fixed on the dark horizon, while I held my breath, terrified of her reply. Finally, she spoke, her voice no more than a whisper. 'I don't deserve to be loved, Santi.'

I let out the breath I had been holding. 'Don't ever think that. You're everything I've ever dreamed of.'

She stared out to sea, her jaw tense. 'I've heard people talking about unmarried mothers – damaged goods, that's what they call people like me.' She winced and put her hand on her belly. 'The baby knows when I'm upset.' She reached for my hand and placed it on her bump. The baby squirmed against my hand, and my heart contracted. I don't know how long we stayed like that, but I felt connected to Margarita in a way I'd never felt with anyone. Eventually, she shifted her position, stiff from not moving. 'The baby is the most important thing right now.

'I'm not going anywhere, Margarita.'

She took a sip of water and turned to face me. 'Have you really loved me since you saw me on the cathedral steps?' she said, a tiny smile playing on her lips.

I nodded. 'I'd never seen anyone more beautiful. And I still haven't.'

'I noticed you, too. You caught me staring, and I thought I'd die of embarrassment,' she said. 'Why haven't you got a girlfriend?'

I paused for a second. 'Because I've never met anyone who makes me feel alive. Until now.'

Her face became pensive, and she reached for my hand. 'I need some time, Santi. He hurt me so much.' Before I could reply, there was a shout in the distance.

'Santi! Where are you, *amigo*?' It was Kiko. Margarita grinned at me. 'Go and see what he wants. I'll stay here for a while. It's so peaceful. I've never heard the sea so clearly until now.'

'I'll be back as soon as I can. Are you sure you'll be okay here?'

Margarita smiled shyly. 'Yes, but don't be too long.'

I raced along the beach searching for Kiko and found him trying to prop up my father – covered in damp sand – on a chair near the drinks table. 'Pa?'

My father squinted up at me, his eyes unfocused and

glassy. '*Hijo*! I've been raising a glass for Somorrostro – but this spoilsport has hidden my bottle,' he slurred, jerking his head towards Kiko, who grinned.

'You've had enough now, Pichi. You need something to eat to mop it up.'

His mother passed by, and I called out to her. 'Loli, can you bring Pa some food from the buffet?'

She took one look at my father and shook her head. 'Ayy, Pichi Calaf, you've never been able to handle your drink!' she said with a chortle and trotted over to the food table.

'Kiko, can you stay with him for a while until he sobers up? I'd stay, but Margarita's waiting for me.'

He raised an eyebrow at me and grinned. 'Okay, but go and tell Eva where I am, will you? She'll think I've abandoned her.'

I jogged off to find Eva and spotted her dancing with Sofia and Kiko's sisters.

'Santi! Come and dance with us!' she cried, grabbing my hand.

I laughed. 'I'd love nothing more, but I just came to tell you that Kiko is sitting with my Pa for a while. Silly old sod has drunk too much. Margarita and I are sitting along the beach. The heat was getting to her.'

Eva gave me a wide smile. 'Take care of her.'

'I intend to. See you later,' I said, unable to keep the grin off my face, and set off in search of some food to take back to Margarita.

59

Margarita stretched her legs out in front of her. All the melancholy and anxiety she'd felt since Artie's disappearance was less pronounced and didn't hurt as much. She thought back to the times she'd spent with Santi. That first night she'd met him and Artie, dancing in Las Ramblas, trips to the cinema. Her head had been so full of Artie that she'd overlooked Santi, always there with a smile, a funny quip and a hand to hold. She had more in common with Santi than she had ever had with Artie.

She recalled the day they had walked past her library and how he'd dismissed it, the way he'd belittled her about her lack of knowledge about Gaudi. Artie had never expressed interest or asked about her life, desires, or fears. Had she been sucked in by his charming persona and blinded by her physical attraction to him?

The pull between her and Santi had been there all along. Unlike her lust towards Artie, her fledgling relationship with Santi was built on a shared interest in learning, a common ground despite their different circumstances. His declaration tonight had come as a surprise, and she felt torn. If she agreed, and they became involved, would everyone assume it was simply because she wanted a father for her child? She couldn't bear people to think that, least of all Santi.

She shook her head, annoyed with herself for overthinking. Tonight, she would relax, enjoy the party, and talk it over with her mother tomorrow. Months ago, she would have laughed if someone had told her that her mother would be the first person she turned to for advice. The lonely years of her childhood hadn't completely faded from memory, and their closeness had been a long time coming, but Margarita was determined to focus on the future. None of them could change the past. All they had was the here and now and the promise of tomorrow.

She trailed her fingers through the sand, smiling as she felt the baby kick sharply. Her hands curled around the bump, and she rubbed it, feeling the baby's foot. Suddenly, the hairs on the back of her neck prickled. But before she could turn, pain jolted through the tender skin of her face, and a hand clamped over her mouth, muffling her cry. Her arm was pulled awkwardly up her back, making her eyes water. The hand was suffocating her, dragging her back into the murky wasteland higher up from the shoreline. She kicked out with her legs, the instinct for survival strong despite her terror. She bit down as hard as she could on the hand, the tang of blood making her nauseous. There was a howl, and a fist struck her hard on the side of her face. Her jaw cracked painfully, and everything turned black.

When she opened her eyes, the music and laughter had faded. She moved her leg and winced as sharp rocks scraped her leg. But then, with a dull thud, she was kicked hard in the back. She curled into a ball, but before she could scream, the air was crushed from her lungs, and her eyes widened in terror as her attacker pinned her down. Face to face with the most grotesque-looking creature she'd ever seen, Margarita's insides turned to water. Malevolent eyes leered down at her, and his putrid, overpowering breath made her gag. She shrank back but had nowhere to go. She screamed, but once more, his hand clamped over her mouth, this time even harder, and the sound of tearing cloth resounded in the quiet darkness. It flashed through her mind that if she stopped struggling, there was less chance the baby would be harmed. As she became still, her attacker sneered down at her, his fingers ripping at her knickers.

'Good girl, you're a fast learner,' he wheezed, flecks of rancid spit spraying her face.

Then, a bellow of anger came from nowhere, and the weight of the man's body was lifted off her. Her whole body was trembling uncontrollably as she gasped to get air back into her lungs. She looked over her shoulder and saw Santi, his face dark with rage and his fists clenched. He and the man circled each other.

'What the fuck are you doing?' growled Santi, stepping closer to the man.

'I heard you telling her you'd take her and her bastard child on,' the man spat. 'The ungrateful bitch turned you down, didn't she? Poor Santi, that must have stung. I thought I might be in with a chance because she's not much of a looker, is she?'

Margarita watched, her terror mounting. This man knew Santi.

Santi launched at the man, grabbing his throat and knocking him to the ground. His hand tightened around the man's throat. *'Hijo de puta, te mataré*, I'll kill you, you bastard,' he screamed. 'You're nothing but a coward. Even your own family despises you – you're nothing to us.' The man clawed at his face, and Santi's grip loosened. With a grunt, the man kneed him in the groin, causing Santi to roll away.

Rubbing his throat, the man barked with laughter. 'Do you think I care? You, the perfect child, the genius of the family, casting your spells with that mad old hag.' Saliva glistened as he licked his lips and sneered at Santi. 'Isn't she dead yet? Maybe I should pay her a visit sometime – perhaps later when I've finished with this one,' he spat, leering at Margarita as she lay quaking on the ground.

Cringing under his gaze, she turned her head away. Her mind was spinning. Was he related to Santi?

With a roar, Santi bared his teeth and launched himself at the man, pinning him down with his arm and crushing the man's windpipe. Before the man could fight back, Santi began pummelling him repeatedly in the face. 'Thank God Mama's not here to see how low you've sunk, you evil bastard.'

Margarita shrank back, her arms tight around her stomach. Her attacker was Santi's brother! How could this monster share the same blood as Santi? In mounting alarm, she watched as the man began to fight back, a twisted snarl on his face as he deflected the blows raining down on his head.

'I'm glad the old nag is dead,' he panted. 'All she was ever interested in was her precious Santi. You'll regret this, *hijo de puta.*' Dodging Santi's punches, the man managed to struggle to his feet. He took a step back and spat in Santi's face. As Santi raised his hand to wipe away the saliva, the man drew his arm back, and his fist caught Santi squarely in the face.

When Margarita felt warm blood soak her face as Santi's nose shattered, she staggered to her feet and limped towards the light of the bonfire, screaming for help. She glanced over her shoulder just in time to see Santi launch himself at the man. A flash of metal glinted in the moonlight, and as if in slow motion, the man slumped forward with wide-eyed surprise and fell to the ground with a thud. Margarita froze on the spot. Her attacker lay on the ground twitching, a knife sticking out of the side of his neck. Blood pumped from the wound, and she watched as a pool of sticky blackness spread around his head. Santi stood over him, staring down, his face transformed from the gentle man she knew into a stranger with the wild eyes of a killer. Several seconds of absolute silence elapsed until Margarita's screams pierced the still night air.

60

Margarita's screams filtered into my consciousness as if I were underwater, distant yet alarmingly close. Adrenaline coursed through my body, and rage thrummed inside me like a drumbeat. Iker lay unmoving, his open eyes glassy and unfocused. I stood over him, elated and horrified in equal measure, until my legs gave way and I crashed to my knees. Behind me came the crunch of footsteps over the rubble, and Kiko appeared out of the darkness. He squatted beside me, and though his lips moved, I couldn't understand what he was saying. When he looked over my shoulder, his eyes widened. I turned. Margarita was sprawled on the ground several feet away, her face covered in blood. In an instant, I was beside her. 'Margarita! *Dios mío, cariño*, what has he done to you?'

She shook her head, her eyes unfocused, with a bruise already visible on her cheekbone. 'Why, Santi? Why did he attack me?' she whispered, her eyes pleading with mine.

I cradled her in my arms, unable to look her in the eye. 'He's crazy, Margarita. I'm sorry, I'm so sorry he did this to you,' I cried, filled with shame. Her hand touched my cheek, and she turned my face towards her.

'He was like an animal. He would have killed me if

you hadn't come.'

My eyes closed, relief flooding through me that I had arrived in time.

'*Qué coño ha pasado*' said Kiko. 'What the hell happened?'

'Look at her, Kiko... look what he did to her,' I said, my jaw clenched and blood roaring in my ears.

Kiko ran his fingers through his hair and knelt beside her. 'Where are you hurt, Margarita? Is the baby alright?'

Frowning, she tilted her head to one side and pressed her fingers into her stomach. 'I can't feel it moving,' she cried, tears streaming down her face.

Kiko and I tensed at the sound of footsteps. It was my father, stumbling drunkenly. He froze as he took in the gruesome scene before him. He stared down at Iker, then turned to Margarita, who was sobbing in Kiko's arms and put his hands on his head in despair. With a howl of anguish that tore at my heart, he fell to his knees beside Iker's body.

'*Dios bendito,* what's happened?' he slurred, searching in vain for a pulse. After what seemed like an eternity, his shoulders began to shake as he closed the staring, unblinking eyes of his son, my brother. Iker was dead.

Shame poked me like a sharp stick as I witnessed my father's torment. Not because I'd killed my brother but because we had all allowed Iker to bully and trample his way through life, hurting everyone around him. I left

Kiko holding Margarita and knelt beside my father, resting my hand on his shoulder. His eyes met mine, and in that instant, I knew he didn't blame me. He'd seen Margarita, her face bloody and bruised, and her dress ripped to shreds. No words were necessary. Hushed whispers rippled through the gathered crowd, pitying eyes watching us. But no one said a word. I knew without a doubt that more than a few would raise a glass to my brother's demise.

Eva was sitting with her arms around Margarita, both of them sobbing. Kiko stood up as I came over. 'Margarita has felt the baby kicking, but we need to move her to somewhere dry and clean her up. Our house is empty.'

I nodded and glanced back at the body of my brother. 'What shall we do with him?' I said, jerking my head in Iker's direction.

Kiko went over to talk to a few of the men and came back, his face grim. 'They'll deal with it. Come on, help me get the girls away from here.'

We lifted Margarita to her feet, and Eva wrapped her in a shawl someone had handed her. But as we set off to Kiko's house, raised voices filled the air, drawing closer. I turned, along with the rest of the group, my eyes narrowing as four policemen emerged from the alley. In all the years I'd lived in Somorrostro, this was the first time I'd ever seen the police step foot in the camp. We'd always dealt with problems in our own way, but now I was terrified – I'd murdered my brother in cold blood.

The agents approached us with wary faces. Four pairs of eyes widened when they spotted the bloodied body lying on the ground. One of them spoke. 'We've had a report from one of the nightwatchmen in charge of the diggers that there's been a disturbance. What's happened here? Who is this man?' he asked, pointing to the body.

My father and I began to speak at the same time, but I caught my father's eye and shook my head imperceptibly. I stood tall and took a deep breath. 'His name is Iker Calaf. He's my brother, and he attacked this woman,' I said, pointing to Margarita, who was being supported by Kiko and Eva.

The agent glanced over at her and then nodded at me. 'And who attacked him with the knife, *amigo*?'

I was about to open my mouth to reply when a clear voice rang out from the back of the crowd.

'We found him like this, *Señores Agentes.*' Tia Rosita came into view, limping slowly, the onlookers parting to let her pass. 'It would seem that someone has meted out the appropriate punishment as befits a violent attack on a pregnant girl,' she said, coming to a standstill between Iker's body and the agents. 'We've been celebrating La Revetlla and are grateful for your concern. But in all my years in Somorrostro, no one has ever interfered in our business. Given that tonight is the last time we will be here, I pray that you allow us to find the culprit and ensure justice is served as we see fit.' She fixed her gaze on them, her face composed and her bright, birdlike eyes gleaming in the moonlight. Seconds passed. The agents glanced at each other and then back at Tia Rosita. A look passed between them, and without a word, they nodded, gave a respectful salute and faded away in the darkness. Their radio transmitter crackled as one of them spoke. 'Patrol 26 to base. There's nothing to see here. Probably kids messing about. We've checked all over the site and are making our way back. Over.'

Relief ran through my veins as they disappeared. I was sure none of them would ever forget the power that emanated from the old woman like a warm *carajillo* on a winter's morning. They would tell their wives, daughters, sons and grandchildren about a murder on a beach called Somorrostro where the *gitanos* had once lived. About an old woman whose plea made four grown police officers turn around without a word. A woman older than the hills of Collserola.

61

Wrapped in Eva's arms, Margarita shivered uncontrollably. Hushed voices talked over her head, but she couldn't understand what they were saying. The face of Tia Rosita, her eyes narrowed, peered down at her. 'We need to get her to my house,' she said, touching Margarita's forehead.

A voice rang out of the darkness. 'Kiko, come and help me.' Strong arms lifted her, and tender hands brushed the hair off her face. It was Santi. Margarita put her arms around his neck and closed her eyes. They reached a dilapidated shack, and Santi carefully eased her through the narrow doorway. The scent of herbs and woodsmoke filled her nostrils, and as Santi laid her down on a pallet covered with soft blankets, she groaned. The stinging on her legs was almost unbearable, and she could hardly see out of her right eye. Sofia knelt beside her, placed a bottle of brown liquid and some torn rags on the ground, and began cleaning the wounds on Margarita's legs. She braced herself, expecting discomfort, but the liquid instantly eased the pain. Santi knelt on the other side of her, holding her hand. She gazed at him through her good eye, recoiling at the sight of bruising on his jaw and his swollen nose. Blood was caked around a cut that ran from under his eye to his ear. 'Sa… Santi,' she croaked, her throat raw.

'Shhh, try and relax.'

She tightened her grip on his hand. 'Thank you.'

'I'd do it again in a heartbeat,' he said, his ashen face strained.

Sofia propped a pillow under Margarita's head and held a glass to her dry, cracked lips. Margarita gagged as she swallowed. Within minutes the agony in her skull had eased to a dull throb. The worried faces of Eva and Kiko at the end of the pallet and Tia Rosita, perched on a stool, swam into focus. 'Is the child moving, *preciosa*?' asked Sofia, dabbing Margarita's face, the tincture cooling the fire on her skin.

'Yes,' she whispered. The kicks had been getting stronger as if the baby had been woken by her tears. She rubbed her palm across her belly, feeling the butterfly wings of movement. Her other hand found Santi's, and she threaded her fingers through his, pushing herself higher on the cushions. Eva edged closer, her pale face familiar and comforting. Margarita reached out to her, and with a sob, Eva leaned into her, cupping Margarita's head in her hands. Over Eva's shoulder, she tried to smile at Kiko, but the tender skin around her mouth made her wince.

'I'm sorry, Margarita,' said Kiko. 'I'm sorry we couldn't protect you. You're my sister. If Santi hadn't arrived first, I would have killed him myself.'

Margarita nodded. He didn't need to tell her.

From behind Kiko, there was a gasp, and Tia Rosita

crumpled to the floor. Santi jumped up with a cry. 'Sofia, get the foxglove drops on the top shelf behind the peroxide,' he instructed and gently gathered Tia Rosita up in his arms as if she weighed no more than a feather.

Margarita struggled up from the mattress. 'Lay her down here. I feel much better.'

As Santi stroked the sparse white hair from her brow, Sofia squatted at his side and passed him a glass dropper. He held Tia Rosita's head and gently eased the dropper between her lips. Her eyes fluttered, and after several tense minutes, she regained full consciousness.

Her gaze flickered around until it rested on Margarita. 'Your daughter will have a long, healthy life, *hija mia*. She will have your sweet nature and the spirit of your mother. But promise me you'll learn from your mother's mistakes – her story must never become yours. The love you have around you will sustain you for the rest of your days.'

Santi's hand curled around Margarita's, and her heart quickened as their fingers interlocked.

Tia Rosita began to cough and took another sip from the glass Sofia held to her lips. Turning to Santi, her eyes softened as she held his gaze. '*Hijo mio,* don't ever feel guilty for your actions tonight. Your brother was a cruel coward who had long been cursed. Never doubt that you did the right thing.' She stopped to take a deep breath. 'Your heart is pure, and love is reaching out its hand to you. Never let go of your dream, *mi niño*. You've brought me so much joy, and I'm grateful for every moment I've spent teaching you.' She hacked again, her chest crackling, and spat into a handkerchief Sofia had passed to her. 'You are destined for greatness, Santi Calaf. It won't be easy. The best things never are. But you will have an angel on your shoulder and a heart full of love.'

Her eyes closed once again, and Santi stood up and made his way towards the back of the shack. Sofia cradled Tia Rosita's head, and Margarita shuffled closer to Eva. As they watched the rise and fall of the old woman's chest, the silence in the confined space was deafening.

62

I tried to unlock the wooden cabinet where Tia Rosita kept the morphine, cursing my shaking hands as I fumbled with the key. I grabbed the bottle and breathed deeply to steady myself. I knew without a doubt that this was her goodbye to me. She had been the guiding force throughout my life, even more than my parents had been, and at that moment, I wondered how my life would be without her. Kneeling beside her, I took her hand, age-spotted and misshapen with arthritis, and held it up to my face. A gentle hand rubbed my back, and when I turned, the love I saw in Margarita's eyes helped soothe the torment in my soul. Tia Rosita's breathing was becoming more laboured, and I exchanged glances with Sofia. I took the stopper out and held the bottle to her lips. She let out a long, shuddering breath, and her eyes opened.

She reached out her hand to Eva. 'Ah, Eva, you have such a gentle aura, *preciosa*. I can feel it all around you,' she said, grasping Eva's hand. Her gaze was sharp as she glanced around the room at each of us. 'I have a story to tell, but I haven't got much time left,' she whispered.

None of us spoke, and I thought I could hear the sound of our collective heartbeat thundering in my ears. Tia Rosita shuffled up the bed with a grimace of discomfort, her breathing erratic.

'Many years ago, my daughter Elvira, Sofia's mother, took in an orphan she found wandering the streets of Les Corts alone. A three-year-old girl dressed in nothing but a thin cotton dress and some sandals in February. It was criminal. Elvira took her to the police station. They said they'd make some enquiries but told her she couldn't leave the child with them and suggested she took the infant to the nearby Santa Maria Del Remei church, where someone would know what to do with her. Well, my Elvira didn't want to bother the nuns and brought the poor child back here. I'll never forget Sofia's face when she thought her mother had brought her a new little sister.' She peered at Sofia, whose eyes were full of tears. 'Don't cry anymore, *pequeña mia*. You'll see them again very soon now.' Patting her granddaughter's hand, Tia Rosita continued. 'Elvira went back to the police station every day for two weeks, but no one had come forward to report a missing child. After those first two weeks, she returned once a week until, almost a year later, the police informed her they were closing the case and, once again, told her to go to the church. She wasn't ours by blood, but she was part of our family by then. Even though we didn't know where she came from, she had the spirit of a *gitana, mi pequeña* Queti.'

It was becoming more difficult for Tia Rosita to catch her breath, and I could almost see the grains of sand running out of the hourglass of her life. But I had no doubt she would see this through to the end.

377

She continued with her story. 'Those years watching the girls grow up brought Elvira and me so much joy. They danced everywhere, never apart, chattering in a secret language that no one else understood. The only time they would leave each other's side was when Queti accompanied me to the mountains to collect the herbs and plants I needed for healing.' Tia Rosita paused, inhaling deeply. 'She had the same gift I'd been given. I always wondered if she'd been born into another *gitano* clan, misunderstood and feared, rejected because of that gift. I've lived more years than I can remember, but none have been as special as those I spent passing down all I knew to Queti. She treasured the knowledge like a *paya* treasures a diamond. Since she left, I've passed all I know on to you, Santi,' she wheezed, her eyes flicking in my direction. 'But I'm straying from the story, and there isn't much time left.' She turned to Margarita, who was resting her head on my shoulder.

'*Hija mia,* what happened to you tonight wasn't the first time Iker Calaf had attacked someone. When Queti was twelve and Iker fourteen, he cornered her in the stable next to Pichi's house and had his wicked way with her, leaving her bloodied, bruised and with child. Elvira and I suffered so much that he might as well have raped us too. I gave her a strong potion that should have got rid of the child, but it didn't work. I spent days and nights testing plants, but nothing worked – so desperately did the child want to be born into this world. We kept Queti hidden at home, not because we were ashamed of her but because she was so terrified of Iker Calaf. We couldn't even say his name out loud without her becoming hysterical. We kept her out of sight to save her from the scurrilous rumours that would have spread through the camp like poison ivy – or worse, if Iker had heard the rumours and demanded a claim on the child.'

I sat with my head in my hands, bitter tears of shame that my brother had done such a heinous thing dripping through my fingers. It would destroy my father if he ever found out, and I was glad I'd killed Iker. Not only for Margarita but also for a young girl called Queti. 'How could you bear to be near me, Tia Rosita, knowing what he'd done?' I asked her, my head bowed, unable to meet her gaze.

'I saw the gift you have for medicine, for healing, and I was determined the sins of your brother would not change the course of your life. You mean the world to me, *hijo mío,* and nothing and no one will ever change that,' she said, her voice weakening.

'Where are Elvira and Queti?' I asked, stroking her face with the back of my fingers.

Coughs wracked her body, and several minutes passed before she could answer. 'They moved to Sant Celoni to live with my brother's family. Sofia and I have visited them once a year every summer for almost twenty years. It was always heartbreaking when we had to leave them to come home. They live a quiet life there, waiting for the day they can be with Sofia again.'

'Why didn't you leave with them to make a new life

for yourself?' I asked, curious as to why she'd stayed in this hellish place when she could have had a new start.

She gave a long, shuddering sigh. 'I had to stay here until the circle was closed, *hijo mío*, and Sofia was adamant that she wanted to stay with me,' said Tia Rosita, her eyes resting on her granddaughter. 'But it's been a long wait – there have been months, years, when I thought I wouldn't live to see this day, to see Iker Calaf reap what he sowed. To finally face the consequences of his actions all those years ago.'

'What happened to the baby that Queti had? Did it survive?' asked Kiko, his face pale in the flickering candlelight.

'I've lived with such a lot of guilt for so long. The conditions here in the camp were hellish, and it was a cruel winter that year. We didn't have enough milk to feed the baby, and we couldn't get a wet nurse because we hadn't told anyone that Queti had given birth.' Her eyes closed, and a tear trickled down her paper-thin, wizened cheek. 'It was all part of God's will, Kiko, but it almost broke me. I wrapped the baby in some rags and took it into the city. I left the tiny bundle outside the police station in Plaza Espanya, praying she would be found before she perished from the cold.' Her eyes darted around the room until they reached Eva. 'And she came home, Kiko. You brought her back, finally. You fell in love with her and brought her back to the place where she belongs.'

Eva gazed around at us, her mouth open, catching

my eye at the exact moment that I realised I was her uncle. None of us spoke as we tried to make sense of Tia Rosita's revelation.

Eva crawled over to the pallet and lay beside Tia Rosita, her face inches from the old woman's. As she took the old woman in her arms, I saw, perhaps for the first time ever, a look of pure peace pass over Tia Rosita's face. 'Thank you for waiting for me. I promise I'll carry you in my heart forever. None of us will ever forget you. *Te amo,*' whispered Eva.

As Tia Rosita's eyelids fluttered for the last time, she smiled. '*Bendiciónes.*'

The sudden drop in temperature made me shiver, and a prickle of cold air ran down my spine. And just like that, the secrets of the past lost their power and turned to dust. In the fullness of time, the universe had finally led us to this moment, revealing with it the destiny of our lives. Without a word, we joined hands in silent gratitude to Tia Rosita for sacrificing the last years of her life to ensure we all came together. As the energy flowed through us, we held her words deep in our hearts. Nothing could dim our light despite our sorrow and pain that night. Finally, we were where we were meant to be. But that wasn't the end of our story. It was simply the beginning.

***

Two months later

The contractions began in the middle of the night. Margarita heaved herself out of bed, pulling on her dressing gown as she waddled through to her mother's room. 'Mama, I think the baby's coming,' she said, turning on the light.

Her mother sat up in bed, one of her rollers coming loose. 'Have your waters broken?'

Margarita shook her head. 'Not yet, but the contractions are fifteen minutes apart.' She winced as another one began. Her mother jumped out of bed, dragged the rollers out of her hair, and pulled on a skirt and a jumper. 'Come and sit down. I'll heat you up some milk,' she said, rushing from the room.

Margarita smiled to herself as she followed behind. Her mother had been counting down the days until the baby arrived, massaging Margarita's swollen ankles and knitting dozens of baby clothes.

'Keep an eye on the milk, *cariño*. I'll pop to Bernat's to ring Oscar,' her mother called over her shoulder, slamming the door behind her.

Margarita leaned against the worktop, trying to ease the ache in her lower back. Half of her was petrified, and the other half was desperate to meet her child. The months since the attack had been a struggle. When she had arrived home after Sant Juan, broken and bleeding, her mother had held her in her arms and sobbed. The anguish on her face had haunted Margarita ever since.

Giving herself a shake, she turned off the gas just as the milk was about to boil and tipped it into a mug.

'He's on his way,' panted her mother, coming through the door. 'Right, where's your bag? Have you got everything?'

'Yes, Mama, everything's ready. It's behind the door in my room. All I have to do is put my toothbrush in,' she said, shaking her head in exasperation.

Fifteen minutes later, the intercom buzzed. Carmen picked up Margarita's bag and bundled her out of the door as Oscar raced up the stairs towards them. 'How are you feeling, Margarita?'

'Hanging in there,' she said with a faint smile. With one hand on the rail and supported by Oscar on the other, Margarita began the slow descent. After stopping to breathe through another contraction, they reached the door to the street.

'I've parked the car outside the Palau de la Música. It was the closest I could get,' said Oscar, taking the bag off Carmen.

'Thank God it's the middle of the night, and there's no one around,' Margarita said, rubbing the small of her back. 'Imagine all the neighbours gawping at me in my nightie?'

Oscar opened the car boot, threw the bag in, and climbed into the driver's seat. Margarita eased herself onto the back seat, and Carmen shuffled in beside her. When they reached Hospital Sant Pau, Oscar dropped them off at the entrance.

'I'll go and park the car. Dr Blanco is expecting you,' he said and screeched off.

Margarita looked at her mother and laughed, shaking her head. 'I think he's more nervous than I am, Mama!'

As they reached the doorway, Margarita stopped, gasping as a wave of pain shot through her abdomen, and grabbed her mother's arm.

'Breathe like we practised, Margarita,' said her mother, her voice calm and soothing as she rubbed Margarita's back. Once the wave had passed, Margarita straightened, wiping her forehead, and they made their way to the maternity ward. Hours later, the shrill cries of a baby pierced their way into Margarita's consciousness. Through a haze of pain, she opened her eyes, and the contours of her mother's face swam into focus.

'It's a girl, *cariño*, she's perfect,' she said, pressing a damp cloth onto Margarita's burning brow.

When her swaddled daughter was placed on her chest, exhaustion was replaced by a surge of joy, and the world stopped turning. She pressed her lips to the baby's fuzzy head and inhaled the scent of her child. The baby's eyelids fluttered, and she squinted, looking straight at Margarita. Nothing could have prepared her for this moment; no words existed to describe the feeling. Everything had changed.

A cough from beside the bed made her drag her gaze away from the child. At last, he was here, his eyes shining as he leaned down and kissed Margarita's forehead, gazing at the bundle in her arms.

'She's as beautiful as her mother,' he said, his voice thick with emotion. 'Have you decided on a name for her now that you've seen her?'

She nodded. 'Isidora.'

With a smile that could have moved mountains, he took Margarita's hand and pressed it to his face. 'Gift of the goddess Isis. Our gift.'

As she stroked his cheek, her heart expanded. With this man by her side and her daughter in her arms, she would never be lonely again. '*Te quiero*, Santi.'

EPILOGUE

Now

The face I've adored since the second she came screaming into our lives almost fifty years ago sits across from me in her favourite armchair. Isidora, her shoulder-length hair falling in soft waves and streaked with grey at the temples. I've been blessed to watch her grow, surrounded by love, from the moment she was born through girlhood, womanhood and finally into her maturity.

She uncurls her legs from under her and stretches. Outside the window, the sky has darkened, and the headlights of passing cars cast shadows that dance on the ceiling.

I clear my parched throat, and without a word, she heads into the kitchen, returning with a bottle of my favourite beer. She draws the heavy velvet curtains and switches on the lamp in the corner of the room. I gulp down the cold beer, trying to rinse away the dusty memories. The sound of laughter and singing, music and dancing, and the aroma of cigarettes and food simmering for hours in huge pans is as clear now as in 1966. Horses were tethered to the side of our shacks, and chickens and goats roamed freely among us. But more than anything, I remember feeling safe in my small corner of the world. Shielded from the stigma of living there, a stigma I didn't fully understand until long after I'd left. I fought tooth and nail to escape my past, not realising how it had shaped me, creating the man I would become. Sometimes in my dreams, though, I hear Margarita's screams, the stench of fear, and I'm smothered to death by the weight of privation. It's only now, looking back, that I bless each day, happy and sad, that I spent in Somorrostro.

I set the bottle down on the low table between us and run my palm over my face as if to wipe away the images swirling around in my head.

'Papa,' she says, fixing me with the same eyes as her mother's. 'I sometimes forget Mama's face – it's like waking up from a dream. All I see are fragments.' She reaches for her packet of cigarettes, ignoring my frown of disapproval, and lights one, inhaling deeply. 'I have to look at her photo every day.' Her cigarette crackles in the silence that follows. 'When you bring her back to life for me, she's real, but as soon as the story ends, she becomes a mirage in the distance again,' she says, rubbing her temple. 'Yaya Carmen was my last link to her... and now she's gone, too.' I hear the catch in her voice and notice the purple smudges of grief under her eyes.

I take another drink of my beer. 'The story never really ends, Isi. Your mother and I, Eva and Kiko, were the lucky ones.' I pause, spent from so many memories, recollections that I often suspect are too saccharine, over-sentimental.

Isidora stubs out her cigarette and pads around the table to sit beside me on the sofa. She takes my old, calloused hand in hers, holding it as tightly as she did when she was a teenager on the day we buried her mother, my beautiful Margarita.

'Do you believe in miracles, Papa?'

I smother a smile. After so many years of telling her that as a neurologist, a man of science, I believe in trial and error, not leaving things to fate or the gods, but I've never really convinced her. I place my other hand on top of hers, my throat tightening. 'All of us who watched Tia Rosita take her last breath in Somorrostro were touched, blessed by something we couldn't explain even if our lives had depended on it. We were afraid our fanciful notions of sorcery and witchcraft would be mocked by those who didn't believe in miracles. But your mother taught me there's magic in everything, in everyone, Isi – all we have to do is find it.' I promised Margarita that I would raise her daughter as if she were my flesh and blood, and it's a vow I've never broken. Isidora has been my greatest achievement, comfort, and teacher – and I wouldn't change a single thing.

Except, perhaps, to see Margarita standing on the cathedral steps in her orange dress. To hold her in my arms and spin her around as we dance in Las Ramblas, just one last time.

The End

Acknowledgements

Oscar Casas Slack, I love you and would choose you as my son a million times over in a million lifetimes.

Gines Carvajal, this book would never have been written without you. *Te Amo*.

Cassie Steward, my niece. I'll be forever grateful for your suggestions, inspiration, advice and love.

Lynda Steward, for encouraging me through each torturous draft. I love you.

To my cyber-friends. Nic Winter, my co-presenter and friend, for your help, chats and shenanigans.

Eva Alton, for always being a message away with advice and friendship.

Darin Nagamootoo, for your friendship and support.

Stuart Knott, for your endless encouragement and advice.

Laura Mackenzie, for being my biggest cheerleader.

Sarah Whitton, for making me laugh with your voice notes and loveliness.

Miriam Didi, the worst arc reader ever – I adore you.

Karen Legg, for your support and friendship.

Elizabeth Moore Kraus, for your love and support.

To my beta and arc readers for their advice and suggestions. Michelle Wolff, Helen Coxhill, Michelle Moore, Louise Hankey, Helen Aitchison & Sara Fritz.

Tiffany Andrea, for helping with the last-minute formatting drama. I'm beyond grateful.

And finally, for two women – both born in 1933 – without whom this story wouldn't have been told.

Margarita Gisbert Blanche, whose death inspired me to go back in time, to create a kinder world, and to keep her memory alive in this book.

My mum, Beryl Slack. Your battle with dementia means you'll never read this story – but I think you would have been proud of me. I love you.

And lastly, to everyone who reads 'The Road to Somorrostro'. Thank you.

'Even the darkest night will end and the sun will rise.'

Victor Hugo

ABOUT THE AUTHOR

Julia Slack has lived in Barcelona for twenty-five years. She's a freelance English teacher, copy editor and proofreader.

Her interest in Somorrostro beach, home to thousands of gypsies until its demolition in 1966, was sparked by French photographer, Jacques Leonard. His marriage to Rosario Amaya, a gypsy from Somorrostro, allowed him unprecedented access to the very closed community.

She spends her free time discovering new parts of the city on her motorbike and walking along the beautiful beach where the tourists remain blissfully unaware of its dark, forgotten history.

She'd love it if you could leave a review on Amazon or Goodreads.

Follow her on Instagram @juliaslackauthor and go and say Hi!

Printed by Amazon Italia Logistica S.r.l.
Torrazza Piemonte (TO), Italy

52216006R00223